FACULTY OF LIARS

FACULTY OF LIARS

R. L. HEBER

A POINT BLANK BOOK

First published by Point Blank, an imprint of Oneworld Publications Ltd, 2026

A CIP record for this title is available from the British Library

ISBN 978-1-83643-177-0
eISBN 978-1-83643-178-7

Typeset by Oneworld Publications Ltd
Printed and bound in Great Britain by Clays Ltd, Elcograf S.p.A.

The authorised representative in the EEA is eucomply OÜ,
Pärnu mnt 139b–14, 11317 Tallinn, Estonia
(email: hello@eucompliancepartner.com / phone: +33757690241)

Oneworld Publications Ltd
10 Bloomsbury Street
London WC1B 3SR
England

For my parents,
with everlasting love and thanks.

Prologue

I know the crash is coming before it happens, time contracting as everything kaleidoscopes in front of me. I cannot release the phone from my grip, or I risk destroying everything. I brace myself for impact. It was only hours before that we'd arrived at the gala, brass band playing in the corner of the lawn, people in all their finery; bright ballgowns, fur stoles, glittering diamonds, long satin gloves, up dos, white tie, black tie. Segments of narrative flash through my mind: everything that has played out in the past months that has led up to this point; everything that has played out on a global stage. In the news, all over social media, my actions laid bare for the world to see. All at odds with the gruesome reckoning in front of me now.

The grey tarmac twists upside down as the car caves in on itself. There's a strange sound next to me. The crunch of something non-metallic. The hiss of an airbag. The car is on its side. I squeeze the phone in my hand. It would just take tiny movements to press the three digits and get help. But something in my brain isn't connecting. I turn to face the driver's seat. There, next to me, are splayed limbs, a face like a melted puppet.

***

There's blood all over my left thigh and my green dress – the beautiful, green dress that had been chosen so carefully – has a huge rip in it on the side and my left nostril is dripping. It's deathly quiet outside. The trees hang over us and there are lights in the distance. Somewhere, about five minutes away, is my home. A strange sound rattles through the car. My attention turns again to the phone, which is slippery in my hand.

Then, silence. The phone screen casts an eerie glow, a digital halo around my pale skin. If we were both to die now, what would the media say? They'd have a field day. I think back to when it all started. The things I'd done, snaking their way around the world. The phone light goes out. I close my eyes. You. Me. Limbs tangled. My love. The images fade to black.

BEFORE

Man is not what he thinks he is; he is what he hides.

André Malraux

The Day of the Announcement

1.

The text arrives at midday, while we're in bed. You've prepared well for my visit – smooth sheets, brunch goodies huddled on your granite kitchen counter – the things you know I like from back home, in England. Strawberry jam, Earl Grey teabags, crumpets. Nothing too original, but you've even found a small pot of Marmite in the campus shop. I unscrew the familiar yellow lid and inhale but hold off from eating it, because last night you told me you hated the smell. I said I'd save it for when you pissed me off.

'Pissed me off.' You'd mocked my accent in clipped tones. 'Anyway. Just you wait,' you'd said. 'Tomorrow you'll surrender to me entirely.'

You hadn't been wrong there. Kicking off a sheet, body still buzzing, I grab my phone.

'Come on,' you say. 'We don't have long.'

'One minute.' Unlocking my keypad, I touch the envelope icon alerting me to the new message. I feel the heat of your breath on my shoulder.

'Who the hell still sends texts anyway?' You turn away

from me so I can see the triangle of tiny moles on your pale back. 'Seriously.'

'Don't be childish,' I say with a laugh, my forefinger hovering over the message. I'm comforted with the thought we both have something to lose should we ever get caught.

The text is from Jeff. He must have got the job; although we've had countless nods that it was coming, we've been waiting all morning for the official announcement. Jeff, being Jeff, would only have rung me if it was bad news so he could complain, hanging up before I could massage his ego. Now he's probably in his current office, JEFF HARKER, PROVOST on the door, sitting in his worn, brown leather swivel chair, fingers steepled under his chin as he muses on academic life. His message will be short. Something along the lines of us celebrating tonight.

I prod you in the shoulder blade with my elbow, but you don't move. You grab your own phone and put on Coldplay. You'd been playing it when I arrived, speakerphone set quiet, lights low. I'd switched off the music when you were in the bathroom. If you'd noticed, you hadn't said a thing.

'Sorry,' I say to no one in particular. I tap on the screen again. Unable to stop myself from using British vernacular, I've saved his number under JEFF MOBILE. I select the message. His text is four words long. Four words signifying that my life is about to change.

It was me that set all this in motion. 'You can do it,' I'd told him a year earlier, after the second time my womb had caved under the pressure of cradling a human life. Or that was the story I'd told myself anyway, alone in the Development office's bathroom. That my body clearly wasn't cut out for it, whatever 'it' was. I'd pressed the toilet flush almost triumphantly, as if proving myself right all along.

'You know you can do this job,' I'd said to my husband, for want of anything else to fixate upon. 'I'll be there to support you.' The look on his face had said it all; a glittering, hollowed-out stare as the knowledge had dawned on him that he was indeed made for the role.

'Shit.' I shut the message, then open it again. 'Shit.'

'What?' You turn around, pulling yourself up against the green velvet bedhead, so incongruous amongst the otherwise plain, simple décor of your University apartment 'What's happened?'

'This.' I twist the screen towards you. 'Not unexpected. But actually seeing the words is somehow different.'

'Shit. Does that mean…?'

'It means we need to be more careful.' I put the phone down on the pillow beside me, careful to lock the screen again. 'Amongst other things.'

Throwing back the sheet, I think about getting ready. This time in about a week we'll probably have moved into The Lodge, a huge, white gabled house for the incumbent University president, with a long, gravel driveway, beautifully manicured lawns and trailing rose bushes. The pay increase, Jeff has told me, will be even more life-changing than it was when he was appointed as provost and head of health partnerships. And once Jeff's settled into the role, we can then try again. Maybe explore other options. My mind won't allow me to dwell on those, so I break the silence.

'I mean, you work here.' I wonder how quickly I can get away to see my husband. 'So does Jeff. Obviously, you live in the arse end of nowhere. I'm bloody glad your paths haven't crossed.' I think about the text message again. *Good morning, Mrs. President!*

'*Arse*. How cute the way you say it,' you say. 'Nearly as cute as your actual behind. And if I get caught sleeping with the new University president's wife? What happens then? And when will I get to see you? You'll be so busy.'

'We won't get caught,' I tell you matter-of-factly. 'You'll have to meet him soon, though. But—'

'But what? We'll meet at the gala. I'll make sure of it. Just to make you squirm.' You laugh, but I detect a warning tone in your voice.

We both fall silent. I'm hurt by your words. *Sleeping with*. This is so much more than that, isn't it? You trace your thumb along my left arm, pressing it into my skin as you reach my wrist. I pull away. Even though we've been telling each other 'I love you' for months, I now wonder if we need to finish things. The thought is unbearable. And something about Jeff's message is also troubling me.

'What?' you ask.

'Nothing,' I snap, torn between fear of you losing interest and thoughts about my future. 'Sorry. Nothing. It's… well. Look, I've really got to go.'

The bed creaks as you get up to stop me. Despite my physical attraction to you, your tall, slim, muscular body, the smattering of hairs across your chest, I am momentarily sickened at the sight of your still-slick nakedness; the raw animality of you is a reminder of the things we've done and the person I've become. I fold both arms around myself as I give an involuntary shiver.

'I promise I'll text you later. Okay?'

'I get it,' you say. 'You're far too important for me now.'

Despite my own internal monologue about us, or perhaps because of it, I don't have the strength to reassure you otherwise. I pick up my phone and wave it in the air. 'I'll text. I told you.'

I think about the familiar blue Telegram icon, hidden behind my other apps. A trick you taught me not long after we first met on campus. 'It's like you've done this before,' I'd said.

I pull on my knickers and a pair of denim shorts. Those will have to go. As the wife of Jeff Harker, Medical School provost, it's not my usual attire of navy, khaki or cream slacks, loafers, a neatly pressed white T-shirt and a Chanel-type blazer; a perfect combination of American and English style. Smart. Classic. A little preppy. I like to play the part. Mostly. But today, I've taken a more relaxed approach.

'Don't be like that,' I manage eventually.

'Like what?'

'Like that.' My voice muffles as I pull my shirt over my head.

'It's you who's leaving,' you remind me. I open my mouth and quickly shut it again, remembering what we've been doing. The way my body gives in to you. How you've discovered a part of me that Jeff never has. How many times you've told me I fill a huge void in your life. 'The minute I laid eyes on you, I knew you were someone special,' you'd said. I tried to fulfil that idea you had of me. I never did and it was only in acceptance of that did I surrender myself to you completely. But now, all I can think about is Jeff and what's going to happen next.

'I will,' I tell you. 'Look. Sorry, it's just that things are going to be a bit different. I still love you. Nothing has changed there. We just need to watch ourselves more. I'll scope it all out and let you know tonight. Okay?' I bend down and kiss your cheek. 'Don't worry.'

A chemical tang fills the back of my nose and throat. I didn't notice that earlier. Your lanyard – UNIVERSITY MEDICAL SCHOOL FACILITIES MANAGER – is next to us on the bedside table, the red cord wrapped neatly around it. I recall the first time I saw you, at one of a series of fund-raisers you helped organise for the medical school all those months ago, I recall the security pass you presented to me in both hands, like a child showing off a painting.

I smell that odour again. 'Bye,' I say, wrinkling my nose.

'Be careful no one sees you leave.' As though I'll have forgotten since the last time you reminded me. You blow me a half-hearted kiss, not bothering to look up from your phone, and I know I've lost you, most probably to your work or a crossword game. You mutter something about getting tons of emails in the past hour, and then you start typing furiously. You suddenly look stressed out, but today I'm not affected by your sudden disinterest in me. All I can think about is getting home.

I grab my bag from your empty sideboard and leave your apartment that sits on the edges of the Headway Woodland. The midday sun is hot on my skin. Closing the door behind me, I scan the area for people. Luckily, your apartment, above an old university storeroom, is the only one in your small block, and there's no one about.

Jeff's message has unnerved me. I can't put my finger on why.

My phone buzzes. I unlock the screen and navigate to the hidden Telegram app, where I open the portal and type in my password. *That was epic*, you've written. And then, *I already miss you, my love*. Relieved I haven't pissed you off too much, I type back a smiley emoji followed by a heart. That will have to do; I can't think of anything entertaining to say. For once I don't double-check myself before I press Send. I lock Telegram, then the phone itself, before sliding it into my pocket.

Tying back my hair, I start the walk home. I'm thirsty and distracted. I work out the timings of my actions: shower and wash hair, choose an appropriate outfit, go to meet Jeff in his office with a bottle of champagne. The thought process loops at a particularly fast and unwelcome resonance, occasionally broken by the swish of trees, the crack of a twig or the squawk of a bird.

I speed up. Fifteen minutes more. There's no one around. Breathe, I tell myself. After all, it'll probably be the last time I do this for a few days. There'll be drinks parties.

Engagements. Jeff's inauguration rehearsals to attend. The lavish medical fellowships gala event in a few weeks. I recite the spiel in my mind that we've been fed almost constantly by the comms team since Jeff's first appointment: the coveted Wickham Medical Fellowships, which were first awarded in the nineteenth century, thanks to a generous donation by Henry Wickham, a prominent physician, and which attract the world's intellectual elite, regardless of their financial background.

I realise that Jeff and I will be hosting the gala and I'll be on show in no time. I remember Suzy, Harley Robbins' wife, at her husband's inauguration: sleek, light-brown chignon, pearl earrings, block heels and a navy shift dress; the way she held herself as she gave a warmly delivered and self-penned welcome speech to her 'wonderful husband', whose dedication to the University had changed the course of many lives after he'd expanded the funding for the Wickham Fellowships so significantly. How impressive she had been.

Good Morning, Mrs. President!

It's only when I think of Jeff's text message again that I realise what's bothering me. It's not the words that are a surprise. After all, I was expecting them. Deep down, I'd known it the minute I'd spotted Harley and Suzy nodding at him after the announcement of the prestigious and world-renowned Rosemont Development Award. Our entry had apparently 'trumped' every other US and international university, after quadrupling our fellowship offering in the past five years with what they described as an 'astonishing feat of fundraising'. Harley had reached over in the audience at the ceremony, and even then I could see the tiny yet complicit movement of both heads. No. It's not the message. Or the words. It's the exclamation point, a grammatical marker Jeff has always found abhorrent. I think about us discussing it at length, about the outward turn of his nostrils. They have their place, I always argue. Ironically or whatever, like everything else. But my UK master's in English Literature from Bath University doesn't cut it with Jeff.

I pick up the pace again, eager to get back to my own home. That exclamation point, so out of place in Jeff's lexicon – could he have meant it as a joke? Knowing my husband as I do, it's doubtful. Instead, this vertical line atop a single pixelation seems to me some sort of omen. Has he changed so much in such a short time? Has something happened? Or has my affair now sullied every detail of my life?

'Silly,' I mutter, laughing. The sound echoes through the woodland. I laugh again and wipe the sweat from my top lip, and, whilst thinking of you inside me, my back arching against rucked-up sheets, and Jeff's text message, I continue the baking-hot walk of shame.

If Jeff could be described in grammatical terms, by his hatred of exclamation points, I had always been an adjunct. At school, I'd been best friends with future head girl Amy Lazarus. At university I was deputy chair of the student pastoral team, a role I was good at. But never good enough to take the next step up.

And here I am again. Still the same. Defined by my marriage to Jeff and if one were to go against my husband's advice to his students and be reductive in their approach, you'd summarise me as follows, and in no particular order: Elizabeth Harker, age thirty-seven; part-time research academic, part-time fundraiser and writer of research papers; bibliophile; lover of UK property shows; lover of toast and jam; slow, thoughtful eater; shiny chestnut shoulder-length bobbed hair; five foot four; slim; neatly dressed. Measured in all her actions – until I'd met you. Can hold her own in an argument, apart from when discussing grammatical matters with her husband, the newly elected president of – University and Medical School.

Cheat.

And yet – yet. Since my phone alerted me to Jeff's text message not even half an hour ago, I've been overwhelmed by the sense that those four words are about to tip the balance. Given that on the face of it Jeff has the starring role, I don't yet know how. No. Not simply the starring role. He's the director. And as we well know, things can go wrong there. An actor turns up drunk. The production budget spirals. Health and safety issues, or worse, crop up. I stand still, canopied by the huge trees five minutes from your apartment. Rubbing my arms, I think of the story that lies ahead. How much of my ensuing life script is down to me, here in this present and how much of that script is informed by the stories of my past; the narrative equivalent of a set of ancestral matryoshka dolls.

My therapist on campus (a perk of being married to a senior member of University staff) is obsessed with stories. 'Ninety-five percent of your daily actions are driven by your unconscious mind and the stories you tell yourself,' she's fond of saying. 'The lens through which you see life and the language you use about yourself. Your patterning. Your perception, Elizabeth. That's what I'm trying to get a sense of here. What limitation you overcompensate for with your words.' In part, she was right. My perception had indeed become reality. Adjunct. Good, but not that good. 'My language changes according to my moods,' I'd said with a laugh one of these times. She hadn't cracked a smile.

I think of you again. The way you left the bed halfway through our time together this morning, your smirk as I cried out for you to finish what you'd started. At that point my husband hadn't even entered my mind. In the space of the past twelve, beautiful months with you, I've gone from 'good, but not that good' to pretty fucking bad.

I don't think me or my therapist are any the wiser even after all these weeks, about where my unconscious and conscious meet. 'Is the disconnect that great?' I'd mused one day. And the forward tilt of her body told me that she thought she was finally getting somewhere with me. That I was opening up like a bird hatching into its first dawn. But she'd been wrong. And to this day I have never veered from that tightly guarded physical manifestation of myself, upright posture, hands cupped in my lap. Not even when we discussed the untimely deaths of my mother and big sister when I was eight. Or the two miscarriages. The only person able to see beyond that version of me, was you. I think of that now as mine and Jeff's home comes into view, the white three-bed cottage I spent six months decorating, perhaps unconsciously (see? that damn word again!), with a baby in mind. The round tables I ordered – no sharp edges. The low sofas.

I think of the way my body responds as you move closer to me. Our heat, the release of any of my internal narratives when I'm around you. I haven't told a soul about us. Not that I have many real friends to tell. I haven't even hinted at it in therapy, and I wonder if she knows. Whether she's able to detect a subtle shift in the way I sit when I think about you, my body burning.

Opening the side zip of my bag, I pull out the key ring Jeff gave me for our second wedding anniversary and open the newly painted cream door to our house, relieved to be somewhere familiar. It dawns on me again that soon we'll be moving into The Lodge. That my life has changed monumentally since this morning. That the universe has listened, somehow, to my pleas for change in the aftermath of the miscarriages and the ensuing emptiness which has resulted in me giving my all to being 'Jeff's wife'. And that my husband's life is transmuting through me. Or perhaps vice versa.

I'm pleased that Jeff isn't at home, even though the gramophone is still playing from this morning. Brahms. His favourite. Hanging up my bag in the coat cupboard and switching off the music, I run up to the shower and start scrubbing off the last hints of you, ready to revert back to doting wife, and out of nowhere comes that chemical smell again. I sniff my forearms, wondering whether I'm imagining things. I lather up the Imperial Leather soap I ordered to remind me of England and breathe in its smell. The suds sting the inside of my nose. After I've blow-dried my hair and dressed, I opt for cream culottes, a black silk shirt, kitten-heeled slingbacks and some gold jewellery in case we go straight out to dinner, finishing off with a spritz of Chanel No. 5. Grabbing a bottle of champagne from the fridge, gifted to us by a visiting fellow, I decide not to take my own car – Jeff, by the looks of it, has taken his – and order an Uber, ready to toast the man of the moment.

Ten minutes later I'm at the Development office wondering what I'm about to walk into. My husband, University president. My husband, who will now be overseeing both the University and the adjacent postgraduate Medical School. I'm filled with relief we've never had a discussion about me leaving Jeff. That the intensity of our relationship and our love has been conditional on me being in some sense unavailable.

After the Uber slows to a stop outside the building, I pull out my compact, applying one last slick of rust-red lipstick. I tuck my hair behind my ears and climb out onto the gravel drive and make my way inside. After I walk through the main entrance, my heels echo along the corridors and something about the building makes me stand taller, straighter. The black-and-white tiled floor, the wooden shields on the walls engraved with the names of previous deans, provosts and University presidents. My eyes skip to the last etching. The gold writing: HARLEY ROBBINS 2019–2025. And next... JEFFREY HARKER 2025– My fingers trace the letters. I'm unsurprised by how organised it all is; the Administration Department runs a tight ship.

A door opens, and the sound of Simon and Garfunkel's 'Cecilia' fills the space around me.

'Oh, Elizabeth dear.' It's my predecessor, Suzy Robbins. 'Wonderful news. Not that it was unexpected. And you and I need a little get-together so I can pass on all my pearls of wisdom. Not that you don't know it all already, of course.' She smells like my grandmother used to: talcum powder, lily of the valley and freshly applied lipstick overlaying something slightly sour. I wonder if this is my future.

'Oh, no. I don't.' I glance over at Harley's name on the board. 'I know nothing about it at all, so I'd love to hear all your pearls of wisdom. Anything you have to share.'

Suzy moves closer. I can see the powder clinging to the fine hairs on her cheeks. 'The one thing I know is that whatever happens, make sure you're the adoring wife. At least in public.' She lets out a long, grating laugh. 'I made it my mission to help him succeed. My law career came in handy, but your life now is here. This.' She indicates the building around her. 'You'll be thankful for it. If you play the game, you'll have a wonderful time. It's a wonderful opportunity. Don't do anything to ruin it.' She laughs again. I hold my breath as I think of you. 'But here's my advice. Your role now is to support Jeff in every way you can. But I should imagine you've been doing exactly that, in order for him to have got here. He chose well with you, Elizabeth dear.'

I'm taken aback by the idea that I apparently had had no agency in the matter of our relationship. Suzy carries on without pause.

'People are going to want all sorts from you. Learn to be discerning in who you trust. And what agenda they have. People are going to resent you. A lot. They're going to complain. Dislike what you're doing. Say nasty things about you. Outsource their own misgivings to you, as well as any issues they have with this great place.' She sweeps her hands through the air again. 'As Jeff's wife, you have to be prepared for all of it. The good and the bad.' She stares at me again. 'Don't take anything to heart. The compliments or the insults. You're the blank canvas on which people can project their emotions about this establishment. That way you'll be able to do your own thing, and you'll both benefit.' Suzy takes a breath. 'And don't forget the power you hold by dint of being married to the president.' She smiles. 'People annoy you, you can deal with that in a manner you see fit. I certainly have. Anyway, what a lifetime of privilege you'll both have. Being at the forefront of education. Being allied to some of the greatest minds this planet has to offer.'

'What an incredible thought,' I tell her, not untruthfully. I think of you again. The idea that I've risked losing all this privilege in exchange for what you've given me. In exchange for you. Is the love we have worth it?

'A thought that is now a reality,' Suzy says with another

laugh. 'Naturally, Jeff's learned his lesson. Last semester was difficult.' I open my mouth slightly to ask *What lesson?* before my brain catches up with me.

'I know.' I'm not going to be caught off guard, and the only way I can reconcile the idea of Jeff having kept secrets from me is by telling myself that we were going through it with the miscarriages and he hadn't wanted to worry me. But even when I think back, he hadn't seemed different or stressed at that time. A little distracted for a week or two afterwards, but otherwise normal. So much so that I'd asked myself whether he wanted children at all, until I'd come to terms with it being Jeff's way.

'We had to learn the hard way at times too.' Suzy's eyes cloud over. 'But we're happy now, and so delighted that the position is going to you both.' *You both.* The floor tilts in front of me and I have to steady myself. 'And with Harley and his medical appointments, we couldn't carry on. So sad after all he did with the Wickham Fellowships. A dream of his, to leave this world a better place. He really did try and hang on a few more months to see it all announced. One hundred fellowships last year. Quadruple that number this year, thanks to the incredible generosity of the community. We're praying that figure is confirmed soon.'

'Confirmed?' I say, thinking about how we've already announced it in our Rosemont Development Award entry.

'Yes. Confirmed.' Suzy gives a tinkly laugh. 'Basically. Just tying things up now. Anyway, Harley. It was his absolute favourite part of the job, ringing every single recipient to let them know they'd won.' She lightly presses her right index finger against the underside of her nose. 'Goodness, look at me, would you?'

'Harley's...' I falter. 'I had no...'

'No, no, we didn't tell a soul. He's been extremely insistent on not telling anyone. Jeff knew, obviously. Had to go through the proper channels.' She winks at me. 'And the role couldn't have gone to anyone better than your husband. And I hope and pray that Harley stays with us to see the final figure announced at the gala. His big moment. A lifetime of work.'

'Oh goodness.' I reach out for Suzy's hand. She stiffens and pulls away from me. 'I'm sorry. That makes sense now.' I stop speaking. It had struck me as odd that Harley hadn't stayed one more academic year to see his efforts come to fruition.

'No need for all that.' She gives me a distant smile. 'Now listen. You just make sure that husband of yours steps into my husband's shoes. Carries on what he started and makes the most of that brilliant network of his.'

'Yes. I will. I'm so proud to be part of all of this.' I sweep my arms around the room as Suzy did. 'And the Fellowship scheme, and everything else that's going on.'

'Yes, Harley has left Jeff with so many plans. It's a wonderful thing my husband has done. His legacy is going to change many, many lives. Honestly. And Jed and Nate have gone off to Harvard and Yale, but they're back and forth to see their Pops.'

I take the bait and indulge her. If I'm going to start

playing the game, I'd best start high, and clearly she doesn't want my pity. I know exactly what is required of me. 'Of course. Clever boys. You must have done a wonderful job with their upbringing.'

'Well, yes, and their countless nannies.' She laughs again, clearly relieved to be fitting neatly back into her own role. 'But they've been amazing, and…'

I drift off at this point, thinking about what Suzy said about Jeff, only picking up snippets of what Suzy says. I pull myself together, reminding myself to demonstrate good manners; they'd come in handy for being the perfect wife.

Suzy's mouth is still moving. 'And Nate…girlfriend… Jessica Fortescue. Banking dynasty. It's all rather… Oh look, here's the man himself.' I turn to see my husband speed-walking with his PA Janet next to him, notebook in hand. He's wearing the same clothes he wears every day: a grey-brown tweed suit, tortoiseshell glasses, brown brogues. He, too, likes to play the part.

Jeff nods. 'Ah, just the person I wanted to see. You must have read my mind.' He gives me a smile. 'Hello, Elizabeth.' His arm hovers behind me as he kisses my cheek.

I think of your lips there not long ago, lingering there for a while before you concertinaed yourself down the bed.

'Very glad you're here,' Jeff says. As the shade of my skin starts to give me away, I force myself to look him in the eye. My husband, University president.

'Congratulations, Jeff.' I cough. 'We're all so proud of you.'

'Thank you.' He squeezes my arm, and there is something

unspoken between us, the unspooling of our imagined future. Jeff's tenure. The Lodge. A baby. All we've ever wanted.

But then my mind goes to you, earlier. Our closeness. The way you propped yourself up on the bed on your left elbow, right hand working its way down my body. 'It's okay. I've got you,' you whispered as I held back before finally giving into you for the second time that hour.

'Congratulations to you too,' Jeff says, looking around him, presumably to make sure he has an audience – which he does, in Janet and Suzy. He nods at me. 'After all, you're a big part of why I'm here. Your constant support.' He gives me a flat, performative sort of smile before waiting a beat and reverting back to form. 'Right. So listen. Janet's booked us a table. Cecconi's. Haven't you, Janet?'

'Yup. Early.' Janet looks at me. 'Congratulations. Jeff has always told us how instrumental you've been in his appointment.'

'Thank you,' I reply, wondering why this is the first time Jeff has ever shown any gratitude towards me in public.

'We're being joined by Abraham – in fact, there are a few things I need to discuss with him, so why don't I go a bit early and get that boring stuff out of the way and you follow on later?' Jeff says. 'He's going to run through everything. We'll celebrate at the same time, of course.' He gives me another smile and squeezes my arm.

'Ow,' I murmur, stepping away. Jeff's normally gentle with me. I'm again reminded of you earlier, the pressure of your thumb on my wrist.

'Love Abraham,' Suzy says. 'Brutal as hell. Knows the

media. Got us out of many a crisis.' She throws back her head and lets out another tinkly laugh. 'Elizabeth, get on his good side. He'll help you out of any spot. The worse, the better for Abraham. He loves a disaster. As our director of communications, he's second to none.' She sounds more serious now, and I notice Janet nodding.

I think of you again and how Abraham would get me, *us*, out of that one if our affair were ever to be discovered. How would we countenance what we'd been doing?

'He even managed to whitewash that terrible stalking incident. Don't know how he does it.'

'Midas touch.' Jeff's voice echoes down the corridor. 'Not that we'll need it. At least we won't now I'm in charge,' he adds. I laugh, expecting him to follow suit but his expression remains the same. I watch him again, the way he holds himself in these hallowed halls, pulling out his phone and holding it up against his ear, Janet keeping up with his great strides. Despite the way I'm feeling, I know that if I want all this, if I want the title, the lifestyle, the kudos, the value of contributing to the Wickham Fellowships, even in some small way – and if I want to protect it all – then you, my love, unfortunately have to go.

By the time supper rolls around, my make-up is gritty around my eyes. I'm exhausted and agitated every time I think about having to end things with you. Harley and Suzy made an exit half an hour earlier, with promises of dinner in a few days, 'before things get hectic with plans for the inauguration ceremony.' As she left, Suzy patted my arm, and I knew any mention of Harley's illness was a closed book; it was now business as usual, however hard things got for them. 'And don't forget the gala,' she added. 'Speaking of which, are you going to give a speech at the ceremony?'

I think of Suzy's words as I dab cold water under my eyes. I stare at myself for a minute. Yes, I'll give a speech. I mentally rehearse how I will stand up at the lectern and try to shake the feeling that I'm not up to the task. Then I do something I've vowed I'll never do: I ring you. But not before gently pressing each stall door with my foot to check I'm alone. There's something about the thought of not being with you anymore. Whether or not I'll bring myself to finish things with you. How will my nervous system respond to the void you'll leave behind? How I'll miss you when all that remains is Jeff's almost scripted familiarity. I feel reckless after the alcohol, giddy at the thought of you watching me onstage at the ceremony. Watching me in a position of power. Heat charges through me.

Thankfully, you pick up on the second ring. I knew you would. You're not working today or tomorrow. I ache at the thought of finishing things with you. Not yet, I tell myself. I need some more time. Before the inauguration. I'll do it before then. The words sound empty, even to me.

'Elizabeth.' You sound bemused. 'What are you doing? I thought you'd—'

'I wanted to...' What did I want? 'I've just had a couple of champagnes,' I say, my tone coquettish.

'A couple?' You snort. 'Wow. Well, I guess you're not

used to it, are you?'

I think I hear footsteps nearby. I move to the back of the bathroom, through some frosted glass doors, and into a small, unused shower cubicle with a yellowing OUT OF USE sign tacked to the door.

'Nope.' I lock myself in and sit on a narrow wooden ledge, one foot against the door. 'But I wanted to hear you,' I whisper. 'You know I can't stay away from you.' I'm aware I shouldn't say those words to you right before I'm due to end things.

You ask me what I'm doing. What I'm wearing. I tell you Jeff's appointment has been confirmed. A charge runs up my spine: the sanctity of our secret; the contrast between how I feel about you and what I know I have to do. The fear my life will crumble if I'm found out. I lower my voice. I tell you the things I want you to do to me. Things I never told a soul before I met you. I'm still surprised by how in sync our bodies are after all this time. You clear your throat. 'What else?' you ask. And… And shit.

'Someone's calling through. It might be Janet. Or something to do with Jeff. I've got to go.' I hang up. *Sorry*, I type. *I'd better go back. But I've got a few more minutes if you want to text.*

Sure. A thumbs up emoji appears on my screen.

What are you doing anyway? I can't bear to let you go.

Working, you reply. I wait for you to carry on, but you remain silent.

On what? I venture.

Home stuff, you say.

Home stuff? What home stuff?

Just…stuff. Nothing you need to worry about.

I'm not worried, I'm just interested in knowing what you're doing? I try and sound light in tone but something about your reticence to talk after I've hung up so quickly is making me uneasy. I start typing out something to show I'm not being needy, but everything I draft sounds wrong and overwrought.

I just miss you. I don't need to know everything about you. It's just that…

I put down my phone. Are you playing some power game with me, now Jeff's the University's big player? Are you taunting me? And even worse, are you going to cause trouble for me?

I pick up my phone again. *Never mind,* I type and press Send, my earlier frisson of excitement fizzling out into some sort of poison which makes the idea of not being with you even more difficult to accept. *Speak later.*

It's only after I've sent the text and waited for a reply that never comes that I realise something. Despite all the time we've spent together, despite how much of my physical and emotional self I've given you, despite our proclamations of love, I don't know much about you at all.

2.

The Uber ride to Cecconi's to meet Jeff and Abraham, the director of communications, feels interminable – too much alcohol pitching against the agitation over whether or not you'd replied.

As we reach the edge of the main street the sky is still bright, forcing its way into my psyche when what I wish for is darkness. I open the car window in an unsuccessful effort to make myself more alert, and by the time I get inside the restaurant, I'm geared up to greet Jeff, who is already seated in a booth with a man I can only assume is Abraham. He's solidly built, with thick, black hair set to one side and features which sit well in his face. He appears relaxed, the sleeves of his white shirt rolled up to his elbows, which are resting on the table in front of him. I cast a glance down at my phone one last time before slipping it into my bag. You haven't contacted me. I concentrate on what's ahead, signalling to the waiter and mouthing *over there* as I point to my husband. 'With them.' The waiter looks over at Jeff, smiles at me and gives a small nod of acknowledgement, and I walk straight over, the buzz of chatter around me and the background jazz mellowing my mood. They're talking intently, and don't see me at first.

'We have to carry on as normal,' Abraham is saying. 'As though this never happened. Put it to one side completely. All right? Oh, and Elizabeth—' Abraham starts as he notices me behind Jeff. He stands up, opening his arms. He is a solid physical presence, tall and straight-backed, with an ease of posture I find disconcerting. 'Hey, Elizabeth. I don't think we've met properly before, have we?' he says.

'I'm not sure we have, no.'

'Anyway, it's great to meet you.'

'You too.' He kisses my cheek. 'I've heard so much about you already.'

'Lovely to be able to celebrate with you.' I'm taken aback by this display of overfamiliarity and extract myself. I don't ask him exactly what it is he has heard, and from whom. My earlier excitement at being in this position in the University has dulled; with the idea of you not being in my life any longer, everything feels flat.

'And you, Elizabeth. We're so delighted,' Abraham replies, ignoring my formality. I want to ask him who 'we' are and what 'we've' had to put to one side. But I make myself forget about that as I decide how best to react.

'And so are we,' I respond with a smile and make a point at nodding over at my husband. 'Really. Jeff worked so hard, and it's so nice it's all paid off. And he has such big plans for the University.' Jeff smiles approvingly, before pointing at the bottle of champagne.

'We saved some for you,' Abraham chuckles. 'Just.'

'Lovely.'

I watch Jeff pour my wine and then Abraham's, his forefinger lifted slightly towards the waiter. 'Another one of these, please.' He flashes a brief smile at the waiter, who appears out of nowhere at our table. It appears my husband has already inhabited his role seamlessly. 'Thank you. Give us five minutes to decide what to order, and bring my wife a menu.'

I scan through the food listing the waiter brings while listening to them talking. Budgets. Where the money will go. Jeff's aims for the University. Problematic areas. Issues that might turn into bigger 'headaches', as Abraham calls them. Branding. Subtle changes of focus. The language around the University and its 'giving'. And the main priorities in the coming weeks and months: the inauguration, the announcements of the Wickham Fellowships, and the big gala.

'Got a lot on, guys.' Abraham tears off a piece of bread from a basket on the table, stuffing it into his mouth. 'I mean, this is all high-level strategy stuff that we'll discuss in our board meeting. Jeff, that's the one right after the inauguration, remember. I'm presenting. So are you. All the governors are coming. Elizabeth, sorry to bring work into this celebration dinner.' He drains his glass. 'Can't seem to help it.'

'It was you and Harley that came up with this idea, was it not?' Jeff puts down his glass. 'Expanding the fellowship scheme. Getting our University into number one position? You have a lot riding on it.' He pulls out his phone and starts to look at his messages, something he's railed against ever since I've known him.

'Yeah, well.' Abraham puts down his bread, and with Jeff now otherwise occupied, looks at me. 'It is. It's my life's work. Can't be seen to fail now, can I?' He takes another slug of his drink and laughs. 'The director of comms needs to do a good job with his own comms.'

'Why don't I get involved?'

I realise that if I want to take a leaf out of Suzy's book, I need to speak out. If I want to really and truly start living as the president's wife, if I want Jeff and I to raise our profiles, I need to get stuck in. If you're no longer going to be in my life, I need to prepare myself for whatever comes next. Make myself proud. Fill the void you leave.

'I've already written some research papers here. I know the ropes.' I look around. Jeff is still on his phone. 'I'd love to do more. And what better way to do that than with the Wickham Fellowships?' I pick up my glass and hold it towards Abraham. 'Number one…' I think about how impactful our work could be. I'm fired up for the first time since you entered my life. 'I could help out with fundraising.' I train myself not to look over at Jeff for reassurance. Not to lift my voice at the end of a sentence. I'm direct. Clear. I have to riff off Abraham. Play my own role. 'I was with a UK charity for five years before moving over here. Raised £3 million for the homeless with the Bed for Life campaign. So I know about raising a lot of cash in a short amount of time. And I'm also well-organised, so I can help out with the gala fundraising event too. I know you might just see me as Jeff's wife,' I add, astonished at the strength of my words, 'but I'm totally invested in making this role of Jeff's work for us both. After all, we're a team. Like Harley and Suzy. So, from a comms perspective...'

I let the words hang in the air. Abraham's gaze flickers towards Jeff.

'Well, from a comms perspective that sounds dang great.' Abraham roars with laughter. 'We do need more bodies on board. And what better than to have the wife of the University's president involved. I'll talk to Virginia in HR in the morning. Set you up with something official. To add to your already very impressive roster.'

My stomach sinks at those words. I'll have to live up to Abraham's narrative about me. I wonder where he got it from.

'Thank you.' I feel the corners of my mouth upturning slightly. 'And cheers.' I catch Jeff's eye and he slides his phone back into his pocket, mouths *Sorry*.

'That sounds amazing, Abraham.' Jeff gives me a small nod. 'I want my wife to be happy. After all, she pushed me to go for the role in the first place. She's been a wonderful support.' He looks at me and smiles, and for the rest of the meal I allow them to talk shop. They discuss the students. The donors. Lavinia, the chair of governors voted in shortly before Jeff started, who will need to see the annual report. What 'stance' Jeff will take. The University's strategy for introducing him to the public.

Abraham looks at me. 'You know, I've just realised you two look very good together. Look the part. So your relationship will be part of my strategy.' He claps his hands and looks from Jeff to me. 'It's like you were both made for this role. Elizabeth, how great to have you on board. I know you'll love it here. No two days are the same. You'll be kept very busy.' It's like he's been reading my mind. 'And you'll both be given media training.' He smiles gleefully. 'Roughhousing with the hacks.'

'Again?' Jeff says.

'Of course. Can never have too much of that.' I listen as Abraham tells Jeff he understands where he's coming from, but needs to align his voice with the values and ethos of the University. 'We need to think about every word very carefully.' He looks like he's still chewing on his bread. 'If you want to position yourself as forward-thinking, as revolutionary but with a traditional core,' he says, pointing at Jeff's suit, 'you look the part. But we also need to demonstrate our ability to change, and to reflect that in our language. To be inclusive. And approachable and confident. But without being patronising. We're moving away from it being a few rich donors supporting everyone. Community and all. Less of a hierarchy. I'll draft something for you and send it over.'

'Even if there are still just a few rich donors,' Jeff says with a laugh, 'we should try and spread the fundraising. Make it a real community venture. We need to keep the elite language, though. People buy into it from right across the globe. It's a hard balance.'

'It sure is, but we manage. Which is why we're exactly that,' Abraham says. 'Elite. Accessibly elite, but not too accessible. Now,' he rubs his hands together. 'Community spirit. Let's do some more events where we get all the locals involved. Some green-fingered initiatives outside our grounds. Show them we care.'

Everyone goes quiet, and the waiter comes to ask us if we're ready to order yet. Jeff waves him away. 'Another five minutes.'

'And the big thing we need to discuss,' Abraham raises his glass. 'The Med School. The new Wickham Wing.'

I try and act normal. Run my finger down the plastic sleeve of the menu, heart thumping. You've never mentioned a new wing. And neither has Jeff.

'Genius of you, Jeff.' Abraham says. 'It's really going to solidify us as the major league player. If we can get the last part of that other funding, we'll be able to demolish the Franklin Wing quickly.' There was no pushback on the comms for that. Jeff? You with me? Better that they leak things slowly than we do a big announcement. Give people time to get used to it, all that new equipment changing. It's a big deal for that department. They've been there forever. Anyway, we've got those biweekly meetings now scheduled for the main players. They can feed back. In time, of course. Let their teams know what's going on, so everyone feels involved. And heard.'

'Yup.' Jeff clears his throat. 'Right. That's enough about work, don't you think?'

The Franklin Wing. Your place of work. You've never said a thing. As one of the main players, I now hold this piece of information which has a direct impact on you.

Your beloved facilities department is going to be razed to the ground.

I think back to a few hours earlier, whilst we were lying in bed and you were joking about meeting Jeff. But now it doesn't seem funny at all. If the Wickham Wing project starts soon, and Jeff is doing his walkabouts as University president, you and he might get more than a simple introduction.

I can barely swallow my drink.

I think about the first time I met you. I'd been out on a limb at a Medical School fundraiser, wanting to talk to someone so I wasn't wandering around like a spare part. You were welcoming people and taking down donations for the silent auction. I was waiting for Jeff to finish talking to some bigwig. I introduced myself to you. You showed me your lanyard and I asked how much we were hoping to raise.

'Just a tiny one, $250,000. Except this drinks thing is so extravagant it probably cost us that much in the first place.'

I gasped and said that was a lot in one night. 'We had a few big nights when I was fundraising back in the UK,' I quickly added, not wanting to show myself up as a total amateur. 'But not as many as this. And we'd do some rounds by traditional post. Lots of cold-calling. I guess I never realised how much went into academia.'

'Oh, you'd be surprised,' you said with a shrug. 'Academia is the worst of the lot. Look.' You pointed at a woman in a green velvet suit. Her grey hair was pushed back with a green velvet Alice band, the type I used to wear at school in England. 'She's giving $40k. Her husband's loaded. She's from old family money.' You pointed out someone else, another old white guy who looked not unlike a cartoon version of Albert Einstein. 'He's big in AI. Wants to put in another $50k towards a virtual reality operating machine. They'll do all that if we raise enough at the gala for the fellowships. Loose change for them.'

'And what do they get in return?'

'There's the rub.' His eyes slid back over to Alice-band woman. 'She gave a donation last year too, and this just keeps things ticking over for her. So she can keep herself busy, I guess.'

'You know a lot about this place,' I said. 'It's good, though, to see people wanting to change things for the better. It's a nice thought.'

Something crossed your face at that point. 'You're sweet.' Your eyes searched mine. 'It *is* a nice thought.'

'And him?' I pointed to a tall man surrounded by a crowd. 'What does he want?'

'Kudos?'

You licked your bottom lip ever so slightly, and something intangible crossed between us. An electrical pulse that had settled deep in my loins. I coughed. 'Excuse me. My husband.' I headed over to meet Jeff, but by then I knew. You knew.

However, despite my constant excuses to visit the Medical School and attend lectures in the Franklin Wing, it was a good half-semester until our paths crossed again. It was another fundraiser and I'd made an extra effort that night, blow-drying my hair, making sure my make-up was on point and even buying a new blusher, which the sales assistant had assured me would soften my skin tone, which I'd always regarded as pale but which she referred to as 'English rose.'

Jeff waves his hand in the air again, bringing me back to the present. 'Let's eat now.' The volume of the music has increased, and the room is hot and fuggy. 'Elizabeth?' It's not so much a question but a command; it's time for me to order, and dithering is no longer acceptable.

I scan the menu. 'Just a...' Jeff's eyes are on me. 'I'll have the puttanesca,' I say. I almost laugh at the irony.

Jeff slaps his menu shut. 'Steak for me. Abraham?'

'Salad for me. The crevette and the fries.' I open my mouth to say I've changed my mind and I'll have that too, but the waiter has already scooped up the menus and gone.

I get through the next two hours with the thought that I know something you don't, and that perhaps I should tell you what's happening behind the scenes at your workplace. I smile in all the right places, drink lots of water. I listen to Jeff and Abraham talking about tactics. How much media exposure we want, if any. Whether our reputation is robust enough to withstand a passive comms approach. Whether our strategies for the #MeToo scandal have worked. How the new outbuildings can be developed in a way that doesn't raise hell with the residents.

'Kids,' Abraham says after we've finished eating. He rubs his hands together. 'We need to do some initiative with underprivileged kindergartners in the area. Maybe some more eco-friendly stuff in their gardens. Get our logos engraved on some signage. I'll get our equalities team on it. Feeds into all that community stuff.'

'It's a good idea,' Jeff replies. 'Nice for everyone.' He looks at me. 'I'm beat. Let's go home.'

After we've paid the bill, dropped Abraham home and reached the cottage, I'm simultaneously exhausted and wired. Jeff, though, wants to stay up drinking.

'I'm sorry,' I say. 'I need to get to bed.'

'Really?' He tilts his crystal glass towards the soft light. 'You, my wife, don't want to celebrate your husband being made president?' He gives a small laugh. 'Our new life?'

'I'm shattered' I murmur, wondering why he sounds so flat. 'But well done again. By the way,' I add, trying to inject curiosity into my voice, 'Abraham mentioned the new Wickham Wing. That sounds really exciting. That's a huge part of your job.'

'It is,' says Jeff. 'It's exciting.'

'Who are the main players?' I ask. 'Should I know this kind of thing now I'm married to the president?'

'Of course.' Jeff seems surprised. 'Sorry. Yes. You're right. Of course. I'll fill you in. Me. Abraham. Some of the donors. It's all a bit under the radar at the moment, so we've got to be careful. The major donors like to keep low-key. Which is why it's all so hush-hush. It's a big part of why I was voted in.' A big part? I've never heard you mention it, and it appears now that the entire direction of the Medical School is about to change.

I say goodnight to Jeff and head upstairs to brush my teeth, wash my face and get into bed. I message you on Telegram. I tell you about everything that happened tonight. I don't tell you about the Wickham Wing, though; that will have to wait. I tell you that you upset me earlier, and that I'm tired. That my body still aches from earlier.

It's only now that I realise I've decided to end things with you. I still need to leave you on a good note, though.

Twenty minutes later, you're still offline. That's not like you. Had Jeff's promotion really thrown you that much? You never cared when he was provost; if anything, it gave you even more of a thrill. Now, it seems, you are showing me your true colours.

Three Days Before the Inauguration

3.

The next morning, I'm exhausted. I'd spent the entire night wide awake, wondering why you'd been behaving so oddly and how I was going to get you to talk to me about it. Just as I'm about to drift off, I hear the hiss of the coffee machine downstairs. I internally plead for Jeff not to wake me up but five minutes later, he comes up, a plate of toast in one hand and a mug of coffee in the other.

'Six forty-five. Wakey wakey.' I pull myself up and he passes me my favourite mug, a large earthenware one we'd bought on holiday in Italy. 'The inauguration. There's a meeting about it later. Three o'clock. In the office.'

'Fine.' I shuffle up the bed, my eyes heavy from lack of sleep. 'Thank you.' I yawn. 'I'm going to give a speech,' I say, more determined than ever to nurture our new lives together, especially since you'd gone so quiet on me. 'Suzy asked me yesterday if I would. Like she did.' I stop myself from saying I won't be as poised as her. 'I want to be,' I sip the coffee. 'Yum. This is good. I want to be a good wife to you.' As I say this, I feel myself changing. The thought of you inside me feels as shameful as it did good only this time yesterday.

'You make an excellent wife.' Jeff puts one knee on the bed and bends over to kiss me. I put my arms around him, and out of nowhere he's taken off his shirt, unbuckled his belt, and I'm filled with the type of urgency I thought I only felt with you. 'God, this feels good,' he whispers. 'We haven't done this for so long.'

I pull him towards me.

'Is it because you want to sleep with a president?'

I laugh, thinking he's joking, but his eyes are already closed as he slides inside me, lost in himself, and within a second the urgent feeling has passed. I go through the ritual, spreading my legs, making the right noises, and I'm about to ask him to slow down but then I start to think of you. I watch the ceiling moving back and forth, and as I'm starting to zone out, he moans, rolls off me and turns to face the wall. 'Sorry,' he says. 'Got carried away. It's you. I can't help it.'

'No need to apologise,' I say. And I mean it. But I wonder if something lies behind his detachment of late, and if those words – *Good Morning, Mrs. President!* – have changed everything. Or simply set something in motion that cannot be stopped?

I prop a pillow behind my back. Will this be it now? For the rest of time? When you're gone from my life, will I be able to recreate with my own husband what we have now? Before you, I never knew such a thing existed.

'There's just something about you,' you whispered to me the second time at your apartment. Our foreheads were pressed together as we were saying goodbye. You led me, slowly, back into your bedroom again right after that, and it was another two hours before I left your apartment for real, the taste of you still on my lips.

I shiver. Pulling up the sheet, I grab the now-cold coffee. I so desperately want to say something to Jeff about how clinical he was with me just now. Or has he always been like that? Have I normalised it? I open my mouth to speak. But the weight of my own shameful actions hooks the words back down my throat.

'Now listen.' Jeff, back to president mode within seconds, is out of bed again. He stretches his neck as he does up the top button of his shirt. 'The plans for later. Three in the afternoon, yes? And your speech.' He bends to kiss me again. 'It's a great idea. You'll be amazing.'

'You think?'

'Nope.' He looks straight at me. 'You're my wife. I'd never have married someone mediocre. I don't think. I know.' I kiss his cheek and he looks at me again. 'Listen, enough about work,' he says. 'You'll be great. Anyway, I've got more important things to discuss with you.'

'What?'

'I've been thinking.' He puts a hand on each of my shoulders. 'About all this. I've got this position and we're going to be here a while, although we'll be moving house soon, and I think it might be time. Which reminds me. I need to confirm with the movers ASAP.'

'Time?' I start to panic. Has the knowledge of my relationship with you permeated every part of my psyche? 'Time for what?'

'I think, well, you… How about we look into…' My shoulders start to hurt as he tightens his grip. 'You know.'

'I don't. I'm slightly irritated. 'No, I don't know.'

'The paperwork?' he says, obviously stalling. 'We could look into the process. If, um, if it doesn't work again. We can keep on trying.' He points to my stomach. 'But start the process at the same time, so we, you know…'

I finally work out what my husband is unable to say. 'Oh my God,' I laugh. 'You mean…'

'Yes. I mean,' he laughs too. 'I've done some research of my own. If we start now, it could take a year. I thought maybe we could look into China. Or something. Apparently the process is relatively straightforward and with my new role, maybe things will move quicker. And in a year or so I'll be well into my time by then. I'll have learned the ropes. You'll have learned the ropes too, I should think. I think it will be a good time to… And if it does happen naturally, then they'll be…'

'Siblings,' I whisper. 'Wow, Jeff, I, I thought, after all this time,' I point to my stomach and give a tiny laugh. 'That you weren't interested. You never said much. I just—'

'Don't cry about it,' he says with a laugh, as much as Jeff is capable when having a serious conversation. 'I've been thinking about it a lot. I wanted to wait until everything was perfect. Until' – he looks around – 'everything was perfect for us. And now it is. Me, president. You, telling Abraham you want to have more input. It's all just as it should be.' He's shallow-breathed. 'And now, well, we'll have enough to pay for some decent help. Just imagine. It's all happening for us. I know it is. It is. It's goddamn perfect.' His energy picks up pace. 'We need to make the best of this once-in-a-lifetime opportunity.'

He lets go of my shoulders and relief billows through me. 'I'm not crying, I'm just...' I'm just what? The luckiest person on the planet right now? Why is the universe rewarding me for the awful things I've done? I think of that time again. The minutes that stretched into hours. The sound of my gasping before pain was replaced by silence. The cold, shiny metal of the toilet's handle as I flushed it. The whirl of water, spiralling into a deep and unending emptiness. 'Thank you, Jeff. Thank you. I love you.' I stretch up and kiss him again on the mouth, and it turns into something longer, and more lingering, until he pulls away and holds my arms firmly in place a distance away from him.

'Right.' Jeff pats his breast pocket to check his phone. 'Much as I'd love to stay with you, I'll see you at three.' If he's ever wondered what I've been doing during the hours in the day I haven't been with him, he's never asked. The English language research project I was working on has run out of funding and I've been so utterly consumed with you I've had no time or energy for much else. But then I think of our new lives together, mine and Jeff's. Me, the University president's wife. Our hopes for a new future. A new start. I think of Jeff's words: *It's goddamn perfect.* And it is, but I question why I can't match his energy, feel what I'm supposed to be feeling. And as I'm thinking about hopes, something unsettling bleeds into my psyche:

the way you behaved yesterday. I'd thought it would be seamless splitting from you. I would use the excuse that you deserve better. That you might like to start your own family. Look for someone younger. I thought you'd be upset but react well. That you'd tell me, perhaps, that it was a relief. But now I have the creeping sensation that you aren't going to go away that easily, that you'll shatter the dream Jeff has so beautifully dangled in front of me. Perhaps you creating that distance will make me want you even more.

We need to talk, I message you as soon as Jeff's gone. *Can I come over for a bit later today?*

Hi, you reply. *Didn't hear back from you.*

Sorry, I say, wondering why you haven't started with your usual effusiveness about how beautiful I am, before remembering that isn't the point of my message. I need to be ruthless and not get tangled up in your behaviour, although it would be easier to let my ego play along with you. *Got tied up with loads of stuff.*

No worries.

Listen, I type. *I've got to be back on campus at three. Just after lunch?*

I can't do today, you tell me. It's as if you already know what I'm about to tell you. *I'm packing up to get ready. I'm going away for a couple days. Fishing trip.*

You are? Wow. Okay. Have a great time. Where are you going? When are you back?

Strange, I think. You normally tell me your every movement. I scroll back through the past few days' worth of conversations. I'm sure you told me somewhere that you had lots of work on for the next week, but when I look back there's nothing to suggest you've told me anything at all.

I pull up the slats of the blinds in the front room and scan my surroundings. I can't see anything or anybody other than both our cars in the drive. Jeff has obviously made the twenty-minute walk across campus to his office. I open the window a fraction.

Tell me everything, I reply, aware I'm getting sucked into in the conversation, but by this point my curiosity is winning out.

College friends, is all you give me. Although you never seemed bothered when I do the same to you. I feel an arrow-like sting in my chest. *Jeff and I are going on holiday. We're going to upstate New York on a theatre trip. We're going on a research trip.* And the rest. All that time you've been there, unquestioningly loyal, and I've almost come to expect it. *Have a wonderful time,* you say. *You deserve it.* Have I been so dazzled by your adoration of me? Is this all this has been? An exercise in propping up my ego, a distraction from what happened last year? A distraction that's turned into something real?

Well, I hope you have an amazing time.

Thank you, you say, without the usual *x* at the end.

All okay?

Yes. Totally fine.

Listen, it's the inauguration next week, so let's meet before then? I type. *Need to speak to you about something.* I hold back from confronting him about his strange moods.

Sure, you reply.

Tuesday? Inauguration is on Wednesday. I'll come over at some point?

I start to type that I'll bring you food, the oat bran muffins from Carey's Deli that you love, before deleting the message and reminding myself I have to be strong. Except I'm feeling more and more unnerved. You love me, don't you? Or has a strange defensiveness taken hold? We talked recently about attachment styles. Have I perhaps given too much away about my own? Tucking one hand under my leg, I wait for your response, telling myself maybe you're just busy and your tone doesn't reflect the way you feel about me, but my gut tells me otherwise.

Tuesday it is, you say finally.

OK. Have a great time away. Tuesday, I write. I wait again for your reply, but your status switches to 'Offline'. I spend the next five minutes staring at the screen, waiting for you to reappear, my hand hovering over the telephone icon, but you remain invisible. It strikes me now that you know. You know. Somehow you know what I'm about to do and you're pre-empting it by distancing yourself. Creating a void you know I'll want to fill. And although I'm on to you, I still find myself falling for it all.

For the next few hours I'm incapacitated, veering between sitting at my laptop researching speeches to distracting myself with baby names and ritually logging on to Telegram, but you remain offline. You told me once that you weren't talking to anyone else on the app, that it was reserved solely for me.

You'd declared your fidelity to me the third time I visited your apartment. 'I'm married, though,' I said. 'It's not like I want you to be with anyone else, but I have no hold over you. So...'

'But you do, Elizabeth,' you breathed, fingers pressing firmly into the base of my skull. You tugged gently on my hair, tipping my head back. You bit my lower lip softly. 'You do.'

And now you're acting so strangely. If you cause me any trouble and our affair ever comes to light, Jeff will leave me. We've discussed it, you and I, time and time again. 'I can't get caught,' I told you. 'Jeff has a red line about cheating. I'd be out. And once he says something, he sticks to it. There's no going back.'

You'd laughed at the danger. 'How exciting,' you said, something which gave me a thrill at the time, but which now makes me feel sick. And with everything that had happened, the idea of Jeff leaving me hadn't seemed so bad because I'd been so caught up in my own misery. You'd managed to mitigate that with the lightest press of a finger against my skin. But now. Now. I wonder whether Jeff's promise would stand, now he's been promoted. Whether divorcing the president's wife will be in Abraham's remit of reputational management.

At midday, as I'm about to get ready for the inauguration meeting, you pop up online, but you don't so much as ping me for those twenty minutes, something which has never happened before. You've always kept me warm with a one-liner, even if you've been busy. *I'm here,* you'll say. *Just doing some work so let's chat later, yes?*

In the hope of you noticing me, I start typing – *Did I do something wrong? How did you know I'm about to end things? Please don't make my life difficult*. But I end up deleting all my paranoid messages and putting down my phone.

I can't concentrate on my speech; my mind keeps wandering back to you and your potential next move. Grabbing the phone again, I open the University intranet and click on VACANCIES. *Join us in changing lives!* it says at the top of the page. I read through the blurb before scrolling down to MEDICAL SCHOOL. There are two jobs going, neither in any way related to yours. I relax a little. By now, if you'd been intending to up sticks, leave town and ghost me, your job would be advertised in time for the end of this semester.

I go back to the speech. Think about my life in the here and now. My opening gambit. *My wonderful husband, who was made for this role. Whose integrity and steadfastness*... I type and delete, type and delete. Blah blah blah. Everything I say sounds like I'm overcompensating for the things I was doing last year, and I can hear your voice in everything I write. How often you've told me I'm a good person. 'Don't worry,' you'd told me. 'You know this is normal? Everyone does it. That's why you're so good. You just don't realise. Your husband, he's probably at it too.' You'd laughed and I'd shaken my head.

I delete everything I've written so far, slam my laptop shut and grab my car keys. Without thinking too much about what I'm doing, I make my way over to yours.

4.

I don't normally drive to yours. But today, I have to race back and put on some make-up and get to the three o'clock inauguration meeting.

Parking at the edge of the woodland, I put on some lip gloss and tie my hair into a loose bun, checking my reflection in the rear-view mirror. I'm wearing a tank top and jeans, the casual, sexy outfit you love, and so I haven't had to make too much effort at least. You like me natural, or so you tell me. Although I plan to finish things with you, I haven't yet broken the psychological pattern that wants you to find me attractive.

I give myself a talking-to, wipe off my lip gloss and jump out of the car, but something about the usually calming woodland sets my teeth on edge: the warning screech of birds, the giant, clawlike branches bearing down on me. It's as though nature knows something I don't. At points I feel so paranoid I check that no one's following me.

Making my way to your front door, I hold up my hand ready to knock three times and then twice more slowly, as we've agreed. It always seemed so exciting before; now it just feels silly and for the first time, I notice the huge cracks in the white paint down the side of your door frame. There's no response. You must be out. Or have you already left for your trip? It crosses my mind that I should try the Medical School, but then I notice a sudden movement at your window. The drop of a curtain. You're in. You're in and you're hiding from me.

I knock again loudly, not caring who might be around, but you don't answer me. I check Telegram and you're online. I ring you, listening out for the tinny jangle of your ringtone, a crappy a capella version of a Coldplay melody. You're clearly quicker off the mark, though, and have set your phone to silent. You told me you'd never do that. That your phone is always turned up loud, in case it's me. The sexiest person alive. The love of your life, who's taught you so much about being good. About doing the right thing. Then you'd stare at me and cup my face in your hands before kissing me softly on the mouth. I'd wonder if Jeff has the capacity for such passion. It was only after meeting you that I realised I'd always mistaken the methodical and self-involved rhythms of my husband's movements as loyalty, the price to pay for the next steps of our marriage: two pink lines on the white plastic wand. The strands of a story that was yet to materialise, in my life at least.

I stand for a few more minutes getting my internal bearings, aware I mustn't react to the intense emotions flaring through me. But it's hard. My lungs shrink, the world around me presses in on my body and my throat foists the breath out of me like the last pathetic note of a punctured accordion. What kind of game are you playing? Do I need to keep you sweet? Do I need to wait until after the inauguration to finish things with you? Do I need to be smarter about this?

Despite everything, the way you're behaving towards me hurts. I turn around and start to walk back to my car, willing myself not to turn back and check if you're watching, but five steps on and I do. I look up to your window. The curtain is still. Did I imagine it all? I replay the sequence of events in my mind. You are in the house. I know you are. And now you and I are playing an even more dangerous game.

I reach the edge of the woodland and stop. Ten minutes later, a resolve anchors itself in the depth of my belly, and I turn back towards your apartment. Be courageous, I tell myself. Ask firmly, calmly, if something is the matter. Don't take no for an answer.

When I get to your door again I knock, this time without our special code. Three firm raps. Still, you don't answer. But then I start to call up to your bedroom window. I don't bother to look around. I shout louder, my voice sounding more urgent. And again. My actions are reckless, but they work. I hear the trip of your footsteps as you rush down the two flights of green-carpeted stairs to your front door. You open up but don't say anything, keeping your body curled behind the door.

'Can I come in at least?' I take a step forward, reminding myself of my earlier self-talk. 'Don't worry.' I glance at the top of your stairs, wondering if you have someone with you. 'I don't want to come up.' But you've already made your own view clear as you move away from the door and position yourself at the bottom of the stairs, arms folded across your chest. You don't say a word. 'I just...what's going on?'

You give a small shake of your head, which makes me want to cry. 'You can tell me.'

'Look,' you reply. 'Best we forget about this. Things have gone a bit strange between us, don't you think? Sometimes these things just happen. It's best we end things now. Right? I...' You clear your throat. 'I don't feel the same about you anymore.'

Although I've come here to tell you the same thing, I still love you, and your words skewer my heart. 'Okay,' I say. 'Do you mean that?'

'Yes.' You nod.

'Was it Jeff? Are you worried he could get you fired? Are you scared for your job?' My words come out in a rush. I think again about what I know about the Franklin Wing – your place of work being replaced with a new, shiny building. For a split second, I wonder if I should say something – my parting gift, a warning to you – but I decide against it. Your behaviour doesn't warrant that part of my energy. Your behaviour doesn't warrant my insider knowledge. Your behaviour doesn't warrant any part of me ever again.

'Listen, sometimes...you know...' You shrug as though I mean nothing to you. 'Things don't work. Do they? Listen. Wait.' You turn away and run back up the stairs. I shuffle my feet, wondering for a crazy second if I should take off my top. Surprise you. Try and seduce you again. But your front door clicks shut. I wait for you to reappear, but it's fifteen agonising minutes before you come back down.

'Sorry.' You look ruffled. Out of breath. Strange, given the amount of running you do. I think about your body. Athletic. Slim. The things you've done to me. I feel the familiar flush creeping up on me. 'Here.' You hand me a pen. 'Take this. Keep it. It's from me. A reminder.'

The pen is heavy in my hands. I glance down at the familiar navy colourway. The University's red eagle crest. It's beautiful. But still. After everything we've been through, is this it? Stationery? I look up, barely recognising the person in front of me.

'Best you go now.'

'Fine.' I lean in for a hug, my lip inadvertently brushing your cheek: a test, maybe, to see if you respond. Just one more kiss. One last time. I think of holding my arms above my head as you lie on top of me, our fingers intertwined. A tiny sound escapes me, and you turn away.

Sliding the pen into my handbag, I tell myself to maintain my dignity. To leave before I do or say something regretful, or even worse, desperate. I stare at you for one last time, drinking in the tiny freckles across your face. The small area of pitted skin on your inner left eye, which I'd kissed after you told me you got the scar after falling onto a sharp piece of metal on a bike when you'd been about eight.

'Fine,' I repeat, giving you one last chance. 'You'll never see me again.'

I pause for one second longer, waiting for you to say something. Anything. You nod, and I think about the pen. The crassness of it all. An old pen? You told me with no hesitation, a matter of days ago, that you loved me. You held my gaze for three beats longer than I was normally comfortable with, but you whispered something as you gently touched me, your fingers working your way downwards, circling, sliding, and I moaned and didn't hear you the first time, but you stared right at me and said it again as my body absorbed your touch – all of you – and I started to cry. *I love you. I love you. I love you.*

You push me gently but firmly out of the front door. Again I feel the familiar dampness on my cheeks as I let you guide me out of your life and back into the suffocating air around me.

Two Days Before the Inauguration

5.

When I got back after seeing you yesterday, I took out the pen, my only physical reminder of you, and held it in my hand until I realised I was running late. I redid my make-up at least twice before leaving home, overlaying the salty track marks on my cheeks with translucent powder and wiping the black smudges under my lower lashes with a damp cotton bud. Then I rushed to the inauguration meeting and sat away from Jeff, thanking my body for getting me there.

I've told myself not to contact you again and concentrate on the inauguration, but my mind is filled with thoughts of us. When I'm alone, I search the University intranet. You're there, handsome as ever in your headshot. You look happy. So trustworthy. So inviting. So suited to the role. I read through staff WhatsApps to see if anyone has mentioned you. I go through a hundred different scenarios about why you might have treated me the way you have. And what your intentions towards me really had been. You've always been so open. Told me everything. Let me in on all the secrets you've kept hidden from those around you – secrets, I see now, that you trailed at my feet the whole time we were together. A bit now, the rest the next time. You'd told me you loved me.

'Darn it this is good, Lizzie Lou,' Jeff says. It's two nights before the inauguration and I've made a salmon and asparagus tart, and a salad with pomegranate and molasses dressing. I had to concentrate on something that wasn't you, or the uncertainty of my future without you hovering at the periphery.

I'd been distracted, though, stalling at every step of the recipe, picking up my phone one more damn time to see if you'd messaged. My stomach had dropped each time I slid the phone back onto our white quartz kitchen counter.

'You okay?' Jeff asks me over the dinner table. I will him to stop chewing so loudly. 'You nervous?'

'Nervous?' I push my plate away. 'No, just not hungry.' I smile. 'Well, maybe a *bit* nervous.'

I need to have some excuse for behaving like this. In two days, I'll be on show to hundreds of people, and I still haven't reconciled pre-president Jeff with this man in front of me here now. The everyday Jeff is still there despite his new, upgraded identity. The way he still pushes his empty plate across the table, towards me, before wiping his mouth and leaving the table. The way he undoes his top three shirt buttons, twisting his neck three times before shaking out his shirt sleeves and slowly removing his cufflinks before bed. The way he lays on me, his body heavy, eyes on an indeterminate point on the wooden bedhead behind me.

'I guess I'm preoccupied about my speech.'

While I'm waiting for Jeff to speak again, my phone buzzes. I grab it from the counter and turn away from my husband, who has, contrary to his own rules, picked up his own handset, fork mid-air in his other hand. He's been spending his entire time on his phone, alternating between reading emails, calling Abraham, and tapping hard on the screen with his right forefinger.

I've set my phone so notifications won't show on my home screen, but I pray it's you. Just one more text. Some sort of explanation. A message to say you still love me. Hands shaking, I go through the motions, opening Telegram. I'm praying for a photo, perhaps. You, fishing. Or a one-liner – a reference to the way you've always kissed my neck three times after we'd made love, a private joke we share. I started to follow up our visits with three X's on Telegram every time I left, and we'd send this message to each other throughout the day as a signal we were thinking of each other in less than salubrious ways. Sometimes, if I was alone, you'd give me strict instructions on what I was to do next.

But instead, there's a message that makes no sense to me on first reading: *Hi B. You didn't turn up! See you later. Getting more and more urgent – I really can't wait much longer. Been waiting patiently all day for you.*

I read the message again. Silly you. Your mistake, I think, safe in the knowledge you'd told me you weren't seeing anyone else, so I assume you've typed the wrong letter. How could I think anything else? You're more than enough for any human, you'd tell me as you'd stroke my back with one finger. But then I notice that you're online, and realise you'll have seen that I'm online too. A couple of seconds later, the message has vanished and there's an empty space between us.

Been waiting patiently all day for you. It was a phrase you used with me. It was a phrase you often used with me after I'd told you I knew we'd meet in a frenzy whenever you said that to me. And why else would you be on Telegram with someone, instead of WhatsApp, email or text? 'The app for affairs and illegal stuff,' you said when you first told me of its existence. And I knew the latter was totally off your agenda; I glance down at my keyboard to check the proximity between the letters E and B. Not a mistake you could have easily made.

Jeff starts rambling along opposite me, the timbre of his voice setting my teeth on edge because he's breaking my focus. 'So I think if I position myself as the bridge between old-school and pioneering, people will trust me,' he says. 'I'm not doing anything too out-there. But I'm, you know, going to push boundaries.'

I don't respond; different scenarios are segueing through my mind. Have you ever mentioned a sister? A friend whose name begins with B? I look down at my phone again, pull up the intranet and search the Medical School support staff list for the initial B. The first one I spot is a governor I recognise, Bella Mayhew. But Bella is elderly, and although you claimed to like me being older than you, I think a possible octogenarian might be a step too far.

I scan through the rest of the names beginning with B, eyes hovering over the ones I think you might have gone for. All the while, I'm making sure to nod in the right places to engage with my husband, murmuring agreement at the end of each of his sentences. I'm surprised by how easy it is to pacify Jeff into thinking I'm not simply listening but hanging on his every word. Is this how it's going to be with him from now on?

'So. Speech?' Jeff says.

'Speech,' I manage, feeling like I might throw up. 'What do you think?'

'Whatever you say will be fine. And you'll be delivering one at the gala too, I hope. We've got plans for you. Me and Abraham. As he mentioned at dinner, we think you'll be very appealing to donors and colleagues.'

I think about what you would have told me. How invested you'd have been in my feelings around public speaking. In what I thought would go down well with the audience. And more importantly, what I'd really want to say. You valued my opinion and often asked why I didn't truly value my own.

Who the hell is B?

Wrong person! I type, breaking my rule never to text you in front of my husband. As an afterthought, I add a laughing emoji, then press Send, but you're offline again, and I have a feeling you'll ignore my message anyway. My finger hovers over Delete. My mind conjures up images of an imaginary B. Buxom to my slender, long blonde hair to my short, strands of it whipping across your face as you take her from behind. You, telling her she's your world. B, who is now a projection in my mind's eye; a mirror for all my own insecurities. I tell myself not to get caught up in it all. That it's a good thing. My future is here, opposite me. And if you have been cheating on me, perhaps it'll make it psychologically easier to come to terms with the end of our relationship.

'What's wrong?' Jeff puts down his fork. His movements are measured, perhaps in a bid to disguise his impatience. 'Why are you crying?'

'Am I?' I force myself to swallow down the lump in my throat. 'I don't know. I'm fine. Just tired. Overwhelmed.'

'It's me who's been made president.' He laughs scornfully. 'Not you.'

One Day Before the Inauguration

6.

The next day is busy again but you're there in my mind with B, pushing at the edges of my entire being, and I end up snapping at Jeff every time he speaks. I try and keep myself busy by actioning things that will positively impact my future, the one without you. Firstly, I do some research into adoption agencies near campus. The Sunbeam Agency looks good and has positive reviews and so I print off their form. I fill in half the information and leave it on my desk ready to complete the rest with Jeff later.

I realise how much there still is to finalise. The rehearsal dinner. Seating arrangements. The Development office's events team have been coordinating everything, looping me and Jeff into all their plans, and their constant messages recalibrate me. Every time I stop, though, I see your eyes, vacant with the softness of B's body. Had you ever loved me at all? Had I never been good enough for you? Thin enough? Sexy enough? Just enough?

I busy myself some more by taking it upon myself to oversee every detail of the inauguration, asking for some-one to call the florist and order more red and white flowers to complement the logo. I check out the meaning of the blooms, so they are in keeping with our ethos; it's something I realise Abraham expects, and it reminds me of my wedding to Jeff, although back then there were only twenty of us in a small church in the Highlands.

Once the details have been finessed and one last meeting fixed with the events team to go over speech timings, everyone feels just about ready to go. But first we have a meeting with Abraham in Jeff's office.

'Right, you two.' Abraham rubs his hands together. 'Inauguration. So soon. So exciting. Jeff, you with us?'

'Huh?' Jeff slides his phone onto the table. 'Yup.'

'You all right?' I ask. 'You look a bit peaky.'

'Things already getting to you?' Abraham doesn't laugh. 'It's a tough gig, this one. You're up to it, though. Now come on. We've got things to do. I've got lots of jobs for you, Elizabeth.'

'I'm in.' Jeff looks at his phone again and swipes the screen. 'Just let me...'

Abraham gives Jeff a look and turns to me with a raised eyebrow. I wonder too what my husband is playing at. He's always maintained that using a phone during a discussion is the height of rudeness. 'What's happening that's so important, honey?' I try and keep the irritation out my voice, but Jeff doesn't respond. Simply gives a small shake of his head.

'Alrighty. Whilst we wait for Jeff, party line. Let's do a super quick run-through, and then I've got someone to do an hour of media training with you both.' He rests both hands on Jeff's desk, shirt sleeves rolled up. 'So, we've got the donors.'

I watch Jeff finally put his phone in his pocket and swivel slightly right and left in his chair, his thumbs circling each other.

'I think the top five ones should have reserved spaces right at centre front.' Abraham turns away from both of us. 'And our main one isn't coming. But we've got to keep the others in top position. And our dean, Kevin Tang. Which reminds me. He's on annual leave after that, so Jeff, you'll have to pick up his work too for the next couple weeks.'

'Great,' Jeff murmurs.

'We've also got Lavinia, our chair of governors. If you do the honours there, Jeff?'

'Certainly.'

Abraham carries on. 'And the sports hall refurbishment, play that down a bit, as we discussed, Jeff. We don't want people to think we're now swimming in cash. Refer to it as a "lick of paint" and then we'll do a quiet opening ceremony later on. And be careful,' he adds. 'About talking to people when you've had a drink. The amount of times I've had to sort out Suzy and Harley after a few too many. Once, they openly disagreed with something we'd been lobbying for. Word got round. Funding was pulled. And if people ask you random questions, it's sometimes the press sniffing around. The hacks here are relentless, especially if there's a juicy story about the University. Remember that we've got generic statements for things like deaths, narcotics incidents, terrorist attacks, shootings, sexual assaults, politically motivated events and protests, and I'm sure you know about those already given you've been here a while, but we'll go through policy on all of them when you start your tenure. And remember the University's zero-tolerance policy for racist behaviour.'

'So, what you're saying is that we're not allowed strong opinions on anything?' I say.

'Well...' Abraham rubs his nose. 'Listen. We've got lobbyists and donors to keep happy. Right? A good endowment fund goes a long way in these parts, and we need to keep the Wickham Fellowships going in perpetuity. Particularly as there's the new Wickham Wing to think about. We've got an exceptional fundraising team, but we need to keep things going. Off-record, Elizabeth – and you must know this already – but here, and at the Medical School in particular, we've got donors with extremely strong opinions, political and otherwise. Not that we necessarily condone those opinions, and most of our donors keep a very low profile and don't publicly showcase their views. Or their faces, for that matter.'

My mind tracks back to Jeff talking at Cecconi's about the new Wickham Wing, and how keeping the big donors on side often means being hush-hush about it all.

'But we've got to keep them happy by being bipartisan, even when they try and lobby us in some way or another. That goes around the dinner table too. Keep anything like that in your own home.' Abraham glares at me. 'This is our big moment. The gala. The Rosemont Development Award we've just won. We're now in the spotlight for the work we're doing at the Med School. Every other medical school in the world is looking to us, wondering how we're achieving these astonishing results, hitting all our fund-raising targets and recruiting the best people, both staff and students.' He taps his fingers on the wooden table, seeming impatient. 'An article in the *NYT* said we had the fourth-largest university endowment fund in America last year. Jeff, I know one of your aims is to get to number one. That aim's on my list too. I reckon we're pretty much there. So, Elizabeth? What have you got?' He stands up, stroking his chin. 'Quick read-through?'

'Read-through?' I look at Jeff as though he'll have the answers. 'Of what?'

'Speech? Tomorrow?' Abraham draws out the words like he's talking to a four-year-old. 'The speech you're giving tomorrow. It's in the programme. We've printed them off already.'

'Sure,' I stutter. I haven't been able to focus enough to write a speech in the first place. 'Actually, it's not finished. I'll do it tonight.'

'I need a check on it.' Abraham leans backwards in a manner both imperious and irritated. 'It's just how things work here.' Jeff looks down into his hands. 'If you could send it over tonight. Oh, and the finalised guest list. There are two hundred and thirty at the last head count. It's in both your inboxes, and the seating plans too. So please familiarise yourself with it all.'

I'm irritated at his tone, although he's probably right to be concerned. I remember tonight's plans. We're having dinner with Suzy and Harley before the handover. I won't have time to write a speech.

'That reminds me,' Abraham gets up from his chair and walks over to me. Something about his presence makes my stomach churn, as though I've done something wrong. I don't like the way he hovers over me, hands jangling the keys in his pocket but otherwise still save for the frenetic bob of his Adam's apple as he mutters what he's thinking. 'Your profile,' he says. 'The media trainers will go through this in a bit too, but I've been through everything online. We didn't find much but we've had a bit of a spring-clean.'

'Spring-clean?'

'HR. When I spoke to them about you getting more involved, they combed through everything you have online. But if you could let me know whether you have any aliases or online accounts not under your own name.'

'Really?' I try and keep the disdain out of my voice.

'Well, yes. It's a matter of safeguarding. Not only our students, but you too. We have to make sure there's no unfiltered content that could get you in trouble. Or Jeff. We had a look before, but this goes one step deeper. And with social media we have to consider what you've been liking. Or commenting on. Who you follow. That sort of thing. Just to check there's nothing potentially harmful to your reputation.'

'Right.' I nod slowly.

'We need to be scrupulous. Oh, and regarding some of your previous jobs. If you keep low-key for now we'll introduce you very slowly. I'm going to get you to do a few op-eds, get some photos of you in community spreads. Position you on LinkedIn as a thought leader for charity work. Sound good?' I don't move. 'Excellent. Perhaps doing some cleaning up of the neighbourhood. Get you out there at the fundraisers. We want your research capabilities out there too, but we'll think of the right time to launch all that. Or rather, you.'

'Can I give you my own strategy? About how I'd like to appear?'

'You can.' Abraham shrugs and walks out of the room, giving me a wave as he leaves.

After Abraham disappears, I start to do my own sleuthing. See what could possibly be misconstrued online. I googled myself plenty of times when I first met you. Did a recce on how I'd be presented to you. What information you could potentially glean from me. I'd been disappointed to find out you'd clearly not bothered. Either that or you'd stalked me online and then pretended to know nothing about me. I type my own name into the search engine.

There's a long Wikipedia page dedicated to Jeff, and someone's added a new blurb about me to the University's website:

> Elizabeth Harker, thirty-seven, wife to the esteemed Jeff Harker, — University and Medical School president. Born in England, Elizabeth was instrumental in the Bed for Life campaign and is now involved in research for the University. She has had three research papers published on Romantic literature. Elizabeth is heavily involved in the University's Development and charitable arm, fundraising so that we

> can provide scholarships to the brightest minds in the world, regardless of their financial position. Elizabeth will be heading up the new Wickham Essay Scholarship under the Wickham Visionaries Initiative.

Is Abraham now directing my work streams? I scroll down. There are a few photos of me taken from various websites, places where I've worked or accompanying interviews I've given on the government policy on homelessness that was implemented in the UK before I left. A couple of them could have been problematic, had someone wanted to query that policy, but when I scroll down further and click on the links to the interviews themselves, I'm redirected to 404 pages. Every single mention of me has disappeared, save for one headshot on the Bed for Life campaign, where I'm smiling. My hair was long then, past my shoulders, and I'm wearing a professional-looking smile, just this side of looking too goofy. I remember the photo being taken before I met Jeff and thinking it would be the first one people would see if they happened to google me. I'd made an extra special effort, deep-conditioning my hair, putting on eyeshadow and lip gloss when usually I wore none. Other than my existence here, my marriage to Jeff and what our future holds within that, it seems that my previous life has been wiped out entirely.

The rehearsal and dinner with Suzy and Harley the night before the inauguration is a roaring success, mainly because I decide to put you out of my mind. Jeff and I have had our media training; we've practised how we're going to deliver speeches and answer questions from the press. All of course in accordance with what the wording of my new online profile tells me I am: wife to esteemed University and Medical School president, Jeff Harker; incantations of what I am to become.

I haven't heard from you since your message about B. There's nothing I can do. I have to act as though I'll never see you again. The uncomfortable sensation that you've been with someone else, that I wasn't enough to satiate you, settles after a glass of wine, and for the first time in a while I start to relax in Jeff's company, knowing we're now a team. That we are now leaders. And not only leaders, parents-to-be.

We spend the evening finalising the formalities for the inauguration ceremony, the timings and sound checks, before moving to one end of the Great Hall, to a long oak table that has been set up for us. The clinks of our glasses echo off the old wood panelling. It feels like I'm absorbing the energy of ghosts of academia past through these walls. And the food, brought to us on silver platters and served by white-gloved staff, is also a sign of what I'm to expect. Langoustines, salads, crème brûlée, paired with the finest red and white wines while we sit with weighty polished cutlery in our hands. The sky outside mutes itself to a purple black, highlighting the filigree outlines of the stained-glass windows. Candles around the room cast intricate shadows across the stone floors.

'Cheers to you all.' I smile, holding up my wine glass, its crystal distorting my view of the people opposite. 'I'm so looking forward to tomorrow.' Every so often, I remember I haven't yet written my speech, but the more I drink and the more swept up in everything I get, the more I tell myself it's okay. That if I speak my truth I'll be okay, especially after this afternoon's media training. I know now how I'm to present myself. As a loving wife, an extension to both my husband and the University. I'll know what to do in any situation, and I'll do Jeff and myself justice. Screw you, I think. You could never deliver me this kind of lifestyle. And yet my ego and heart – and my body – still need tending to. I look around. All these intellectuals in one room here to toast my husband, and by proxy me. Except Jeff's presence dulls their interest in what I have to say. Their eyes hunt him, seeking his attention, and their own inner narratives drown out my words. He is their key to something. Something bigger than them.

'And so the ramifications of that were huge,' Suzy is saying. I nod. Grin. At that point I start thinking of you again and I feel like I'm in some purgatorial déjà vu, a feeling that lasts right up until I'm back home again and out of my clothes.

'Shouldn't have had that last whisky,' Jeff says with a yawn and climbs into bed. I wonder why despite everything I still feel like I'm cheating on you with my own husband. 'Just felt like celebrating. All of this.' He waves his hand around the room. 'I can't believe that this time tomorrow...' He sounds like a small boy before Christmas. Then his voice goes quiet. 'It definitely feels like a lot.'

'It is.' I don't mention the speech. Jeff may have forgotten about it. But Abraham hasn't. By the time I check my phone, he's sent one email and a WhatsApp asking me to deliver it to him. *Yes* I message back. My first mistake. By the time morning comes round I realise I've not only over-promised, but I've also lied.

The Day of the Inauguration

7.

'Morning.' A tiny shaft of sunlight crosses Jeff's face. 'Today's the day. Shall we?' His hand lies on my right thigh, warming it.

'No,' I tell him. 'I've got the hairdresser and make-up soon.' Any excuse I can find, even though my hair appointment isn't for another two hours.

'Right.' I detect slight irritation in his voice and start to feel guilty about my own misgivings. This is Jeff's big day, and my only thoughts for the past few days have been about you. 'Actually,' I roll over, moving closer so my mouth is next to his left ear. 'Maybe I've changed my mind.' I shut my eyes. Perhaps, if I pretend I'm with you, Jeff might open up a bit. He might relax into his own body. Or at least relax into mine. I take his hand. 'Listen, honey,' I whisper. 'Why don't you...' I draw it downwards, pressing his fingers into the places you knew by heart. You'd always found new things to discover about my body, however familiar it was to you. 'Like this. Slowly.' It feels shameful taking the lead with Jeff. Seducing him anew. 'You know, maybe we should...' I move his fingers to the left. 'There. Look.

Maybe if we just take our time.' I think of you. How you'd spend hours, hours. Stopping. Starting. Learning. 'I could show you.'

'Show me what?' Jeff replies, almost mocking. 'How I should be doing it? Are you going to be teaching the president a few things now?' He laughs and rolls on top of me. I look away. He bends down and sucks on my left ear, hard, so my eyes smart, before using the weight of one knee to open my legs and pushing himself inside me. 'We'll see about that.'

It's over in minutes. Jeff's eyes are closed the entire time before he rolls off me, sighs and leaps up to go to the bathroom. I lie still; my body is aching, aching for you.

I hear Jeff singing in the bathroom. The sound of the hot tap. When he comes out and gets dressed, he doesn't look at me as he puts on his shirt, shaking the sleeves down and putting on the rest of his tweed suit. 'Anyway,' he says. 'Have a great day. And remember...'

'Yes?' I look at him from my prone position. 'What?' I soften my tone, hoping it'll be a hook for him to say something nice. For Jeff to say that he loves me.

'Oh. Abraham. He's on at me.' He gives me a cursory nod before smoothing out his jacket. 'Speech.'

'Okay.' I feel the sting of tears.

'Listen. I'll see you there, will I? I've got to go and collect my robes from the Development office later.' Jeff looks at me again. There's a dawning that this is the moment. His big moment. Our lives changing forever.

'That's okay. My hair and make-up are being done later, so I'll see you there. Hey.' I go quiet. 'Listen. I'm proud of you,' I tell him, wanting to make things okay between us despite the way I'm feeling. 'You deserve this.'

'I do,' he says before turning to look at me. 'Don't I?' It strikes me as odd, this insecurity. This self-doubt I'm not normally privy to.

'You do.' I sit up and squeeze his hand. 'You really do.'

'Whatever happens, you deserve it too.'

I laugh, but don't respond.

Hours later, as I'm slipping on my shoes to go with the cream silk pussy-bow shirt and navy fitted suit I've chosen, I look in the mirror. Sergio has styled my hair so it shines, just above my shoulders. The make-up I've had done brings out the green in my eyes. Megan has layered my lashes with some falsies. Subtle, I'd told her as she was talking about Kyle, her husband, kirby grip between her teeth.

'They're simple creatures,' she said. You want their attention or you want to distract them, you show a bit of leg. Make them think they're going to get some. Metaphorically, of course. Or ignore them. But it's as easy as that, isn't it?'

Ha, I thought. She'd carried on talking as she dabbed coral pink on my lips. I was thinking of Jeff all that time. The rush this morning. The way his mind had seemed to be somewhere else.

'Pop,' Megan commanded. And then she swept a soft brush upwards over my cheeks, with a more neutral shade of blusher, highlighting the cheekbones I'd forgotten I had.

I've been meaning to practise a speech, but I've been distracted by the idea of you and B and the silent competition this idea has bred. I look in the mirror again. My skin is almost luminescent. Megan's words run through my mind. *Show them a bit of leg. Make them think they're going to get some. It's as easy as that.*

I grab my phone, set it to portrait mode and hold it up to the light. Then I gaze at the camera as though I'm about to sleep with you. You used to love that expression of mine, and I'm sure this will hook you back in. You always told me you could read my thoughts when I posed like this. *You're thinking about what I'll do to you, aren't you?* And most of the time you were right. And so now, one last time, I simply want some reassurance that it's me you preferred. That it's always been me. I click the camera button but don't write anything. I press Send.

You, of course, will know what day it is today. Everyone knows. It will be filmed. You've told me you can't make it, but you'll probably watch my speech online later. I think of you looking at me on that stage, Jeff's hand brushing mine as we pass each other, as I stand at the lectern, take a deep breath and introduce myself to the audience.

Putting my phone on silent, I take one last look at reflection, smooth down my suit and grab a small black clutch my sister-in-law sent me last year from Canada. I've ordered a University car to collect me half an hour before I'm meant to be anywhere. Each minute has been carefully accounted for, and if I'm late I'll throw off the entire agenda. The phone flashes. An incoming call. Abraham.

'Hi, listen. The speech. I've—'

'No.' He laughs. 'I've given up on expecting that. But that's not to happen again. I need to run through the wording next time. You don't seem like you're going to go rogue, but I need to make sure we're all on the same page. Anyway, look, just to let you know that the press are coming. They'll be covering this one. We've managed to get William Harbottle from the *Gazette* to do something, and it's going to be livestreamed on our YouTube channel to some of our governors who are overseas at present, and all the others who can't attend. I'm sorry. I meant to tell you this but it slipped my mind. It's potentially going out to thousands. So, well,' he stops, making sure I've digested this piece of news. That I fully understand the gravity of the situation and that I'm not to let anyone down. 'I think that's everything. Is it?'

'It's okay. It'll all be okay,' I say, acknowledging Abraham's need for reassurance that I'm not some renegade whilst being careful not to fall into the trap of feeling like I need to prove myself.

'I know.' His tone sharpens. 'I'm spearheading this. I know it'll be okay.'

'Sorry, I…' I go quiet, removing myself from this power play. 'You've done a great job.'

'Anyway, Jeff knows all of this.' Ouch. A swift reminder of who's really in charge here. 'Just so you're aware, you'll be miked up all the time. There was a bit of an issue last year with Suzy talking about one of the big donors, so I remember. Called him a megalomaniac. I'll loop you into all comms.'

'Wow.' I'm so relieved he's not on at me about the speech that I start laughing. 'Oh, my car's here. Listen, thanks. It's all good. We'll put the University in a good light. Not that it needs it.' I take my bag, lock the door, run out to the waiting car and climb into the passenger seat. 'Anyway. Good luck.' I hang up and glance at myself in the rear-view mirror. My make-up still looks good, my eyes are bright, and for the ten-minute journey I stare at my phone, waiting for my photo to be delivered to you, wondering what you'll do – or say – next. My finger hovers over the 'Delete for All' whilst there's still only one, as yet undelivered tick, but by the time we pull up, another has appeared. You've been on Telegram. You've seen my photo. For a split second, my screen shows you typing, and then, as quickly as you appeared, you're gone.

The idea that you've 'seen' me, albeit digitally, gets me through the half-hour meet and greet before we all sit down for the ceremony. You certainly know how to get my attention, even if it freaks me out and makes me second-guess myself. The atmosphere is electric, made even more so by the thought of us being back in contact. The thought that I might be the one to finish things for good.

As I'm talking to Janet, I feel the phone vibrate in my clutch bag. It's you. Surely. Excusing myself, I walk into a quiet part of the hallway and stand in a doorway. But it's only my sister-in-law, and it's a text for Jeff: *Hi! Please tell my brother to call me back. H.*

I head back to where I was before. I look over at Jeff

and he winks at me. Mouths something over the buzz of chatter. I can't tell what he's said, but I pick up his subtext: we're a good team, you and me.

Abraham waves me over. 'Elizabeth. We're set. Timings are crucial. I'll hold a hand up when you've got sixty seconds left, like we went through yesterday.

'Did we?' I frown. 'God, my mind's gone. Lucky you reminded me.' My mind is now back on you. I regret sending you my picture. Your lack of response has left a shame-filled chasm.

When the music starts, we follow Abraham into the Grand Hall. I can't help but gasp. The flowers have been placed beautifully around the room and the lectern where the speakers will stand and there, velvet chairs lining the stage. My name is printed on a laminated card placed on the chair closest to the stage wings. I smile at nobody in particular. The room is darkened, save for a spotlight on the lectern, and all around the room are huge banners reading — UNIVERSITY AND MEDICAL SCHOOL, with INAUGURATION. JEFF HARKER underneath. I start to feel light with the excitement of it all, as the buzzing voices reach a certain pitch before softening as we all take our seats. The orchestra in the pit below us starts. Beautiful, low cello tones begin as a female singer performs 'Pie Jesu'.

The music quietens, and Jeff appears at the end of the aisle in his blue robes, carrying a golden staff with the University crest down the side. *My husband*. He's followed by Suzy, Harley, Abraham, Kevin Tang, and some of the governors. The top donors have all taken their seats at the front. Harley takes to the lectern, and Jeff sits next to him. He's looking old but more relaxed than I've seen him for years, and I think about what Suzy said. How much he's put into the University, only to not see it through to the end.

'I'm here to talk housekeeping,' Harley begins, which elicits a laugh. 'As you are all aware from the consent forms you were sent earlier, today's ceremony will be broadcast.' He glances over at a huge multimedia camera. 'So if you feel like falling asleep, be aware it could be shown to someone's aunt back in the UK.' More laughs. 'Who might also be asleep. But only when I'm talking.' He makes a few more jokes, before changing tone. 'But really I'm here to say goodbye to you all. Our University was founded by a wonderful family, headed up by James and Dilly when they donated enough money to build an academic centre of excellence. And of course the most generous and eminent physician, Henry Wickham, who put us on the map by allowing us to build the Medical Centre, a place that puts us at the forefront of education, research and innovation. A centre that breaks barriers, which is what we and our students have been doing for years.'

Harley grabs the lectern in front of him and looks around the audience. 'This is a historical moment for the University, and a pivotal one, with some quite astonishing plans in the offing for the Medical School, which is doing pioneering work with the best minds across the globe – thanks to our students and also to the generosity of our donors who have contributed to the Wickham Fellowship

Scheme, which has now been expanded considerably. They are the ones who transform what living means. They are the ones who are going to shape the future of medicine and what it means to be healthy. What it means to be human. What it means to be alive.'

The audience erupts in applause. Harley waits, nods, then holds up a finger. 'And that's just the start. But our work is not done.' He scans the room, stopping, it seems, at each person here, and adopts a more sombre voice. 'Our Wickham Fellowship initiative is at the true heart of what we do here. Giving opportunities to the brightest minds, who might not otherwise have access to places like this. The best on the planet. We find those people. We bring them here. Some of those who have passed through these great walls have already dedicated their own lives to research and changed the course of medicine. And you too can be a part of that by making sure that every single person who deserves to can study here, and change lives regardless of their economic situation.' He grips the lectern harder. I feel a deep sense of pride of the institution I'm a part of. We are, indeed, changing lives.

Harley clears his throat. 'And on that final note, I'm going on holiday, so from me it's goodbye.' I laugh along with the rest of the audience. 'And in the meantime, ladies and gentlemen.' I hold my breath. 'May I introduce you to the incoming president of — University and Medical School. He's someone who brings with him a wealth of experience as the current provost and head of health partnerships at our Medical School, with a resume to make your eyes water.

He's had forty academic research papers published, won the Fulbright, twice, has completed a degree in Biochemical Sciences, after which he won a scholarship for a one-year field study in the Amazon rainforest, where he published a book on his research on the function of medicine in plants in Indigenous tribes and how to integrate those findings into Western medicine. His breadth of knowledge is quite astounding, and his Harvard MBA and five subsequent years at Hollings Bank and their investment arm make him the right person for this job, especially in these politically uncertain and globally turbulent times. We can trust him to steer our place of learning into an even better future. He is also known amongst us all as a wonderful orator and a great friend, who is curious and has a way of thinking that supports the values and ethos that this place of learning stands for. He is also known for his love of tweed.' Everyone laughs yet again, and I look over at Jeff, who is now staring at a point towards the back of the room. I try and reconcile this man who is being lauded to thousands of people right now with the husband with whom I live my everyday life.

'Please welcome your one hundred and thirteenth president…' Everyone starts to clap, and my husband's name is drowned out. Aware I'm being filmed, I sit up straight, a loving smile fixed on my face, as I watch Jeff being sworn in. I listen to his speech. How we've raised funds for the University. How many lives we've changed. He and Abraham have been talking constantly about how to use the correct language so as not to appear patronising (*Do not use the word 'opportunity'. That has to be implicit.*), and my husband rises to the challenge beautifully. His speech is rousing enough to get more donors involved. To remind them that we have to keep their eyes on what truly matters – giving our future generations the education they deserve. He makes no mention of giving money, instead making it clear that philanthropy runs through the veins of this building.

I'll have to give my speech soon.

Jeff looks over to me. 'And of course, I couldn't have done any of this without my wife.' The room goes quiet.

I notice Abraham on my side of the stage, behind a thick red curtain in the side wings, doing something on his phone. I breathe through the adrenaline coursing through my body and a deep feeling of peace settles over me. The noise of my own guilt is replaced with an emptiness. My body feels lighter. I sit up even straighter, hands in my lap. It might even be time to tell my therapist about you. End of a chapter. I look at my husband behind the podium standing upright, strong. I've heard him practising in his study, but I've never listened to the whole thing before.

I smile back at Jeff, the way I've seen many wives do in the past. I shut my eyes briefly and then the floor vibrates and the sound of clapping fills the air and my bones as Jeff sits back down and another piece of music starts to play.

How could I possibly have risked losing all of this for you? It's only now, with my future dangling in front of me, that I realise how wrong your behaviour had been. The strange way you'd behaved when I'd last seen you. And then B. That sliver of hope hooking into me time and time again. That four-letter word, *hope*, turned poisonous. How close I've been to losing everything because of my inability to understand how much you'd affected my nervous system when it was pliant in its grief over the loss of my pregnancies. But still, part of me loves you. A part I'm not willing to examine too closely. Perhaps the part that was awakened when you first looked at me closely, your breath intermingling with mine. Perhaps the part that gave into you so fully I could barely breathe, my desire for you reaching ever-expanding heights. Perhaps the part of you that pushed me away. I thought I loved you, but perhaps I don't really know what love is. Perhaps.

Briefly shutting my eyes, I centre myself again. You're not here. I have to think about my future with Jeff. I ready myself to give my speech, absorbing the rousing cello solo into my body, the beautiful melodic vibrations of the violins as they speed up and slow down.

Then I hear it. A low, gasping sound. No one else has noticed. I look to my right and see that Abraham is white, shaking, holding on to the curtain. 'Jeff,' he hisses over the music. 'Get him.'

'Jeff,' I hiss, covering my lapel microphone so it doesn't pick up my voice. I wave six chairs down to get his attention. He looks over at me and I nod towards Abraham. Jeff slides himself past the back of the chairs and into the wings. No one seems to notice, because the conductor is standing as the last crescendo hits and the music is slowing.

The emcee stands as the notes soften to silence. 'Next,' she says, smiling at me, 'we have Mrs Elizabeth Harker, wife of our new University president.' I hear the clapping.

I notice the tiny red light on the camera zooming in on me like a sniper's sight. I look over at my husband. Abraham now has an iPad in one hand, the screen covered with the other; he's facing the audience and it's visible from where I am. In fact, I can see it directly. Jeff is holding a hand over his mouth, looking at Abraham, shaking his head. I read his lips. *No,* he's saying. *This cannot be happening.* Then, curling the curtain around himself to make sure he's not visible to the audience, he adds, *Fuck. Fuck. Fuck. Fuck. Surely not now?* I lean back to get a better view. In the years I've known my husband, this is the first time I've known him lose control like this. I walk over to the lectern. Try in the glare of the spotlights to process the image I've just seen.

'Ready?' the emcee is saying. 'Elizabeth Harker?'

'Ladies, gentlemen.'

I look towards Abraham, who nods at me. *Carry on,* he's mouthing. But the words don't come. I stare out at the audience. My future in real time, right in front of me. These people we are meant to be leading. And now this.

'Ladies. Gentlemen,' I try again. 'Esteemed guests.'

My voice is nothing more than a whisper. Pull yourself together. I remember Jeff's words about Abraham. *Midas touch. Not that we'll need it.* One image. One image that will destroy the University's reputation. The ramifications of what I've seen start going through my mind. I look over at the two men again. Abraham's eyes are down, fingers squeezing the bridge of his nose. Jeff is looking at him as though willing him to do something to get us out this god-forsaken situation.

'Sorry,' I say clearly into the microphone. 'It's been a long morning.' A few scattered laughs break out across the room. I try and talk again, but all I can hear is the whirr of the camera.

I recognised you in the photograph straight away. Your top was off, as was normal for you when you were out for your morning runs. You were hunched over, a red puddle to your left seeping into the ground below. There, in your back, was a knife, lodged neatly in your skin.

The camera in front of me beeps. The red light flashes.

You are curled over, dirt in your lungs. Your left hand is outstretched like a spider, reaching for the phone. You, my love, are dead.

8.

I'm talking to a crowd of people, but all I can think about is you. The slump of your body. I'm scared, terrified to open my mouth again in case I let out a scream.

A montage flashes through my mind. You. Me. Bodies together. I wonder if you thought of me as you took your last breath. I wonder if I featured in the timeline of your life that played out in front of you as your brain and heart shut down. That damn camera keeps whirring as it trails my every movement, livestreaming it to thousands.

And as I'm about to open my mouth again, I get it. My last sign of you as you were typing. Typing. You were alive at that point. I think about the forensics now, sealing off the area, sweeping up the dirt around you into tiny plastic bags along with your phone. Your phone. The photo. The photo I sent you. The image of me was one of your last trails of communication. I look at Jeff again; both hands are wrapped around the lower half of his face. I think of my decision moments earlier. My future alongside Jeff. How much I have to lose. Don't scream, I tell myself.

Abraham is speaking to Jeff. *Listen to me. Listen to me. We've got this.* His posture is upright; he's pacing in tiny circles. Then he's nodding. Jeff's nodding. *Okay,* I see my husband saying. *Okay.* Then Abraham puts his phone to his ear, relying on me to distract the audience. I've planned two minutes for my speech. I reckon they're going to need at least five.

'Ladies and gentlemen,' I repeat again. I hear the tremor in my voice and I clear my throat, squeezing the sides of the lectern. The man with whom I've been cheating on my husband is dead. If anyone finds out I was with you, I'll be considered a witness. Or a suspect. An acid taste settles in my mouth. I've been reckless. It had taken twelve months of you to shatter the facade I've spent years creating. I push down a sob.

'I'm so honoured.' I clear my throat again. 'To be standing here in front of you today in this place. I've been thinking about what to say to you here.' I feel nothing; I'm aware of no one. Thank God. 'But what I realised' – I move my mouth closer to the microphone – 'is that I could plan all I liked but that this moment, this moment here, is all we have. So we want to thank each and every one of you here today.' My vision starts to blacken. Not now. Not now. I smile into the camera in front of me and carry on talking, oblivious to the words coming out of my mouth, until I come round again. 'The people who keep this place alive, who empower our students, our staff – from the new University president, to the domestic staff who keep our buildings running so smoothly.' I stop as I think of you again. That smell. My fear of doing something wrong. But I'm the conjurer who's brought this entire thing into existence. 'The catering staff...'

Act like nothing has happened. Don't act suspiciously. Sort yourself out.

'All of whom run this place like a tight ship and to whom we are so grateful. Here, at — University, that's what Jeff Harker, our new University president, strives to give you. The chance to be yourselves. Jeff and I will make sure you have room for that.'

I think of you again. *I love you for all that you are, Elizabeth. The good and bad parts of you.* It struck me as strange at the time, offensive, even, because it seemed that other than cheating on my husband, I'd only presented my good parts to you. Or what I thought they were and what I thought you wanted them to be. And when we'd first slept together, my body had reacted in ways I'd never imagined possible. There were still parts of me I'd kept hidden from you – mainly because I'd hidden them from myself, even as I'd opened up my whole body to yours. *I love you, Elizabeth. I love you. Don't you get that? You have shown me what I should be doing with my life.* And it strikes me now that you knew me in ways I could never have imagined. That you'd seen through my facade.

'And we hope to create a welcoming and wonderful atmosphere for you all. And we want you to know that our door is always open.' I stop, look around the blurred audience in front of me. 'Thank you, and I hope you have a wonderful day.' I stop again, smile. I glance over to Abraham again and he's nodding slightly. I know I've done him proud by managing to keep afloat.

The audience stamp, clap. But then things go silent and Abraham takes to the microphone to tell everyone that 'there are a few technical difficulties. Please bear with us.' Jeff smooths down his robes and fiddles with his glasses as I step away from the podium. He passes me, his fingertips brushing mine, and as he moves I watch Abraham sidestep down the stairs and go around the audience, talking to a few people I recognise as the senior management team and some of the governors. They all remain expressionless other than Suzy, who holds up a hand to her mouth but quickly removes it. I understand why they have been chosen for their roles. Abraham motions towards the conductor, who starts up another song, but I can hear the audience shuffling around in their seats. And after about ten minutes, I glance towards Jeff. They can't keep everyone waiting much longer; people are starting to talk. I hear chairs scraping the floor. Impatient coughs. I watch Jeff run his right hand down his robes one more time and then adjust his posture. He turns to Abraham. *Cameras.* He motions for them to stop rolling. *Done.* Abraham nods. *Already done.* I hold my breath. *And microphones,* Jeff hisses and points towards his personal microphone. *I'll sort it out.* I pull apart the wire on my own.

'Ladies and gentlemen.' Jeff is now back onstage and bending towards the microphone branded with the University crest. There's a silence and the energy becomes something deeper, more palpable. I listen to him make the announcement about your death. I listen to his words about you. I watch people pulling out their phones. The rustle of fabric as they hurry to look up the news, the latest word on socials. Abraham carries on talking. *Can't divulge any more information. Need to tell you immediately for security protocol. Follow orders. Process in place for this eventuality.* His voice turns into an indefinable sound and I can only make out snippets. Something about the victim, and the authorities believing it to be 'one of our own. A member of staff.' Can't release the name to the press yet. Formal identification needed. 'But the image is circulating, and so we have to...' He carries on. Something about your name getting out online. A terrible shock for staff. People start to cry. I know Abraham must have his reasons for telling everyone here that it was you. I can't fully digest what he's saying. Something about informing next of kin. Something about an alarm sounding throughout the rest of the University. Cops...here soon. They'll be stationed right outside this building. Everyone remain seated... Drill...safe...security everywhere...

A clank of metal echoes through the hall as someone bolts the door. A woman starts to weep in the middle of the audience. All I can think about right now is your next of kin. Who is that? Then I think about the cops. Your phone. My photo. Oh God.

Jeff is onstage now. Entirely calm. Talking.

He tells the audience that the University has shut down the woodlands and surrounding areas. That they need to for the investigation. Tells the press that for security reasons they must not publish anything until everyone is safe.

That people are to avoid talking about it on social media from inside this room.

This. This is why my husband has been voted in as University president. He's stuck to the rules of the game. He's kept his cool where death is concerned. He's the steady hand. And, although your killer might be on the loose, it seems that from my speech, I am too.

I turn to Abraham, mumble something about going to the bathroom. He doesn't hear me as he's busy shouting at everyone to stay put until they have word it's safe to leave. Voices become higher-pitched, the atmosphere more chaotic. People get to their feet. 'Stop. Everyone. Stop.' Abraham once again yells into the microphone.

Jeff takes over. 'Please,' he commands, his voice reverberating around the room. 'Everyone remain calm.' People start to sit down. Another person starts wailing. 'It's all right.' He keeps glancing over to the shatterproof windows. Again, there is a sudden swell of movement: the press, going crazy despite Jeff's pleas. Click, click, click. What about security? Are they sure the deceased was a member of staff? Why would they have been targeted? How could we allow this to happen? People want to know; they are getting angry.

Coming down from the stage and making my way down the aisle and past the audience, something which is most likely against the rules, I head for the bathroom, slide down the white-tiled walls and curl myself around the loo, where I'm wretchedly and violently sick.

***

I lie there in my nice clothes for what feels like a long time. My overriding thought is that you never said goodbye to me. I never found out who B was, and you didn't reassure me about her. And for that, there's part of me that hates you.

I try and work out what the fallout from this will be. Whether you would have come back to me. Whether we would have been able to resist each other or there would have been one last time, despite my protestations that I had to stay loyal to Jeff. Our connection was too strong. Or so I had believed. My mind is still muddied, and thoughts fade in and out without giving me a chance to dissect them into something useful.

Every so often an image of you, face down, comes to mind. After what feels like a few minutes, I get out my phone and unlock the screen. There are more than one hundred notifications. None are from you.

I open WhatsApp, scrolling to the first post since your death. It's the image of your death I was witness to not long ago. Who the hell took your photo? How was it disseminated around the University? I zoom in. There you are, nothing but a bunch of pixels on the screen. The exclamation point in Jeff's text message only a few days ago flashes through my mind. *Good Morning, Mrs. President!* I zoom in further to examine the phone just out of your grasp, but it's too fuzzy and I can't make anything out on it. But then I think of the forensics combing through our conversation and making their own links. The wife of the University president! Having a full-blown affair with a member of campus staff!

I check for more information. A brief statement has already been put out by Jeff through the main University channels, asking people to remain calm. To follow University policy on security and to wait until we know more. God, he's fast. God, he's good. I skim through the other threads, absorbing as much information as I possibly can and then head over to the social media channels, where the image of your body, albeit blurred out, is spreading like a disease. One anonymous X account, @StudentInvigilatorX, which has only twenty followers, says the following:

> Dead body. — University in lockdown. Follow here for updates. 🧐☠🧐

I watch as the follower count rises, and I wonder how the hell the comms team are going to handle this.

> @StudentInvigilatorX Cops trying to find out if premeditated. Forensics crawling the place. Terror on campus. 🧐☠🧐

I think of the only areas with signal in that woodland. The walkway near your apartment. I know it intimately. I think about someone taking your photograph as you lay bleeding out. Calling the cops. Trying to resuscitate you. In which order had they done these things?

I scan through more notifications. Staff announcements to students. Staff WhatsApps about you. No one can believe it. Reams of text about the impact you made in the Medical School. People are in shock. Terrified. Seeking counselling. None of the employees speculate about your death, except one person, a Ray Govindra in the labs, who has provided links to the @StudentInvigilatorX threads: *Here. You'll find all the latest.* I try and make sense of all the information coming in. *We're sealing off all areas. You're not allowed out. We're calling parents. Don't go anywhere alone. We're waiting for the authorities to alert us. Things are in hand. Police officers are crawling the area with sniffer dogs and guns. We need to inform you about the next steps. Don't release the photo.*

Someone's posted a link to a news story written by the *Gazette*, even though Jeff explicitly told everyone to avoid publishing anything that might compromise us. I click on it. There, at the top of the article, is a photo of Jeff.

Murder on Campus

During the inauguration of the president of — University…

I read on.

Our reporter at the scene…

There's not much other information in there about your death. No photo of you. Just some stock shots of the woodland. A promise that there are more updates to follow.

I wonder about your parents, your family. The knock from the police, telling them. Their shock. It dawns on me that you rarely mentioned your family. 'We've got better things to do with our time,' you'd said when I'd asked you once, before kissing me gently. A wave of guilt rips through me. Guilt and something terribly, shamefully, close to desire.

Then I see it in my notifications. The tiny white telephone icon, clear as day, alerting me to a missed call. Not on Telegram. Not on WhatsApp. An actual phone call. The only people who ring me these days are perhaps Janet, when she has a message for Jeff and she can't get hold of him directly. My sister-in-law. My eighty-five-year-old second-cousin Susan, from England, pretty much my only living relative I have left since my father's death four years ago. Next to the icon is a voice message alert. I select it.

'One new voice message, 12.40 p.m. To listen to your message, dial six.'

Oh, for fuck's sake, hurry up, I think. And then I hear your voice.

'Just about to start running. But I wanted to phone you. Thanks for the photo.' You clear your throat. 'Look. Things…' You breathe sharply and murmur something about someone following you, but the message crackles and I can't hear the rest. 'Shit,' you say. You lower your voice. 'Just tripped. Listen. You've made me think about things differently. Reasons…can't explain right now. But Elizabeth. All of this. It's all because of you.' What the hell is all because of me? Your breathing is harder now, as though you've picked up pace. 'So before I go I just want to say that…' The line goes quiet for the next ten seconds or so. 'Believe me. I'm sorry for what happened. You have no idea how hard the past few days have been. How hard it was to tell you to leave. I'm sorry. I'm sorry if I hurt you.'

You go silent again. I will you to carry on talking, so I can hear your voice one more time. You'd loved me. Or had you? I'd lost trust in the words you were telling me after our last meeting. But then I think about what you just told me in your message. Despite the way we'd left things, and although I'd been planning to cut you out of my life, you'd still made me see things about myself that no one else had. Perhaps you were a good person after all. Perhaps this hot and cold behaviour... Perhaps...

'It's...' The sound goes crackly again, and I'm sure you say something important, but I can't make it out and I'm too terrified to rewind the message in case I inadvertently delete it. 'And one more thing...' Then I hear it. A movement. You're talking to someone else. 'Oh God.' You let out a small laugh. 'Sorry, you gave me a real—' Followed by a muffled noise. A groan and then a gurgling.

I look at my phone, at the damp imprint of my fingers left on the screen. I hear Abraham outside the door, and I lower the volume. Even though it's not on speaker, I'm terrified someone, somewhere will hear.

You'd never meant to hurt me by ghosting me and you'd never known I planned to finish things with you. You'd died thinking you'd upset me and hadn't been able to rectify things before the ground below had absorbed the life-force of your blood. I cover my mouth, stifling the noises threatening to burst into the open air. I think of your words again: *It's all because of you.* What was all because of me? *Believe me.* Such an easy and empty thing to say. Two words to try and convince me of your actions. I whisper them. Feel the ease with which they flow into the air around me.

But how can I believe you?

'Elizabeth?' Abraham's voice is steady. 'Elizabeth. You in there? You okay? I've come to check on you. Check you're all right. You're not technically meant to be anywhere alone. It's not safe and it doesn't look good. We need to keep everyone in one spot. Especially while we're still waiting to hear more.'

I wait, fill my lungs and slowly end the voicemail. I shake my head. 'I'm good. I stand up shakily. Fine. A bit shocked, that's all. I'll be out in a second.'

'Fine. I'll go back to the hall. We're in lockdown. We've managed to keep things calm. The cops have told just me that the killer's fled. No witnesses, but they've scoured the area with sniffer dogs and there's no one around. But we've got to stay put until we get given the all-clear, and not tell anyone either. The press are still here, and there's coffee, and…remember what I told you? About comms. We need calm alignment. You're in charge now, Elizabeth. You and Jeff. You need to be out here. People need to see you.'

'Yes,' I say, trying to sound as engaged as possible. 'Yes. I haven't forgotten.'

'And the cops…' he's saying, but my mind goes to you again. 'The cops. We'll need you and Jeff on this. Jeff will need to be…oh, look, Elizabeth, hang on…' I hear his phone ring. 'Hello?'

Please, I inwardly plead. Go away. Please. I think of the cops again. Of your last call to me.

'Yeah. Listen to me. We've got to manage this alongside the cops. Security are here now anyway.'

I listen to him drone on because my head is full of your voice – and the sound of your final breaths. *Sorry, you gave me a real—*

All I can think about is you trying to convince me that you'd had good reasons for ignoring me. How worthy you'd made yourself out to be. All I can think about is you pinning this all on me. *But Elizabeth. All of this. It's all because of you.* I don't even know what exactly 'this' is. All I can think about is that when the cops investigate your murder, when they go through your phone, they'll find out that the last person you spoke to on this earth, before you took those last breaths, was me.

AFTER

'I never lie,' I said offhand. 'At least not to those I don't love.'

Anne Rice

The Day of the Murder

9.

Things move quickly after that. At least compared with usual University processes. Everything is very orderly. Abraham gives everyone instructions, ticking checkboxes on his iPad about the emergency steps we're meant to take, the procedures we're meant to follow, who we're meant to speak to and at what points. We're all supposed to have read the policy documents all over the University intranet, and only now does it become clear that Abraham and my husband, the consummate professionals, are the only people in this room who have bothered to do so.

Jeff keeps order in his own inimitable way. Calm, dignified. Brilliant. And yet there are still no answers. For the next twenty minutes, Abraham stands in the wings, on his phone and pacing up and down, directing Jeff to keep a damn tight lid on this. I want to tell them to stop. That too much control will turn into chaos. All I can think of, though, are those last jagged breaths of yours – and the fact that I am now a witness. That I might hold the key to finding your murderer. That if I don't confess, and if I get the cops to shut down the investigation, I'll be doing something illegal. It occurs to me that I might be put in jail. Publicly derided. If someone from the precinct leaks the message, everything will come out, all my communications with you. The things you told me on Telegram to do on my own in the bedroom. The number of times we professed our love to each other. How I'd never felt this way before. All for the public to pick apart.

I imagine Jeff's reaction, and press my hands to my cheeks as reality distorts around me. I try and process it all – the things I've done that might have led to this, the fact I will never see you again – but all I can hear in my mind are your last, desperate drags of oxygen. I sit paralysed by the thought of you, phone in my hand, your voice reduced to a series of digital vibrations locked inside it. People are sitting in groups around me; some are silent, some are crying after two hours of people getting up and down, demanding to know if we are safe. I no longer care about anyone's safety. I sit, mute and numb, facing the prospect of my own future and how to handle it.

'All right, folks.' Abraham appears on the stage. 'Listen up. The forensics are still in place, sweeping the area for evidence, so we can't trample around the grounds. But we've got security all over campus, and, as we've told you, there's also security surrounding us here. Sniffer dogs. A heat-seeking helicopter. Drones. The whole hog.' He pauses. 'We've organised coaches to take you all off-site, where we'll have security measures in place too.' He wipes his forehead with the back of his hand. 'We've got you covered. Everything's good. Everything is fine as far as your safety is concerned.'

His voice is low and reassuring. 'But please go around in threes and fours. We've told all students they must stay off-site for the next few days at least. The person who did this isn't on campus anymore. There are extra security cameras being placed around the Woodlands, and we'll get more up when the forensics give us the all-clear.'

There's a scrabble of noise, questions being hurled out across the room. What security measures? Was the attack premeditated?

'We're not sure yet, but we'll let you know as soon as we have any more information. But I will do everything in my power to make sure you all remain safe.' Jeff speaks slowly, careful to choose the appropriate language. Careful not to use the words springing up in my own mind: serial killer; random attack; targeted. Which had it been?

People stand up after that and leave quietly, many of them still sobbing; either they knew you, or they felt connected to you somehow.

After what feels like forever, I'm left alone in the room with Jeff, Abraham and a group of people I recognise from our website and whom I've met at various functions: all the governors, Kevin Tang and the senior management team. Abraham positions three tables side by side, motioning for everyone left in the room to bring a chair and join him. I find myself barely able to move.

'We're just waiting for Janet.' Abraham points to the table. 'Please take a seat until she comes.'

'It must have been random,' I mutter to no one in particular.

Who the hell would want you dead? Despite your behaviour, despite B, whoever that was, despite it all, you were a good person. You had strong morals. You always wanted what was best for the Medical School. You wanted to save lives.

'Jeff, what's happening?' I say, forcing myself to steady my voice. My husband keeps looking over at the door.

'Crisis meeting. Janet's being escorted here by security. She'll be another five minutes or so. She's sent me her live location.' Jeff holds up his phone.

'I need to go home,' I whisper. 'Please. I need to get home.'

'You can—'

I start to leave but Jeff grabs my arm.

'When I go. Not before. We're a united front, you and I, Elizabeth. You need to,' he takes a breath. 'You need to pull yourself together. People are watching how we manage this.'

I need to act like the University president's wife. I need to stand up straight and show composure and dignity in the face of the unimaginable. I need to work out what I need to do next.

After a while, the door opens and Janet appears. She sits at the table wordlessly with her notes and a laptop.

'Right.' Abraham squares up at the end of the table. 'We need to get on with things. It's a shock to everyone. A member of our own staff.' He continues speaking. I watch as Janet types, her face unreadable. Abraham's voice cracks every so often.

Then it's Jeff's turn. He tells the governors each step he's taken, repeating to them how he delivered the news, as though reassuring himself he did the right thing. They discuss whether he followed the correct policy. Whether he could have done anything differently. The official statement that will be given to the press. Whether our comms have been watertight.

Lavinia, the chair of governors, stands up straight. She scans the people around the table, taking everyone in.

'Before we work out the motives for this attack it is our absolute duty to make our staff and students feel safe again. Whatever that takes. Their well-being is my absolute priority right now. I've apportioned money from the emergency fund to go towards extra security measures. I've hired the services of Glenn and co, who will sort the logistics. Who will station patrols around campus.' She looks at Jeff and Abraham. 'I do not want a single person on-site feeling worried for their safety. This is our community. I do not want people going to bed panicking that they might not wake up in the morning. Are we all clear?'

'Yes,' Jeff says. He looks down at his phone.

Lavinia carries on. 'And then we make sure things aren't affected on a wider basis.' After this statement, there's a silence in the room that I can't quite fathom. 'We've all worked incredibly hard,' she says, looking around the table again, 'at making this place a number one destination for our stakeholders. We're recruiting the very best staff. The top minds in the world. We don't want this to overshadow our hard work. Much as I'm mindful of this poor man's death, of this utterly awful tragedy and the impact on his family and loved ones, we also need to think of all of you, and your livelihoods. Generations to come. The Wickham Fellowships. The future expansion of the Medical School. All of it. Does every one of you understand me?' She doesn't say another word and instead picks up a pile of papers from in front of her, straightens them out and gives a tiny nod to a tall, grey-haired man in glasses who has just appeared in the doorway. 'Ma'am. You ready?' He takes her bag, and they start to leave together.

On the way out, Lavinia stops and turns. 'Jeff, my dear,' she calls out, 'I can rely on you, can't I?'

'Of cour—' Jeff starts to answer, but she's already gone.

10.

More police arrive ten minutes later. I see the blue lights first, streaking through the windows, and then there is silence.

'Why are they here?' I say, my voice pitching upwards. I will myself not to sound desperate, but there's a part of me that thinks I'm about to lose it entirely. 'Jeff, I thought we already had cops stationed outside. What's happening?'

'Elizabeth,' Jeff hisses. 'Calm down. They've come to talk to us. That's all.' He lowers his voice. 'Security are still here. We can't be seen to be freaking out.'

'But aren't you?' My voice cracks. 'Freaking out? Someone's dead. Someone's been murdered in broad daylight where we work. Where we live.'

'Of course I'm freaking out.' Jeff takes my elbow and moves me away from the other governors still here. 'But I've got to be careful now. Do you understand what will happen if I put a foot wrong here? If *we* put a foot wrong?' He tightens his grip. 'We're being watched from every single angle. The governors. Staff. Students. Their families. The surrounding community. Not to mention the wider damn world. You've seen the news. Social media these days. This story is a goddamn global shitstorm.' For a second, I nearly laugh. Tell him he's been picking up bad linguistic habits from Abraham. 'We cannot afford for anything to go wrong at all. Everything has to be perfect.' He sighs. 'Otherwise, my tenure here will be over.' He looks around. 'Do I have to spell this out to you, Elizabeth?' I try and nod. 'We damn well need to be seen to be doing the right thing.'

'Rather than what actually *is* the right thing?'

'Look, this here,' he says, scanning the room again, 'will all be over before you can say "murder". The adoption. My career. Your role within this University. Finished.' He draws a hand across this throat. 'Leadership. That's what we need to show. We're leaders here.'

'All right. I get it.'

The door clanks open. 'The cops,' I whisper again, right hand damp around my phone: my last link to you. I clench every muscle in my body to stop my nervous system going into free fall.

'Hello there,' Jeff says. He releases my arm and walks towards two men and a woman in full uniform. 'Thank you for coming. Abraham?' he calls over to the other side of the hall, motioning for Abraham to get off his phone. 'If we could park ourselves over in the corner.' He leads the way back towards the front door and points to the coffee urn, and my brain filters everything into slow motion as I watch. Them shaking their heads. Jeff ushering them further out of earshot. Him talking expansively, back facing me, gesturing with his hands. I force myself, to put one foot in front of the other from where I'm standing.

I stumble across to sit next to Janet. 'You all right?' I ask.

'I'm just about all right,' his PA replies. 'Sit down. You look white as a sheet.'

'Do I?' I adjust myself in my seat, berating my body for giving me away. 'Is there any update?'

'There's plenty of press around. I'm not sure how they got in. But it's highlighted weak spots in our security, so I'm sorting those out now and hoping no one gets wind of them before I can get that done.'

'Wow,' I reply. I think back to Jeff's earlier words about showing leadership and try to come up with something useful to say, but I go blank. I keep staring over at the cops in the corner, watching for any clues in their body language. Anything that tells me that they're here telling my husband I was having an affair with you. That tells me that your phone, which will by now have been scoured by forensics, has shown them you and I knew each other well. They'll see me staring from the screen in a way not even Jeff has seen before. Unless I can delete both sides of our conversations – something you told me is now possible on Telegram – they'll see me topless, lying on my bed, *I'm waiting for you* underneath it. They'll see me cupping my breasts, legs apart, the photo softly blurred, alongside the message *You're not getting all of me now*. You'd messaged me right back again after that one: *You are incredibly beautiful*. They'll see me exposed for all I am: a liar and a cheat. And now, a potential witness – or worse even, a suspect. An indistinct sound escapes my mouth.

But Elizabeth. All of this. It's all because of you.

'You all right, honey?' Janet asks but doesn't wait for an answer, filling the space. 'Anyway, your husband. And Abraham. They've been working so hard lately. Getting the University into the best possible position. And now this.' I can't concentrate and her voice turns into a drone. I want to tell her to shut up and get on with the job at hand before Jeff gets in real trouble, but I'm grateful that she's talking to me and it looks like I'm doing something useful. 'I just feel so much for that poor man,' she's saying when I'm able to focus again. 'The idea of him bleeding out with no one to help him. One of our own. It's unconscionable. Terrifying, really, to think someone is still out there. If it was a random attack. Wrong time, wrong place.'

'Right.' Bile rises up my throat.

Jeff talks to the police for another half an hour. Twenty of those minutes I spend in the bathroom, haunting myself with old messages between us, finger hovering over the option to delete our chats. When Jeff sees me return to the room, he comes over. 'Let's get out of here,' he says. 'Abraham's coming back with us. It's time to go home. We'll get some food in.'

As we walk, I listen to the two men talking about you. They discuss the wording they should put out around your death.

'You wouldn't have been expected to know him personally, of course, as you're new to the job,' Abraham tells

Jeff. 'But at the same time, the public will expect you to know who all the members of staff are. They don't show much mercy when it comes to death.'

Jeff's jaw tightens. 'Right.'

'And anyway, I've checked all the safeguarding with HR and I've run his security checks through the system too. They were, thank the lord, all in order and up-to-date. I had to congratulate Virginia there.' Abraham's shoulders slump. 'So it's been quite the day.'

They talk about leaving no stone unturned. Jeff tells Abraham to delegate, or he'll drop a ball somewhere.

'Speak for yourself,' he replies, silencing the conversation. 'You all right, Elizabeth? You've hardly said a word. I know it's been a horrible shock for everyone.'

'I'm good, Abraham. Thanks.'

We get in Jeff's car, which is parked outside, and he makes me sit in the passenger seat, presumably as some sort of message to Abraham and yet I couldn't feel less in command of the situation. I shut my eyes. I want this all to end.

'Damn hacks,' Abraham mercifully changes the conversation. 'On and on at me. Wanting details. Names. I've given them the statement.'

Jeff speeds up the car. 'Let's go through it all when we get back.'

As we turn into the driveway, I think about how you'd never been to the cottage. I thought it too risky. You'd tried to tell me it was okay, once, when Jeff had gone away for a night.

I want to see how you live, you'd typed. *I want to imagine where you are when you tell me you're in the kitchen. I want to imagine you doing those things every day. I can't stop thinking about you.*

I'd taken photos of myself that day, in every single space of my home. I spent a long time working out the best shots. Pre-empting what you might be wondering about the place where I lived with my husband. Your life had seemed so free. Would you sneer at the set-up, the way we had two of everything, placed side by side? Two coffee cups on the shelf; mine on the right, Jeff's on the left. Two sinks. Christ, we even sat on our own set chairs at mealtimes. At home we were still pretty normal, for all Jeff's power at work. I wonder if you'd seen me as nothing but an extension of that power.

When taking the photos, I'd positioned myself in areas I believed showed me in a more exciting light. I placed two books on the Romantics, a candle neatly on top of them, on my side of the bed. Lay in the bath, leg hooked over the side. With you, at least, I started to enjoy myself. But then I snapped myself in Jeff's study, sitting on his desk, legs crossed. *The big boss!* you had written back, unwittingly highlighting the pedestrian nature of my home life and the fact that when I was with you, I revealed a part of myself no one had seen before. A part that was defined by the power I had over my own desire. I'd told myself that it wasn't Jeff's fault; my husband has power and agency elsewhere. I hadn't responded to your message, instead deleting the photo minutes later. *What did you do that for?* you'd replied.

After getting through the front door, Abraham and Jeff go through into Jeff's study and I wander into the kitchen, phone in hand, still trawling through months and months of communications between us. I look for anything unusual. Anything that should have rung alarm bells. Names of people you might have upset. Any reason why you would have written that this was all because of me. But there's nothing. Your murder must have been random. I keep thinking of those words – *It was all because of you.* I replay things I said to you. Things I did. I tell myself I'm being ridiculous. As Janet said: wrong place, wrong time.

I creep out of the kitchen two or three times and walk past Jeff's study, but the door remains firmly shut and I can't hear anything at all. Just the occasional creak of the floorboards. I order in food, chicken schnitzels and fries, and let security know to look out for the driver; I'm grateful for the distraction, even though I know I won't be able to eat. It's only when the delivery arrives that I wonder if Jeff and Abraham are going to have a go at me about let a stranger near the house despite the increased security, but neither says a word about it when I call them into the kitchen.

'God, Lizzie Lou, well done. I'm starving,' says Jeff, grabbing the brown paper bags off the table and picking up the pile of plates I've laid out. 'Not in here. Let's go into the living room and watch this in front of the news. I don't want to miss anything, but I'm getting a damn headache from staring at my cell.'

We sit side by side on the huge sofa, me, Jeff and Abraham in what otherwise might have been a cosy night in. Jeff gets out the takeaway, screwing up the brown paper bags and demonstrating a winning aim at the bin. 'Here we go,' he says. 'Now don't tell me this isn't a weird situation.' He flicks on the television. There's something unfamiliar about his movements as he repeatedly jabs the remote control, tutting, cursing under his breath. He stops on CNN.

BREAKING NEWS. There you are. There are pictures I've never seen before and that weren't in the footage I watched on my phone earlier. You looking tanned, your hair windswept, freckles out. You wearing a wetsuit, surfboard under your arm, running past the camera, laughing, waving. I wonder who's behind that camera. And out of nowhere I'm gripped with terror again. 'God,' I cry. 'It's all so awful.'

The ticker rolls across the screen: 'ELITE — UNIVERSITY CAMPUS SHUT DOWN AFTER BRUTAL STABBING OF MEDICAL SCHOOL STAFF MEMBER. I turn to Jeff and open my mouth but no noise comes out. A blonde news anchor appears on the screen.

'We've since heard that the University is closing for at least three days. An official statement earlier from a spokesperson at the University' – Abraham coughs – 'said that student safety is paramount, and that although they can't be more specific comments whilst the investigation is ongoing, they can assure everyone that they are working very closely with the lieutenant in charge of the case.'

'You okay?' Jeff asks. He's back on his phone despite complaining just now about it giving him a headache. 'This story,' he says, his tone neutral, as though he's asking me whether I want milk in my coffee. I make a slight movement of my head. 'Listen, Abraham and I might have to go back to my office later. But I don't want you left alone here.'

But, Elizabeth. All of this. It's all because of you.

I barely register what Jeff's saying as I watch you on-screen. The news anchor's words float around in my mind. 'Brutal stabbing... America... lockdown... a witness.

'Witness. Who's the witness? Did they say there's a witness?'

'The guy who found his body.' Jeff's typing, distracted. 'Don't know if he saw or heard anything useful.'

Useful? I want to shake him. How can he be so dismissive? So cruel? Despite the intense heat, I start to shiver.

'Don't worry,' I say in response to Jeff's previous comment. 'Go. I'm fine here. I would prefer to be on my own, actually.' I nod towards both men. 'I just want to get to bed.'

'Fine.' Jeff nods at Abraham. 'As long as you're sure. I'm going to ask security to patrol around here and for one of them to be stationed right outside. I'll be back in a few hours, I should—'

'My God,' I say before he can finish. 'It's us,' I whisper, hands shaking. 'Footage. From the inauguration. Copyright William Harbottle. That's the *Gazette* guy, isn't it? He must have made a buck. You told everyone not to say anything that would put us in danger.'

Then there you are again. Next to you is a small boy. Strawberry-blond hair, a shade or two lighter than yours, freckles spattered over his face. You both stare into the camera, sun on your faces. And there it is on the rolling ticker: you leave behind a wife and a six-year-old son.

A son. A wife. You had a son?

I turn to Jeff. 'In fact, I'm going to bed now,' I say. 'I'm exhausted.'

'Hmm,' Jeff replies. 'Fine. Fine. Okay. I've texted the security team. They're going to station themselves outside until I'm back, and probably until the morning. Abraham, Donny all right at home?'

'Donny's fine,' Abraham replies. 'We live so far from campus that I don't think there's an issue.'

They carry on talking, but I don't hear any more. Wife? You had a wife? You'd never said a thing. And you'd never mentioned a son.

Excusing myself, I head upstairs, slip on an old T-shirt and climb into bed. I lie there, knowing I'll never get to sleep, whilst four gasped words, play over and over in my brain. Four words was all it would have taken to tell me you had a child.

I pick up my phone, google your name and the word 'wife,' but nothing comes up.

I look for more information about you. I read online comments. I check the news sites every three minutes or so. Eventually the police lieutenant issues another statement from outside the University.

'We are doing everything we can to investigate what we believe to be an isolated incident. We will not stop until we find out who did this. We are committed to keeping everyone here safe.'

The Day After the Murder

11.

The slam of the front door wakes me with a jolt. Jeff, coming back. I place one hand on the bedside light and clasp my phone with the other. It's only when I hear the familiar jangle of keys on the sideboard, the rustle of Jeff's coat and the soft murmur of voices from the television downstairs that I drop my hand from the light. It's 1.30 a.m. and I've only just fallen asleep. I lie back down, dizzy from the adrenaline surge, wondering when Jeff is going to come up to our bedroom.

He'd texted me at around midnight, reminding me there was security right outside the house, which had ironically freaked me out even more and led my mind into strange, dark places connected with why that was necessary in the first place.

I look at Jeff's message. *PS,* he'd typed. *Call the cops if you need anything at all. They're all over this, and Abraham and I have spoken to them, so if they know it's you, you'll get a quick response. Here: Newton's direct dial to follow.*

I look at Jeff's next message: *A contact: Lieutenant Newton.* Pulling the decorative cream eiderdown from the bottom of the bed over me, I curl up on my side and pull up our conversations again. Reading back over them, I look for clues about who you were. Anything at all. Whether you'd ever shown me any inconsistency in your behaviour, other than in more recent days. You hadn't. Since the day we had first spent time together, after the second fundraiser, you'd always been open with me. There had been nothing to suggest your feelings about me had ever waned. Nothing at all. I look through our final messages, from the last time I slept with you. *That was epic. I already miss you, my love.* Why had your tone changed in such a short space of time?

The entire history of our relationship is tied up in this one app. At the beginning, you had told me about the things you liked doing: getting fit (*you look after yourself so well,* I'd told you countless times); reading medical journals (*I have enough of those around my house,* I'd said); being with me (*It's weird, isn't it,* I'd said, *how well suited we are*). Then you'd told me you preferred our intimacy face to face. That although it was great to have these chats, you didn't want them to replace real life. *Come over later?* you'd asked. That was what you had referred to as our third 'date'.

We'd had a few conversations about the University at the outset of our relationship. How much you loved it here. How the Medical School was doing 'great things' and that you were happy to be a part of that. There had been a few occasions where I'd asked you for reassurance about our relationship, but the patterns and shape of our communications had largely remained steady throughout. Equal footing. Sometimes I'd send long missives. Sometimes you would. Normally at around 9 p.m. our conversations would heat up even more, precipitated either by you or me saying *I can't stop thinking about you xxx*. Sometimes that would happen in the middle of the afternoon too, when you knew I was home alone and you were stuck in the office. *I know I shouldn't,* you'd type. *But I wish I was with you. I wish you could just come over now.* There had been the few occasions I'd been able to, when Jeff was away at a conference or visiting a research fellow or giving a lecture. I'd asked if you thought I might be spotted as I sneaked out of my place in the pitch-dark. *I don't think anyone is going to be watching,* you'd replied, then a smiley emoji followed by *Just wait till you get here*. I'd brush my teeth and throw a coat over my silk nightdress and get in the car. You'd often try and persuade me to sleep over. *I'll set the alarm,* you'd say. *No one will see us. No one ever comes to this part of the woodland.* But I'd always driven back home, normally after you'd pulled me back; one movement of your palm against my stomach, your thumb softly massaging my skin, was all it took to persuade me to stay 'just one more time'.

Other than the obvious betrayal of my husband, you and I had been a perfect and mutually respectful match. I'll never find anyone like you again. I miss you and simultaneously can't reconcile this with the fact that you'd lied repeatedly, betrayed me with B, and then brutally cut me off.

A strange and bitter laugh escapes me.

Jeff starts snoring downstairs. Selecting 'incognito mode', I look up the length of time it takes for police to access mobile phone records as part of murder investigations. I try and work out the chance of them missing our messages. The possibility that the cops won't be scrupulous about going through your phone records and every single conversation you had. Some sites say twenty-four hours. Some say a week. I look up our district office and Lieutenant Newton, whom Jeff had told me to contact if necessary. I read about all the cases he's been involved in. The fraud case that was the talk of the town last year. The twenty-year rape mystery he'd solved after reopening a cold case; that guy had got life, and Newton had been interviewed about it in the *Gazette*.

Now the shock has started to wear off, I realise it's only a matter of time before there's a knock at the door. This is a high-profile case they'll want to solve. And as it's high-profile, the district office is more than likely to leak information. I have to get myself out of this trap.

I listen several times to your last voicemail. The quickening of your breath. Your voice, laden with what I now recognise as fear. The sound of footsteps behind you. Oh God. I stop the message before I hear your last moments. I haven't yet been able to desensitise myself to it all. I put my phone on screen lock wondering how I will get out of this.

Kicking off the sheets, I listen out for Jeff. He's still snoring downstairs. Normally I'd shout down, tell him to come to bed, or go and gently shake him, but instead I sit up and place a pillow behind my back and set about downloading an online Dictaphone. Again, I play the voicemail from you, this time recording it. I then set up a new email address and send the file to it. Next, I select the entire year of communications with you and copy that into a second email. When I'm sure I've backed everything up, I switch off the phone and pull out the SIM card. I hold it between my fingers. If I get rid of it now, I might be in the clear. The police might not find out about our affair. No one will ever need to know. Putting the SIM in the top drawer of my bedside table, I try and clear my mind, weighing up each option carefully.

I think about the enormity of what I'll have to do if I come clean. Whether somehow I'll be seen as an accessory to your murder. Whether they'll find evidence tying me to your death.

I put my pillow down again and slide the phone under it. Now, under my own roof, I'm holding on to something that not only could show the entire world what type of person I really am but which could also obstruct the course of justice.

12.

I sleep for around an hour. When I wake up again, I have Jeff's words in my mind – *they're all over this* – and the lieutenant saying that they will not stop until they find out who has done this. I bring up the news on my phone and there it is again on loop, the lieutenant repeating those words. I imagine the police going through your phone history, cross-referencing the numbers with the telecommunications company, as I'd seen done so often in crime documentaries. My phone number flashing up.

Although I didn't hear Jeff come to bed last night, he's fast asleep next to me, right hand resting on his stomach. I watch the slow rise and fall of his chest.

There's a thumping sound from somewhere. My body tenses before I realise it's only the hot water revving up. I swing my legs out from under the covers and sit on the edge of the bed trying to keep calm. I revisit my thoughts from last night. My lines of enquiry feel altogether clearer, starker.

As the sun starts to seep through the blinds, I get dressed silently: a simple pair of navy jeans, flats and a ruched black top. I brush my hair. Other than a slick of lip balm and some moisturiser, I don't bother with make-up. Then I head out, rushing past the security guard outside the front of our house and climbing into my car.

Gone to the Development office, I text Jeff. *Don't worry. Security everywhere.* Then I stop and type him another message: *Also, just wanted to say I love you.* It's not often we tell each other that. I can't remember the last time. Perhaps before the miscarriages. But if anything untoward happens, I want my husband to know that some part of me, despite you, still loves him.

It's half an hour before I find somewhere off-grid that's not too far from the district office. It takes me another twenty minutes to work up enough courage to make the call. My head resting on the steering wheel, I think of my mother. For the first time in years, the picture of her is clear in my mind. That half-cocked smile, her Farrah Fawcett-style dark hair, the way she'd open up her arms for me ready to fly into, my sister by her side in a blue woollen jumper, left sleeve unravelling. *Darling. Elizabeth. I've missed you.* Then the image cuts short and darkness descends on me as the memory of the knock at the door seamlessly inserts itself into the narrative. The two policemen, helmets clasped to their chests, heads bowed. My dad, pushing me into the living room. *We're so sorry, sir. Car overturned. We're sending over a family liaison officer for you and your little girl.* I sit with the emotion for the first time in years. I wonder what she'd say to me if she were here now. *It's okay, darling.* Her voice would be soft and safe, leading me to my own decision. After that, it doesn't take me long to pick up my phone and make the call.

Another twenty minutes later, after I've managed to send Lieutenant Newton my what3words location – a tiny clearing off a country road, where there's been no other life since I parked up – he makes his way to my car. I reach over and open the passenger door, nodding for him to sit down.

'Mrs Harker. Ma'am,' he says. 'Here – I bought you coffee.'

I take the cardboard cup gratefully, wrapping my hands around it, absorbing the warmth into my bones even though it's hot outside. 'It's good to meet you properly, Lieutenant Newton,' I say. I clear my throat while looking at his side profile. He's wiry. Thin brown hair and long sideburns. Age indeterminate; some elements of his face are childish but his forehead is etched with wrinkles. 'Thank you. For coming, I mean. I've obviously got no legal representation with me. But I thought we could have an initial chat and see where that goes.' I take one hand off the cup and clasp the wheel in front of me. 'Look, I—'

'Do you mind?' He pulls out a tiny silver metal rectangle. 'I'll need to record all this.' He also takes a pen from his pocket. 'I'll be making notes too, and you'll need to give a formal statement if this happens to be anything other than just a chat.'

'Of course.' I think of my mother again. *Be brave.* 'That's fine. Listen. I'll take a few notes myself.' Putting my coffee in the drink holder, I lean back and grab my handbag, a notepad and the pen you gave me. I feel the weight of it in my hand and think of you encouraging me to do the right thing despite wronging me at the very end. I look straight ahead. 'I need your assurance that this will go no further. Between you and me, I know there are leaks at times. Or strategic moves to alert the press to goings-on, but—'

'I can't promise you a blackout on this, ma'am.' I watch as Newton switches on the Dictaphone with a swift move of his fingers. 'First you need to tell me what's going on. Then I can decide.'

'Well, I can give you information,' I tell him carefully. 'So you can discount me as a person of interest. Or anything else. I have nothing to do with this whatsoever.' I can hear the panic creeping into my voice. My tone getting higher and higher. I battle its pitch back down. 'Listen. Neither me nor my husband. Neither of us.' I hear the tremor in my words. I promised myself I wouldn't bring Jeff into this. A promise I've already broken. 'I want to tell you that for the past twelve months, I have been having an affair with the deceased.'

'All right.' Lieutenant Newton puts down the pen and glances at the Dictaphone, the red light flashing accusingly in his lap. 'Go on,' he says.

'We met at a fundraiser.' I stop.

'It's all right. Continue.' There's no impatience in his voice, but a muscle in his left cheek moves ever so slightly. 'It's okay.'

'We were together since then.' I feel myself slump in my chair with the release of telling someone about you. 'A year.' The most intense year of my life. 'We always met at his apartment. Never outside.'

'And what did you know about him?'

'That he is – was – a good man.' I pick up my cup and remove the lid, blowing on the coffee. 'A gentleman.' I take a sip; the scorch of heat distracts me from the pain of your death.

'What about extracurricular interests?'

'Sorry?'

'You heard me, ma'am. Anything he enjoyed doing that was maybe troublesome to him? Gambling. Drugs.' He looks directly at me, his watery grey eyes searching mine. 'In light of all this, I'll need you to be straight up with me now, ma'am.'

'Nothing,' I state clearly, initially offended he's implied I might be anything but and then reminding myself that given what I was up to, he has every right to query my words. 'I promise you. Absolutely nothing. He was invested in his job at the Medical School. He liked to run. He never mentioned his kid to me. Or his wife, but…' Instinctively, I know that with Newton I mustn't try and excuse our behaviour. 'When it came to me, he was…' I fiddle with the rim of the cup. 'He was good. There was someone, I think. Someone else.' I look towards Newton. 'Maybe?'

'And why would you think that, ma'am?' If I think I'm going to get reassurance from a cop who is investigating your murder, again, I am clearly mistaken.

'He messaged me once.' I glance down at the phone in the pocket of the car door. 'I think it was meant for someone else. A person he called B.' I look at Newton again to see if he gives anything at all away. 'I never got to confront him properly, though, because… Did you find anything? About this…B?'

'No, ma'am.' There's pity in Newton's voice. Pity, perhaps mixed with contempt that I'm using this conversation to try and garner information about your extracurricular proclivities. 'I'm sure we will though. We've got the best cops on this,' he adds quickly. 'And they're going through the telecommunications over the next few hours, so if there is anything, we'll soon know.'

He grills me with another forty minutes of questions. They seem so random that I can't unravel their lines of enquiry about why you were killed. He asks why you loved your job so much. He asks in depth about the last time I saw you. Your frame of mind. We go over the same things again and again. The moment I found out about Jeff being made president. Or rather, the moment it became official. He asks about the last time I went to see you. I tell him I was intending to end things with you, but that you'd pre-empted things and blown me off. Presumably for B. Out of all of it, it's that part that still hurts. I tell the truth about everything. I even tell Newton, when he asks, that I loved you.

'You really did?' he says, pushing me for more. 'Love him? Or was it just—'

'Just what?' I snap. 'Yes. I love him. Loved. I loved him.' And it's at that point I wonder where my love for you has gone now you're no longer here.

I watch as Newton's pen scratches the notepad. I think of the last time I saw you. The way you handed over that ridiculous pen. I curl my hands around it. 'Wait,' I whisper, pulling out my phone from the door, wanting this to finish. 'There's more.'

I don't look at him now as I press Play. We sit in silence, listening. I sip slowly at the rest of my coffee and stare out of the window as your last breaths play out.

'Holy shit.' Newton rubs his chin. 'Holy goddamn shit.'

'I'm sorry,' I say, my voice flat. 'I'm so sorry.'

'You didn't think we might have needed this sooner?' he says. 'Or is that why you're apologising? Because you thought you'd hold up the investigation for us?'

'I'm sorry,' I repeat pathetically. It's only now that I realise the true ramifications of withholding the recording. I watch Newton as he listens again. I want to ask what is going through his mind. If there are clues in there I've missed. Oh God. What do you want?

'We'll need to hang on to that.' Newton's hand hovers over mine. 'Your cell,' he says. 'Now. Please.' I hand him my phone without arguing, and he puts it into a small, see-through plastic bag he pulls out of his pocket. 'Thank you. You also need to tell your husband.'

'I can't.' I shake my head firmly, sick at the thought. 'It'd be over. Him and me. He's president. Of the University. We can't be seen to—'

'Be having an affair with someone? Especially someone who's just been brutally murdered?' I flinch. 'You need to tell him, because if this gets leaked, then... We've got a small, tight-knit team on this, Elizabeth.' I wince as he uses my first name. 'Some stellar brains. But there'd sometimes be reasons for word to get out. If it helps the case. You know that as well as I do, and if that's the case, we'll look at doing so. We can't be hiding an affair if it's going to hinder the investigation.' He looks me in the eye and takes another sip from his cup.

I look away. 'Give me some time.' My voice is flat. 'Please. Let me—'

'Look, Elizabeth, you'll need to come in. For formal questioning.'

'But I'm not a person of interest or anything, am I?' I feel my voice rising again.

'Was there a reason for the delay in giving us this crucial piece of evidence?' he says.

'Yes.' I glance at my phone in the plastic pouch. 'The affair. Look. Just give me some time. Please. I'll tell my husband, if you think that's entirely necessary. Give me two weeks to get myself sorted. In that time, I'll help you as much as I can with your inquiry. Please. Anything you need to know about him. Anything at all. I'll tell you everything. Telegram.' I point. 'We did everything on Telegram. You'll find it all on there. But please. Please don't ruin my life. My marriage. We'll lose everything. Please.'

'Anything else while we're at it?' Newton voice is cold. He does nothing to reassure me. 'Anything else you might feel the need to tell me? Anything you've got of his. Anything that could be more evidence and that you might have failed to tell us about?' His tone is glacial.

'No,' I whisper. The pen slides down onto the floor. I reach down to grab it, banging my head on the steering wheel as I come back up. 'Ouch.' I rub my scalp. I start to cry. 'Ouch. That hurt.'

'Two weeks then? To tell your husband?' he says finally, after an almost contemptuous pause.

'Okay,' I murmur. Surely I can manage it so that in two weeks I won't have to tell Jeff a thing?

Newton continues, smoothly interrupting my thoughts. 'You'll need to come in sooner rather than later, and I'll need to get all this signed off and on file. And you'll need to come in for more formal questioning too, but we'll have to probably arrange that off-site, given the media presence around this.'

'On file?' I ask. 'I mean, like I said—'

'We do things properly.' He swallows the dregs of his coffee. 'And I can try and manage things my side, but there's a limit to what I can do depending on how the investigation is looking. Understood?'

I nod dumbly.

'And if I think anything might leak or I'm aware anyone else has got hold of the information, I'll call you,' he adds, not unkindly. He sighs. 'Look, I've got to go. As you know, all eyes are on us right now. Abraham is doing a good job, but we're also having to do our own comms on this. The national press has gone wild over it. So if you'll excuse me.' He waves the plastic pouch in front of my face. 'Oh, and…' He hands me a card. 'My direct dial. If you need it.'

'Wait.' I watch Newton open the car door and slide out. I crunch my now-empty coffee cup in my fist. 'Wait.' He turns towards me. 'Do I need someone?' My voice peters out to a whisper. 'A lawyer.'

'Only you know the answer to that.' Newton looks at me again and something sad crosses his face. I see myself through his eyes. Bored wife slightly losing it and getting her rocks off with a younger guy. Probably deluding herself, thinking they'd run off into the sunset. Probably obsessed with him. Was that how it had been? I think back to our time together. The way you'd looked at me, how desired you'd made me feel, and how you'd told me constantly that I'd had that desire within me all the time, that it was just ignited by you. How you'd listened to me. Really listened to me. And how you'd always asked what I liked. What I wanted. And you'd always followed through, watching my reaction every time. *Here? What about here?* I start to feel light-headed thinking of you. I shake myself out of it.

And not only that, Newton must be thinking, but she's married to the president! Wasn't he enough for her? Did he not satisfy her? What did you have that he didn't? I start to burn up again and realise it's not just myself I've shamed.

Newton waves at me through the car window. 'Hey, and ma'am?'

'Yes?' I whisper, thinking again of Jeff. How he's been pushing for the adoption. Supporting me. Setting up our lives so we can both be fulfilled. My eyes smart. He doesn't deserve any of this.

'I'm sorry.' Newton places his right palm across his chest. Then I realise he's talking about you.

'I'm sorry for your loss.'

13.

I sit in my car in the clearing, feeling a creeping discomfort that news about you and I will leak out. I imagine people talking: *Did you hear the rumours? Ridiculous. But rumours always start somewhere, don't they?*

I watch Newton standing outside, making a call, and as he hangs up, a text arrives from Jeff on the navigation screen: *Med School hall. Staff meeting.* My phone is still linked to my car's Bluetooth.

Given I no longer have any mode of communication, I type a route into the car's satnav and head straight over to campus, pulling up a few roads away from the Development building before making my way on foot to Janet's office. My cortisol is spiking.

I walk fast along the black-and-white-tiled corridor, trying to keep up with the blood whirling around my body. I notice Jeff's name again on the wooden board. PRESIDENT.

To calm myself, I go via the bathroom. Last time I was in here, I'd been talking to you. I step into the tiny shower cubicle where you and I last spoke, remembering what had happened in those three seconds between us sharing our secret desires and it feeling like you'd gone off me for good. Then I come out, let the tap run and then pat cold water on my face and neck and around my eyes. I redo my hair and put on some more lipstick, an old red one from the bottom of my handbag, and I force myself to stand upright. Even if coming clean to Newton might end up having disastrous consequences, it's made me feel stronger. I have two weeks to work things out. Maybe. Leaving the bathroom, I make my way to the office adjoining Jeff's old one, where Janet sits.

'Janet,' I say urgently, then I slow my words. 'Listen. Sorry to be in a rush. Meeting Jeff soon. But I've done something awfully stupid.'

'Oh, honey, I could go over the stupid things I've done today a million times over,' Janet says. She stands up and walks towards me. 'I'm glad it's not just me. Now what can I do for you?'

'My phone.' I wave my empty hand around. 'I can't find it.' Knowing University protocol as I do, I'm aware this will be a security breach. Especially as it's the president's wife's phone. 'It's probably at home. But we've started packing up. And the whole house is a complete mess. It was on silent, stupidly, and it's probably dead by now. The phone, I mean.' I laugh nervously. 'God knows where it is, but I've got quite a lot of stuff I need to do.' I will myself to stop talking. 'Funny how reliant I've become on it. But could I borrow one? From here? Only for a bit. I know you keep a few spares.'

'Oh, moving. Honey, you must be exhausted, what with all of this.' Janet reaches out an arm. 'Of course you can borrow one. No, don't you cry, honey, it's okay. Look, let me get you the Development office's events cell. No one's used it for a while. They use it for the fundraisers. Here.' She grabs a key from the lanyard around her neck. 'Wait there.'

Something about Janet's comforting words has set me off, but by the time she's back, I've managed to sort myself out with the thought that she'll report back to Abraham and my husband on my emotional state otherwise. However, as she re-enters, she seems to pre-empt my concerns. 'Listen,' she says. 'Don't worry. I'm not one for sharing things in this office. People know that if they have a problem they can come to me. We're all human. Now look.' She hands me the phone. 'This here. The PIN is 1840. I'm so sorry. This cell. It's pay as you go. I've looked and there's twenty dollars on there, but there's unlimited data, so that'll last.'

'Founding date.' I manage a laugh, relieved that there's no contract and I can do what I like with the phone. 'At least I recognise that much.'

'Indeed.' She smiles. 'Much as I love the place, the University is entrenched in every darn thing we do and every move we make. Now look. I'll leave it as it is. I've logged out of everything.' She shows me the screen. 'So don't worry about that.'

'Thank you so much.' I take the phone from her. 'Appreciate it, Janet. Appreciate you.'

Then I think about how much Janet knows, and how much sway she has in the University and Medical School.

***

I walk over to the square on campus in front of the main entrance and find a bench with nothing behind me. No CCTV. It feels strange with no students around, and I have the place to myself other than the security guards looping the area. The grey stone building to my left, the Medical School, which is adjacent to the main building, is bathed in sunlight and looks beautiful. I'm in awe that me Jeff and I have been pulled into its orbit.

Opening up the Development office's phone, I go through everything on it. There's not much. Photographs of past events they've organised, all sorted into folders. I go straight to the second fundraiser, where we'd kicked things off, you and me. I scroll through. There's one of the backs of our heads, but nothing else. I look through the rest of the albums; nothing there either. I read through the Development office's email account, but it's mostly general stuff and queries about raffle tickets. The auction process. 'Save the date' messages. I log out and delete the account, then wipe the history and cookies and log in to all my own accounts. My email account is easy, but then I realise I can't access my WhatsApps without a verification code.

I call Newton's direct line. 'Newton. Listen, I'm so sorry. Have you got my phone number?' I listen to my own words tumbling out. 'I'm about to send my number a verification code for my WhatsApp. Listen, please do me this favour. As the wife of the University president, I need to have access to all comms.' I'm not sure I'm making sense, but the idea of missing information about you on the University's WhatsApp groups is unbearable.

Newton sighs. 'Ma'am. Listen. I'm not here for—'

'Please. Listen, I'll do anything. I'll find out anything for you. Please.'

'Fine.' He sighs again before reading out the digits. 'That best be all.'

'You can do what you like with the phone now. Honestly. It's all yours.'

'My team is already on it,' Newton says somewhat smugly before hanging up, but I'm too relieved to care. Having access to WhatsApp again is making me want to cry with the relief that I might now not miss any clues about B's identity. Or anything about you that I don't already know. I log in to the app. There are more updates about you from staff. Hints that the media are saying you might not have been the man you'd said you were. I catch a few words: *Awful. Sickening. If only the press knew. A good colleague.*

I scour the latest social media sources about you. Your death seems to be making quite the stir. @ StudentInvigilatorX, which seems to be the go-to account about your murder, now has 300,000 followers waiting for updates. There are stories about you everywhere. Wild theories abound that there's a killer on the loose on campus. I scan through the latest.

> @StudentInvigilatorX Cops on the hunt for CCTV footage. Witness is a student who is now recovering from shock. 🧐☠️🧐

Closing the feeds, I go onto the official news sites. More about your death. Drone footage of the University. ELITE

MEDICAL SCHOOL SHUT WHILST STUDENTS FEAR FOR THEIR SAFETY. The media and socials are going with the narrative that the attack was random, fuelling fears of a serial killer on the loose. There are talking heads and medical students giving their two pennies. Some say how well it's been dealt with. Some say they would be too terrified to come back. More footage, this time of Jeff outside the building, the flag now flying at half mast, the sky shaded mauve. It must have been filmed late last night.

'We are deeply committed to the safety of our students, and we have followed all policy. We are doing everything in our power to get people back on campus as soon as it's safe to do so, and have put extra security measures in place.'

The footage pans back to the Headway Woodland. Your apartment is in the background. I pause the video and stare at your window, willing your face to appear. I think of your smile when you'd seen me at your front door. *Coming*, you'd mouth, face pressed to the glass. Had there been others? Do I have to worry that awful stories will come out about you? I'm not sure how much more I can stomach after finding out about B.

My phone pings. Another text through the University comms stream. It's Abraham.

All Staff: Med School meeting at midday. We're meeting on Med School campus but must proceed with caution. Please enter through the Franklin Wing. Front is all blocked off although apparently will be reopening soon, but please still take the back route. Please avoid going near lecture theatres and side rooms, especially in the Facilities dept. A reminder to all staff that social media posting from any on-site event is currently prohibited, as is talking to anyone from the press. Many thanks. A.

Midday. I look at my watch. It's still only 10.30; clearly Jeff has forgotten to tell me the time of the meeting, but I make my way over anyway. Attending a meeting on the premises where you worked every day is unlikely to arouse suspicion and will make me feel closer to you.

I walk right up to the huge facade looming over me, — MEDICAL SCHOOL engraved on the front in block writing. There are three security guards at the front, one stationed on the side entrance to the Franklin Wing. 'I'm Elizabeth Harker,' I tell him. He nods whilst scanning the area behind me. 'I'm early. But I've got work to do. I'm married to—'

'I know,' he tells me. 'Go on in, ma'am. And have a good day.'

'Thank you.' I wonder how much else security know about me.

As I walk through the single wooden door, I find that the building is completely empty. My frenetic thoughts fill the vast interior. Although I've visited the Medical School regularly for fundraisers and when accompanying Jeff to various dinners, I've never spent time absorbing everything in the building, and never without crowds of people present. I stand in the central foyer looking around at the white busts of historical figures from medicine. The hanging portraits. The framed, yellowed books on the walls denoting historic landmarks in the field of medicine.

I go straight down the long corridor past the main lecture hall and down to the research rooms. To the left is another entrance, into the depths of the Franklin Wing. Your domain. I open the two doors that lead into the wing. I stop, waiting, seeing if I can sense anyone's presence in the vicinity. After a few minutes of no one appearing, I go through the doorway and down another long corridor, where there's a big sign on the left-hand wall, emblazoned with the eagle crest. Facilities. I know from Jeff and Abraham's conversation last night that the forensics have already scoured your office. I know it has been sealed off. After my conversation with Newton, I dread to think what will happen if I get caught doing anything out of line.

Pressing myself against the wall, I walk on tiptoes in an effort to silence my footsteps. I keep stopping, starting, checking no one is following me, but the entire place is silent. My mouth dries as I walk down and down until I reach what feels like the bowels of the Medical School. There on the left-hand side, door wide open, red and white tape covering the entrance, is your office. The reminder of the police's presence is stark. From the doorway, I scan the room. Your desk is clear save for one pen holder and a blank piece of paper. The chair has been pushed to one side of the door and has a large ball of Poster Tack stuck to its armrest. Reaching over, I grab the ball, turning it over to see if I can find evidence of the whorls of your fingerprints. Nothing. I squeeze it tightly in my palm and look around again.

I think I hear footsteps and so I press myself tightly against the door, breaths coming thick and fast, but no one appears. I return my attention to your office. On one wall is a large, wipe-clean calendar with a square box for each day of the year. Nearly every date has either a meeting or is overlaid with a Post-it. You were clearly busy.

Glancing around again, I duck under the police tape and take a quick photo with the phone, reminding myself to check the picture hasn't gone into the cloud and to reset factory settings if I ever return it, when something strikes me: the date you'd told me you were going on a fishing trip. You've written one upper-case letter in that square. Its neatness is at odds with the rest of the entries, but it's definitely your writing, the two semicircles stacked neatly on top of each other. It's enough. The blood drops to my feet and for a second I grab your desk, thinking I'm going to faint. I wonder again what she'd had that I don't. I look down at myself. My narrow hips. My breasts, which you'd held so often, telling me they were perfect. And yet they weren't were they? At least where you were concerned. I feel pressure in my head, and hear footsteps again. Before I can think again, I sneak out of the room and walk as fast as I can, one step at a time, until I can bear it no longer and break into a fevered run.

I go the opposite way from where I came. It's only when I'm further into the building and away from your office that I start to calm down, and at that point I realise I've just passed the morgue. I imagine you there, dealing with the logistics of death in order to save lives. You never discussed that element of your job with me, instead telling me you never got squeamish and that it was necessary. 'It's all part of the bigger picture. Information for us all. An opportunity to make things better.' And now I wonder exactly what that 'picture' was.

Slowing further, I walk past huge plaques listing the names of our most generous donors right from the 1800s, beginning with Henry Wickham before finally I find myself back in the foyer. The impotent anger over your lies and treachery, your infidelity – could I call it that? – stands me in good stead to get through the next few hours, as does the relief that I've got away with being so near you.

Whilst I've been trawling through your calendar, someone has been busy sticking up sheets of paper with arrows directing people to one of the side rooms off the main foyer. In the room, coffee urns, biscuits and rows of chairs have all been laid out for staff. There's a table at the front, next to a small podium. On the table is a beautifully bound book and a pen. A candle burns to one side.

Lavinia and a couple of the other governors come in and sit at the back of the room. She waves at me and gives me a nod. I smile back, reassured by her presence; this alone will be silently steering this situation for the good of all concerned. Then I go and stand next to Jeff as he's thrown question after question from staff about safeguarding ('We've followed policy, and so far there's been nothing to worry about where that's concerned.'). About future risk ('We're working very closely with the cops to mitigate any future risk. The attack may have been targeted, in which case the risk to our staff and students is lessened.'). About who would want you dead, and why ('We're not sure. We are waiting for the investigation to reach a conclusion.'). About security ("This will be kept in place for the remainder of the term, although we will be scaling back when we get word from the cops that it's safe to do so. We're liaising with them on an extremely regular basis.'). About fundraisers for his wife and child ('Staff are entitled to do what they like in their personal time, but anything with the Medical School name to it needs to go through Abraham and the comms team.'). About the best channel to get comms out. And finally, about your memorial. I listen to my husband. His voice is strong, clear and sure as he answers everything with the grace and courage I'm now wondering if you ever had.

I hear Abraham in Jeff's responses, but the delivery is all his own. His steady hand. His calmness in the face of collective trauma. He's good, my husband. In fact, he's excellent. Had my desire for you fuelled me into jeopardising what Jeff and I have? And will all I have now be enough to compensate for the lack of sexual desire in my life? Almost reflexively, I reach for his hand, nodding whenever he speaks. His fingers are cool and dry against mine. There's no electric charge, like when you touched me. Instead, he is a presence anchored in reason, his loyal wife by his side. Funny how my perspective has changed now you're dead.

The manic energy on my arrival in the meeting room is replaced by a quieter, more sombre atmosphere as someone starts to play music. Lavinia stands and leads people to sign the commemoration book.

Jeff speaks into the microphone again. 'We'd love to capture any memories,' he says, guiding his hand towards Lavinia, 'so please do sign the book. And please, again, no photographs of anything on social media. Many thanks, all of you.'

My husband and I sit and watch the staff walk up in twos and threes to sign the book dedicated to you. 'We'll use them,' he tells me, 'for his memorial. I've spoken to his wife. She wants a copy too, and we're going to get quotes on a big screen running throughout the event, with photographs of him on the digital boards.'

'I'll do it,' I tell him. 'I'll do the memorial. I'll arrange it. I need to do something. I can't just…' I squeeze his hand. 'Please. I'll talk to the wife. Maybe best coming from a woman. I know how busy you and Abraham are.'

'Let's discuss it later.' Jeff squeezes my hand as he nods and smiles at passing staff, not looking at me directly. 'Thank you for coming at such late notice,' he tells them as they walk towards the book. 'I'm sure that's fine. I just need to run it by—'

'Abraham?' My tone is slightly mocking. We both go silent. I hear the air conditioning whirring over the music.

'Fine.' Distracted, Jeff takes the bait. 'Go for it. Thank you. Yes, hello, Miss Kinko, hello.' He shakes the hand of someone I recognise as one of the Med School lecturers and turns away from me to talk to her.

Pulling out my phone, I go to the corner of the room and email Abraham, cc'ing in Jeff, my hands shaking. I'm firm in my use of language – Abraham, you've been a good teacher.

Subject: Memorial.

Abraham,

I've spoken to Jeff and I'll be running this. I wanted to let you know before any further plans are made. See you later,

Elizabeth.

I press Send before rejoining the other staff, who are now talking freely about you. They tell each other what a good man you were. How much input you had had into the Medical School. I listen for talk about other women. I listen for talk about your wife and her whereabouts all this time. I listen for any single piece of information about you that I can store in my mind for later. That I can then dissect and chew over until I have a clearer picture of the person you were.

An hour passes. People start to file out of the building, with Jeff herding everyone towards the door, thanking them ever so much for their support and goodwill following this terrible event. Telling them that they are all so much appreciated and that this won't be forgotten. His words seem to make the staff more buoyant; they clearly revel in the attention and praise. Once everyone's gone, two people in navy University-branded uniform start sweeping up and collecting all the mugs.

Lavinia appears, posture straight as always. Her eyes look right into mine as she places a hand on my arm. 'Dear, how are you?' She doesn't wait for a response. 'That went well. Your husband...'

'I know,' I tell her. 'I know.'

'A marvel,' she continues. 'A true marvel. What he's done already, how he's commanded this situation at every turn. Him and Abe.' She stops and looks around for a second. 'But listen.'

'Yes?' I hand an empty mug from the stage next to me to a tiny man with dark, slicked-back hair. 'Here. Thank you,' I tell him.

Lavinia nods. 'Abraham tells me you are a good presence.' She rubs my arm. I feel the warmth of her hand seeping through my skin, and out of nowhere I think I'm about to cry again. She and Janet seem to have that effect. 'That he thinks it will do no end of good, dear, for you to be seen a bit more. And in truth, dear, I've seen it in you today. You standing up on the stage like that with him. Holding hands.' Someone passes, and she waits until they're out of earshot. 'A feminine presence is always very soothing. Don't you think? We're strong leaders just by being visible.' She looks over at a huge portrait of Henry Wickham hanging above the stage. 'And I can sense you have this. You're a wonderful counterbalance to Jeff.'

'Thank you,' I tell Lavinia, glancing over at the commemoration book. 'I'll go and see what everyone has to say.' I walk over to look through the comments people have made about you. Jeff has opened it with a beautiful and cleverly worded statement. How you made the Facilities department your own. How you will be deeply missed and mourned by those who loved you. He's finished it off with a quote from Ecclesiastes and signed it in cursive. I stop for a while, absorbing his words, then make a decision to follow suit. A tiny nod to you. I take the pen you gave me from my handbag and carefully remove the lid. Its metal is cold in my fingers.

With best wishes, and may you rest in peace. Elizabeth Harker.

I deliberate over the next part, especially because of your betrayal over B, although I'm still wondering if I have any right to be angry, given that I am married. You'd lied to me. Again and again. In the end, I put three tiny *x*'s at the bottom of my signature. Blowing on the ink, I wait for it to dry before sliding the pen back into my bag, which I hold against my body as a way of feeling close to you. I wait for some emotion, but there's nothing save an undeniable heat ripping through me. I shake my head, trying to rid myself of all thoughts of you. Your touch.

Elizabeth. I love you.

I distract myself by leafing through the rest of the pages, learning more and more about how you were viewed by others. More quotes. People thanking you for all you'd done, all with 'good humour' and 'kindness' in what was a 'busy' department. You had clearly been good at your job. People talk about your love of good coffee, your double espressos from Martino's. (Had B been a waitress there? I wonder.) Your love of talking to the students about their latest research. Your love of spending time absorbing more knowledge in the research rooms. Your good hand in guiding the medical postgrads with their work, and how much time you'd spent with them. It hits me that I might have been looking in the wrong place on all the staff boards; B could be one of the postgrads. Despite you saying you liked older women, perhaps you also liked younger ones.

I thumb through more of the pages.

Near the last entry, there are five tiny sentences. Non-joined-up handwriting, so neat it's as though it has been typeset.

You were so excited about the new wing, it reads. *You couldn't wait to get started on the huge project and had been planning every last detail of the incredible facilities with the team in the past few months.* The words blur in front of me. *I'm so sad for you that you didn't get to see it through. You'd dedicated your life to making things better for the Medical School. I'll make sure I put as much care and thought into bringing your vision to the world. Rest in peace.* It's signed *Richard.*

I think back to the dinner at Cecconi's a few days earlier. My overriding thought when they'd been speaking about the new Wickham Wing and the demolition of the Franklin Wing was that you couldn't possibly have known about it. That you would have told me, even if it had been under wraps. You'd once said you'd never hide anything from me. I thought you'd have told me if there was any way you'd met or were likely to meet my husband, like you'd promised.

I unlock my phone again and pull up the photograph I took of your calendar. There's nothing that looks like it relates to the Wickham Wing. No mention of Jeff. You'd used people's initials to show who was at the meetings you attended, and neither Jeff's nor Abraham's are there.

It hadn't been necessary to keep this information to myself. It hadn't been necessary to protect you. Because you knew. You knew all along.

14.

For the next three hours, the only way I can calm myself is to look up adoption agencies and imagine myself in a different future than the one currently playing out. The one where I'm having to be represented in court. Or the one where I'm already in jail after having explained to Jeff that I was cheating on him. Or the one where I don't end up telling Jeff. Where I still have to live with the guilt. I never felt particularly guilty when we were lying in your bed.

I blame your death for the way I snap at Jeff as we get in the car after the staff meeting. He looks around before gently pushing me into the front passenger seat, slamming the door shut and getting into his own seat.

'Look,' I tell him. 'I'm sorry. It's truly awful. And stressful.'

'I understand.' Jeff grabs my hand in the car, a move unlike him. 'I'm feeling it too. Really.' I tell him what Lavinia said to me about his management of the situation. I tell him things I wouldn't have said this time a few months ago. That I'm scared. That your death has made me question whether I want to be in this place at all. That the expectation for me to perform as his wife currently feels like a burden. He listens to me as my hand rests gently in his, and then places a hand on my knee for the entire drive home and I feel bad for taking advantage of his good nature to console myself. For pretending that I'm scared in order to garner his sympathy and be reassured that he still loves me, and that my life isn't going to fall apart. I wonder whether your death, in some sick way, has reconnected me and my husband. I squeeze Jeff's hand again. Your lies and your betrayal have made me realise what I have right in front of me. A good, honest man, who is doing the best he can in the face of your horrific murder. A good, honest man who's steering a globally renowned medical school through the horrors of your death. Who will probably go down in University history as one of the greats. A good, honest man who will probably never speak to me again if he finds out about us. I hold my other hand over my mouth as I try and get that idea out of my head.

By the time I'm in the safety of our own home again, I sit on our sofa and make the executive decision to do something positive. I read more reviews of the Sunbeam Adoption Agency, already feeling a twinge in my chest. Whomever we manage to adopt will have the most wonderful father, I promise you, I whisper into thin air. And not for the first time this week, I start to weep.

For the rest of the day and night we sit quietly at home, Jeff in his study writing up more statements about you, writing comms to the staff and students, their families, the community. Abraham sets up a 'Memorial Planning' WhatsApp group, adding me as an admin. I pick up on Jeff's job of getting in the removals team and working out the best day for them to pack up, ready to move into The Lodge. *I'm not sure when's best,* Jeff has texted me. *Harley and Suzy are moving out tomorrow, so the choice is ours.* I reply that there's no real hurry, but of course there is. The sooner we're settled into our new lives, the sooner all this could be over. If in two weeks' time there have been no further breakthroughs in your murder, and nothing needs to come out about our affair, I'll be home and dry.

Despite what I told Newton, I'll orchestrate it so I won't have to tell Jeff about us. And I won't be reminded of you every time I take a step in my own home, every time the floorboards creak as I move away from my marital bed, as they did when I'd spend hours downstairs alone, or in the bathroom, talking to you, texting you, listening, fizzing with the thought of the things you wanted to do to me. With you telling me that you couldn't ever envisage the end of us. Telling me how you were falling for me like you'd never done before. And even after everything you did, I still miss you.

My phone pings again. It's Abraham, on the Memorial Planning WhatsApp.

Elizabeth, great you're on board. I hope you don't mind if this keeps you busy. I think there's quite a lot to do on it. Glad you've volunteered. Thank you. What do you think about these? He'd typed and sent over three versions of an order of service. *Subtle branding, but we should have it nevertheless. Thoughts? By the way, Lavinia told me how great you two were today. Thank you! Sorry I couldn't be there.*

Something about me standing up there onstage with my husband has changed things, and for the first time since moving out here, I feel like part of something. Part of a team. Part of something bigger than me, despite it all being wrapped up in your death. The next few hours I spend in bed, trawling through comments about you on social media. The keyboard warriors seem to be going wild about why you were killed. Word on the street – or rather from @StudentInvigilatorX, who now has over half a million followers with a new slick, black profile avatar with a red graphic of a magnifying glass in it, has it that you were in debt. That perhaps – with nothing to back up this theory – you'd been stealing meds from the research rooms to sell, and that was what had ultimately got you killed. That there was some *good stuff* out there. An anonymous user, allegedly a medical student, has posted a reply about rumours of a *blazing* new drug that is going to revolutionise pain management; *and partying* has been added on, with a winking emoji. *Perhaps he'd been on someone else's turf*, says another reply, which garners three hundred likes in the time I'm looking at it.

Gambling? someone else has written. I cast my mind back to all of our times together. The only time I'd seen you distracted or agitated on your phone was when you'd been doing the *New York Times* crossword. And you'd been entirely against recreational drugs. The accusations don't seem like you but have hit a nerve with the general public, who seem enamoured with the idea that you'd been selling them. Clips of news stories from as far away as Japan, stories I've never seen before, are being posted all over the internet. Memes of your face. Snippets of Jeff talking. Theories abound. People talk on the forums about how handsome you were. It seems that in your death, you've struck a chord. You, my love, are famous.

About an hour later, I hear Jeff's heavy tread on the stairs. I put down the phone and switch off my light before he can disturb me. I watch as his shadow fills the wooden floorboards from the doorway. 'You awake?' he asks. I don't reply, but he must have seen the light on. 'I'm going to take a bath.' Jeff had once been a five-minute shower man, but I'd managed to convert him when we first met, and now he likes nothing more than soaking himself for hours in hot water.

Jeff pulls at his brown belt, curling it around his right hand. As he drops his jacket onto the wooden chair by the window desk, I watch his back in the darkened room, that back so familiar to me. I imagine the indents of my fingers deep in his skin. Over the last four years we'd slept together on a monthly conception timetable. It dawns on me now that I've given myself so wholly to what I believe to be his needs, and invested so wholly in creating a new life for him – and for us – that I've never shown him my true self. At least not the self you were privy to. The true self that wasn't set in routine. The true self that allowed me to abandon everything when I was with you.

I shudder as he walks over to my bedside and sits down. I think about trying to get him now to see me as you did, but he stretches and yawns. 'It's been a long one. I need to unwind. My goodness, I'm tired. Abraham hasn't stopped all day.' He heads for the bathroom, leaving his phone next to where he's been sitting.

'Enjoy then,' I murmur, the decision made for me, and I don't have the energy to go any further in actioning things with him. Instead, I lie still, waiting for the sound of water running. His sigh as he settles into the bath and then the stillness, save for the low, reassuring murmur of the shipping forecast on the waterproof travel radio I bought him last Christmas.

When I'm sure he's going to be in there for a while, I slide across the bed and pick up his phone ready to put it onto his bedside table. The screen lights up. It's Abraham again. Something about the gala dinner. *Should we go ahead as planned? I think we should. It's all for the best cause, and it's not for another few weeks. No one's going to begrudge us doing a celebration for the Wickham Fellowship recipients. I think it would be worse comms if we were to postpone. Anyway, catch you later!*

I think about you again. How you never said a word to me about the new Wickham Wing. I tap in Jeff's passcode. Despite Abraham's pleas about compliance with security protocols, *even with your most loved ones*, I'm in.

First, I go into his emails, scrolling back to last year and scanning anything that looks like it might be relevant to his conversation with Abraham earlier. Nothing out of the ordinary. Mostly comms forwarded by Janet. I then type in 'Medical' and 'Wickham Wing'. Lots of emails come up. Development costs. Tenders for architects. For builders. At what stages things need to be ordered. Potential donors. All run-of-the-mill, although I'm surprised by how advanced the plans seem to be, given that they've only just been announced. There's nothing to or from you. Before I can deliberate much further, and out of curiosity about whether or not you've ever come up in conversation, I type your name into the search bar. After a couple of seconds, the screen fills with a group of emails under your name.

'Lizzie Lou,' Jeff shouts out, making me jump. 'You want to join me?'

'No.' I put on a slow, sleepy voice, although my adrenaline is firing. 'I'm good, just feeling sleepy.' I read the email. Reread it. It's nothing out of the ordinary but at the same time everything out of the ordinary. Biweekly meeting requests, sent by Janet. To both you and my husband, and one other, a Richard Teddington from the Medical School, entitled 'Wickham Wing Development Meetings'. You had accepted every single meeting request, with diarised dates right up to 2027. The first ever meeting that had been called, and which you had accepted, was two months ago, has a short note on the diary invite:

PRIVATE AND CONFIDENTIAL

As discussed at our last confidential gathering, Jeff Harker requires your presence at biweekly meetings to keep up to speed with all things Franklin/Wickham Wing. The main players are required at each meeting, your input is valuable, and we'd like you to start gathering information to feed back to your colleagues in good time. Minutes will be taken and attached to an email.

Kind regards,

Janet, PA to Jeffrey Harker

So you were one of the main players.

Touching Jeff's screen so it doesn't time out, I use my other hand to look up my own phone calendar. A random Friday morning, eight weeks ago. I scroll back. Jeff and I had been away that Saturday, at a big concert in Ohio run by the University's music staff. My husband had been on good form, but despite talking relentlessly about his work, he never said a word about the wing. We'd had a lovely time, though, walking, talking, eating, and for the first time in forever I'd felt connected to Jeff after everything that had happened. The miscarriages that had been around the time I'd first met you and which had, in part, been the catalyst for me starting our affair; my grief, unacknowledged at the time, had settled in my body's cells, fracturing my neural pathways. Or perhaps, as I'd come to learn in my therapy sessions, electrifying the ones already formed. The following Monday I'd come to you. You'd asked me time and time again if I'd slept with my husband while we were away. 'I've got no right to be jealous,' you'd told me. 'None at all. But I can't help it. I bet you don't react to him like you do to me.'

And you'd been right. I recall again all the times we'd spoken about my husband. The times you'd asked me about him. What he was like. Whether he was a good man. ('Yes, overall'). Whether he was good in bed ('At times'). Whether he was bigger than you ('Hmmm, not too dissimilar,' I'd said with a laugh). You'd been inspecting your arms at the time as though checking for your own imperfections, fine hairs standing upright as you blew on your skin.

'I'm good too,' you'd said. 'Despite this. You. And me. And—'

'And what?'

You'd gone silent for a while. 'And nothing,' you'd eventually laughed, and we'd started all over again. I'd been betraying Jeff. Had you also been betraying me?

I do a few more searches around the date of the meeting. There's one email from you.

> Thank you for organising, Janet. Please find attached the relevant documentation from what was discussed in today's meeting.

You'd signed off with your first initial. And that was it. There is a budget spreadsheet attached. I open it up. At the top you'd written *Attendees,* with Jeff's initials, plus Richard's, Abraham's and your own. You'd then inputted information about three new digital AI dissection tables at the cost of $200,000 each and some other medical training equipment, along with some forecast costs on insurance. I berate myself for being so damn trusting to think you hadn't known about any of this. You were facilities manager. Obviously you'd known. You ran the logistics of the entire Medical School, which was a huge role. Maybe you'd simply been doing a good job keeping things on the down-low, not discussing confidential matters, and then it had got too late to mention that you'd met my husband. Maybe. My chest tightens.

Whilst I'm looking through Jeff's emails from Abraham, I hear the slosh of bathwater, a great sigh and the radio turning off. Shutting down Jeff's emails and making sure I've closed the spreadsheet, I slide his phone back onto the bedside table and twist myself over so my back is facing his side of the bed. I shut my eyes. I hear the scrub of a towel on skin, then the sag of his side of the bed, always the one closest to the door. He gets in between the soft linen sheets I make sure are ironed each week, and switches off his bedside lamp. He puts his hand on my hip to see if I'll be receptive to his touch, but with my skin stinging and the blood whooshing around my body, and while I work out what the hell to do with this new information, I level out my breathing and play dead.

Two Days After the Murder

15.

It's nine o'clock when I wake up. I've slept in fits and starts, sweating into the sheets, with dreams that felt almost hallucinogenic in their vividness. You, looking into my eyes. Me, pulling you closer to me, as close as two humans could possibly be, my legs wrapped tightly around you, when out of nowhere I'd wake up clawing at myself, still seeing your face but now gnarled and ugly, your last gasps rattling in my ear. I'd woken up at one point clinging on to Jeff, as he'd kicked off the sheet and rolled over, my leg hooked over his. It's 9.20 now and still I'm unable to get out of bed. Jeff tells me I look peaky and that I'm to stay quiet whilst he gets more work done in the study. I don't have the energy to disagree. I'm meant to be the perfect wife, but today you are a demonic and terrifying intruder into my thoughts. Your spirit seems to have reanimated itself, burrowing its dark, formless way into my psyche.

'Jeff.' I speak without much conscious thought. 'Listen. Abraham's been really on it. And I've got to get this absolutely right. Both in terms of organising and planning and in terms of how we want to portray ourselves.' I commend myself for starting to behave like Abraham. 'Thinking about the memorial, do you want to say a few words? I mean, did you meet him at all?' I test my husband, steady my voice as I wait for his answer. 'Ever? Were you introduced? If so, it might be an opportunity to open up the conversation. Give it some gravitas. Some sort of grounding.'

'Well, funnily enough,' Jeff says, placing both hands on the desk. 'Abraham tells me I did meet him. At one of the new Wickham Wing meetings a few months ago. It's awful, but I can't actually remember him. He was sort of...' Jeff's eyes track the ceiling as he searches for the right word. 'Unmemorable.'

The word hangs in the air.

'Right.' A strange hiccupping sound comes out of my mouth and I manage to turn it into a laugh. 'Does that mean you won't say anything at all?'

'How can I? I need to be authentic in what I put out there, Lizzie Lou. You're the one who always tells me that. Anyway, listen. I need to get on with this. Can you cast an eye over it?'

I lean over Jeff's computer screen, even though I'm not entirely sure what I'm reading. Another damn statement about security. The same wording we've given out a hundred times before. *Following safeguarding protocol. Students. Policy. Security on campus. No stone left unturned.* I don't have the will to ask him what it's for.

'Looks good. Listen, Jeff.' I seat myself on the edge of his desk, touching the piece of paper he's been working on. I tell myself to behave as though nothing untoward is happening. Unmemorable was the word he used to describe you, saying he hadn't met you properly during your meetings with each other. There had been something artificial about his tone. His exaggerated frown had made me think that my husband, who remembers lines and lines of poetry he's read only once and who tells me I always have to tell the truth to get out of a dinner engagement ('I don't care if it's hard, Lizzie Lou. Do the honourable thing'), was also lying. 'We have to pack,' I say eventually for want of anything else to discuss. 'Or at least think about booking the removals people.' I massage my scalp with my fingertips. 'This is bad.' I rub my face. 'We've got all this to sort out.' I look around the room.

'It's all right.' He doesn't bother looking up from his screen. 'Look, it's all right. When we get into The Lodge we can relax. Start again. This was a once-in-a-lifetime incident. Nothing like this is going to happen again.' He reaches for my hand but I turn away, unable to participate in the conversation, wanting to move away from him. Everything, it seems, has caught up with me. The shock of your death. My sadness that you are no longer here. B. The strong suspicion that my husband has just lied to me. Like you did. Jeff taps my leg to get my attention. 'And we can book a weekend away. I thought we could fly to New York for the opera.'

'I'd love that,' I manage.

'Listen,' Jeff says. 'I've got a meeting with security soon. I've got three days left with them covering campus, but I might add on another week or two until the cops confirm the killer's motivation. God alone knows why they've asked us to wait that long to find out.' I think back to the timing I agreed with Newton. Two weeks. I wonder if they had other reasons for agreeing to that timing, or if they knew something I didn't and I was in for a nasty surprise. 'Lavinia's keen to keep going with it anyway, just until the students feel safe, even if we dip into another budget. She thinks that's all that matters. Which I guess is the right thing to do. Rodrigo, outside' – Jeff tilts his head towards the window – 'he'll spearhead it.'

There's a knock on the door. Three rapid bangs. Jeff shakes his head.

'Don't know who that could be. Speaking of the devil, Rodrigo is meant to be calling up if we have any visitors.'

'Jeff,' Abraham calls. 'Quick.'

'Oh, Abe,' Jeff mumbles. 'Listen, Lizzie Lou. Why don't you go back to bed? You look awful tired. Do some memorial research if you can, maybe. Stay on top of removals. If we book someone in for three days' time, this will all have died down. We can then focus on what's in front of us.' He looks at the door then down at his phone. 'All right?'

'Yes,' I reply, knowing I'm incapable of making any type of decision. I say a brief hello to Abraham as I pass the front door, motioning for him to go through to the study. I don't even have the energy to talk to him about planning the memorial, but thankfully he doesn't try and talk to me and heads straight through to find my husband. I go upstairs to the bedroom, but even there I can hear Abraham's voice. Then Jeff again.

'That fucking Harbottle,' my husband rages. I still can't get used to him swearing, I thought he'd be more careful with his language now he's University president. 'What the hell does he want now?'

Harbottle. The *Gazette* journalist who'd been busy publishing stories at the inauguration.

Jeff's study door shuts and I hear nothing else after that, because my mind goes blank and I pass out, into an empty slumber.

The paranoia sets in two hours later, when I wake up again. It has taken a total shutdown of my body to process everything, and it seems I'm still pulling at the threads of what's going on. The betrayal in all corners of the Medical School. I've run through every reason you might have lied to me about meeting my husband, and why Jeff, much to my surprise, lied about meeting you. I've asked myself whether you'd been gathering information on him. Whether you'd been playing games with me. With Jeff. Whether Jeff was trying to protect me from something by lying about remembering you. And so it comes to pass that I have to play my cards close to my chest.

Going back on my phone, I look fruitlessly for new information on you. Anything that's come up in the investigation. There's a news story published by the *Gazette*, with Harbottle's byline – STUDENTS UNSAFE ON CAMPUS: GAZETTE REPORTER GETS PAST SECURITY AT PRESTIGIOUS UNIVERSITY – which must have been the reason for Abraham's earlier visit. Underneath is an article about how Harbottle had managed to get on-site by claiming to be a member of staff.

I think back to how Janet had been dealing with all of that when the cops first arrived after your murder. A statement from Jeff appears at the bottom. The usual wording about safeguarding. Keeping the students safe. Assuring people we've followed policy.

A notification comes in on my phone. It's Abraham, pleading with staff again not to talk to any journalists. *Due to the nature of this story and the public interest in it,* says the message, *we again implore all staff to keep silent on University matters. If anyone is found to be in breach of this, they will face instant dismissal.*

I get out of bed and make my way across the landing and down the stairs to find out what Jeff intends to do about this. I tell myself to act normal and not to let my anger and distress get the better of me. Another notification comes down. It's Abraham, messaging the memorial planning group with a mobile number. The area code is unfamiliar and he has given no explanation. I open the study door, waving the phone in the air. 'Is this going to cause problems?' I ask Jeff. 'Abraham's text. I'm planning the memorial right now.'

'I'm now having to write to all staff members, and our students and their families, to reassure them. Again. That weasel Harbottle.' Jeff sounds resigned. 'There can't be much more, surely? Interest has to be waning. This is absolute madness. All these theories. Why can't people wait until the official line comes out?'

'Which is?'

'Which is that this guy,' Jeff says, resting his head in his hands, 'was up to no good somewhere and paid for it with his blood.'

'Right.' I stop myself from saying any more and return to a topic I know is relatively safe. 'Listen. Removals.'

'Go on. Tell me. What's the latest?'

I tell him the latest, wondering if we'll only be able to discuss 'safe' topics for the rest of Jeff's time here. Going back to my phone I contact the removals company and make the arrangements Jeff requested. Then I start googling your name again, looking fruitlessly for new information on you.

The phone rings. I've had to change the tone to something less piercing, and it's a couple of seconds before I realise it's mine. I pick it up. 'Abraham?'

He starts talking before I can say anything else. *The memorial. Chaplain. Eulogy. All set.* I tell myself just to get through these next few days. To get through your memorial and moving house. Not only do I owe that to you, but I also need to get more information.

Then Abraham's talking about making the phone call. That it would be best coming from me. Don't I think? Softer. More amenable. If I don't mind. I have that way about me. For a split second I don't want to admit I have no idea what he's talking about.

'Thank you. But I'm sorry, Abraham,' I venture. 'Let me stop you there. Which phone call? To whom?'

'The number. I sent it to you earlier. Just now. To the group. I'm sure I did. Didn't I?' There's a distant tapping sound down the line. 'I did. Yes. Right here. Look.' He reads out the digits. 'Hang on. Let me look. That dial code, it's…' More tapping. 'Arizona. It's Sedona. Jeez. So it'll take… hang on, let me look up timings.'

'Sorry, yes. You did. But I wasn't sure what the number was. Or whose.' Jeff motions for me to leave the room and close the door. I go quietly.

'Arizona. She's in Arizona. The wife,' Abraham says. 'That number. For you to call. To arrange the memorial. The number. It belongs to his wife.'

Again, it's another three hours before I'm able to do as Abraham has asked. To 'steer the ship' where the University is concerned. To find out what your wife wants in terms of your memorial. Whether indeed she wants anything at all to do with it.

Nicola, Abraham texted me shortly after his call. *She's called Nicola.* And that was it. Nothing else. I prep myself, telling myself to be careful not to give the game away. To let her talk. To avoid spiralling into nervous dialogue. But before I ring, I spend a long time researching Sedona, a place you never mentioned having visited. I look on Google Maps, trying to get a sense of it, imagining you breathing in the air there. Would you have loved the beautiful red rocks surrounding the area? Would you have mocked the New Age shops, so prevalent in the area? Enough. I need to focus again. I text Nicola. I tell her I'm going to call. It's half an hour before she responds.

Thank you so much for reaching out. I'd love to talk. I'll call you when I've dropped my son with the childminder.

Mention of your boy kicks me in the gut.

To delay phoning Nicola, I walk to the mirror and put on my make-up. Foundation, which I never normally wear, blusher, mascara and a pat of dark cherry-coloured lip gloss, at odds with the casual outfit I've chosen today: cream wide-legged trousers and a light blue off-the-shoulder linen top. I notice Rodrigo outside, scanning the area, and then I hear Jeff downstairs in the kitchen. When his study door clicks shut again, I make the call. I give the usual platitudes. How sorry I am. How I never met her husband, but that I'm here to help with everything. 'And your son?' My voice catches. 'How is he?'

'He's doing really great' she says, her voice warm. 'I know that's a strange thing to say, but the truth is, he barely knew his father.' She goes quiet.

Your son. I clear my throat, trying to keep my feelings in check. 'Oh goodness.' I mime a grimace so she can't detect the emotion roiling inside me. You had loved someone else. You had another life with her. I both love and hate you, and an ugly part of me wants to hurt your wife. 'That's... I'm so sorry to hear that.' I make a concerted effort to soften my brusque tone. 'Listen, I know that must have been hard to tell me. But that's helpful to know. It's good information for me to have when we're doing the memorial. The dynamics of your relationship. How you shared the load.'

I feel terrible about conning your wife into telling me about you. But with Newton knowing what he does about you and me, it's an absolute necessity to be pulled into this even further.

'Shall we have a chat about that quickly now?' I ask. 'You can fill me in and then we can talk through how best to manage this. With the press rummaging around, best to be forewarned. But don't worry, I'll be there for you. We all will.'

'Oh goodness. Thank you, Elizabeth, I didn't know you'd be so caring. So considerate. Especially after what I've told you, and given that he and I hadn't spoken for so long. But really, that's so kind. And you know what? I've had the press on at me all this time too.' I think of Harbottle, wonder whether he's been haranguing her. 'My friend Casey, she's told me I have to ignore it all. I mean, I've hardly been out. Tommy's school has been good though. Keeping an extra-close eye on him at all times. Offering him counselling. Not that I think he needs it. In some ways I think it only highlights everything, given he was used to his father not being around. But that's for another time. Anyway, where were we?'

I'm almost hypnotised by your wife's voice. She's so softly spoken. So sweet and breathy. Had that been part of her appeal to you?

'You know, I'd been keeping all of this to myself,' Nicola says. 'I had no one to talk to apart from Casey. I couldn't admit, could I, that there was a part of me that was so angry he left that for many months I could barely say his name in our house? I tried. You know. I tried so, so damn hard in that time to keep the thought of his daddy alive for my baby. When he was old enough to understand.'

I will her not to break down.

She pauses. 'I never wanted him to feel abandoned.'

There's something about the way she says this that makes me want to break down myself.

'But sometimes in the dead of night, when I was exhausted, I was so angry with him for deserting us. I'd scream those words – "Where are you? You left us. You left us."'

'I'm so sorry,' I whisper. Which is the truth. I am. How could you have done such a thing? Your beautiful boy. 'Where did you guys meet?'

I don't intend the question to come out, but she launches into an answer seemingly without recognition that it might have been in any way intrusive and unprofessional. 'Oh, that's a funny story,' she says with a laugh. I hang on to her every word as she tells me how you'd both been on separate dates in a tiny bar; you'd been on a work trip and your date had failed to turn up. You'd noticed your wife-to-be sitting across the room, also on a date, but one which was clearly going wrong.

'We settled down quickly after that. It all seemed so right. He easily got a work transfer. He was doing research at the time, so he could work lots from home. He travelled a fair bit. South America. Russia. Loads of places. Until we had Tommy, and then he was around all the time.' She pauses. 'We had it perfect. We really did, Elizabeth. Goodness, I thought I was over all this. I was. I am. I promise you.'

'You don't need to justify anything to me,' I say, meaning it. 'You can be over him but miss him too, you know. Things aren't always so binary.' Which was something you used to say to me.

'Anyway.' The line goes muffled. 'He came to save me. He was good at that,' she says more forcefully. 'He was good at that. Until, of course, he wasn't.'

'And how come he left?' Again, I berate myself for being so brazen, but I can't seem to stop myself. 'I'm so sorry,' I add quickly. 'Just so we can manage the press on that one. So they don't start inventing their own narratives.'

'What, aside from the narrative they've already built? That he was taking drugs? That he was stealing them from the Medical School and selling them? That's going to be great for Tommy to read about when he's older, isn't it?'

'I'm sorry,' I tell her. 'But from what I've heard about your husband, I don't believe any of it. He was obviously a good man.'

'You know, I still don't know why.' Her voice goes quieter. 'Why he upped and left shortly before Tommy's second birthday. He never told me. Just walked. I came home and all his stuff was gone. I thought initially he'd met someone else.' I withhold a gasp. 'But looking back on it, I think he was stressed about work. Something had happened. It wouldn't have been like him just to leave. He and I were honestly never perfect together, but you know what, he'd never have left Tommy unless there was a good reason to. He loved him. He really did. That whole time, he doted on him. I sometimes had to fight him to spend time on my own with my son.' She gives a tiny laugh.

I decide to stop right there.

Despite wanting – needing – more information and my surge of internal rage that you'd chosen to leave your son and my mother had had that choice taken away from her, I decide to stop there. If anyone finds out how much I've been asking about you, it'll be a red flag. Instead, I change the subject and ask Nicola about herself and Tommy, hoping for some clues I can piece together about your life before me. She tells me snippets about your son. She tells me how she was late to drop him at childcare because hearing from me had been traumatic and my message had made her husband's death all the more real. How Tommy had been asking for hot dogs for his tea. How she thought she'd leave him with her mother or Casey for the duration of the memorial. That she won't tell anyone how you abandoned your own son. We both go quiet.

Flashes of memory come back to me. I'd found it too painful to talk about my miscarriages with you. I preferred just to be with you as your lover, and as myself, without any other reason than to satiate my desire. It's only now that I recall you'd mentioned that you thought you'd be a good dad. I'd agreed with you. Kissed you on the mouth. And the next time we'd slept together, I'd opened myself up to you even more. Trusted you even more. The sting of the memory, especially now I know you were already a father, makes me agitated. I start to pace around the room, thinking about how my own husband would be as a father. A sob nearly escapes me as I imagine him explaining the science of a molecule to our child. The earnest seriousness with which he'd undertake it all. Where the hell had things gone so wrong?

'Anyway,' Nicola says with a sigh. 'That's all over now, isn't it?'

'It is indeed,' I state. I'm exhausted by the pretence of it. Your lies. Jeff's lies. Having to live with the knowledge of all these betrayals.

I change tack. Ask her about the finer details of the order of service. The music she wants. The readings.

'Hmm,' she says. 'I'm pretty ambivalent, in truth. You guys probably knew him best more recently. I meant it when I told you we weren't in contact much over the past year or so. And even before then, he'd only think to ask about Tommy sometimes. But…' She pauses. 'Anyway. No use dragging that all up. So please. Go ahead. If you like, you can run it through with me, whatever you're planning. How does that sound?'

'That sounds good,' I tell her truthfully. 'Look. I'll get some information about your husband from his colleagues and put something together. We don't have much time, so it'll be fairly simple, but we've got an amazing choir who've apparently agreed to come in to sing. As we've just discussed, I think the press will be around,' I add. 'But if you come and meet me first, we'll go in together.'

For the first time since being put in charge of the memorial, I'm energised by the thought that I'm contributing. And also by the thought that I'm getting close to finding out more about who you were and getting to know the woman you'd married. Or at least learning about the different versions of you we each saw. Nicola and I talk a bit more. About the University. How difficult things have been. How wonderfully we've handled the PR side of things.

'I've seen a lot of your communications to the students,' she says. I don't ask her how, nor does she offer up any more information. 'And they're exemplary. Exactly the right tone. And I'm very grateful for all your efforts in this. Especially given that you didn't know him.'

'Well, I'm now leading the charge with my husband Jeff, so it's a privilege to be doing this for…' For you. I could still take ownership of the day. I could still do what I think you'd have loved.

'Hey. Actually,' Nicola goes quiet. 'There is one song. But I'd love it a capella. Would that be possible? To get the choir to sing it a capella? It's a big ask, I know. The arrangement shouldn't be too difficult.'

'It's fine. Absolutely fine. We can do whatever you like. He was a much-valued member of our community and we need to show our respect for him.'

'Okay,' she replies. 'It was from the album he played on repeat when he first told me he loved me.' I stand still. 'I know we were estranged from each other, but I still miss him you know. Anyway…' She lets out a tiny noise. 'It's Coldplay. "Yellow".'

Everything around me seems to go silent. I think of the times you'd played me Coldplay, and the times afterwards. When you'd first told me you'd loved me, you'd staged the scene beautifully. The soft sounds of 'Yellow' from the other room. Candles. The movement of your hands. Kissing me. The way you'd told me that night that it was my turn. The album had restarted, and as that particular song had started to play again, you'd said it as you'd looked into my eyes. *I love you. I love you. I love you.* I never owned you. I'm married, for God's sake. And yet here I am, being territorial about a goddamn song.

'Hello?' Your wife's voice echoes down the line. 'You still there? Anyway. That's what I've decided. It's my only request. I'd like you to play that.'

I thought I'd been special to you. Turns out you'd seduced me the same way you had seduced your wife. Then you'd abandoned us each in turn. That much at least we had in common. And with that one request, your wife had blown what was left of my world right apart.

Coldplay. 'Yellow'.

I love you.

You'd been playing me all along.

Five Days After the Murder

16.

The next few days are a blur, for which I am grateful. There are times, though, when I'm going about my day, planning the memorial, booking florists, music and the like, when I find myself clutching at my phone, drenched in sweat, waiting for Newton to ring and tell me the game is up. Every time I hear a noise I startle, and at one point, when I think there's a knock on the door, it takes two hours for my heart to settle back into a regular rhythm.

On the face of it, at least on campus, things have gone back to normal. The students have started to return with a new energy. They move around in groups, books under arms, backpacks on. At lunch they drape themselves across the front lawn, confidently louche; books and devices are strewn around them on the grass, as are sandwich wrappers, twitching in the gentle breeze. Most lectures have started up again. A few students have opted for online learning instead, but they have been told by the comms team that their mental health comes first and that they won't be marked down for this in their end-of-semester grades. It's unsettling that I'm carrying the burden of the things I've done when everyone else seems unhindered by guilt. How lucky they are.

In between organising your memorial and the move to The Lodge, I keep thinking about all the lies. Jeff unexpectedly telling the truth about meeting you, even if he had tried to manipulate me into believing he barely remembered you. His expression when I'd asked him about you: something close to contempt. *Unmemorable.* I keep thinking about when you'd first told me you loved me, how you'd played me the same music as you had your wife. Had you hoped that by repeating your actions things would be different the next time? That the connection would be more real?

As I become less certain about what you'd felt for me, I become less sure of myself. I drop things. Cry at random points during the day. Muddle my words.

Twice, Jeff asks if I'm okay.

'That lurgy,' I say the second time, sensing that he is losing patience. I tap my throat. 'So strange. Whatever it was that sent me under the other day, I can't seem to shake it.'

'Look,' he takes me in his arms. 'You've been amazing throughout all of this.' I relax into his chest despite the mistrust I feel for him. I have no one else. 'I haven't told you that enough. I know the last few days' events have probably taken their toll, but after this,' he says, squeezing me, 'the rest of our tenure here will be a cinch. And we've got everything to play for. The Lodge. The adoption. We've just got to get through this first.' Jeff's physical presence grounds me in a way you never did. But perhaps that in itself was part of your appeal.

'Ha,' I tell him. 'I've seen what goes on in academia. You can't fool me.'

For the next few days, Jeff is in his study the whole time, and when I'm least expecting it, when the adrenaline has finally subsided, I get a call from Newton. I can't read his tone when he asks me to meet him for questioning.

'All okay?' I ask.

'I'll see you where we last met. You sent me the what-3words. I'll send it back to you, given I have your cell.' At the mention of my phone, my mind starts to fill in the gaps. Have they found something on it? Could they have misinterpreted something you'd said?

'Okay.'

'Now?' he says, although I know it's not a question. 'How long will it take you to get there? Twenty?'

'Wait,' I say. 'I need time to get legal representation.' But then I start to panic. Will Jeff find out if I do? The only lawyer I know is Harry Bellwater, who sometimes deals in-house with the University's legal cases, of which there are many. I can't ask him. And I don't want to start googling 'best local lawyers for murder cases' on my phone. Or on my computer, for that matter.

'Well, we do need to see you now, ma'am.' Newton's tone changes. 'We're willing to wait a little while for you to find legal representation, but you would need to be quick.'

I look in the hallway mirror; my hair has come loose from its bun. I've sweated off some of my mascara and my lipstick has smudged, I start to rub my skin repeatedly until I leave red marks under my eyes and around my mouth. I tie my hair again into a tight knot at the nape of my neck.

'Listen, ma'am, this isn't going to be anything too intense. We're just wanting your help with some things.'

'Fine,' I say, unable to think further. The idea of sourcing anonymous representation feels like it's about to tip me over the edge. And in any case, apart from what Newton already knows, I have nothing to hide. 'I'll see you in twenty.'

I call Jeff after I've got into my car. 'Listen,' I tell him. 'I've got to run a few errands. I'll be back later.' But he's hung up before I can continue. Relieved I don't have to tell more lies, I focus on the endless grey tarmac in front of me as I drive. Normally I enjoy the shade of the trees overhead and this beautiful place around me, but today there seems to be darkness within every shimmering molecule.

When I pull up, Newton's already there, pacing around in the tiny clearing, from the road, sleeves rolled up, pressed shirt tucked neatly into his belted trousers. This time he's with a woman in a T-shirt and navy uniform trousers. Nodding at me, she sticks out her hand and I wonder if this is some weird, good cop, bad cop set-up.

'Hey, I'm Tamara.' She flips her long black plait over her shoulder. 'Good to meet you, Elizabeth.'

I look questioningly at Newton, who shrugs. 'Would you mind?' He points to his car, which he's parked under a tree so it's barely visible to any passers-by.

'No.' My voice shakes. 'No,' I say more forcefully. 'Not at all.' For a second, I think they're about to handcuff me and take me away. And in that split second I nearly let out a scream, but I manage to hold it together, at least until we get in the car. I sit behind the passenger seat, and Tamara joins me in the back. Near my right leg is a tiny tear in the leather, yellow foam poking out. Someone's tried to cover the tear with masking tape. I have to stop myself from ripping the entire thing off so I have something to concentrate on other than the indignity of it all.

Tamara pulls out her Dictaphone and notepad. 'I'm going to record this.' She holds up the shiny black device. 'Should you wish to stop the conversation at any point, I'll be describing your actions into the microphone.'

'You said you'd give me two weeks.' I hear my tone and will myself to stop sounding so whiny. 'If you don't hear anything else, if nothing happens, can we just leave it there?'

Newton twists himself round in the driver's seat and looks over his shoulder at Tamara. 'We'll have to see. It might be in our best interests to do so, but we'll have to let you know about that.'

'We'll let you know as soon as possible,' Tamara says, softening the atmosphere. Good cop.

'Could you please tell us' – Newton is now staring straight ahead out of the windscreen so all I can see is the side of his head, the tic of one eyelid – 'where exactly you were when you first heard about your' – he coughs – 'lover's death.'

'Yes.' They already know where I was. Where the hell are they going with this? 'I was at the inauguration. My husband's inauguration. I'd arrived early. We were all seated.

Apart from Abraham.' I think back to that moment. Your photograph. 'None of us knew how to react at first.'

I will myself to be quiet. I'm here alone so have to be careful to choose words that can't be taken out of context. I silently thank Abraham for organising media training for us. The trainer had repeatedly told us to find a narrative that suits us, one we can work with.

'I'd sent him a photograph.' I stare directly at Newton. 'Just before. Of myself.' I lift my chin in defiance, pre-empting the shame that never arrives. 'He didn't respond. But I saw that he was online. He was online while I was in the taxi on the way to the hall. And then he disappeared again.'

'Right.' Newton tilts his head, obviously mulling over this information. 'And your husband? Why weren't you with him in the car on the way to the inauguration?'

'He was there early. Rehearsals.' I don't seem to have the mental capacity to leap ahead to where he is going with this. 'I'd been to have my hair and make-up done.'

'Did you know he wasn't going to be there? At the inauguration?'

'I, well, yes. We'd talked about it.' I swallow. 'I thought he might be watching though. Somehow. Abraham told me they were livestreaming it. I figured he might have got the link. Seen me.'

Shame creeps up on me this time as I remember how I thought as I sat onstage that you might have been thinking about me.

'And your husband. Back to him.' Bile rises up my throat. 'You guys have a good relationship?'

'We do.'

'But you were…'

I look at Tamara.

'Tell me how that works for you,' Newton says.

'It simply works. Okay? I mean *worked*.'

'So let me get this straight,' Newton continues. 'You love your husband, but you also fell in love with another man, with whom you'd been having an affair for a year? Forgive me, ma'am, I'm not quite getting it.'

I wonder how best to answer. Do I truly love Jeff? Had I truly loved you? Or was it simply that you opened a desire in me that I'd never experienced before? That I'd been able to explore a part of myself that had been hidden until I met you? When I was with you, shame hadn't been a buffer for my internal desire being played out in my external reality. You, my love, had allowed me to be all of myself. Those secret parts of me that I had barely been able to face myself. 'You like that?' you'd asked me, your eyes searching mine. 'What about here? And when I do it like that?' And it had surprised me every time when my answer had been yes. 'Yes. I do. More.' Then you'd start to hold off until I begged, and I'd asked once or twice whether you enjoyed controlling me like that, and you'd told me yes, but that you knew I got off on it too.

The truth of it was that yes, I did love you. Do love you.

'Ma'am? Ma'am, are you listening?'

I jump. 'Yes. Sorry, what did you say?'

'I asked you how you could claim to love your husband but be having an affair all this time. For an entire year.'

There's something accusatory in his tone. In turn, I'm riled that he's after information about my love life, and that the subtext of his questions has taken on a sexual tone.

'Look, I'm not comfortable with this line of questioning.' Tamara nods so slightly that the movement is barely discernible. 'So maybe I'll contact my lawyer now.' I glance at Tamara again out of the side of my eye. She's staring intensely at the back of Newton's chair. There's a tiny black stain right in the middle.

'Listen, ma'am, I'm only trying to get things straight.' Newton stretches out his arms, placing both hands on the steering wheel. 'Tell me about him. Did he ever mention drugs? In the Medical School or outside it? Ever complain of headaches?'

'Sorry?' I don't have to fake the confusion in my voice. At first, I'm unsure whether my answer could be used to prop up the narrative they're creating around you, then I remember the way Newton had asked in our previous meeting if you'd ever been into drugs or gambling. 'Never. A headache?'

'You ever see him taking anything?' Newton turns the steering wheel from left to right like he's on a racetrack.

'Never.' I frown. 'At least…' I think. 'No. Never. I can be sure of that.'

'You never see anything lying around? Medication, that sort of thing?'

'Sorry, I'm not quite—'

'Just answer the question, ma'am.' Newton looks to his left, out of the window. I think back to Nicola telling me about the prevailing theory that you were both a druggie and a dealer who had been stealing from the University's medical supplies.

'No.' I remember rummaging through your bathroom cabinet the second or third time I'd stayed with you. Like a bookshelf, a person's bathroom cabinets contain a lot of information about a person. But you'd had nothing much to give me on that front. You'd liked to stock up in packs of three. Toothbrushes, toothpaste. Three roll-on deodorants. I'd even looked at the price tags to see where you'd shopped, imagining you in the Market Basket, arms flexed under the weight of your bags. I'd found an old tube of sun cream, the plastic rolled over at the bottom, and I remembered wondering if you'd been seeing someone at the time you'd bought it. If you'd massaged cream into her shoulders using those stroking techniques, you'd used with me. I'd felt a strange mix of jealousy and excitement at that point, and I remember being shocked at myself. I'd gone back into your bedroom then, and after a few seconds I had leaned over and taken you into my mouth. I clear my throat. 'No. Nothing else. He barely kept anything like that.'

'Nothing at all?' Newton taps his fingers on the wheel.

'Nothing,' I repeat, determined not to tell the police anything that would make you seem less than normal, even now you're dead. I can't figure out where Newton is going with his line of questioning, and it's throwing me.

'Listen, I do have to get back at some point.' I'm ready to add a line about my husband running the University. 'I've got some important stuff to be getting on with.'

'A few more questions, ma'am,' Newton says, reclaiming the power. 'Did he talk about work a lot?'

'He was work-focused, that's for sure,' I say, truthfully.

He turns again to look at me now. 'What do you mean by "work-focused"?'

'Well, he cared about his work,' I say carefully. 'He cared that he was making a difference. That he was helping the masses.'

'And did he talk about anything to do with his work?'

'Not specifically.'

'And would you say he asked you about your husband? Did he want to know anything about the University? Or the Medical School?'

'Not at all. The topic of Jeff was off limits.' I don't tell him that you'd often ask me to compare the two of you. 'So was anything I knew about the Med School.'

'And how was he when you last saw him?'

'Off,' I say truthfully. 'Like he was upset at me for something I'd done.'

'Something you'd done?' Newton sounds shocked and I think about backtracking, before realising that would make things even worse.

'I hadn't done anything, though. Like I told you before, I'd gone over there to finish things with him. The only thing that had changed between us was Jeff's new role. I thought that was probably the reason why.'

'Right.' Newton goes silent.

'Is that it now?' I make as if to open the door. 'Am I free to go?'

No one says a word. Then something is unleashed inside me, and I'm flooded with emotion.

'Do you know anything?' The question comes out in a whisper. 'About who did it?' I feel as though I might cry. 'Surely you have some ideas.'

'We're looking at some interesting leads.' Newton nods towards Tamara. 'As I said, we've got a good team on it. I will tell you, though, that it was someone with a motive.'

'A motive? How do you know?'

'We know because we're good at what we do.'

I clasp my hands around the door handle. 'And what about B?'

'B?' Newton seems taken aback.

'I told you about B. I told you I thought he was seeing someone else.' The words are knives to my heart. 'Did you find out who she is?'

'That's all pertinent to the investigation.' Newton stretches out his arms again. 'So we'll be keeping that in-house.'

'Right. And listen,' I plead. 'Jeff. You didn't answer me. I'll help you with anything I can. Please tell me after two weeks if I don't need to keep doing so. If I don't need to tell Jeff.'

Newton doesn't answer. 'You can go now,' he says in a monotone. 'Thank you for coming over. We'll contact you again if we need anything.'

I'm kept busy after that with Abraham contacting me constantly about your memorial service, and with the move. I can't seem to stop thinking about the first grilling from Lieutenant Newton. Had I said the right things at that point? Why hadn't I kept my damn mouth shut?

And what had you been trying to recreate with me when you'd played me Coldplay? Had you just been playing your standard seduction card? Had you also dimmed the lights when you'd done the same with your wife? With B? Had you held her softly by the hand and taken her into your bedroom? Had you slipped off her top whilst stroking her shoulder with your right knuckle? I think about all these things as I wonder if my marriage to Jeff is over, and as I prepare myself to say goodbye to you for the last time.

For the next six hours, the removals team trample around the cottage. It's a feat to act normal after having seen Newton, so it's good to be occupied. I watch as each room empties: a dismantling of everything as I know it. Jeff and I direct the team as best we can, whilst also tying up the last details of your memorial. The orchestra. The choir. The flowers and the eulogy, which will be delivered by Richard, your successor. I also go through the order of service, the logo we'll use. Everything needs to be perfect. After all, says Abraham, we have to assume as if all eyes are going to be on this. Press included. Somehow they'll get in. They must already be aware it's taking place, and Nicola's presence will add more of a personal angle.

Your wife flies in tonight, and both Abraham and Jeff want to be ready to go so we can tell her that every detail has been checked and double-checked. That if, or rather when, the press turn up, she has nothing to worry about. That our University and Medical School deserve the reputation of being one of the – if not *the* – finest educational establishments in the world.

I look around the cottage, noticing tiny piles of dust around the skirting previously hidden by our furniture, imprints where paintings were, moth-eaten sections of carpet that we had never noticed.

'You think we'll be able to fill The Lodge?' I ask my husband as we sit on a tower of boxes.

'I do. Harley and Suzy have left a load of furniture behind.' Jeff sips at a cup of coffee. 'And we've got an allowance, remember. A good budget to make any changes we want. So I think you and I should go shopping whilst we're in New York. God, I can't wait for a break.'

'Sounds amazing.' Jeff had proved himself worthy a million times over during these past few days. I kiss my husband, feeling uplifted for the first time in forever and deciding to park my knowledge that he lied to me about meeting you. Perhaps he'd signed an NDA. Perhaps he, too, had simply been doing his job. I think about a weekend in New York. Opera and shopping. I'll buy some new underwear. We'll start trying again. I look at Jeff's side profile. How physically unassuming he is. But he had commanded the stage, the embodiment of the word *respect*. He had ably managed this entire crisis. Crisis. His word, not mine. For me, this was a tragedy.

'Listen,' says Jeff. 'We're eating in the University Hall tonight, with the wife.'

'Nicola.' Jeff's dismissive tone makes me surprisingly defensive. 'You mean Nicola?'

Jeff doesn't react. 'Nicola. Yes. I've ordered the silver service menu. Smart.'

'Fine.' I've already worked out what to wear when I meet your wife. A dress you loved. Green velvet. Long. A sweetheart neckline, not too plunging. Demure, but not too demure. And I'll wear heels. Smart black heels that you also loved. You'd begged me to wear them naked with you; I'd never got around to it.

I think of you when I stand in front of my bedroom mirror and put on the heels. Jeff has gone on ahead for a meeting with Abraham before drinks. Before slipping the green dress over my head, no knickers on underneath, I think again about how you saw me for all that I am. I then blow-dry my hair before putting on my make-up. Nude lipstick. Minimal mascara and a darker blusher. The candlelight will pick up my bone structure, and I hope your wife will say something complimentary about my appearance. It's my fucked-up way of both trying to prove a point and keeping my connection open to you.

The landline in Jeff's study is flashing when I go downstairs, although I hadn't heard it ring. I then pick up my phone to call for an Uber and see a grand total of fourteen missed calls. I open my home screen, praying it isn't Lieutenant Newton. It's not; it's Jeff, probably wondering where I am. But then my phone starts to flash again. Abraham. He'll leave a message if it's important. And he does. I listen to his voice telling me that I'm not to go the normal route to the University. A car is on its way. There are press swarming the place, trying to get people to talk.

I WhatsApp instead of calling. My adrenaline is firing so hard I don't trust my own voice and my chest feels like it's about to cave in on itself. *Oh no. What's going on?*

There are more rumours flying around, Abraham responds. *Just make your way here. Don't worry, we've got you all the way.*

His words seem strange, but I'm reassured by the tone of the message. I leave the house, lock the door behind me and get into the car that has already arrived. 'Rodrigo, we'll be back around eleven,' I call out to security before closing the car door.

When we get onto the main road, I dare to check my phone. There are no more messages from either Jeff or Abraham, but I'm getting loads of notifications. I go straight to the @StudentInvigilatorX account, which seems to have become my source of all knowledge about the investigation into your death. I scroll past the pinned posts about you and reach the latest. It's one sentence. I laugh when I first read it. How ridiculous, I think. I look at the comments; everyone is going mad. Links to other sites, more conjecture about you, more rumours.

> @StudentInvigilatorX Check this out, guys. It seems he was having an affair. With someone important!!!! When this breaks it's going to be absolutely wild for the murder case and the Med School. 🧐☠️🧐

There's another post underneath. I open it up and shut it again.

> @StudentInvigilatorX And here's today's photo for you all. 🧐☠🧐

There, beneath @StudentInvigilatorX's profile, is a side profile photo of a woman. A shoulder-length bob. Even features. Nothing too extraordinary save for a teeny-tiny birthmark on her right cheek. My vision turns to pinpricks and I lean forward between the car seats. That woman is me.

'Please stop the car,' I say. 'Down a side road. I need to make a couple of phone calls.'

'Certainly, madam.'

I wait until we're somewhere quiet and ask my driver to let me out. I look around for anyone who can hear me, and also scan the area for rogue CCTV or camera doorbells. When I'm satisfied I'm fully alone, I whip out the card Newton gave me and ring the number on it.

'Lieutenant Newton,' he answers.

'Lieutenant, I'd love a word.' I'm on the verge of being sick, but somewhere, in a place that feels very distant to me, I hear my words running into each other. 'Can we talk?'

'One sec. Just finding a quiet spot.' His footsteps echo down the receiver, then there is the clank of a metal door.

I wait, blood thundering in my ears.

'Mrs Harker?'

'Lieutenant Newton. Listen, I know we spoke earlier, but—' I take in a sharp breath. 'Why did you do this? You told me—'

'Ma'am, please,' he says quietly. 'Please. Calm down. No leaks came from our department, I can assure you of that. I know what you're referring to, though. I saw the socials a moment ago.'

'How?' I snap. 'How then? These things don't just come out like that.'

'Listen,' he says soothingly, before I can go any further. 'They haven't made a direct link.' He goes quiet, presumably waiting for me to process it all.

'Which means they don't have proof?' I start to sob.

'It means exactly that,' Newton responds carefully. 'It means it's currently a rumour. The socials will probably break the story, but they haven't yet got irrefutable evidence or at least two confirmations which would stand up in a court of law. It means they'll know they can post it and not be sued for libel or defamation. Once it's clear that the socials have broken the news, the press will soon follow suit. I'm sure you know all this already, Elizabeth, but you sound—'

'I don't,' I tell him. 'I mean, I do, but—'

'But you're terrified and trying to work out who could have leaked this? Who knows about the two of you? I've seen this many times before in my line of work, Elizabeth.'

'Right,' is all I can manage. My phone beeps. Abraham, on the other line. I decline the call. 'So they insinuate that he was having an affair, then they make the link in people's minds that it's me by putting a photograph of me underneath the post?'

'Exactly. It's enough to get into people's psyches. The photograph means nothing. It's not even clear it's you.

But it apparently took the keyboard warriors all of twenty seconds to find your name through Google's reverse image search or something.'

'They've got no evidence then?' I imagine everyone's speculating about me on the socials right now.'

No amount of reassurance is going to calm my tornado of thoughts. My fear that everything is over for me. The move to the Lodge. The adoption. And then there's the public humiliation, and the thought that people might think I had something to do with your murder. For the first time since your death, I think of my parents, grateful they aren't here to bear witness to all of this.

My throat closes. I have so much more at stake than I did this time yesterday. I'm even more certain now that I can't screw things up with Jeff. That I'll overlook his lies to me so I don't lose all this. 'Is there any way to find out who leaked the information? Who knows who that was? Maybe I can tell them to...'

'From experience, my best advice to you, Elizabeth, is to leave it. Don't say a word. Don't fuel the rumours. People can talk all they want, but if you keep your head held high, they don't have a leg to stand on.'

'But what if there's photographic evidence? What if...'

My mind ricochets through all the possible ways someone might have found out about you and me. Were we ever careless? (I don't think so). Did you tell anyone? (I also don't think so). Did anyone have a grudge against us? (By the sounds of it, possibly you. Given I barely knew anyone in this place, unlikely to be me, except by proxy.) But the seed has already been sown. Every interaction we ever had is being played out in my memories.

'You still neither confirm nor deny,' Newton says. 'Rule number one. But if irrefutable evidence does come out, then you'd better work out how to manage it all. I've been speaking to Abraham Cohen a lot throughout this. He'll have some wisdom. He's trustworthy too. I've told him lots of things we've never told anyone else, and he's always dealt with them sensitively. He's probably your best bet.'

'But he and my husband—'

'Abraham is good at his job. His work is more important than any personal relationship he has with anyone, I can assure you.'

'How do you know?'

'We grew up together. Small place, this, when you're teenagers. I know him well. He's been good to us. Worked really hard to get funding for the new district office and our new facial recognition software. As I said, we've worked on other incidents. To do with the University. Remember that stalking case?'

'I vaguely remember reading about it,' I murmur.

'And that lady who got done for fraudulently claiming hundreds of thousands of dollars of expenses?'

'Yes, that too.'

'And countless others. There's an awful lot that goes on behind closed doors at the Medical School, Elizabeth, that Abraham shuts down. Or attends to in a brilliant manner, so the public don't hear about it. In fact, I'd say that man damn near being a genius, and he loves this place. A lot.

You know he was one of the first scholarship recipients here at the University?'

'No.' I shake my head. 'I had no idea.'

'They kept him off the streets. He feels he owes this place a lot. He wants it kept clean, and that's his only motivation, even if his methods seem brutal at times. My intuition tells me to speak to him about it. You can tell him I said so, if it comes to that. He'll think of a plan.'

I go silent as I try and work out how the hell I'm going to admit to Abraham what I've been doing. Tell him that I've already been to the cops. That I'm tied up in something far bigger than I could have imagined.

'Thank you,' I say, and I mean it.

'Listen.' I hear Newton open and close a door. He lowers his voice. 'Maybe it will make you feel better if I tell you that we've been through everything with a fine-tooth comb. All your movements. You're not under suspicion.'

I'm filled with relief. 'That's good to know. Really good. But who is? What's going on with the investigation right now?'

'You know I can't give you that information.'

I recoil, feeling like I'm being told off at school all over again.

'But we're looking into other lines of enquiry right now.'

Pulling my screen away from my ear, I look at the time. It's only ten minutes until your wife arrives for dinner and I'm still at least fifteen minutes away from the Great Hall after the diversion. 'Listen, I've got to go. But thank you. It's appreciated. Much appreciated.'

I hang up and spend the next couple of minutes in the car, scrolling through more posts about you. Everyone has gone wild over the speculation that you'd been having an affair with someone 'high up' in the University. It seems to have triggered wider speculation about whether the identity of your lover has been confirmed, also more and more theories about why you were killed, each more ridiculous than the last. But the idea of a secret lover has romanticised your death. You're no longer just a local murder victim. You're an international sensation. Thousands of posts mention the University and Medical School. Jeff is now being dragged into this. Some ask whether he had ordered your murder as revenge after finding out his wife had cheated on him. Although Abraham has clearly set things up so no one can tag either of us, our names are out there for all to see. The University has already been tarnished by your murder, and now it is being dragged through the mud even more. I think about Henry Wickham. The funds he left for the Medical School. How that one simple act of generosity and good intention has been obliterated by your death. And by my actions.

17.

My only course of action now is to hold my head up high, as Newton said. To face both Jeff and Abraham as though this story is an inconsequential nuisance. To brush it off. Be dismissive. It works for Jeff, and it's going to have to work for me. The only difference is that Jeff never seems to care.

'You all right, madam?' asks my driver.

'I'm good.' I breathe deeply, in and out, in and out, staving off what feels like an impending panic attack. 'I'm fine. I'm fine.'

But when I get to the Great Hall and through security, everyone seems jolly, as though nothing's going on. There are about ten of us in the Great Hall's foyer, along with two waiters holding silver trays of champagne.

Even Abraham seems his laser-sharp self, despite something happening that might have external ramifications. He calls me over as soon as he sees me. 'Elizabeth, come meet Nicola.' I walk to them, taking tiny steps like I'm on a tightrope. He grabs my hand. 'We've just been saying that the Medical School will honour Nicola's husband by creating a Wickham Fellowship in his name.'

Jeff is standing next to Abraham and I hold on to him to steady myself, wondering if your wife has seen any of the commentary on the socials. Whether I should mention it and make light of it. 'That sounds wonderful.' I'm aware of my mouth moving. Sounds coming out. But nothing else, only the hum of noise around me and the distant echo of glasses clinking. If Nicola thinks I was using our last conversation to get information about you after seeing the online rumours, that I trapped her into talking about you whilst using the University as bait, God knows what she'll do. And as for Jeff…

I'm transported to being back at school and being called in to see the headmistress after doing something wrong, except the feeling is amplified to such a degree that I have to grab onto Jeff even tighter to make sure I don't pass out. He doesn't tense up, and I hope his reaction means he hasn't read the rumours, or that he doesn't believe them. With my other hand, I wipe way the cold sweat around my neck.

'Gosh, it's hot in here.' In a bid to change the topic to something mundane, I look around to pretend I'm searching for the air conditioning. Anything that's going to bring me back down to earth. I wonder how much longer I can cope. Whether the end result will be worth all this pain. Then I tell myself that Nicola's son has lost a father. That I need to be kind to her. That I need to pull my damn self together. That the more peculiar my behaviour, the more suspicious people will become. I focus on that energy and concentrate on your wife.

'I know we spoke on the phone, but I want to say in person how very sorry I am.' Even in the state I'm in, I can tell how disingenuous I sound, but she replies with the same warm tone she used when she spoke about her son.

'I appreciate that so much,' Nicola says. 'It's so wonderful of you to do this for my husband.' I think back to her words about you and her being estranged. She gives me a tiny nod. I give her one back. There's a complicit and mutual understanding that she doesn't belong here. I know it. She knows it. Knows she has to keep up this charade to play her own part.

'We're so glad we're able to,' I say. 'Even with all this noise and speculation going on around us.' I will my cheeks not to go red and I glance at Jeff, who nods and says something about people not having anything better to do with their time. But I still feel an underlying sense of unease that no one seems particularly perturbed by the rumours swirling around us.

Lavinia and the other governors arrive, and three violinists start playing some Mozart in the background, with Nicola getting carried along in a tidal wave of people offering condolences.

I'm left alone with Jeff. 'Listen,' I hiss. 'There's stuff going on. Online. Rumours.' I try and look helpless.

'Not now,' Jeff says through clenched teeth. He takes a swig of his drink and looks around the room, acknowledging one of the governors with a hand gesture. 'Not now. It's an absolute...' He takes another swig to steady himself. 'Leave it, would you? Like Abraham said.'

Abraham?

Excusing myself from Jeff, I make my way to the bathroom and lock myself in a cubicle. Pulling out my phone, something which Abraham has strictly forbidden around guests at public events, I check my emails.

> Dear All—
>
> In light of recent online speculation, please carry on tonight as per—we're now focused on Nicola and I don't want any of this to be a distraction. Don't worry, we've got it all under control, but I need you all at the top of your game here. No mention of anything! Please! I'll talk to Nicola about it before and put her mind to rest about these absurd rumours that are, frankly, getting out of hand rumours. No one is to panic.
>
> Abe

Then a separate one to me:

> Don't worry. We've got this. Abe.

By missing his emails, I've actively ignored his instructions in front of Jeff.

I can't stay in here much longer. Smoothing down my dress, I come out of the cubicle and check my face for sweat tracks. When I'm satisfied I look normal, I force myself to go back into the hot swell of the room.

Somehow, I get through the drinks, though I wave away the canapes on offer. It's only when we sit down, when I'm seated next to your wife, with Jeff on her other side, that I can relax a little.

Nicola points to my midriff when we sit down. 'Your dress, it's so beautiful. I've been admiring it all night,' she says. 'It's so lovely to meet you face to face after our conversation. Everyone here has been so incredibly supportive.'

'Thank you so much.' I don't feel as I hoped. Just a tiny charge of shame that I've been so cruel in wanting to demonstrate my ownership of you.

Your wife is a softer, curvier and altogether fresher version of me. She shines. Her blonde-brown hair is piled up so strands of it fall around her face, and her skin is smooth and plump. I feel altogether too plain, too forced. Too put-together in my quest to look like Jeff's wife that I've forgotten who I really am.

I think back to the time I wore the dress with you. I fidget in my seat, trying to rid myself of the sensation of impending doom snaking its way down my spine.

'I've had to really improve my wardrobe since Jeff took on this job. Only a few days ago, as you know,' I say. I've read an article somewhere about my namesake, the former queen of England, with whom my mother had been obsessed, and how she had made conversation at state dinners. I almost erupt with laughter at equating this meal with a huge royal banquet, but it works.

'Wow,' says Nicola. 'You've gone to such a lot of effort.' I nod as the waiter behind us appears with a beautiful silver platter, lifting its lid. We make due expressions of delight as our food is tonged onto our plate: delicate pinkish salmon fillets with bouquets of asparagus and butter-drenched baby new potatoes.

'We can only imagine how hard it's been on his relatives. On you.' I stop and wait for her to talk.

'His mother, Bren...' Nicola says. She cuts into the salmon and looks at me. 'She's got Alzheimer's. She's in a home. We go and see her. Me and Tommy. But she's got no recollection of her son. Or her daughter either.'

'Daughter?' I frown. You'd never mentioned a sister.

'They were estranged too. My husband seemed to make a habit of it.'

'Habit of what?' I spear the salmon and put it to my mouth. I nearly gag.

'Disappearing.'

'Really?' I force myself to chew the flakes of fish. 'That's hard for you. What actually happened? You did mention it before, but I didn't want to press you.' I try and keep the tremor out of my voice. My fork clanks down onto the plate.

'It was hard on Tommy,' she replies. 'Not so much on me. He spent a long time crying, and his behaviour was all over the place. Well, I blamed the behaviour on my husband anyway.' She laughs.

Nicola then tells me in more detail than our previous phone call about how you'd walked out on her when Tommy was two. How she'd been left rearing him whilst earning a living. Why had you done it? Listen to the way she talks. The register of her voice when discussing you. She moves her head closer to mine and glances around the table. 'I'd love to say some horrible things too, but I can't here. And he's still Tommy's father, after all.' I will Jeff not to insert himself into the conversation at this point. Luckily, he's immersed in discussions with the chaplain who will run your memorial tomorrow, and I get fifteen unadulterated minutes of you.

You had apparently been the perfect father for the first two years of Tommy's life. Doing the night feeds. Being attentive to Nicola. Taking Tommy out so she could rest. Bringing her steaming mugs of beef bone broth so she could recoup her strength as she nourished your child. Insisting on taking Tommy to his childcare on your way to work.

'And what work was that?' I ask. You'd told me you'd always worked in project management. I'd googled you many times, but your digital footprint had been limited to your University role, with a brief bio underneath your profile photo that told me that you had worked on large-scale projects specialising in logistics.

'The same as with you guys,' she replies. 'Just less of it. He was very present.'

'Then what happened?' I tilt my head to one side. 'I mean, you told me a bit before, but—'

Nicola's tone sharpens. 'What happened is that one day I got back from work – I'd only just gone back full-time as a paralegal – to find all traces of him gone. No note. Nothing. All his things had disappeared. Right down to the tiny china owl I'd bought him as a joke on our second anniversary.' She looks down at her plate, pressing her fork against a tiny flake of salmon. 'He was gone. For an entire year. After which I get a message from him asking to see his son. And that was it. There was no explanation for his behaviour.'

'And you let him see Tommy?'

'I held out for a bit. I'd done my grieving. Tommy had done his. He turned up one day. Passing through, apparently. On his way to San Francisco for a conference on medical supplies. He looked well. Tanned. Didn't look like he'd been suffering without us.' She dabs the white linen napkin against her mouth. It's the first time I've heard her voice crack.

'And where had he been?' I push. 'I mean, did he tell you?' I try and keep the desperation out of my voice.

'He'd been working. Apparently.' She looks directly at me. 'Gave me thousands of dollars anyway, as recompense. Guilt money. So he must have been earning a fair whack.'

You'd never displayed any type of wealth to me. I think about your apartment. You liked living there, you told me. It was out of the way. Easy. Everything organised for you. You hadn't wanted to rent your own place off-campus. It certainly made it a hell of a lot easier when you wanted to up sticks and leave.

Nicola is talking again. 'He'd left his passport on the table while he'd gone to the bathroom, though, and I couldn't resist taking a look. There was a recent stamp in there. Ecuador. I thought he must have gone there for work during his time away. It was dated a couple of weeks after he left, and he'd been there for four months. Or maybe he'd had some sort of breakdown. Needed to reinvent himself, or had met someone. Any number of reasons. But God only knows what he was up to.'

'And you never confronted him on it?' I pull back my own line of questioning, aware that it sounds like I'm almost blaming her for not seeking out more information. Ecuador?

I try and remember if you'd ever mentioned being abroad for that long. I was sure you hadn't, and I'd asked lots of questions; I'd wanted to know everything about you.

'Stupid of me really, wasn't it?' She turns her face towards me, the candlelight flickering underneath her huge blue eyes. 'Not to ask more. I didn't want to risk making a scene. I was also busy trying to rebuild things and look after Tommy. It's crazy, the things you do when you think you're in love.' We both fall silent.

Jeff leans in. 'Nicola.' He nods at me. 'So glad you could be with us.'

For the rest of the dinner, I latch onto one of the governors across the table from me, asking him questions about how he became such a 'crucial' part of the University. I know, the minute the question comes out my mouth, that I'll get an elongated answer. That I'll be able to detach myself from his stream of egotistical consciousness and consider the potential consequences of telling Abraham what has been going on. I'll also be able to listen out for anything of interest in the conversation between my husband and your wife.

When dinner is over, and the chat around the table has mostly petered out, your wife is escorted by Lavinia to her room, which is in the accommodation building for visiting fellows and is hired out for functions. Security staff are stationed outside, and it has been decided that it will be safer for her to stay here so she won't be accosted by any errant press.

'Jeff.' I corner my husband, who has been talking to one of the governors. 'Listen.'

'I know.' He holds up a hand. 'I'm sorry. I'm so sorry. I can't believe they've dragged you into this. I tried to talk to you, but you were late and I just, well, listen to me.' He squeezes my shoulders. 'Please listen to me. I promise you, like I already told you.' I surreptitiously watch Abraham on his phone. 'Lizzie Lou, are you listening?'

I nod, not fully grasping what he's saying.

'Look. I'm sorry. I can't believe it. All through dinner, I've tried not to let it get to me. I could barely look at you knowing the things they've been saying about you. I'm really… I'm sorry. All right? That you have to put up with this for my sake. For the sake of all of us. We want to apologise for what's going on. And we're looking out for you here. All of us. It was grim, having to pretend everything was hunky-dory.' Jeff nods towards the dinner table, where the gleaming silverware still sparkles and the white tablecloth is smeared with food. The candles have been snuffed out and dripped wax has solidified down their sides. 'But we'll get through this. I'm not having my wife's name being tarnished. People insinuating all these crude, crass things online. This afternoon has been dreadful.'

'What's Abraham saying?' While I need reassurance and am happy that everyone is on my side, I'm also hurt by them finding the concept of me having an affair so utterly ridiculous. I've inadvertently managed to hoodwink everyone into believing I'm the injured party. My good girl image has played out well.

'You have nothing to worry about. We'll smooth it all over.' I hold on to my husband even tighter.

'What about you? The things they're saying about you?' I ignore the stabs of guilt. 'That you murdered him as an act of revenge?'

'If I ever found out what they were saying was true,' Jeff says, giving a rueful smile and looking around the room, 'they'd be right.' He kisses me on the cheek. 'Anyone going near my beautiful wife?' He kisses me again. 'I probably *would* kill them.'

'I just need to talk to Lavinia,' Jeff tells me as the last people start to make a move. 'Give me five.' He bends down and brushes my ear with his lips, and the thought that he is so damn trusting makes everything seem even worse, if that were possible. All I can think about is Newton, urging me to tell Abraham. To seek his wisdom. If I tell him, perhaps I won't be so burdened with it all.

My phone goes. There's no one watching, so I pull it out. It's a message from your wife: *Hi Elizabeth. I hope you don't mind me contacting you like this. I just wanted to say how deeply sorry I am about all those people online. Abraham mentioned it. The trolls are awful.*

I wonder what it is about me that makes people think I'm incapable of having an affair. Not that I'm complaining. I imagine your wife finding out that I've been lying to her all this time, that my kindness towards her has been an act. What would you say to me about that?

Keep your head up. Don't let yourself be pulled into it all. They'll soon move on.

This was the advice my friend Casey gave me when the press were outside my home. I still appreciate so much the way you looked after me on the phone the other day. Your kindness in trying to make things okay for me before I arrived at the University. I'll never forget it.

I read this last part several times.

The room spins around me. I can't believe she's naïve enough to have swallowed the narrative that I'd never do anything wrong. It had been bad enough that I was married, but that the fact you'd been married too. Although I'd had no idea about that at the time, I struggle with the thought of how it will play out in your wife's mind. I have to do something. I have to draw someone else into my web of deceit. I no longer have the capacity to keep the truth to myself.

'Abraham.' I force myself to walk slowly towards him. He's on his phone, head down. 'I need to talk to you. Now.'

He gestures with a free hand towards the corner of the room and I give a tiny shake of my head. 'Somewhere else.' He quickly slides his phone into his pocket, realising I'm not here to discuss something innocuous.

I follow Abraham into a side room I've never seen before. It's full of files and old marketing materials. Huge posters of the Medical School from various stages of its existence. Vast banners on metal rollers. — UNIVERSITY. THE FUTURE OF MEDICINE IS HERE in gilded curlicue atop a sweeping image of the grey building itself, majestic in all its historical glory. At the front is the campus square, the green's richness an explosion of colour beneath the blue sky. Then, underneath, SINCE 1840. I shudder, thinking of my own actions, the unfolding timeline.

'I was sleeping with him,' I blurt out. 'I was having an affair. The rumours are true.' I speak clearly and slowly for the first time since you died. 'Nicola.' I wave my phone in the air. 'She's just messaged. Here.'

Abraham scans the screen.

'I loved him. You have to know that. Jeff cannot find out.'

I watch the shake of Abraham's head. I wish to God I'd got his assurances first that Jeff will be kept in the dark about this, but it's too late now.

'I've already been to Newton,' I add. 'He's not going to say anything.' I don't add *yet*. 'He did suggest I come to you with this. Only recently though,' I add, pleased to have Newton on side. 'Anyway, listen.' I lower my phone before Abraham can see anything else. 'Need you to help me navigate this. If not for me, for this place.' I gesture towards the banner. 'To protect it.'

I can see Abraham's mind working. The way he's weighing up every eventuality and every possible strategy to mitigate the situation. My own focus on the situation has been so telescopically narrow, I haven't been able to think beyond my own immediate needs.

'Listen...' He stops. 'Right, you need to tell me everything.'

I spill as much as I can in the next quarter of an hour. Tell him that his friend Newton has, on the whole, been supportive. That I haven't yet sought legal advice. That I'm not an obvious person of interest in the murder case. That I've helped the police by giving them my phone. That Jeff will probably kill me if he finds out. That I have no idea how the public found out about you and me. I let out a hiccup as a sob rises up my throat.

'Somehow they know. I think. It's too random to be a coincidence. Someone knows, and they're using it against him. Me. How the hell else would this have got into the public domain? I don't even know where that picture of me has come from, or what I was doing when it was taken.' I exhale, slowly, before I start getting hysterical. The relief of sharing this with Abraham seems to have unleashed all the emotion that has settled in my blood, bones and all the spaces in between.

'Right. Elizabeth. Stop.' Abraham gives me a look. 'Listen to me. Stop talking,' he repeats. 'I'm going to deal with this. Don't worry.' He shakes his head. 'Okay. Listen. Here's what we're going to do. The basic plan. I'll need some time to finesse this, but it looks as though whoever did this might know something but doesn't have any evidence. Which is why there's no clear connection. And that's also why it's not made the local or national press – there's been no confirmation. We've received no request either for confirmation of the story, or for a statement.' He's mirroring exactly what Newton said earlier. 'So what I need you to do is damn well hope there's nothing else. Only speculation. Perhaps from a look you two shared, or something like that. Might someone somewhere have seen you together?'

'Only at public events,' I say, truthfully. 'Maybe they sensed there was something between us. But we were very careful.'

I think back to the last time I'd seen you. When I'd been yelling up at your window, oblivious to anything else. Before that, I'd never gone in and out of your apartment without repeatedly checking there had been no one around to see me. And you'd always kept your blinds shut when we were together.

'No. No one could have known. Unless he'd told someone. Which he wouldn't have done. He valued his job too much.' That much I know to be true. You would never have risked your position. You were, if anything, more mindful than me.

'Right. So perhaps someone just assumed. Saw you flirting or something. Best-case scenario. We can deal with that.' Abraham draws a breath. 'Then things will die down. People will get bored of it when more facts about the case are released, which I should imagine might be soon. I know Lieutenant Newton and his team are fully invested.'

'Right.' My voice shakes. 'I can't believe they've latched on to the story.' I start to cry, ashamed and embarrassed. 'Me and him.'

'That's the part I'm coming to.' Abraham squeezes his eyes shut. 'And for God's sake stop crying.' His harsh tone brings me round. 'Is there any evidence of you, save for you two being in bed together?' Abraham raises his eyebrows at me.

'No,' I gasp. 'No. No, never. I wouldn't have let him.' I don't let my mind linger on the thought that you might have filmed me without my consent.

'Right. So, unless something like that turns up, we can deny any other photographic evidence. Right?'

'Right.' My mind goes back to our meetings. We'd never so much as touched each other in public. In fact, the more powerful the spark between us, the further we stayed apart. 'It makes things better,' you'd whispered as we were together later. 'There's more sexual tension that way.' And, as usual, you'd been right.

'How did the two of you communicate?' Abraham steps forward. A leak is clearly his main concern.

'Telegram.' I wince. I can't believe I'm saying these things out loud. I can't believe I have to admit my wrongdoings to someone at my husband's place of work.

'Anyone who could have accessed your cell?'

'No,' I say truthfully. 'Newton's obviously got it now, but I kept it on me all that time. Even at night. I never let it go. I was…' I think about how I'd kept hold of my phone when you had been alive, my grip on it tighter the more I missed you. I'd will you to contact me. Will you to reassure me that you still wanted me.

'And what about *his* cell?'

I shake my head. 'Not as far as I know. Like I said, he was worried about his job. Much of the time he was the one telling me to be careful. Reminding me to watch out whenever I left his place. Not to get complacent. But what do we do if there *is* evidence of us? If he told a colleague or something?'

'Elizabeth, I can't think with you behaving like this.' Abraham rubs at his temples. 'Look. Just go now. In any eventuality, I need some space to work out what to do. And listen.' He looks me directly in the eye. 'Nothing in writing about this. Do I make myself extremely clear? Nothing. No texts. No WhatsApps. Nothing alluding to it. Zilch.'

I nod, knowing better than to argue with him or ask for any semblance of reassurance. I've done enough damage.

As Jeff and I are being driven home in the dark in what feels like a brand-new car, I feel like a child once again, cosseted by the smell of leather, the soothing hum of the engine. We pass University buildings and other cars, street lights casting a glow on the satisfyingly smooth tarmac, other strangers criss-crossing our path in their own version of this great matrix of life. Pulling my arms around myself, I lean against the window, replaying Abraham's look as I told him the truth. Jeff is next to me, clicking the keyboard on his phone.

'That went well,' Jeff mutters. 'Don't you think? She doesn't seem like she's going to cause any trouble for us. Nicola, I mean.'

I listen to my husband talking some more. How it's one thing off the list. That the public has a lot to answer for. I nod, though he isn't even looking at me. I turn to face him. I should tell him right now. I can't hold this feeling in my heart for much longer. But then the driver turns and asks Jeff about his day. Whether he's had a good one.

Jeff laughs. 'Funny you should ask that.' And he tells the taxi driver that he had a difficult day, but wasn't that all part of the rich tapestry of life? He laughs again. I rest my cheek against the cool window, and I'm left wondering what part of my sinful soul has generated this into existence.

I let Jeff lead me inside the cottage. I tell him I'm overwrought by all these rumours flying around about me. That the murder has terrified me that we're all about to be killed in our own beds. Pushing me gently down by my shoulders onto one of our kitchen chairs, he opens up a small box I kept back when the removals people left. It contains coffee paraphernalia and kitchen utensils, along with a small bottle of whisky I keep to hand for Jeff.

'Here,' he says. 'Sit. I'm making you a hot toddy.'

When he's done, I drink it up. Although I hear Jeff's words, telling Abraham seems to have pushed me over the edge. I've pulled myself together long enough and can't seem to digest anything else.

'Listen.' He speaks slowly. 'I know this has all been a lot. But you're running the memorial tomorrow. We need you to be on top of this. So you need to get a good night's sleep. Take one more slug of whisky, it'll knock you out.' I do as I'm told. 'I need you to snap out of this.' Jeff squeezes my shoulder. 'Look, focus on what you can. Ignore all the noise. I saw you tonight with our guest of honour. The trust she placed in you. All these ridiculous rumours don't matter.'

'I know.' I look up at my husband, his gentle face, the crinkles at the side of his eyes fanning out like tiny butterfly wings. How can he trust me so much that he hasn't even asked if any of the rumours could possibly be true? I think about the adoption agencies I was looking at earlier. About the future in front of me if all goes to plan. About what will happen if it doesn't. Me, alone. No house, no money, no child, no future. And if Jeff ever finds out. I shudder. 'I know. Ridiculous rumours.' I manage a tiny smile. 'Silly, really.'

'Exactly, so don't let them get to you. It'll all go away soon.'

I head upstairs, slip off my dress and hang it over my chair. I don't even remove my make-up. I get into bed.

Jeff was right. The whisky seems to have anaesthetised the maelstrom of thoughts and, as my therapist would call it, my catastrophising. Except is it catastrophising when the worst has already happened?

Partly due to the drink's effect, and partly exorcised of my inner guilt by having confessed to Abraham, I manage to fall asleep. I'm on the periphery of dreams, mainly about you, when Jeff's phone rings. I haven't heard him come up to bed, but the sound has woken me. I don't move.

I hear Jeff sliding the phone from the bedside table. 'Yes,' he sighs. 'Jesus. It's one in the morning, Abe, you need to get some sleep too.'

Abraham's voice is a tinny echo down the handset. I'm sure he says something about acting normal. Acting as though nothing has happened. Surely he can't be telling Jeff about our earlier conversation?

'Listen, I'll wake Elizabeth if I'm not careful.' A muffled voice again, something about me and the memorial. About organising it beautifully. Jeff lowers his voice further. 'Yes, that's true, but tonight she was acting weird, so I need to make certain.' I'm sure Abraham says something about me potentially not going to your memorial tomorrow. 'If the press see her they'll go mad after all these rumours online,' Jeff says. 'Imagine. Elizabeth next to his wife. The widow and the alleged mistress? It'll spread like wildfire.'

Abraham talks about protecting me from socials. How he'll recommend I stay offline for the next week or so, until this dies down. Just until after the gala. Then the focus will be on something else.

A week? I think. I can't take much more of this.

I hear the bedsprings creak as Jeff gets up and walks towards the door. The sound is familiar from all those nights I'd spent talking to you. It's another hour before he comes back to bed. He's never been one to need much sleep. We always used to joke he was like Margaret Thatcher, only needing four hours a night.

I can't stop thinking about what Abraham was saying about acting normal. He'd already told Jeff that before, at Cecconi's. And Jeff hadn't sounded shocked by Abraham's call. If something truly bad had happened, he would have leapt out of bed and run down to his study. So why on earth had Abraham called in the middle of the night? I lie staring at the ceiling, waiting for the light of the morning, for clarity to emerge from somewhere.

The Day of the Memorial

18.

It's seven when I wake up properly. The first thing I do is grab my phone. Squinting against the ferociously bright light on my screen, I go through the motions of looking up news about you and, by extension, me. @StudentInvigilatorX has posted a small bio of me, taken from the University staff page. Nothing else. Only my name and three lines about my work. And underneath, people have started to make all sorts of tenuous links to my research into Romantic literature and love affairs. To Jeff's work. More and more rumours are spreading and have now even reached the tabloids, who in particular seem to love the story, linking it back to the original social media post from @StudentInvigilatorX whilst taking no responsibility for whether the story is true or not.

PRESTIGIOUS UNIVERSITY FOR THE
ACADEMIC ELITE – MURDER VICTIM LINKED
TO UNIVERSITY PRESIDENT'S WIFE!

I think about Abraham. How delighted he'd be with the

mention of the University alongside the words 'prestigious' and 'academic elite'. Who cares what the actual story is, he'd say. All that's going through people's minds is that we, as an academic powerhouse, are worthy of this story going global. Except now my husband's name is linked with a murder and the public-turned-detectives are baying for blood.

'Jeff?' I shout down the stairs. There's no answer. I look out of the window and his car's gone. I call Abraham from my bedroom. 'Listen, thank you. For yesterday,' I say, despite knowing he isn't doing any of this for me.

'I've been turning it around in my head all night,' he says. 'We can't go after them for libel. Because that would confirm that the story's true and give it legs, even if we took the approach that it's smearing your good name.' I bristle at his wording, given the things I've done. 'Psychologically, it gives them something to springboard off. And that's not what we need right now, even if it distracts the general public.' I ask myself whether he's so tied up in his own thoughts that he remembers he's talking to me. 'I'm going to go with the line that it's hindering the investigation and deal with it that way. Tell them the cops will have to get involved and that there'll be further legal filings if that happens. Listen. I've got to go. I'll see you later.' He hangs up before I can say anything further. I tell myself I have to trust him. That by protecting the University he's also protecting me.

Half an hour later, Jeff comes home. I hear the rustle of paper and the jangle of his keys. 'Lizzie Lou. Bought you some almond bread. That stuff you like from Everly's.'

'Thank you,' I shout down.

'Need sustenance before the memorial,' he yells back up. 'I'm putting it in the oven, all right? Come down soon and I'll make coffee.'

At the mention of your memorial, I remember Jeff and Abraham's conversation in the early hours. I email them both about some last-minute plans and confirmations that no one but me can handle, before either of them can tell me that I can't come and that my presence will attract too much attention. Abraham fires back an email within two minutes.

> No problem. I've arranged it with the chaplain that you and Nicola will meet in the crypt beforehand. I'll drop you both away from the press. There's a back door to the University chapel that is used for deliveries. Be ready for 11 a.m.!
>
> A

I've had a shower and am drying my hair when the doorbell rings. I'm about to go to the window to see who could be at ours when I hear Newton's voice.

'Lieutenant Newton.' Jeff's voice reverberates up the stairs. 'Good of you to come. Really. I called you on the off chance you were around. Please do.' I hear the door open. 'If you would wait one moment please, I'll just head through to my office and press Send on this email. Do take a seat through here. I was about to make some coffee, but I'll ask my wife down. Lizzie?' Jeff calls up. 'We've got a guest. Lieutenant Newton. He's in the kitchen.'

'Coming.' I pull on some jeans, putting my hair up in a claw clip and feeling a bit stronger now I have Abraham onside. I make my way downstairs.

'Hello, Lieutenant.' I force myself to sound cheery and polite, praying he'll play the game.

'Mrs Harker.' He departs from his usual 'ma'am' and is careful, I note, not to say it's a pleasure to meet me.

'Elizabeth,' Jeff calls through from his study. 'I've called in Lieutenant Newton to give us a steer on the investigation. Since everything that happened yesterday. All the online...' He pauses, obviously searching for the right word. '...fuss.'

'Great.' I busy myself with the coffee, filling the machine with grounds, pulling out the best fine bone china. 'And Jeff's just bought some delicious almond bread.' I look towards the oven. 'Smells delicious.' The only thing I can do right now is go into wifely mode, hosting on behalf of my husband as he is seen to do the 'important' stuff. It's the only way I can both distract myself and prevent the conversation from going down unwanted paths. 'Have you ever been?' I point to the brown paper bag Jeff has left on the table. 'They do the most amazing breads and pastries.'

We carry on making banal chit-chat until Jeff reappears. 'Right.' He claps his hands together. 'The coffee smells delicious. And the bread. Did you get the butter out?'

'Oh no.' I quickly walk to the fridge, trying not to see this as a rebuke to my hosting skills. 'Here we go.'

We sit, eat and drink for a while as Jeff discusses the madness of the internet.

'Anyway,' Jeff says in a businesslike tone after we've finished our coffee and bread. He looks at the kitchen door. 'Thank you, Elizabeth. I really appreciated all that. We haven't got too long, though.' This is my cue to leave. I try not to smart over my dismissal, upset that I won't be there to hear the narrative being spun about me. 'We'll have to get ready and leave in an hour or two.'

'Lieutenant Newton.' I stand up and hold out my hand. 'See you later, and thank you.' I speak slowly, still wary of my words. 'For everything you're doing around the University. We're all very much in your debt.' I look straight at him.

Newton smiles. 'It's all part of the job. Anyway, ma'am, I hope it all goes according to plan today.' He squeezes my hand and there's something complicit in the way he holds on to it for a second extra than necessary. I choose to interpret the gesture as him leaving things up to me, and as I go upstairs, I reassure myself that Newton and the police are there to help and that no one at the University, bar Abraham, believes the rumours going around.

I sit in the chair at the bedroom window with my phone. My first instinct is to go to the @StudentInvigilatorX account. There's nothing there. All the threads about us have disappeared. All the comments. I nearly cry with relief. I slump back for a good thirty seconds.

Abraham. I start typing out a message thanking him, but then I remember what he said about not putting anything in writing. Feeling marginally better, I rub my temples and tell myself that it's your memorial today, and that this is now your time.

I'm still sitting in the same chair, looking out of the window, when my phone rings. It's an unknown number. Normally I'd ignore these, but my body seems to be doing things of its own accord. When I pick up, I'm surprised to hear Lavinia's gentle but firm voice. 'Elizabeth,' she says.

'Yes?' My first thought is that I've done something wrong.

'I'd like you to come over. After the memorial. To mine. I'll send a car to you. A ladies' get-together. You and Jeff have had a tricky start. It's only fair that us oldies give you a breather.'

'Well…' I'm exhausted and can't imagine I'll have any kind of will to sit and be polite after I've said my goodbyes to you in a public setting, but my voice deserts me when I attempt to decline and instead I make a small sound of agreement.

'Good, dear,' she says. 'Then that's all settled.'

My phone goes again.

Dear All—

Not long to go. Just to remind you that should you need anything at all at today's memorial, please go and find Elizabeth, who has done a phenomenal job in organising this celebration of our esteemed colleague's life. And to say we're all here to support each other through this very difficult time.

I wonder what Abraham's agenda is here; it certainly isn't to protect me. The enormity of it all, the sensation of being rootless and alone, alongside the responsibility for your memorial, an event where everyone will be looking at me, makes me want to curl up and hide.

Instead, I go into the bathroom, locking the door behind me and look at my phone contacts list. Other than a few female colleagues I worked with on recent research papers, there's no one I could confide in at all. I scroll down further to my dead father's number, finger hovering over the call button, before closing my address book entirely. It's something I used to do on repeat after he had died. I even think about calling Jeff's sister in Canada. Instead, my therapist will have to do.

She answers on the second ring and tells me she's been waiting for my call. She says she's been keeping abreast of the news. That she wanted to reach out but at the same time recognised I would need space. The kindness in her voice sets me off. I tell her that I just need someone to be there. That I cannot share what's going on. I start talking about loyalty to the University. Things needing to remain in confidence.

'Listen,' she says. 'You don't need to explain. Least of all to me. And, in any case, I'm here for you. I can be that person,' she says, and I'm thinking *but you're being paid, and that makes it worse,* and I realise that the only person I want around, that I could really talk to about this, is you. But not only did you betray me, you're also dead. And so for the next half an hour I do nothing but cry down the phone to her as she listens to me silence.

***

After finishing the call, I'm grateful for my meltdown. It means I've been able to redirect my anger at not being able to confront you about your lies. About B. I've cried myself out in the brief therapy session and then iced my eyes to get rid of the puffiness. Although I feel emotionally spent, I know I'll be able to keep it together throughout the service.

It's 10 a.m. when I arrive at the chapel through the crypt entrance, ready to run through everything and to make sure every detail is covered. The flowers are all set. The digital boards behind the lectern are working and the orders of service have been placed on seats. You're expected to pull in a good crowd.

Abraham comes in to update me on the press presence. 'It's all right for now.' He keeps glancing towards the main doors, though, which is making me nervous.

'Listen.' I lean forward. 'Thank you. For earlier.'

'It's fine.' He nods and looks back at the door again. 'Look, I'm expecting all to go to plan, so let's get this over with and we can start to move on.'

'Sounds good to me.'

The chaplain opens the crypt door and comes into the main chapel with Nicola. 'How lovely to see you,' I say, walking up to your wife and giving her a brief hug. 'Listen. Thank you,' I tell her when Abraham has done his hellos and is out of earshot. 'For your message. It was helpful. For many reasons. It was thoughtful.'

'How stressful it must have been for you.' She comes closer. 'These awful cowards.'

Other members of staff start to arrive, and Nicola and I have to stop talking. I press myself against the back wall in a bid to hide myself but they all keep coming up to me, telling me how desperately sorry they all are about everything these 'internet freaks' are putting me through. I briefly shut my eyes, willing it all to stop. How much have they read? Have they lapped up every single theory about you and me? Have they texted their other colleagues to dissect each thread posted?

'Let's go back into the crypt,' Nicola says after a little while, nudging me. 'Get some quiet before things start.' Whether she's doing this for my benefit or hers feels unclear right now, but we move away into the cool, dark quiet. Our voices echo off the stone statues and tombs surrounding us.

'Gosh, your husband did cause quite the stir.' I trace my hand over a marble bust of Henry Wickham.

'He did,' says Nicola. 'And now you've been dragged into it.'

'Yes,' I manage, wondering at what point it will cross her mind that the rumours might be true. 'Listen. Any news on what actually happened? Any leads? I've been so busy moving house, I've missed what's been going on.'

'Mistaken identity,' she says. The organ starts inside the chapel, warming up. 'It must have been. I've been over and over it in my mind. The rumours that he was a bad person. That he'd been stealing drugs from the Med School and selling them. That he was a druggie to boot. It wasn't in him to do any of that. And I know they're now more than rumours. Newton has been asking me all sorts.' I gasp and then let her continue. 'He's been keeping me up to speed on everything. I think he thinks that as Tommy's mother I must be the first port of call.'

I clutch the marble under my fingers. I had felt safe around your wife, knowing you had left her, but it's painful to think that she's number one in Newton's eyes.

'He rang this morning, actually. He was driving somewhere. And he's coming here now to pay his respects.' I nod as though I am also in on the intel. 'What else has he been saying?'

'That's what they're going with. The drugs angle. But it wasn't like him. It really wasn't.'

I want so desperately to tell your wife that I know. That I know absolutely, assuredly that you wouldn't have been involved in any such thing. I want to reach out and tell her that I knew you as well as she did, if not better. That I still love you, despite your betrayal.

'I knew him. I know he left me, but I knew him, Elizabeth,' Nicola says, as though it's me she needs to plead to for his innocence. 'He was probably a womaniser.' I have to stop myself from physically reacting as she continues. 'It's the only conclusion I can come to that explains why he left like that, given how much he doted on Tommy before. But I've never heard from anyone else he was with. Nor do I want to know now. I'd managed to get over him. I don't want to dredge it all up again. That said, he had strong moral values. He did.'

'Could he have changed? People do. Not always for the better.' I think of B and how you couldn't have changed that much. And of course you were sleeping with a married woman. The last thing I want to do though is sully your wife's memories of you.

'Maybe.' She shrugs.

'And are they looking for anyone else? Got any concrete leads?' My thoughts about B have reopened the still-fresh wounds. 'Anyone or anything he was involved with?'

She shakes her head. 'Not as far as I know,' she says. 'But they've been good about keeping all that away from me too. To be honest, it wouldn't be that big of a deal for me now if he had been seeing someone. They did ask me repeatedly if he'd talked about being in danger, though.'

'God, that's...' I shudder. 'Scary.' I think of the lies you told me to facilitate your other relationship. You'd been so honest at the outset of our relationship, telling me you'd never lie to me. And I'd thought it was true. Whenever I'd asked you a question, you'd always tell me what you believed to be the truth, even if it was hurtful to me.

'What I adore most about when we're making love,' you had told me, 'is your innocence.'

I'd been offended at the time. Tried to prove a point to you by acting differently. I'd made my actions more confident, taken the lead, done things I'd only read about in magazines. I'd given you countless opportunities to rectify yourself. To change your opinion, and what I thought was my worth. But you'd held firm as you'd embraced me afterwards. 'Look, Elizabeth, I told you I'd never lie to you,' you'd said as you stroked down to the base of my spine. You have to trust me on that.

'I'm just wondering if he could have changed,' Nicola says, her voice cutting into my thoughts. 'His moral values were still the same.'

I press my palms against both cheeks, trying to cool the burning sensation rising inside me.

'I don't know why I believe that so strongly,' she told me. 'But I also know it to be true. I've remembered a perfect example. I tried to get him to book Tommy a cheaper theatre ticket only six months ago by pretending he was under five. He downright refused. Said he'd never do that kind of thing. So he paid for it himself. I know it was a small thing. But still, it's a thing.' We both fall silent until we register the time and return to the chapel to sit in our seats.

When the organ music starts up, I let things unfold without thinking about how I've been in charge of it. It's all mine and Abraham's work. There's nothing more that can be done except to get through the next forty-five minutes and pray to God that during that time nothing else will be unearthed about me whilst I'm unable to look at my phone.

Nicola and I sit, with Jeff between us. The music is moving, and I'm pleased to see our official photographer there, unobtrusively moving down the aisles and capturing those giving readings. We hear from members of staff who say they were particularly close to you, and from Richard, your replacement, who'd let it slip earlier when he revealed that you'd known about the Wickham Wing. Your eulogy is given by an unprepossessing man with a comb-over and tiny, darting eyes.

I look across at Nicola in her striking turquoise suit. Her head is bowed low. I'm about to reach across to tap her on the arm to show her some solidarity, but I realise she's chewing on a knuckle, trying to stop herself from laughing. She glances over and I will myself not to react despite hysteria rising up in my stomach. I give her a tiny smile whilst clenching my whole body tight, and then Richard introduces the next song by the choir, the a capella version of Coldplay's 'Yellow', as photographs of you are shown on a projector screen behind the lectern. You, throwing your son up in the air. You on a fishing trip, hair swept upwards, grinning at the camera. You in your running gear with all your students, holding up a medal and an enormous cardboard cheque for three thousand dollars, made out to the — University Wickham Fellowship Development arm. It's only now that I hear a sound from your wife, and I look over to see her crying.

The swell of emotion dissipates as the organ music rouses everyone back out of the chapel. Nicola and I leave via the crypt. Abraham clocks me from the front and gives me a muted thumbs up. I nod at him and smile. It all went beautifully. We did you proud. And once again I'm thankful I cried myself out earlier.

In the chapel, Nicola takes both my hands. 'Listen. It's beautiful, what you've all done at the University. Keeping things under the radar, without a fuss. You've all treated me with such respect. Other than Lieutenant Newton I'd have felt out on a limb, so I can't tell you how much I appreciate you all.' Your wife gives my hands a squeeze.

She is so genuine in her emotional response, so giving in her energy, that out of nowhere I feel a rage directed at you. Why had you left her? And your tiny little boy? And me? Had we not been good enough for you? The more I think about this, and about B, the more the sheen comes off you, and by the time I get in the car to Lavinia's, I'm simultaneously energised by my anger and exhausted by my dormant grief.

Twenty minutes after I leave the chapel, my ride pulls up to Lavinia's enormous house, which is painted white, with olive-green gables and a wraparound terrace overlooking the sparkling sea. Her butler leads me through to a sumptuous drawing room. 'Would madam care for a coffee?' he asks.

'I'd love a coffee,' I smile. 'And your name is?'

'Ernesto.'

'Ernesto. Lovely to meet you.' I look at my watch. 'Listen, I'm early, but I'm happy to wait until Lavinia's ready. I don't suppose you have an agenda for this meeting, do you?'

'No, madam.' He shakes his head. 'Madam Lavinia has just requested that I look after you very well.'

'Thank you. I've just come from a memorial, so if you don't mind, I'll take the next quarter of an hour to recalibrate.'

'Of course. I won't let Madam Lavinia know you're here quite yet. She's out with her nephew in the boathouse.' Ernesto makes his way out the room.

After five minutes have passed, I stand up, smoothing down my dress, and go to find a bathroom. 'Ernesto?' I call. But there's no answer. Only a distant clanking sound that I assume is coming from a kitchen. I walk past a huge central marble staircase and turn left down a seagrass-carpeted corridor. All the doors are shut. I open a few, calling Ernesto's name so no one thinks I'm snooping, but there's nothing resembling a bathroom. There's a library and what looks like a shooting room, and a few hall tables bedecked with both ornaments and interior design hardbacks. Then I reach the end of the hallway and open the door of a small room. There's a shiny walnut desk in the middle which overlooks the most incredible view of a seemingly never-ending lawn, a sheet of blue in the distance beyond. On the desk is an old-fashioned inkwell, a pen to its side. I'm reminded of the pen you gave me, and remember that I need to find it again after I last used it during my first meeting with Lieutenant Newton. It's my last link to you. There are two pieces of paper with architects' drawings on them: what look like plans for the Wickham Wing. There's still silence around me. I take two more steps in and look closer at a stack of papers on the desk. On the top one is a line graph with a small logo at the side which looks to me like the outline of a tiny flower. *Helianthus* is written in small letters at the bottom and the graph is tracking what look like investments; on top is a Post-it: *To be filed under Bellamy Ventures*. It takes me a few seconds to understand what I'm seeing.

There's another clanking sound in the distance, this time much louder. Turning on my heel, I rush back to the drawing room without going to the bathroom and sit down again. Finally, there are footsteps, and the tinkle of conversation and laughter. I stand up, and Lavinia walks in with none other than Suzy.

'Good afternoon.' I greet them both, remembering Suzy's advice from when she was in my position: *Make sure you're the adoring wife. At least in public.* And now your memorial is over, I have to act as though I'm an innocent party. 'So lovely to see you.' Both ladies move in for air kisses, and Lavinia gestures for me to sit again.

We talk for a good half an hour about everything that has happened. I'm aware that every move I make will be scrutinised. That Lavinia has the power to end our tenure, just as she had the power to begin it. I pull out all the stops.

'Dear.' Lavinia clasps my hands between hers. 'Gosh, your hands. They're very cold.' She rubs them between hers. It's the first time someone's done that for me since I was five and visiting my grandmother. 'I've brought Suzy with me here today. I thought we could have a bit of fun.'

I smile. 'Wonderful.' I wonder what constitutes fun for them.

'Very well done today. I watched how Nicola was with you. And at the dinner last night. She trusted you. See? Feminine power? These men do a fantastic job overall, but there are some things that should only be left down to us women.'

'Isn't that true.' Suzy pats her knees in excitement. 'It's why Harley was so reliant on me during his tenure.'

'Now, dear.' Lavinia sits forward again as Ernesto brings in a tray of coffees and petits fours. 'Here we go. A lovely drink for you. And do eat up. You need to keep well fed in this job. That is something I've learned.' She pats my hand again. 'Jeff tells me you're moving in tomorrow. To The Lodge. The memorial is over. It's time, isn't it?'

'Time?' I ask.

'Time that all of us forget about this horrible incident. Don't you think? There'll be others, of course. Not necessarily like this, God forbid. But we have Abraham.'

'I agree,' I tell her. I want to believe her so much. And as she holds my gaze, I finally do.

'Oh, you will *so* love it,' Suzy says. 'It's *such* a wonderfully inspiring place. All those huge brains who've lived there before. And Harley, he does miss it so already. Please look after it for us.'

'Of course.' I feel a fluttering of excitement at the thought.

'And there's a wonderful room for a nursery.' Suzy's eyes shine. 'If you decide to go down that route.'

I sit up, thinking about the adoption agencies I've looked into. 'Now you mention it, we have discussed it, Jeff and I.'

'Oh.' Lavinia nods. 'That's wonderful. Crossing everything, dear, for a smooth ride where that's concerned. This place needs some tiny joy in it. Albert and I...' She looks over at a black-and-white photograph of a man in a suit. 'We could never.' She takes a sip of her drink. 'Anyway. Enough about that. You'll need to let me come visit all the time.'

'Of course.' I start getting carried away, forgetting both about everything that had happened now my future is being dangled in front of me. I forget that there must be a reason I've been invited here right after your memorial.

'Now, listen,' Lavinia seems to read my mind. 'As I was saying, Suzy and I thought we'd run something exciting by you.'

'Of course,' I reply yet again, sipping at the coffee, thinking it's a little odd that Suzy's involved in all of this. 'This is delicious. Thank you.'

'The reason I've asked Suzy here today is because she was editor of the — *Medical School Tribune* last year. And given she's leaving; I've agreed to take over. But with her expertise at hand. What fun this will be.'

'Goodness, such a lot of fun.' Suzy and Lavinia look at each other.

'Right,' I say, slowly, looking at them both as they smile at me excitedly.

'And so, speaking of feminine power... We'd love for you to be introduced to our community properly. It'll put all this other nonsense to bed, dear.'

'I'm not entirely with you.'

'Well, Abraham came to me with his usual genius.' Her eyes twinkle. 'We've got to show them. Stand firm in who we are.'

'Show who?' I don't want to appear ignorant, but she's making it hard for me to keep up.

'Those social media bullies. Those trolls. Isn't that what they're called?' She laughs. 'Sadly for them, the Medical

School won't be cowed. We'll carry on as normal. We don't listen to nonsense. We're saving lives. We have better things to do with our time.'

'That's right,' Suzy adds. 'And we know they've gone after you because you're fresh to the game. You know. It's like being back at school. Picking on the new kid. Things were the same when I started. When things were adjusting. Not like this though.' I will her to stop rubbing it in. 'People were attacking me for all sorts. Mainly things Harley had implemented. Outsourcing their annoyance to me. Stopping me at dinner parties to complain about this and that. In the end,' Suzy sniffs, 'I'd just agree. "Yes, yes," I'd say. And then never do anything about it. Leave it at the front door.'

'Although we do realise,' Lavinia hastens to add, 'how awful this has been for you. We're in no way minimising this awful experience. But we do want to show you our support. Show people we know it's nonsense. Show a total disregard for it all. And that clever man, getting it all taken down.' I gasp. 'He said he'd worked his magic. I don't know how he does it. But we're all totally behind you. I mean it.'

'And so…' Suzy looks over at Lavinia, who all but claps her hands together.

'Front cover,' Lavinia says. 'We would love you to be on the front cover of the *Tribune* this month. It's being distributed at our gala event, where we announce the Wickham Fellowships. After we won the Rosemont Development Award for all the fundraising we've done, we're upping our game even more. All eyes are on us, as Abraham keeps saying. Anyway, dear. The magazine, it's distributed globally.' If Lavinia thinks she's selling this to me, she's wrong, and she obviously senses it. 'Of course, the UK is a huge part of it. Back home. What an honour for you and your family to see how far you've come.' I don't tell her I have barely any family left, but she's certainly managed to feed the starved part of my ego. 'And we'll interview you too. You can edit the wording however you see fit. Say what you want.' She leaves the silence dangling. 'We'll get your hair and make-up done. And a wonderful professional photographer. Sam Tate. He's just darling. Glorious. Did that shoot of the Obamas when they first got in.'

'Wow.' I think of my self-imposed role as adjunct. How I'll be elevated substantially. How I'll be able to concentrate on something else other than you. How this will change public opinion of me. How the social media bullies will see who is in charge.

'Look. I know all of this has been a terrible strain on you and Jeff. The first few days of your tenure. What do the young call it these days? A terrible trauma?' She smirks. 'But I think this is the perfect way to start your time here anew.'

'You don't think things have gone too far?' I'm unable to say that my reputation has been tarnished by association, by all the speculation that I've been having an affair.

'We think this will help matters, certainly.' Lavinia waves a hand. 'And anyway, it'll all go away. Abraham will make sure of it. So just agree to do this. Let Abe do his job. We need to focus on this place. We need to make sure that this institution remains at the heart of all that it stands for. Academic rigour. The gold standard in education. Innovation. And the Wickham Wing, the renovations. I know it hasn't yet been announced officially, but I'm sure you've heard all about it from Jeff. We're keeping it all under wraps due to donor sensitivities and still working out how to present it to the public. But I'm sure you know the overall plan.'

'I have.' I wonder if my husband would have even mentioned it if Abraham hadn't mentioned it when we'd met at Cecconi's. And why Jeff had felt the need to be less than transparent with me about it all.

'With our funding target nearly reached, we'll soon be able to tell the public more. If your husband pulls through this last bit.' Lavinia gives a dry laugh. 'And so we want you to be pushing that, and for you to support Jeff's publicity. Because that's what's going to put your husband and this place on the map. We're already in the elite. We want to stay at number one. Because that's what we are. The best, really, in the world. We can't beat that, can we?'

'No.' I think about the solid grey bricks, the Medical School crest. The foundations for everything Henry Wickham had created, spawning the global elite in medicine and beyond. I think about my role in all of this. 'We can't.'

'So dear.' She squeezes my hand tight. 'For the sake of your husband. For the sake of you, dear, please, do say yes. Let's put all this silly nonsense behind us, shall we?'

NOW

The worst part about being lied to is knowing
you weren't worth the truth.

JEAN-PAUL SARTRE

After the Memorial

19.

The next few days are a whirlwind. We move into The Lodge, except I'm still stuck in a liminal state; part of me hasn't accepted we've moved on from the cottage. While the removals happen around me and the team ask for instructions on various matters I don't have the answers to, my mind is on Lavinia's words. *Silly nonsense.* As though you were just some blip on the horizon. Something that had to be 'dealt with'. But it seems you had been dealt with and Abraham has indeed done his job, though I'm still overshadowed by the feeling that two weeks will pass and I'll get a call from Newton, telling me I have to be honest with Jeff. I think about Abraham once again. The way he's already sorted out things so far. Although everything is calm on that front, the feeling of terror still periodically invades my thoughts.

I snatch glances at my phone when I can, mainly while I'm on the loo or late at night. It's midday when I finally get some proper alone time; the removals team are on a break and Jeff's in his office. For the first time in ages, I make myself lunch and sit down at our old kitchen table in the vast space around me. The latest is that there is more speculation about your death. Crime podcasts being published. Maps being drawn, pointing to where the murderer might have gone. Dissection of the photograph of your body. Clues about the weapon. The position in which you'd lain slumped on the ground. People seem to have forgotten that at the core of all this is a human being. The overriding theory is still that you were involved in drugs. I scan through the latest missives; the @StudentInvigilatorX account is once again active.

> @StudentInvigilatorX An informant has told me that the University is cleaning up their 'access to drugs' policy. Could this be in some way related to the #MurderOnCampus? 🙄☠🙄

There are thousands of comments which seem to have descended into talk about campus nightlife, underground raves and the like, and people posting flyers for the latest club nights. I read the latest comment:

> @StudentInvigilatorX @Nicola_Paralegal123 seen on the University campus talking to Lt. Newton, who is leading the case. #MurderOnCampus 🙄☠🙄

This comment has spawned a whole new conversation, this time about how you'd effectively deserted your wife and child, and another thread about how the University's recruitment process had failed spectacularly when they'd managed to hire a drug pusher (#MedicalSchoolSortOutYourHR!).

The new narrative, bolstered by the online warriors, is now around Nicola and the fantastical theory that she herself was involved in a mass drugs ring that she headed up with her husband, which involved illegal trade in medication stolen from the Medical School, medication thought to be worth hundreds of thousands of dollars.

> **@StudentInvigilatorX #RememberingHarvardBodyParts Scandal #ItWasntJustTheJanitor #MurderOnCampus 🧐☠🧐**

Two hours later, my phone pings. A statement, this time from the University.

> Dear All,
>
> Please see a letter attached from Jeff Harker that has been sent out to all students.
>
> Kind regards,
>
> Janet Mayhew, on behalf of Jeffrey Harker

I skim through the letter. It's a reminder to all students about their use of social media, with a link to the University's policy around social media and digital communications. It highlights the contract that everyone signed at the beginning of their 'student journey' at the Medical School: that social media is not to put the University, including the Medical School and the Wickham Development arm, in a bad light, and that anyone found to be repeatedly in breach of this contract will be sanctioned according to the

University's behavioural policy. It then goes on with a more human plea about Nicola. Tells us that we must now, as a globally revered institution, do the right thing and 'let your wife and family grieve in peace.' For a split second, I wonder why they haven't mentioned the social media rumours about me, then realise that Abraham's thinking must be that he doesn't want to spotlight the alleged affair. That doing so, will give the rumours more traction. This, I think, is his deflection technique. It has played out perfectly; for the minute, I have been saved and will be forever in his debt. Now, it seems, your wife has taken the fall for me. If only she knew how she's been used to protect the building. To protect the University's good name. To protect the ambition both shielded and fuelled by those perfectly laid grey bricks.

For that, Nicola, I'm profoundly sorry (See? I'm beginning to get the hang of Abraham's wording), and my gratitude towards Abraham for getting the threads about the affair removed takes on darker shades. It's at this point that I tell myself I can't go on existing in these shadowy corners. That I must now trust the University, Abraham and Jeff to do their jobs. That my role is to do as Lavinia said. To put all this silly nonsense behind us.

The calm steadiness of Lavinia's voice had made me think Jeff and I could do this together. That your death was now mine alone to grieve, in time. That whatever was thrown in my path could be handed over to Abraham and it'd be sorted. Putting down my phone, I relax. I think about our new home, which will soon, I'm praying, be filled with the sound of a child's laughter. Now this is all over, I can concentrate solely on the adoption process.

I thought the size of The Lodge would be overwhelming, but it manages to feel cosy amongst the grandeur; the wonderful furniture, a mix of modern and antique, set amongst our own things, means Jeff and I feel we belong. That our tenure here can start properly. Jeff does indeed fill the space beautifully, as though our new home was built with him in mind. Except that for the next few days, whilst I'm unpacking and organising the house, he locks himself in his new study on the top floor.

'Few things to manage,' he murmurs the first time, and with the chaos of everything else, I don't query what he's doing. I notice that he looks drawn, tired. I take him plates of food, which I leave outside his door until this particular bit of work is over. During these days, I keep myself occupied by driving in and out of town to buy things we need for our new home.

Lavinia has sent a memo saying that things on campus can largely return to how they were before the 'incident', except the University will now have more CCTV cameras on-site and a full-time operations manager to oversee security measures.

The memo seems to trigger a discussion about how much of a distraction these 'online sleuths' are in crime investigations. This splinter conversation becomes another narrative surrounding your death, and at the same time Lavinia's memo goes out, there is a new development. Newton has released a pre-recorded press statement to the local television station and online local news channels. I watch on my phone as he stands with Tamara, head bowed, by his side. He clutches at a fluttering piece of paper, which he looks at briefly, before speaking direct to the camera. I don't move as I watch the screen.

'We've had significant developments in the murder case at — University.'

I wince as I hear what has been going on behind the scenes.

'With huge thanks to the amazing district police, and especially my colleagues, who have been working tirelessly to see that justice is served, we can now release the information that the case is indeed now being treated as drugs-related, and that we will now be working with our dedicated vice squad, who will be heading it up from here on in. Now over to my colleague. Detective Sergeant Cooper,' Newton turns and nods at Tamara, who steps forward, her long plait in a tight bun at the back of her head.

'Good morning, everybody.' Tamara's voice sounds much deeper, stronger than when she was with me, and I wonder if she'd been merely playing the role of 'good cop' that time. 'I'd like to thank our wonderful team. We've made significant breakthroughs in this case, and we'd like to thank the public, too, for their role in giving us information that has, in parts, led to one or two major milestones in discovering who committed this heinous crime. We'd like to add that we believe this was a targeted attack, and we hope that this will put people's minds at rest that such an incident will not happen again. Thank you.' The screen switches to a local news anchor who has brought in a retired chief detective to discuss the case.

I turn off the screen. The focus has now changed drastically. From the University, to you. From me to your wife. I wonder if I can move on too, but then my phone goes and it's Abraham. I pick up, thinking he's going to give me the good news. Tell me I can forget all about it. Instead, he shouts to someone in the background, and then his attention goes back to the call.

'Elizabeth.' His tone is curt. 'She's about to call you. Lavinia. In about fifteen minutes, when she's out of her meeting.'

'Hello,' I counter. 'How are you?'

'She wants you to go over now to hers.' I hear the drum of his fingers down the line. 'For the photo shoot.'

'Right,' I say, wondering why this is relevant to him.

'You've said yes, right?'

Ah – I think I know. He's checking up on me. My first instinct is to tell him no. That I'll make my own decisions when Lavinia rings me herself. That if he wants me to front the University with my husband, I need to be in charge. I imagine my life at his beck and call as penance for what I've done. My life without the desire you sparked in me. My life without the connection we had. It's almost too much to bear.

When I don't answer, Abraham speaks again. 'Don't be silly about this.' His voice is quiet. 'If you carry on as you're meant to, exactly like Suzy did, we'll all be fine. This will go quite some way in salvaging our – your – reputation.'

'Right,' I say. By comparing me to Suzy, he knows exactly where to hit me. Squeezing my phone tight to stop me from calling him something deeply regretful, I weigh up my options. Should I capitulate? Something inside me is saying no, that I need to stand firm. But I can almost hear the words on the tip of Abraham's tongue and feel the hold he has over me, and before I know it, I've adopted the identity expected of me and told him that yes, of course I'll go over to Lavinia's.

Even my husband has seemingly calmed down from the fallout after his period of isolation. I can hear him from the other room, humming to himself, as I make a start on his study. While I'm doing some unpacking in there, I get the call from Lavinia. As per my earlier conversation with Abraham, she tells me that Sam Tate is free. He's flown over as a 'special favour' from Los Angeles, to take my photo.

'It'll be a keepsake for you. Yours to take home with you and put up in The Lodge. A reminder of who you are,' she says down the line, her voice strong. 'And a reminder of who you've become. Now please, do come along in an hour.'

I want to tell her that I can't. That I'm unpacking. That I want, or need, to stay at home, away from people. That I'm still digesting the recent press statement from the police. But I hear Abraham's voice in my head and remain silent.

'If you could wear a button-down shirt,' she says. 'Express wishes from make-up.'

'Thank you.' I kick myself for saying that, as though she's doing me a great favour.

'Jeff?' I call out when Lavinia has finished. 'I'm going to Lavinia's now.' I tell him about the photo shoot.

'What about me?' he asks.

'What about you?' I laugh. 'It looks like I'm the star of the show now.'

The photo shoot is as I'd expected, and although initially reticent, I fully give into it all. Both Suzy and Lavinia are on hand. The stylist gives me an entirely new look, muted but with a 'strong eye' and dark lip.

'Your cheekbones.' She brushes away the excess powder from my face. 'Stunning. Let's highlight those. They'll look amazing with natural lighting. And of course in Sam's pictures.' And she's right. I sit in Lavinia's conservatory, the sprawl of green behind me. I've done Abraham proud; I've checked everything in shot. Nothing that can be taken out of context. No literature that suggests any political persuasions. The result on Sam's camera so far shows me framed by blue sky, tomes on the history of the Medical School and the architecture of the University in shot.

For the first time in hours, you come into my mind. I imagine your reaction if you could see me now.

'Smile,' Sam says again. 'You don't need to hide yourself so much. Give us more of yourself.'

'See?' Lavinia claps her hands, overcompensating for me not playing ball and obviously thinking her words will sway Sam's opinion about me. 'Didn't I tell you, dear? That she was worth it?'

'Great. Head to the side, one last time.' Sam looks down at his camera screen. 'Good. I think this one will do.'

The next two hours are spent in Lavinia's drawing room.

'We thought we needed a more feminine touch. There's something about her.' Lavinia passes around a plate of biscuits and smiles at me before looking at Sam. 'Don't you think?'

'I do. Now, how's things at the University and Medical School?' Sam asks. 'Awful with everything that's gone on. I hadn't wanted to mention it before, in case it put you off, but you've done a fabulous job.' Sam looks at me. 'Now, I'm sure Lavinia's been a strong, calm leader.'

'She has,' I say, playing into Lavinia's wishes. 'Absolutely wonderful. She's steered the University through. Along with my husband.'

Suzy chips in. 'Who has also been wonderful. A great choice to take over the place.'

'And the dear man has managed to secure the last bit of funding for the new Wickham Wing we're building, despite everything,' Lavinia looks at me, eyes shining. 'So we're in an excellent place for next year.'

'It's been incredibly stressful, but we've managed it now. And we can announce the news at the gala, along with the expansion of the Fellowship scheme, so we really are thrilled. It's a huge coup for the Medical School. We've been beavering away on it for the past year or so, so it will be an utter relief when it's all out in the open.'

'Jeff's fantastic,' I murmur. I wonder how I can possibly be on the front cover of a magazine when I've been kept out of the loop on something so monumental and I'm reminded of Jeff's earlier humming. How he'd been in a much better mood.

When I get back home, I change into a comfortable pair of leggings and a T-shirt before I go and confront Jeff.

'I'm meant to be your partner in this,' I say, my voice rising. I hold back on the line that I encouraged him in the first place. 'Do you know how humiliating it was when I was doing the photo shoot, which by the way I'm doing for the University to then hear second-hand about this? I'm meant to be your wife. You're the president. And here I am looking moronic.'

'Listen.' He leads me to the kitchen. 'See?' He opens the enormous fridge-freezer. 'Look.'

I follow his gaze to two beautifully cut steaks from Ferndene's Deli. Next to them is a sauce Jeff makes, an intricate blend of finely crushed peppercorns and some other ingredients that are hard to find and which he knows is my absolute favourite. And on top of that is a small box from Everly's, who make the tiny desserts he knows I love.

'This is what I've been doing this morning.'

I look around the kitchen: no sign of any mess, which also means he's made an extra effort.

'I've been planning for us to spend time together. I was going to light candles. Run you a bath. I wanted to do it on our first night here. I was waiting to tell you tonight, but there's one last tranche of funding that's been promised but not secured. We're waiting on it, so it's a bit premature. But,' Jeff's eyes widen. 'I think we're there.'

'Oh, honey.' I wrap my arms around him, inhaling his familiar smell, something indefinably and comfortingly close to woodsmoke, and it strikes me that maybe I can feel desire when I'm not with you. 'I'm sorry. I really am. This is amazing. I'm proud of you. Thank you. And Lavinia,' I say. 'She was raving about you so much today. With Suzy.'

'She was?' Jeff nods. 'That's good.'

'She really was.' I kiss him on the cheek. 'You've made an incredible start to this role. Now, with the new Wickham Wing, you've really guaranteed your legacy here.'

I think of Suzy and Harley, and how it is now our turn.

Our legacy.

After our candlelit dinner, where we discuss nothing but Jeff's work, I barely see him again for the next few days, and it's only when he's called over to see Abraham that I go to the top of the house to do more work on the unpacking and take swatches of paint up there. With our decorating budget, I've worked out which interiors I want changing, and Jeff has given me carte blanche to do as I please. With our calendars suddenly jam-packed with social engagements, openings and fundraising dinners, I don't have much time to work it all out. Jeff still hasn't fully unpacked his study, and towers of cardboard boxes are pushed into the corner of the room, but his desk has been organised and is perfectly neat and tidy, probably something to do with the fact that Janet has sent over a load of stationery and some of his files.

Janet also starts to send me invite after invite. Or at least confirmation of Jeff's diary commitments, with my initials added if my presence is required – which, it seems, it mostly is. Events in the Medical School and University. Abraham calls lots of meetings about the upcoming gala, which I'm also required to attend. It seems that my management of your memorial has made its mark and my input has become a necessity, with Abraham relying on me more and more to make decisions about the gala itself. He's told me in no uncertain terms that other than the seating plans for dinner, for which he'll be responsible, he'll leave me to head it all up. The music. The tablescapes. The lighting. The podium. And I've taken on the job because it seems I'm beholden to everything Abraham asks me to do, and that for the time being there can be no pushback.

In parts I enjoy the work – it's a distraction from you – despite often finding myself worrying that I should be getting Abraham's sign-off on everything I do. But in my efforts at being the wife I'm meant to be, I learn to ignore his voice in my head and absorb it as my own.

I order in huge neon signs with the University logo for the after-party, and flashing disco balls, smoke machines and confetti for when the final fundraising figure is announced. I hire huge projectors and commission the marketing team to film talking heads of previous Wickham Fellowship recipients to talk about how life-changing the scheme was for them. I ask the team to choose former students who have changed the medical industry. Ideally those who have come from the most financially precarious backgrounds, for maximum emotional impact. So our donors know their money is going to an excellent cause and that we aren't even nearly finished. So they know that they too are helping the generations of the future. There's Olivia Bell, who was sent from foster home to foster home and is now leading medical research in transforming treatment for oesophageal cancer. There's Nadim Suleiman, a top neurosurgeon in Wisconsin who has pioneered a new type of surgery using robotics and who came over to America with just the clothes on his back. There are Victor and Christine, who have been working in countries without easy medical access and are both leading surgeons in their field. When the first video is unveiled to me in the marketing department, I can't help but be overcome with pride at what our University is all about. It is this that I want to be a part of.

Although my days are non-stop you've hooked yourself into my psyche; the shadow of you ever present. Memories of you surface at seemingly random times. When I'm mid-discussion about whether the gala lighting should reflect the colours of our branding. When I'm eating a salad on the run between appointments. When I'm about to meet a potential donor for lunch with Jeff.

And my body, too, heats up with desire for you at certain times. I try and ignore the feeling, but sometimes it's so intense I find it hard to think. It's normally when I'm dressing up for a night out with Jeff. Cocktail parties or black-tie events are the worst, when I'm sliding on a fresh pair of satin knickers beforehand. Or straightening my leg as I pull on a pair of see-through stockings and slip my feet into a pair of vertiginously high heels, which I've taken to wearing more and more often.

Jeff and I, though, we make a formidable team, perhaps even more so now you've gone. We arrive together at events and work the room separately in a circular fashion. Abraham is always there, bringing the most important people to us: potential donors. Anyone who's a pioneer in new treatment. Medical researchers. And at times, I feel like the power balance between me and Abraham has somewhat evened out. The donors, though, mainly seem to be brought in by either my husband or Lavinia.

It still surprises me that Jeff has been so influential in the networking side of things. His love of academia has always been at the forefront of everything he does, but he has seamlessly taken over the role of bringing in more money to the University. Proved himself a trustworthy leader. His academic background and huge brain make him magnetic. And as Lavinia repeats time and time again, having me by his side has only made things all the better, and Abraham knows it. I make a point of smiling over at

Abraham sometimes, nodding to him and reminding him of my presence.

I ask Lavinia time and time again when the magazine will be ready for me to see, ready to make any edits, but she keeps fobbing me off, telling me she'll send me a copy as soon as it's ready and that she's as excited as me. That the text I sent over in response to her questions was perfect and will make people like me even more. In any case, the copies have to be ready for the gala, she says, so in any case I'll see them soon.

I'm back at the house one day, moving boxes, clearing space, booking in the decorators for as soon as possible, when out the blue, I get a phone call from Suzy about going shopping for a gala dress.

'Come on,' she says down the line. 'It's not far off now. If you've already got something, you can wear it for the Wickham Gala. Either way, I'll take you to my lady. My treat. But I think that when you see what she has, you'll want to wear it as soon as you can.'

'Well…' I don't like shopping at the best of times. 'Listen, I thought I'd—'

'Nonsense, nonsense. I won't take no for an answer. You need a break.'

After arranging to meet soon afterwards – it seems things don't change where timing and expectations are concerned – we end up on the high street.

'Here. Come in.' Suzy pushes open a door to a tiny shop with two simple rails on display and only about four pieces of clothing on each. 'Simone will look after you.' Simone does indeed look after me, taking my coat and handing me a freshly chilled glass of champagne. It's like she's known all along that I'm coming in.

'Thank you so much.' I look at the pieces on display, structured dresses simple at first glance but whose stitching and intricacies reveal them on closer inspection to be more like museum pieces.

'This is what you've got to get used to these days, you know.' Suzy looks at me. 'This really is a role that has wider importance. Not just for the University and Medical School, but for education as a whole. Keeping tradition alive from nearly two hundred years ago. You're contributing to history here. A history my husband has been very much a part of too.'

'I am,' I whisper, stroking the fabric of the shiny green dress Simone has brought out and draped across the velvet bench. I wonder, not for the first time, if there's a warning tone to her voice that I have to step up to the plate. The dress is soft under my fingertips. 'This is just divine.'

'Here.' Suzy stands up and motions for me to follow suit. 'Go.' She picks up the dress and hands it to me. 'Try it on. The changing room. It's over there. I'll look after your bag. Go. Shoo!'

'Listen. I'm not used to all this, but—'

'What did I say?' Suzy laughs. 'Shoo.' I do as I'm told, stepping into the huge, plush changing room. Taking off my light blue trouser suit, I step into the most glorious dress I've ever seen. It's heavy satin, off the shoulder, with a bow on one side. It drapes over my body perfectly.

Simone knocks on the door. 'Here,' she says. 'A pair of heels. 'They're the correct size, I hope?'

'How did you know?' Although I'm feeling uneasy about everything, especially with Suzy's obsession with me behaving in a particular manner, I still take the shoes from under the door and slide them on. I open the door. Twisting my hair around itself, I fasten it back with my claw clip and step out of the changing room.

'Goodness me,' Suzy gasps. 'Wow.' My reflection tells me Suzy is not lying. I look at myself from all angles, unsure what to do next.

Simone nods. 'You really are gorgeous.' She looks over at Suzy. 'Shall I?'

'Absolutely.' Suzy holds up her bag. 'Wrap it up please, dear. That was easy, wasn't it? You're going to be the belle of the ball. Mark my words.'

'How is Harley?'

My words seem to catch Suzy off guard. She gazes off into an unknown distance. 'He's doing very well. He's tired. Exhausted after everything. But stoic in that way of his. Nate and Jed are home this weekend with their partners. That always keeps him going.'

'Will he make it to the gala?'

'I don't know about that yet,' Suzy says. And then, after a few seconds, 'All set, though? For the gala? I heard you were running the show.' I wonder why she's still involved, and at what point she's going to step back and let me do my job.

'Yes,' I say, staking my claim. 'It's all sorted.'

'That's great.' Suzy's voice goes quiet. 'I remember last year we had the most fabulous sponsors. They gave everyone favours at the end of the night. It really did make all the difference. Elevated the evening that little bit more.'

'Oh.' I go quiet. Abraham has never mentioned party favours, and they haven't crossed my mind. I have to remind myself not to sound defensive.

'A good way of getting a message across,' she says. 'Would you like me to introduce you to last year's sponsors? I'm sure they'd be happy to help again.'

I think about the dress. Suzy's insistence that I come with her. I should have known this isn't out of the goodness of her own heart. I wonder how much she's doing behind the scenes.

'Well, I did already have some things in mind...' I'm careful not to cede control entirely, but at the same time I don't want to shoot myself in the foot by pushing back too much. 'But that would be lovely. If not this time, then next.'

'I'll email you over their details.' Suzy pulls out her phone. 'They gave everyone a lovely gift last year. It's important we nurture these relationships, as you know. And I've spoken to them recently. Told them I'll still showcase them via our wonderful events team. They got in contact again earlier this week. I've still got my gift from them last year, you know. It's very special to me.'

'What was that?' Something about her tone is making me feel faint. The emphasis she's placing on the sponsors. I can't quite grasp the subtext of what she's saying.

'Something significant. And with our branding, too.'

Her words fade in and out of my mind. I need her to stop talking. I clutch at the bench underneath me as though my body is keeping me steady, preparing myself for something terrible.

'Goodie bags. Lovely pens.' She shuts her eyes briefly. 'Just gorgeous. So generous. Really high quality. Beautiful, weighty ink pens. We asked them if they could brand the pens with our logo, and they agreed to do it. Couldn't have been more helpful.'

I am no longer listening. The only words going through my mind right now are 'pen' and 'significant'. Despite my humiliation, I'd still used and cherished your pen. But last time I'd looked for it, I hadn't been able to find it. I think of you rushing up the stairs when I'd been at your apartment for the last time. How offended I'd been at your parting gift.

Simone presses the beautifully wrapped tissue parcel into my hands. 'Enjoy,' she says. 'The most beautiful dress in our store. It doesn't look as good on anyone else.' I just about manage to smile and nod.

Suzy pulls out her wallet and passes Simone a mint-green credit card with the words UNIVERSITY on it. She has the decency to look somewhat ashamed when she realises I've noticed that she'll be expensing items for me, to her old card.

But had I really expected this to be a gift from her?

The pen. Silly, I think. You'd been trying to get rid of me, hurriedly pushing me out of the door. How insulted I'd been that you thought I'd go that easily. Here. Take this.

A consolation for the fact that I don't want you anymore. That I've been lying to you. A piece of metal. A damn nice one, I'll give you that. But a piece of metal nevertheless.

And I now don't know where the hell the pen is. Something in me wants it back. It's my last link to you.

20.

When I return home, Jeff is in his study again. I hang the dress in our shared dressing room – another bonus of The Lodge. I knock twice on his door, telling him I need to start getting things ready for the decorators. 'They'll be here tomorrow,' I lie.

'Coming,' Jeff yells the third time I go into his study. 'Two secs.' He's ashen-faced. Only this morning I would have put his paleness down to too much time spent indoors, but now I wonder what else is going on.

I make a big show of looking for a tape measure and start to note down the distance between each wall. 'Carpet,' is all I say. 'And I need to work out how much paint.'

'Could this not have waited?' Jeff snaps, looking down at his computer. 'Why now, of all times?'

'Really?' I squat, pulling some cardboard boxes towards me. 'Are we going there? I want your study and the rest of our house to be ready, and I'm doing all I can to make that happen, and you're having a go at me. Go downstairs and take a break.'

'Fine.' He rubs his eyes. 'Look. I'm sorry. Just trying to—'

'Sort something out?' I snap.

'Look. I'll go down. Make supper for us. It's a rare night we don't have anything on. I'm sorry. I'm just—'

'I get it,' I say, not wanting this to turn into a row. After all, I have to pretend I'm fine. That I'm getting on with things as normal.

'Lamb chops? I think I might take a drive to the butchers.'

'Sounds like a great idea.'

I will Jeff to hurry up, and eventually he switches off his computer and leaves. The minute I hear his car leave the driveway, I try and log on to his computer to see what could be taking up all his time and energy, but it seems he's changed his password; the screen judders accusingly every time I type in different suggestions, and I stop, terrified I'll lock him out. Dammit. Grabbing a Stanley knife from his desk drawer, I start slicing open all of his boxes. The pen. It must be in there somewhere. And now it's in my mind, I feel unstoppable. I pull out a load of filing trays. A box of old light bulbs. An old pottery vase we'd bought in the Lakes, in neutral greys and browns. He loved the heft of it, the way it made him feel grounded. I place it on the shelf behind his desk along with some other ornaments he's collected over the years. There's another box full of bits that should have been thrown away long ago. Small jars full of paper clips; a few rocks and cowrie shells we collected on the Isle of Skye after our wedding. Some tiny bowls with other random things in them. I think of all the other boxes in the house still to be unpacked.

Pulling up the removal company details on my phone, I quickly ring George, who had been in charge of loading the truck, and ask him if he remembers seeing a box with stationery in it. 'I'm sorry, ma'am,' he says. 'I think we put everything like that in Sir's study.' I thank him and hang up before sitting on the floor. I look at the mess I've created and bang my fists on the carpet. I curse you for ever coming into my damn life.

It takes me a while to get my breath back, but after my initial outburst, I start to feel calmer and more methodical. I lift up the boxes I haven't opened yet, shaking each in turn to guess what they're filled with. Many are filled with books, and I push these to one side with my leg. One feels like it's half full of books and half full of smaller objects that are rattling around inside, so I slice it open slowly.

I hear Jeff's car swing into the driveway. I go to the window and see him on his phone, leaning against the side of the car. I pull out a few books from the box, and then I notice it. One of Jeff's books, published by Oxford University Press. It's about Indigenous tribes in the Amazon. How companies use Indigenous wisdom to contribute to Western medicine. Distracted from my original aim, I look at the blurb. It talks about psychedelics. He'd been ahead of the game there. Much to my shame, I've never read it. He'd presented it to me on one of our first dates, and I'd been impressed but had never read past the first few pages. It was a book that had won critical acclaim amongst his peers but hadn't been a bestseller. No matter for Jeff, who had wrapped up the idea of publication in the unyielding mass of his own ego and moved on to the next instalment of his life. It still amazes me to this day how understated in his success my husband is.

I open the book, looking at the publishing logo at the front, which Jeff has struck a line through, and his spiky signature in black underneath, underscored with a long, zigzagging flourish. I scour his words. I leaf through each chapter, noting how he crafts his prose, varies sentence length; he would have thought carefully about the rhythm of the text. Each chapter is named after a plant, and each begins with a quote, the selection of which he would have also put a lot of thought into. The quotes probably have a double or triple meaning. I skip to the acknowledgements section at the end. It's a page long. Jeff isn't one for sentiment, and before I start reading I almost laugh imagining how functional his thank yous will be – unless he's writing post-dinner party, in which case he'll write reams upon reams of witty and considered prose about the evening and the guests. I wonder who at that time in his life was important enough to have been thanked and highlighted in his life as a main player. Whether he'll mention any women. He never refers much to his past girlfriends, other than a woman called Anne-Marie, whom I'd met a few times when we'd first started dating and who was the sister of his Harvard friend Patrick. I glance at the first couple of paragraphs. A bunch of names I've never heard of. His mother and sister.

'Honey, Lizzie Lou.' Jeff says as he opens the front door downstairs. He slams it shut behind him and even though

I'm expecting the noise, I'm still not used to the sounds of the house and it makes my heart pound. 'I'm back. I've got a bottle of red.'

'Coming,' I reply.

'I'm going to start cooking,' Jeff calls up. 'I'll shout when we're good to go.'

'Great,' I shout back down. The size of The Lodge makes it much harder to be heard than it was in the cottage.

Grabbing the cushion off Jeff's chair, an old cream one with good lumbar support, I wedge it behind my back and lean against the wall. When we'd bought the cushion, we'd joked about Jeff getting old and needing the support, but as I sit there, I appreciate its comfort. I turn the book around in my hands, read the blurb again, skim through some more of the text. Then I return to the acknowledgements and reach a paragraph discussing some information that had been compiled and checked meticulously and which adds that the book could and would not have been published without all the hard work and efforts of a 'superstar' PhD student, who had spent days and weeks in the depths of Harvard's research library and in the 'far reaches of Ecuador'.

Ecuador. How funny, I think. You'd been there too, visiting after you'd left your wife. I carry on reading. I wish I could ask you about your travels. I wish you were here. I wish I could ask you about B. I keep reading the paragraph, and as I reach the bottom, there, in black type, is your full name. The letters blur in front of my eyes. Turning back to the front of the book, I double-check the publication date.

Twelve years ago. You and Jeff had worked together back then. You had worked together until your death. I think of the Wickham Wing. Jeff's expression when I asked him if he had met you properly. The curl of his lip as he'd looked up at the ceiling, as though reaching into the depths of his mind. The word he'd used to describe you: *unmemorable.* And you, telling me how you dreaded meeting my husband properly.

You'd both been lying to me.

You'd known each other for more than twelve years.

You'd worked together, for God's sake.

I try unscrambling the thoughts in my mind and make sense of what the hell has been going on.

I read Jeff's thank you to you again: *Your work will have a far-reaching effect in showing the importance of Indigenous plant medicine in the role of Western drugs and I'm incredibly grateful for all the time, effort, and dedication you put into this book. Your work will be invaluable in demonstrating the value of Indigenous plant medicine in the pharmaceutical industry, and I would like to express my gratitude to you for all the time, effort and dedication you put into this book.*

The narrative that you were involved in drugs is no longer so far off the mark. But just not in the way everyone is being made to think.

You must have gone back to Ecuador years later, after you'd done the initial research for Jeff's book. I do the calculations. As Nicola told me, you'd left Tommy when he was two, and you had been earning good money, whatever you'd been doing. She'd spotted the visa in your passport and knew you'd visited the country four years ago, spending four months there, not long after you'd left. I try and piece together all the information, but all I can think about is that both you and Jeff lied to me.

You had been mining for medical information all this time. But for whom? Had you kept it between yourselves? Doubtful. Abraham would have known. And I wonder if Newton was involved too. After all, he'd been at pains to tell me how close he'd been to his old pal. Which meant that I was the only person who hadn't known a damn thing about any of this.

I read my husband's words again. I understand that they involve something much bigger and darker than I previously realised. You and my dear presidential husband were complicit in something, a shadowy force behind the University walls and beyond. And this, my love, this is why you were killed.

21.

Despite your death, despite everything that's happened in the past few days, despite the discovery of B, this betrayal feels the worst.

I'm almost paralysed by the enormity of what I've discovered, but I'm clinging on to the knowledge that I know you both lied, even if I don't yet know why. This knowledge is gold dust in itself. Whether or not it'll be enough to sway things in my favour is a different matter, but something in me senses that it will.

Everyone has tried to cover their tracks, just not hard enough. I look back over at Jeff's book. The adoption papers sit in my eyeline on his desk, so many possibilities held in the questions laid out on the form.

I hear the faint sound of saucepans from the kitchen below, Jeff singing to himself. Something has made him happy. If I delved into this deeper, though, all we have would be over. Despite all you did, you're the only person I'd be able to talk about all this with, and it feels even more important now for me to have something of yours that might act as some sort of guiding force.

I phone Jeff downstairs to tell him that I haven't finished, and to give me a call when supper is ready. He tells me that once he's finished cooking, he's been asked to film himself giving an acceptance speech for a fundraising award, and he's far too consumed with talking to Abraham about where best to film and whether he should mention the Wickham Wing. He thinks it's a perfect opportunity to make the announcement without fanfare.

Leaving the study, I tiptoe through to the nursery-to-be – if I can still call it that. I slice open the boxes in there, tipping the contents out onto the floor. It's all miscellaneous stuff. An old stapler. Booklets from international medical schools. A tape measure. Random cables. A Sellotape holder. Dried-out tubes of superglue. But no damn pen.

Then it hits me. I've been so distracted the past few days, I've never thought to look in my car. I've been assuming I brought it into the cottage after the meeting with Newton. Now I remember dropping it. Hitting my head. I race downstairs. Tomato-based smells are wafting out of the kitchen and I can hear something bubbling, the sound of a knife hitting the chopping board. I tell Jeff I'm popping outside because I've left my make-up in the car, but he doesn't reply.

Grabbing my keys, I run out to the car. I'd been sitting in the driver's seat at the time, but I can't see it there. I slide my hand under the seat. It's not there either. Then I look under the passenger seat and see a glint of metal. I reach my hand out, but it's only the seat lever. Just as I'm about to give up, I spot the pen in the side pocket of the door.

The relief at having found it is unbelievable. As I reaching down for it, I almost forgive you for the things you've done. Almost.

I take the pen back into the house with me.

'Lizzie Lou?'

Wiping my forehead and steadying myself, I squeeze the pen tight, holding the cool metal against my chest.

'Found it.' I run upstairs again.

Suzy was right: the party favours were good. Significant. It's an expensive pen, a matt navy topped and tailed with silver. The sponsors had printed the red Medical School logo down the middle, and alongside it, in tiny print, is a square logo and the words Aurelia Wellness.

Finally, a piece of you. I sit on the carpet in the study. The idea of never seeing you again is almost too much to bear, but holding something you gave me comforts me a little. I squeeze it again with the thought that somehow I'll be able to conjure you back into reality. Stupid, I think. But you touched this. *Take this. Keep it. It's from me. A reminder.* I absent-mindedly click the pen on and off and turn it over in my hands, and my fiddling partially loosens it. As I unscrew it further, there's a rattling sound within the internal chamber. Opening the two halves, I shake out what's inside. It's what looks like a USB drive. I drop it; I'm aware my hands are sweating so much I could do some damage.

'Oh my God,' I say out loud. You'd given this to me for a reason. There must be information on here. You'd wanted me to do something with it. I squeeze the pen again, wondering what the hell it is, why you'd given it to me like this, almost throwing it away. What does it mean? Am I in danger now?

I tell my internal voice to slow down. Being married to Jeff makes me feel safer, but knowing what others are capable of, I can never be certain of my safety. I trusted Abraham with my secret. I told him too much. Will he hold me hostage with it? Will he use it against me? Why the hell did I trust Newton when he told me to tell Abraham?

'Don't hyperventilate.'

I say the words out loud to dispel the fear that I'm also about to get murdered. As my therapist has shown me, I squeeze my eyes shut, trying to think of my happy place. It takes me about twenty minutes to calm myself down, but the awful truth is that my happy place is still you.

I eat a quiet supper with Jeff, who mercifully spends all his time on his phone, then I tidy up and tell him I'm going upstairs to prep for tomorrow morning. Running up to the study again, I take the USB stick from the back of a drawer and, holding it carefully between my thumb and forefinger, slide it into an old envelope. I replay my last interaction with you. You, looking harassed, out of breath. As I recall your expression, it hits me: you hadn't wanted to finish things with me. You'd been trying to warn me. I think of your eyes darting around behind me, the tremor of your hand as you'd led me back outside. You'd been scared. How had I got it so wrong? How had I been so wrapped up in my own obsession with you that I'd missed what was right in front of me?

I take the envelope through to my bedroom and put it into the drawer in my bedside table before changing into my nightie. Then I get into bed and lie wide awake. I can't resist opening and closing the drawer every ten minutes, checking the envelope hasn't magically disappeared, and in between these checks I research phone and computer repair places, using generic terms in case my search history is scrutinised. Thankfully, my searches return results that give me the information I need. Eventually I plan out my journey tomorrow, so that even if I'm being watched, to the naked eye my movements wouldn't look suspicious.

Jeff doesn't come into the bedroom until about two in the morning. I hear him pull off his belt and trousers and unbutton his shirt. He half groans as he slides into the bed next to me, and for once, he turns his back on me without touching me at all. I open my eyes and watch as, terrified for my own safety, he folds his pillow in half and within a minute or so is fast asleep. I lie awake the whole night looking around the room. Shadows cast themselves across the walls from an indeterminate source and everything seems to take on the energy of the University itself, something more powerful than I could have ever imagined.

***

The next morning, I down a coffee and grab my car keys without telling Jeff I'm going out. My extensive googling the night before has given me all the information I need, and I've discovered that Medical School policy forbids external USBs being used on internal computers. The place I've found is over an hour away, and I've rung them to discuss what I need and to make an appointment.

With everything meticulously planned, I spend the hour's drive with an empty mind for the first time in days. It seems that being tipped right over the edge has had its benefits; my brain imploding means it's only capable of a black, empty space where my thoughts used to be. My body, though, seems to have other ideas. As I'm driving down the open freeway, I veer between shaking uncontrollably and sweating through my clothes. I turn the radio on and off, needing the soothing voice of the presenter but quickly finding the noise too jarring. I look repeatedly in the rear-view mirror. If someone had been following you, and knew your movements, they surely know mine. There's one car that takes the same route as me, a small, shiny red Fiat. And just as I'm about to take a different route, it turns off the freeway.

After what feels like an eternity, I arrive in a tiny town which initially seems to have the grand total of a motel, a bar called Nancy's that looks like it's made of tin, a pink neon sign on its exterior, and a row of clapboard houses. I do a U-turn and drive back up the empty road, parking up a distance away. The day is clear and bright; there's an expanse of blue above me, around me.

I eventually find the address I'm looking for. Fast Repairs is a tiny shop over a cafe in a square white building. I go into the cafe and am directed to a tiny set of steps up into a huge loft space that contains a couple of sagging brown corduroy beanbags, a row of computers, and a T-shaped desk behind which sits a woman in a baggy old white T-shirt with shiny chestnut hair tied tightly in a bun high up on her head. Pulling out the envelope from my back pocket, I open it up and show her the contents.

'Hi.' I slide the envelope towards her. 'We spoke earlier.'

She nods. 'Yeah. I'm Laura.'

'It's this.' I point to the USB stick. 'I need your help.'

Laura nods in a curtly efficient way that is both reassuring and terrifying. 'I can certainly help you.' I go over again exactly what it is I need, my words coming out in a rush. She nods again. Tells me to be patient and give her five minutes to finish a job for another client. In the meantime, I'm to make myself comfortable. I look around. Other than the beanbags, there's one small, paint-spattered wooden stool at the back of the shop.

'I'm good,' I tell her.

'Okay.' She looks up and gives me a flat smile. I carry on standing at the desk until she's finished. 'Right. All done. Now. First things first.' She disappears and comes back with a laptop under her arm. 'You can take this. Eight hundred and fifty dollars for the computer and for my services. The laptop is refurbished but it's fine. You'll be able to use it for what you need.'

'Eight hundred and fifty dollars is fine.' I think about how it would normally have seemed preposterous to me to be spending that much money on a random Tuesday. 'If we could just...' I tap the counter. 'Look, sorry. It's just that...'

'Don't worry,' Laura says. 'I get it.'

'I'll have to go to the ATM. I can't transfer the money from here.'

'There's one down the road, at the motel on the corner.'

Feeling panicky, as though my body can't keep up with the adrenaline surging through me, I jog to the cashpoint and withdraw the money from my personal account, wondering how I'd explain needing a large sum of cash in a random town. I return to the shop and hand over the wad of notes to Laura, who slides it casually into her own back pocket.

'Right. Let's get this started. I'll—'

'By the way—' I jump in, but before I can finish she holds up a hand.

'Yes,' she sighs while starting the laptop. 'Of course. None of this has anything to do with me. You've paid me, we're good.'

'Thank you,' I say. 'You must have done this kind of thing lots of times before?'

'Oh, if only you knew,' Laura replies, sounding almost bored. She doesn't even look up, just types some more. I wait for twenty minutes and the suspense starts to become unbearable, but every so often she tells me she's nearly got there and to hold on, and then finally she sighs again. 'At last,' she says, and with a flourish presses the Enter key.

'Right. All done.' She slides the computer towards me so I can better see the screen. 'Except for one file that's going to take me a bit longer. I've got most of them though. This one might take me a day or so.' Then she points to an icon on the screen, sounding more energised. 'Click here and you'll be able to read all the other files I've unencrypted. Whoever did this was good. Thorough. Normally this would take me five minutes. But they've done some serious work to hide all this.'

'My God,' I murmur as I look through all the files you'd hidden. The spreadsheets. The communication trails.

'Are you sure you've backed everything up properly?'

She goes through the entire process with me again. 'See?' She taps a long scarlet nail on the keys with a satisfying click. 'Look. If I press this.' She taps again, and the screen starts to fill with hundreds upon hundreds of documents you'd collated. That, after scanning through a couple once or twice, make me think I'm going to vomit right there and then. And there's one particular document that I imagine is the reason you were killed. Now I'm also party to the information, perhaps I'll be next.

Laura shows no interest in the information on the USB. She doesn't react when I tell her I need to sit down. When I keep asking her if the information is safe, that it's not simply going to 'disappear'. 'Here.' She grabs my arm. 'Photograph them. With your phone. All the documents.'

'But there are hundreds,' I tell her.

'Look, it's okay.' She takes the computer again. 'I've uploaded them to a folder on the Dark Web, which means you can access them but no one else can. They're all safe. Believe me.' She nods at the screen. 'I've worked with some much darker stuff than this.'

I think about your murder and I want to tell her that I don't think she has, and that this might have wider-reaching implications than anything she's seen before, but instead all I can do is shake my head and think about you. For the third time, I wonder how I'm going to get out of this alive.

'Jesus.' Laura goes over and picks up the stool, putting it behind me. 'Sit. Put your head between your legs.' She gently massages the back of my skull. She tells me to take however long I need. 'It's normally affairs I'm asked about,' she says with a laugh, before taking a bottle out of her drawer and pouring liquid into a small white cup that's sitting on the desk. 'Drink up,' she orders. 'Whisky.' I down it in one. She picks up the bottle that she's put on a shelf and pours me another slug. 'Here we go. One more. You still look like you're about to pass out.' Laura spends the next half an hour working her magic, and when she's finished, she tells me that all the information is backed up and saved on a private drive which she'll keep in her safe. 'You should see how many other USBs and hard drives I have in there.'

Laura shows me other functionalities on the computer, too. How to access privacy settings so no one will find what I've been working on. How to search the Dark Web. And countless other things that will serve me well until I finalise what I'm going to do.

As I leave, Laura grabs my hand and tells me that whatever it is I'm doing, whatever it is I'm working on, I'll be okay.

***

On the drive home, I think about how long you'd been investigating this. How you'd done all this research. You'd spent the last months of your life investigating the Medical School, collating documents and information. The first date on the trail of communications between people matches that of the message I'd received from Jeff – *Good Morning, Mrs. President!* – shortly before midday.

I think back to the last proper time I was with you. The text that changed everything. I know now that Jeff had just found out the real reason he'd been made president, the reason why Harley had left the role. Why he hadn't stayed his full tenure to see out the expansion of the Wickham Fellowships and the development of the Wickham Wing, which was going to put — Medical School not only at the forefront of medicine but a step beyond that. I wonder if Harley is even ill. Jeff had just been told, right before he'd texted me. Despite knowing what was going on, my husband had still chosen to accept the job. Or, and much more likely, he had done what he had to secure the role.

Again, I feel a sense of foreboding thinking about the exclamation mark. So out of place in Jeff's lexicon. And now I know why.

I think back to the way you'd lost interest in me that day as I'd started to leave your apartment. You'd been looking at your phone, focused on something else. You'd looked stressed but I'd ignored you, been far too self-involved. I realise now that if we'd carried on, maybe none of this would have happened. If I hadn't made you question what was going on in the University, maybe you wouldn't have decided to be the whistle-blower.

Good, but not that good. Grateful I never divulged anything to you about Jeff or anything sensitive to do with his role, I wonder what prompted you to want to pull the rip cord on the Medical School. Had you been planning to take action for a long time? Or had I been the catalyst? I look over at my phone on the passenger seat, then in my rear-view mirror again.

My one consolation in all of this is a selfish one. You hadn't been cheating on me. You never had. I'd seen some of the communications between you and B. All those stories I'd told myself about her, the lens through which I'd imagined this fantasy woman of yours, were a reflection of my own issues, the idea of her activating deep wounds within myself that I'd never even known were there. I replay in my head the contents of the emails, wondering how it all could have been right under my nose. How you had been feeding B information from the Medical School all this time.

> You didn't turn up! See you later. Getting more and more urgent – I really can't wait much longer to see you. Been waiting patiently all day for you.

It had taken a while to process it. His sign-off: Bill. His email address, william.harbottle@gazette.com. You'd told him you'd got something on the Medical School. Something that tied us to a bigger scandal. Bill – William – had asked for evidence. You'd said you'd work on it. You'd sent him bits and pieces before Harley had quit. But those hadn't been enough. Then you'd struck gold.

And after that, my husband had been made president.

I think about Lieutenant Newton, how he'd told me he'd known Abraham forever. It seemed par for the course in this neck of the woods; although you hadn't grown up here, you and my husband had somehow managed to follow each other around the world. And in your job, you had been party to all communications. You'd been Jeff's trusted right-hand man. His spy to make sure everything was going according to plan, masquerading as facilities manager. You'd been called in by Jeff to help manage things. And yet something, or someone, had convinced you that you were doing a bad thing. You'd decided to turn in the Medical School. All the main players. And you'd decided to turn yourself in too. How had you thought they'd let you get away with it?

22.

By the time I return home, Jeff has gone out. He hasn't left a note, nor has he texted to tell me where he is. I spend this time going through anything I can of his. I leaf through folders and files; I try his laptop again, but the password entry field still shakes defiantly back at me on the screen. Then I remember the iPad he used to show people drone footage of the Medical School and development plans he's had drawn up. Rifling through all his drawers, I find the iPad in the second one down. It's fully charged. As with the phone I've borrowed, his passcode is 1840 and within seconds, I'm in. I log in to Waze to track his most recent journeys: nothing out of the ordinary. I look through his search history. I keep hearing noises and prepare myself to shove the iPad back into the drawer and pretend I've been working on my phone, and when I'm sure there's no one around, I return to the iPad. I log in to the sites of newspapers he subscribes to, and look at the ads to see what companies were targeting him with, hoping they'll give me an indication of some of his previous searches. Nothing there: they're all to do with gardening.

I sync his work emails so the latest ones will upload to the iPad; I'm sure Jeff won't notice. I go through them all, but there's nothing to give him away there either. It seems that despite what I now know about your death, despite the lies and cover-ups, my husband is, on the face of it, as clean as a whistle.

I can't find anything insinuating that either my husband or Abraham – or anyone tied to the University, for that matter – has ever set a foot wrong. Everything has been documented beautifully. Everything is in writing. There's not too much new about you on the internet, either, although there is a fair bit about Nicola. She seems to have made quite the impression, and her alleged 'drug queen' status seems to have turned her into an online icon.

After walking to the window and checking that Jeff's car isn't pulling into the drive yet, I start to feel impatient and ring Laura to ask her if she's managed to decode the last file on the USB stick.

'Not yet. I've had to draft someone else in,' she says. 'I promise I'll get it to you soon. I've asked Darius to help. He'll be here tomorrow. I'll call you when we're ready.'

Next I ring Jeff. 'Hey, where are you? I didn't catch you this morning.' I try not to sound too needy; the last thing I want is for him to appear whilst I'm so tied up here.

'Sorry. Gala stuff.' He sounds distracted. 'I'll be back tonight. Or I'll see you later if you want to drop by.'

'I'm just heading out quickly to deal with some sponsors.' He doesn't ask any questions, and before I get dragged into any gala admin, I hang up.

A few minutes later, I'm on my way to the second nearest high street, still checking that no one is following me. Once I arrive, I go to a tiny internet shop that sells cheap handsets and buy an old Nokia. I use it in the back of the shop to ring William Harbottle. A receptionist answers and I tell him it's someone from the Medical School; I give him a fake name to pass on. When Harbottle finally comes to the phone, I tell him that I'm leaving him something important at the counter of the shop I'm in. That I'm associated with you. That I know pretty much everything he knows, and more. That he must never say anything about this conversation and must use the code word Sunflower when he comes to collect the USB stick. I give the man behind the counter a hundred dollars to hand the envelope to the gentleman that will arrive in around an hour, and that he is to ask for the code word.

I drive back to The Lodge via the florist, where I buy myself a huge bunch of flowers, and as I set them in a vase at home I imagine Harbottle opening up the files. The documents in their hundreds which I've been trawling through. I've gleaned enough from the information in there. But there's a lot of work left to do, and not a lot of time in which to do it.

I've added a page of instructions for the journalist to cross-reference. His starting point is the communications about the suggestion of 'a new wing in the Medical School'. That had been from Harley, who had been contacted by *an old acquaintance and potential donor. It'll be fully funded,* he'd added. *We will be leading the future.* I think about Harbottle scanning the following documents. He'll know parts of it already. Things you told him. But then he'll find the more recent evidence you'd collected ready to give him; he'd not turned up due to what I now know was a family emergency. After that, I can't imagine what he will do next. I tell him that he is not to contact me, but that if there's any type of emergency he can use the burner phone I've bought, and that he must always use the sign-off B. My own little joke.

After this, I concentrate on the present. There's nothing else I can do other than play ball. Show that I'm devoted to the Medical School.

Over the next few days, Lavinia and Suzy ring me repeatedly to make sure I'm still on board, that I'm excited about the magazine front cover being unveiled ('no, dear, we can't show you yet. We've decided we want it to be a complete surprise').

It takes every single ounce of strength for me to carry on with the charade. I block out every thought of you, and I tell myself time and time again that this is for the greater good.

One Week Before the Gala

23.

I revert – on the face of it at least – to being the loving wife. Things settle into a quiet but busy rhythm. I have to put everything else aside. Laura has managed to uncover the last document, and I've now collected it from her.

Each morning as I wake up, I read those words to myself to remind myself why I'm doing what I'm doing. Jeff and I both rise early every day, between 5.30 and 6 a.m. Jeff makes coffee. I work on my emails, and so does he. Some mornings I exercise, something; it feels important right now to focus on other things too. Some mornings I can only sit and think of you and do nothing else but look at your image online.

I finish unpacking, and we even start to entertain at The Lodge: a couple of cocktail parties on the lawn, fully catered and funded by the Medical School. Intimate dinners I cook for, trialling new recipes I think befitting of a president's wife and in keeping with the theme of the particular night. Esteemed guests visit, some of whom fly in especially to see Jeff, some of whom want to discover how we have achieved what we have. Some of whom want to have his ear on certain issues within the University or approach their conversations from a wider, more political perspective; what, for example, might be included in the funding for the next academic year. At these events, sometimes people offer Jeff large donations for, say, changes to the curriculum. But he always sticks to his own moral code; at least the one that remains public or could get him into trouble. In private, he, Lavinia, Abraham and Harley still meet regularly. And me, all that time, continuing to play my part as adoring wife, obedient woman and perfect host.

Harbottle and I communicate through my burner phone, and only when necessary. If he thinks at any point I'm getting cold feet, he texts me random links. Sometimes he texts me from his own burner phone, telling me to be careful. I don't ask him for details. I don't ask why. I keep myself to myself and make a show of dedicating myself to the University. Play your part, he says. What he doesn't know yet, though, is that I am playing my part, and more.

I'm playing my own game. I work hard on projects and being a faultless presidential wife. I choose community-led work that will have a 'wonderful' and 'positive' impact on the University, as Lavinia requested in the most recent governors' meeting. In that meeting, we'd had to each talk about our own contributions and what we believed our role to be within the Medical School. I'd had a lot to say.

I told them I'd been busy, which elicited nods from all around and a subtle thumbs up from Jeff the other side of the large wooden table. I felt the relief from everyone in the room that I was aligned with the ethos of the University and Medical School. I could see in the faces of everyone involved that they believed I had now agreed to turn a blind eye to your murder. Lavinia. Abraham. Jeff. Suzy. And now Kevin Tang is involved; he seems to be playing a more major, front-facing role in the Medical School.

With all this ongoing, the time leading up to the gala whizzes past, and I barely get any time alone with my husband. Doing what I see as the right thing – which is probably the same thing that led to your murder – and attempting to avenge your death has taken me down different paths.

While William has been busy working on outing the shadowy figures behind your death, I've also been digging. Using the laptop from Laura and the phone I've bought, neither of which are logged on to the University Wi-Fi, I use data from my phone and hotspot it to my laptop. If at any point I start to worry about my own life, I go to the University staff list and look at your photo, which now has *Greatly missed. 1986–2025. In Memoriam* underneath it, followed by a link to a memorial site dedicated to you.

I spend half my days and most of the evenings after we've finished entertaining combing through all the information you left on the pen drive. I also do my own due diligence; I'm not constrained by editorial regulations the way Harbottle is. I start with the apparently random names you wrote. I don't realise at first why they warrant their own document until I type one of them into Google. At first I find nothing, until I scroll down and hit gold when I cross-reference the name with the author of an interesting thread I've found on a random forum. This changes the course of my own investigation completely, giving me an entirely new piece of the jigsaw.

It's at midnight that Harbottle texts me on the burner phone. He doesn't apologise. *Elizabeth,* he writes. *Editor wants full copy asap. Wants to publish in a few days whilst the University is still in the limelight. Are you on board with this? Otherwise we might have to go ahead separately. Yours, B.*

I'm still up at my laptop. Jeff has gone to bed early, which is unlike him, and I'm dissecting, investigating, researching. Unravelling a horrifying and knotted web of information from around the globe.

Hi B. Look, I'm sorry, I reply. *I can't give you final sign-off yet. If you go ahead, you'll be missing a major piece of evidence, which I'll pass on to you when I can.*

What evidence? he replies. *I thought you gave me everything.*

Not quite, I tell him. I can't afford for any of this to go wrong, and I need to hold the journalist off until I'm ready. And every time I think I'm done, I uncover more.

'Elizabeth,' Jeff calls out. I thought he'd be asleep by now, and I jump, unused to him bothering to ask where I am. 'You coming up? It's late.'

'Yep,' I say, shutting the laptop down.

When I get upstairs, I feign tiredness, before slipping into my nightie and climbing into bed. 'Sorry. Didn't notice the time.'

'Being the president's wife tiring you out?' Jeff says. 'I'm the president himself and I can't sleep.'

I wonder what that has to do with me, and whether there's something he needs to discuss. 'All okay?' I look at my phone, eager to return downstairs before it gets much later and I have to be up for the following day.

'Yeah. All good.' He edges towards me, pressing his body into mine. 'Thought you might like a little time together.' His familiarity feels almost sickening, but to avoid arousing suspicion by saying no again tonight, I adopt the role of dutiful wife. I lie, head on one side and cheek pressed to the pillow, as he climbs on top of me, his stubble scratching at my chin.

'God, that's exhausted me,' he says with a laugh five minutes later, as though he's done me a great favour. 'You like that?'

'I did.' I stare at a fixed point on the wall in front of me.

'Would you hand me a tissue?' I pass him one and watch as he wipes himself clean before passing it back to me. 'Bin.'

Play the game, I tell myself as I walk over to the bathroom and flush the tissue down the loo before cleaning myself up too. Not much longer.

'Oh listen, Lizzie. Tomorrow there's a dinner invite that needs to be extended to Sam Hilton from the Philanthropy Fund in New York. Can you action that?'

'*Action that?*' I repeat, smarting. 'I'm not your PA.'

He completely ignores me. 'And that reminds me. They want to interview me for *Vanity Fair*.'

'Wow,' I say flatly, aghast at the sheer arrogance of it all. 'That's great.'

'Isn't it?' He rolls over, flattening out his pillow. 'Night. Sweet dreams.'

It's only when Jeff starts to snore, that I slide myself out of the bed and make my way back to my desk to carry on my work.

At the Medical School, I make a beeline for the admin office so I don't have to think too much about what I am doing. All my brain power is spent on my own investigation. My days are spent with Janet in the Development office, methodically filing, working out how much spend we have for gardening projects with the youngsters, ordering in plants and seeds – ensuring in general that the Medical School is seen as a force for good in the community. My role would be enjoyable if I didn't have another motive in mind. I align myself most with Janet, because she's worked in the Development office for over thirty years and knows the most about what's happening in the Medical School. It's only when she starts to hint at how disgruntled she's been lately at the way things are being run there that I start to suspect she'll give me information.

I'm given a desk in her office under the pretence of wanting to learn more about how things are run, and while she initially annoyed me after your death, I grow rather fond of this painstakingly detailed, organised woman. She takes me under her wing, showing me how everything works whilst telling me about her husband Ted, who has multiple sclerosis. She tells me how Harley has given them lots of money to install medical equipment in their house, something which confuses me. She tells me about Jeff's predecessors. How there have been a lot of superficial changes to the University and Medical School but that their core ethos has always remained the same; when I ask her what that is, though, she doesn't seem to be able to explain herself. She tells me about the dynamics in the Medical School. In short, she becomes a mine of information, and I start to rely on her heavily. At times, I question whether I should trust someone who works in the building, but I treat her simply as a source of intel about the place. I don't allude to anything bigger. I act as her ally; I get things pushed through that she'd like done. And she and I start to develop a mutual respect and understanding.

'Our benefactor,' Janet tells me one quiet day when it is just me and her, 'it was his intention for the Medical School that made it the place it is today.' Given what has been going on underneath it all, I wonder what his intention had originally been, and how its roots have spread to harness such evil.

In time, she gives me access to everything because I've become so indispensable. Spreadsheets containing passwords. Financial documents. Access to all of Jeff's and Abraham's folders. Our relationship builds so much that at times I forget what I'm really meant to be doing, other than building community and sorting out the gala, most of which I've done weeks ago.

'Why do you love this place so much?' I say one day as I bring Janet a steaming cup of coffee from Martino's. Since the place was mentioned as your favourite cafe, I've been in there every day I've gone into the Development office, in the hope of finding out more about you. I haven't, but in any case it makes me feel closer to you.

I ask her if it's okay if I spend the rest of that morning updating all of our passwords, telling her that it's for security purposes.

'Oh, Elizabeth, you really shouldn't be doing all these menial jobs.' She nods towards my computer. 'But I'm so grateful. I've been meaning to get round to that for ever. Now what did you ask? Why I love this place so much?'

'Exactly.'

'It's...' She stops and looks at me. 'I guess I'm just used to it. The way it all works. And in some way I feel like I'm contributing' – she spreads her arms – 'to this. The wider world.' She looks sad. 'Or at least I used to.'

This week, Abraham has tasked me with ringing half of the Wickham Fellowship recipients to let them know the good news. It would have been a career highlight had I not known what I now know and had I not been dangled carrot after carrot to keep me invested. And one night we have a celebration with staff members who had been particularly close to you, in order to launch the Wickham Fellowship in your name, which since your death, has been taken so horribly in vain. In just a couple of days, I plan to right that wrong.

Two Days Before the Gala

24.

When gala week comes, there's another surprise waiting for me. I get a text from Abraham, who wants to go over the final details and for me to come to the hall to go over timings. I come with a checklist: Link the videos to the projectors. Time the confetti to go off as the fundraising announcement is made. Ensure the lighting and music will coincide with the appropriate speakers.

I speak to the sponsors after three emails from Suzy – a woman from Aurelia Wellness, who tells me they can provide last-minute party favours and bags. It seems Suzy has already done my job for me, as they mention that the bag could also hold the Medical School *Tribune*. A lovely, thick, good-quality tote, says Katya, the woman on the end of the phone. We'll put some wonderful wellness essentials in it. Our latest green powder. Our Skincare range and our health monitoring ring that collates all your data and turns it into a powerful tool for enhancing your life. I'll send you our latest upgraded version. It's got three tiny rose quartz crystals in it, she says perkily. The devil is in the detail, I think. And we're all set.

'We ready, guys?' Abraham yells to no one in particular. 'Gotta check the last bits of tech.' I walk over to where he is standing up on the main stage. He links his computer to the main projector. 'You'd have thought we'd be a bit more cutting-edge by now. Remind me to do something about that. Damn HDMI cable.' He clicks it into place. He pulls up his screen. 'Hang on. Let me test it.' He pulls up a Word document entitled 'Health Partnerships Scheme 2027'. Innocuous. He knows I'm watching. He must have chosen the pages that will put him in the best light. Always thinking about his own comms. Clicking on his keypad, he presses a button on his laptop and the page changes to the next screen on the PowerPoint and appears on the main projector screen behind us, showing four laughing children planting trees. 'Fantastic,' he says. 'All good.' He clicks another button on his keypad, which inadvertently brings up an on-screen keyboard.

'Oh hang on, let's get rid of this.' He taps something on his computer and the screen disappears, but it's too late. I've seen it. He doesn't know anything is wrong. He doesn't know that the cogs of my brain are trying to process what I've seen – three tiny graphics in the 'most-used' emoji toolbar. There, in the personalised keyboard on his phone, which is now linked to the projector for the entire room to see, are three small pictures. A logo of an investigator, and right next to it a skull and crossbones, then another investigator icon. Had I not been looking, I wouldn't have thought twice about that sequence of emojis. At least not in everyday life.

Excusing myself, I go to the bathroom, the one I'm so familiar with when bad things happen. Firstly, I google the emojis. An investigator emoji, followed by a skull and crossbones and then another investigator. See if they had some generic meaning. They don't.

Pulling up my X account, I go straight to the @ StudentInvigilatorX account and go through all the threads posted since your death. There, as the hallmark layout, and the signature of the profile, are the three graphics, in that order. I scour the text with the dawning knowledge that this has almost certainly came from Abraham and that he's been masquerading as @StudentInvigilatorX. I search for similarities, and now I'm looking for it, I can see the rhythm of the syntax later on in the timeline of your death – perhaps when he got sloppy in not adopting a different 'persona'. The positioning of his grammatical markers. The way he uses an exclamation mark mid-sentence for no reason. Using an AI tool, I copy and paste the X threads into a website, and alongside it I digitally compare some other text of Abraham's that I collate from WhatsApps he'd sent me. I click 'Go!', a timer icon flashes up on the screen, and after a few seconds a message comes up: *This text was written by the same person – 100%!* I look at the exclamation mark tacked onto the end of the sentence. I think of the initial text message that started all of this off: *Good Morning, Mrs. President!*

It was Abraham, all along. Writing from Jeff's phone to me. It all makes sense. It wasn't Jeff who wrote to me that day. For some reason Abraham took it upon himself to do it, his control of me starting from the beginning. I dig my fingers into my arms.

It takes me twenty minutes to unlock the bathroom door. Last time I was here, I listened to your voice, the last intake of oxygen into your body. I owe you this much, I whisper out loud. I think about Abraham. How I told him about you and me. Asked him for his help. How he then pretended not to already know.

I read through the messages on the @Student InvigilatorX threads. He was the one to leak the subliminal link between your affair with a 'high-profile' person and me. The photograph of me which I had no idea where it came from. He had it. Abraham had it. How long had he known about our affair? I remember his face again when I told him. The feigned look of shock and horror. How he carried out an entire charade to me that he was going to 'sort it', when all he had to do was log on to his own account and delete. Kudos, I think. His acting skills almost surpass mine. Almost.

'Abraham, all good,' I remind myself of what's at stake here. Namely you. I'd spent another five minutes in the bathroom. 'I think we're ready,' I clap my hands. 'Listen', I test him. 'Do you mind if I have a quick word?' I nod towards the corner of the room, away from a technician who is working on the stage lighting.

'Course not.' Abraham looks at his wrist. 'You're so darn efficient, Elizabeth, that I've actually got ten minutes until my next meeting. Normally I'd whizz off some emails, but I'd enjoy hearing what you have to say. As long as it's not the bombshell you hit me with last time.'

We both laugh. I'm getting good at this. No, screw *good*. Excellent. I've been exemplary in playing this part and yet I'm filled with such rage I'm barely able to see straight.

'Listen.' I put on a faux-worried expression. 'I need your reassurance. There isn't any fallout from...you know, what I told you? About me and...' I bite my lip. 'You don't think anyone else knows, do you? I haven't heard a thing, but I'm worried it's all going to appear in the newspaper. Or something. I just can't seem to relax. And I've heard nothing from Newton, which is making me even more nervous.'

Abraham shrugs. 'It's fine. I wouldn't give it a second thought. Newton won't say a word to Jeff.'

'How do you know? This Student Invigilator X person seemed to know stuff. How do I know he or she doesn't have more up their sleeve? I'm expecting things to explode at any given moment.'

'It won't. I've sorted absolutely everything.' Abraham shakes his head. 'I don't want to discuss anything anymore. Okay? Lavinia's given her orders. We're all to move on. And I can't go round wiping your tears now and sweeping up your dirt.' He looks at me. 'Look, I don't mean that harshly. But it's a fact. All right? And in any case, Jeff...' I nod and we both go silent, me creasing out the internal anger I'm feeling that he's putting the actions of the Medical School onto a mistake I've made. 'Do you miss him?' Abraham asks.

'No,' I say without hesitation. But I feel the familiar ache across my chest. 'Not at all. Stupid. Really stupid thing I did. Nearly lost all of this.' I look around, playing into Abraham. 'For what?'

'For a bad man. A really bad man.'

'What do you mean?'

'Him stealing drugs from us. Selling them.'

Interesting he's still going with that line.

I play dumb. 'Yes. Bad. Really bad.' The pen is in my pocket. I recall what's on it. And who it was that had you killed. Abraham knows. Harley knows. Suzy knows. My husband knows. Lavinia knows. They all know. And now I do too. But they have the perfect alibi. The inauguration, livestreamed for the entire world to see. The audience as our corroborating witness. Their collective weakness; how much they all love a show.

The Night of the Gala

25.

I spend two hours getting ready. Megan comes over to do my hair in a loose updo. I ask her a lot about her boyfriend, Jordan, knowing she'll spend a long time talking. She also does my make-up, blowing powder off my face, applying subtle false eyelashes. I think about your reaction to seeing me. I imagine it frame by frame, and for the first time, instead of feeling the heat of desire, or the terror of being caught, I feel the warmth of respect and awe over what you were doing all that time when I thought you were cheating. The integrity of your actions, even if you appeared to me to be deceitful and weak. Even if you were inconsistent in your behaviour, there was at least a damn reason, and now that reason is manifesting itself as me, against the Medical School and those unseen forces behind it. I shiver.

'Someone walked over your grave.' Megan sweeps the last of the blusher across my face.

'Something like that,' I laugh.

Holding my chin in her hand, Megan inspects me from left to right before helping me step into the green dress. She steps back. 'Wow,' she says. 'Wow. You look incredible.

Here. Shoes.' I slip them on and stand in front of the mirror in the bedroom. 'This is your moment, Elizabeth. Your proper introduction to the Medical School.'

William will now have formed a clear picture of what's been happening. He'll be trawling now through the next bit of information but getting sidetracked, as I had. Researching data. Names. Facts and figures. The bits where Harley had started to suggest bringing in Lavinia to oversee the new Wickham Wing. That a 'wonderfully generous' donor offer had been confirmed and that 'talks' about the funds had been under way. I think now about the bargains made in return for that money. How many lives have been ruined.

I'm nearly done, I write to William, keeping him updated. The last thing I want to do is for him to go off-track. *Has your editor given you leeway with timing?*

Yes, he replies immediately. *But this story keeps on giving. Just as I think we're getting somewhere... I'm uncovering more and more. Also corroborating all evidence proving tricky in parts. We're drafting in another hack to help. A freelancer specialising in investigations. I'll keep you posted with what we find, but so far, all good. Few queries, but I'll go through with you later.*

'Elizabeth?' Jeff shouts up the stairs. 'Ready to go?'

'Yes,' I call back, trying to remain calm that William has drafted in someone else and not told me which I know, rationally, is ridiculous. When I get downstairs, Jeff hands me a box. 'Elizabeth I'm a lucky man,' he reaches out an arm. 'You look mind-blowing. And I got you this,' he says. 'I've been waiting to give it to you. To wear tonight with this dress. Suzy told me she'd arranged it for you.'

'It's beautiful,' I tell him truthfully. A silver necklace with a diamond pendant. I tip my head forward for him to put it on.

'There.' He fiddles with the clasp and lets the cool metal drop against my skin. 'Beautiful. My wife. The perfect showpiece.'

The drive to the gala is quiet, both me and Jeff in the back seat of a car. The roads are generally clear, the spaces open, the views drenched in greenery and a dusky sky, until we reach the more enclosed campus. Students roam around, walking slowly, waving, talking fast. With my dress and make-up set, I try not to fidget too much even though my body has other ideas.

'All right?' Jeff says without looking up from his phone.

'Yes, of course.' I make a big show of looking over at what he was doing. 'Something important going on?'

'Newton,' he taps his screen a few more times and slides the phone back into his pocket. My blood runs cold.

'What does he want?' I steady myself, wishing to God I hadn't asked.

'Nothing,' Jeff shakes his head, but it's too late and I'm starting to feel the familiar slither of paranoia.

'You look handsome,' I say, filling the silence, desperate to keep Jeff on an even keel and get things back to normal. Or at least to make everyone think I'm behaving 'normally'. We'll be making an entrance, and the press may or may not be there, but there will certainly be a photographer and videographer present, and I can't set a foot wrong when there are people watching. My game face has to be perfect at all points. And I have to be the perfect president's wife.

We pull up, to see the entire front of the hall covered in a light show of the Medical School logo. That eagle crest signifying strength and freedom of this age old and elite establishment. There's red and gold bunting criss-crossed over the front lawn from oak to oak; there's a tiny brass band playing in the front left corner of the lawn. People have started arriving in their finery. Bright ballgowns, fur stoles, glittering diamonds, long satin gloves, up-dos, white tie, black tie. When we pull up, Jeff opens my side of the car and holds his hand out. I take his lead, the perfect couple, ready to front the evening. We greet people as we go past, although we don't stop to talk. And as we enter the building, Jeff tightens his hand around my arm.

'Good evening,' says the waiter. 'Would you care for a champagne?' I take one and so does Jeff, and then I gasp as I notice copies of the — *Medical School Tribune* fanned out across the red linen on the table pushed up against the wall.

'Wait,' I tell Jeff. 'Hang on. It's me. On the front cover. I can't believe it. I look so different.' Sam Tate has captured something whimsical about me that I don't recognise; my eyes look into the distance and there's a tiny smile on my face. It's as though I'm emulating the Mona Lisa, and I'm about to tell Jeff this, when I see the headline directly underneath the front cover.

ELIZABETH HARKER ON HER EXCITEMENT OVER THE NEW WICKHAM WING!

I gasp. When the hell had I talked about the Wickham Wing during that time with Lavinia and Suzy? I had talked about how proud I had been being part of this University and contributing to the Medical School. I had, though, never once mentioned the Wickham Wing. They'd never asked me to mention it. They'd never hooked me into any discussion over it at all. I'd been extra sure to stay away from topics like that, in case Abraham had words with me. So they must have added it in after, on the thought that if they'd risked asking me during the interview, I'd say I couldn't talk about it. And I remember Lavinia talking to me about the Wickham Wing and how to sell the ideal to the public: *We're keeping it all under wraps due to donor sensitivities*. And I was the bait, all along.

I scan through the pages. Everything else is as I've said. Juggling marriage with work. Jeff's role and my part within that. Community-focused. Donations. Fundraising. Blah blah blah. Then a paragraph about the huge, exciting changes coming up. How proud I am of the generosity of the donors and how I want to introduce this amazing development to the community. How excited we are as a couple that this is happening. Whoever has done this has set me up entirely, knowing it makes me complicit in the wrongdoings of the Medical School. That it will make it harder for me to remove myself. I squeeze my eyes shut. They've put me on the front cover, orchestrated me being in the Medical School's public domain. Put words into my mouth. And I played into it, Venus flytrapped by my own ego.

'Elizabeth,' Jeff whispers. 'Come on.' There's an edge to his tone. I slide the magazine back out of place, with Jeff shaking his head. 'People are waiting for us.' I put on a smile and walk through the huge doors into the glittering party before me.

I down two glasses of champagne, something I vowed not to do when I'm in this position, but tonight there seems to be no alternative. My nervous system feels completely combustible, everything seems sharper, clearer, brighter. We do the rounds, Jeff and I. A wonderful team. Jeff shakes hands with as many people as he can, clapping them on the other arm at the same time, whilst looking straight into their eyes. He remembers everyone's name. Even though my insides feel like they've been obliterated, I follow up with my own conversation. Soft. Connecting. And when I feel like I can no longer carry on, the microphone screeches and the audience quiets and Abraham rushes up to both of us, shepherding us closer to the stage. 'Guys, you're both next.' He looks around. 'The press are here.'

'Which ones?' I look around, certain William Harbottle won't have made his way in and hoping that right now he'll be working out his editorial strategy. No one answers.

'Okay. Listen, I just need to double-check the video link to the Fellowship recipients.'

'It's all fine,' Abraham says, 'but do go ahead.'

Pulling up my dress, I make my way onto the stage and to the projector and adjust the settings, then make my way back down as the lights dim and Harley appears onstage. Clearing his throat into the microphone, he welcomes everyone to this splendid evening of joy and celebration. He looks good. Abraham whispers something to Jeff.

Harley adopts a sombre tone. 'It's been an astonishingly difficult term, but Jeff Harker, our president, has been phenomenal, along with his team, and he's given me the honour of announcing something I started at the beginning of my own tenure. And so now' – he stops to push up his glasses and fiddle with the sheets in front of him on the lectern – 'for the moment of truth.' He looks behind him as the projector flashes on. 'Here,' he says, circling his hand and taking a bow. 'Ladies and gentlemen, we are so profoundly grateful for our community. For the fact that we all came together to make this happen. All of you here tonight in one way or another...' Harley stops to take a breath and for a second I worry he's going to collapse, but he straightens up again. '...have contributed to the future of global health. To the health of generations to come. Tonight.' He closes his eyes. 'And this is no exaggeration, because we're the first medical school not just in the United States of America but in the world—' The audience starts to clap and whoop. 'The first in the world to have grown our fellowship programme to such a degree that our Medical School admissions process has become completely need-blind.' The audience roars. 'And...' he adds, holding up a finger. 'And...' I scan the room for William Harbottle. Harley carries on. 'We are here and now able to teach our students with this new, cutting-edge medical equipment with the most futuristic of robotics and AI machinery.' He looks around the room again, shaking his head as though having to convince himself of his own input into this. 'The future of medicine, ladies and gentlemen' – the lights dim – 'is here. Right now. Between these four walls. Your University and Medical School. And we have another big announcement to make.'

The room goes quiet.

'The generosity of our donors, some of whom are here tonight, means we will now start development on a new project. We will be building an entirely new wing, to include all the latest state of the art machinery and medical equipment. The Wickham Wing named after our founder, Henry Wickham. Thank you to our anonymous donor, who gave us an extraordinary donation so we could hit our target.'

Jeff must have got the promised funds in that we'd told everyone we already had in order to win the Rosemont Development Award. Another coup for my husband.

'Ladies and gentlemen, again. Please put your hands together and celebrate with us.'

The audience goes wild. Clapping fills the air and when Harley holds his hands out like a composer, everyone stops.

'I'd like to now say once again goodbye. Thanks to research that has also come out of our very own walls here too, with our brightest and best Wickham Fellowship recipients and their research into Dolanexin, or, as it's now been named, Neurolume – my own cancer treatment has been aided. It has been a dark time for us all here, and I've watched from my bed, but thanks to the generosity of financial donations, academic excellence, and innovative breakthroughs, here I am onstage right now with the ability to manage my pain. With all my gratitude to our very own.' The audience is silent, then the noise fills my ears again. 'Thank you. Thank you,' Harley puts out his hands as he had done during the inauguration. I wonder why Harley introduced the Wickham Wing and not Jeff. 'Now, I'd like to introduce Jeff Harker to the stage.' Harley walks off and greets Jeff halfway, clutching his hand and holding his arm. We did it, he's saying. We got there. Jeff takes to the stage. My husband. He's started to hold himself differently now, jogging up to the lectern, waving out to the audience in a relaxed way as though he's geeing up fans on a campaign trail.

'Hello everybody.' Jeff waves and gives a tiny bow. My husband seems to have adopted an entirely different persona in the past few weeks, the fluidity of his movements suggesting invincibility. 'Thank you, Harley, for those inspiring words and yes we're so grateful to our genius superstars. And our enormous thanks must go to a very special guest tonight, Lieutenant Newton, and his incredible team, who led the charge so well in what has been an incredibly dark time for our University. Who fought through thickets of false leads. Who maintained their own dignity through the awful and misleading speculation that reared its ugly head on the internet.' The lights shine onto a table at the front, and Lieutenant Newton nods to more cheers. He avoids looking at me, his smile rigid now as he realises he's been caught with his hand in the pocket of this great University.

'And before I introduce you to your next speaker, I'd like to say that we've still got important work to do. We've still got to break barriers. As far as I'm concerned, this is our first stage. With the best minds in this amazing country of ours, who knows where next. So please dig deep. Save lives. It's up to you. And now I'd like you to meet someone incredibly special.' Jeff continues, the spotlight shining brightly upon him. 'You might have already met her. She seems to be making waves here. You might well have seen her on the front cover of our wonderful magazine. If not, you'll find a copy in the goody bags from Aurelia Wellness, our sponsors this year, and so ladies and gentlemen, please do see your cover model for this special edition.' Jeff goes silent and the lights dim. He stares at me with a strange look across his face, as though he's woken up from a deep hypnosis and doesn't know where he is. 'The woman who has organised all of this for you tonight and who also happens to be the woman who has stood by my side throughout my initial tenure here. Ladies and gentlemen, please, hands together for my beautiful wife, Elizabeth Harker.' The lights sparkle in front of my eyes. The music plays and Jeff says my name again.

'Elizabeth?' he laughs. 'Thinking about joining us?'

I go cold as I think of the last speech I gave after finding out you were dead. Me giving a speech hadn't been part of the plan. Again, it was something they'd sprung on me.

I think about the pen, and how right now, William Harbottle – or Bill, as you so affectionately called him – will be trawling through the finances and communications between an anonymous donor known only to Bellamy Ventures and Lavinia, Abraham, Harley and my own dear husband. And, of course, you. You, who had been preparing to blow the whistle all this time. You who had been doing the right thing.

I look at Jeff, then Abraham, my thoughts frenzied in what feels like a complete vacuum of time and space, the entire contents of your USB flashing through my mind. The truth about everything. The Wickham Wing. The anonymous donor, brought in by Harley, nurtured by Jeff, who had promised the development of the Wickham Wing in exchange for favourable results of the Medical School's clinical trial for Neurolume, the new global drug of choice for pain management which also had the benefit of mental clarity and focus, with a minuscule amount of a new psychedelic drug, harvested straight from a previously undiscovered Amazonian plant that enhanced neural connections. The lights shimmer in front of my eyes.

And you, my love, unwittingly or not, were brought in to manage all this by my own husband before he was even made president. I look around at the crowd waiting for me to take to the microphone. You were brought in by Jeff to make sure the trials were a success. I see the documents and communications with a laser-sharp clarity, remembering Lavinia's instruction to 'sort them out'. And her email:

> Unfortunately, the promised funds from Bellamy Ventures, which includes Helianthus Holdings and Aurelia via an extremely generous donor, cannot be delivered for both the Wickham Wing and the Wickham Fellowships, until we see a marked improvement in results.

You failed, though, my love. Those clinical trials had been a disaster. People had died. Developed psychosis or heart problems. Or both.

I put the pieces together as I read the communications between you and Jeff. My husband's written orders to you that you 'sort this out' immediately. The Wickham Fellowships. Everything. The award too hinged on the Fellowships' development fund. Our written and filmed entry, with all the supporting documents, specified that we'd raised enough funds for the Fellowship expansion as per Harley's initiative.

All of these messages sent to and from Jeff's email with you and Abraham cc'd in, which you stored on the USB and which had subsequently been deleted from Jeff's email. You, later on, telling him you would sort it out. That you'd do the best by the Medical School. You'd hate to see the funding lost, but on the other hand you 'definitely couldn't envisage pushing through the results'. But someone had. They'd changed. Someone had skewed the data. Someone had passed those results on to their 'contact' at an external agency, who had subsequently had them investigated and approved in a short time frame, due to 'extenuating circumstances' and a 'great need' for the drugs themselves.

A reminder from Abraham on WhatsApp to perhaps regularly 'review' communications on your devices to do with the Wickham Wing and the funding.

And then an email from you, sent to Jeff shortly before midday, the last time I'd slept with you and about half an hour before he'd been made president of — University and Medical School. The one that got you killed. Those words you said in good faith, thinking things would change, that you could put some good into this world. *You make me see things in a different way, Elizabeth.*

Dear Jeff and Abraham, you'd typed. Cc'd Lavinia.

> It's good to see people wanting to change things for the better. It's a nice thought. But knowingly putting people's lives at risk is not something I want to be a part of anymore, and I've since decided that we need to inform external agencies that more trials need to take place for Neurolume. That we are now uncertain of our own trial data. It won't be a problem if we come clean now. Or at least present our data in more transparent ways. I'll give you five days or so to rectify before taking matters into my own hands.

The words you'd written – *it's good to see people wanting to change things for the better* – had rung a bell, and I remember they were the ones I'd said when I'd first met you at the fundraiser. How you'd mocked me afterwards. That tiny smile. And the later communication from Jeff: *That's not what you said four years ago when we were paid full whack to hightail it off to research in Ecuador*. I hadn't even recognised those words in Jeff. Full whack. It appears that in his ambition, my husband had morphed into a totally different human being. Or he was now finally stepping into his true self; he'd simply needed the catalyst to do so.

And from Lavinia: 'An end needs to be put to this immediately. Please keep the trial data as is, and the drugs in the wonderful and useful light we know them to be. Saving lives. Healing people. It's all incredibly exciting, and so is the Wickham Wing and the direction we're heading in with the Fellowships.' I had scoured through the rest of the communication. You, eventually capitulating. Telling the 'main players', you'd carry on. Except you'd already spoken to William Harbottle in secret. But little did you know that you were being watched. Very carefully. And subsequently, so was I. The photograph that had leaked to the media. I didn't recognise it for a reason; because I'd been totally unaware it was being taken.

I had only made a slight headway into some of the figures you had pulled together. You, my love, orchestrating everything behind the scenes for the University and Medical School's clinical trials and research into the wonder drug Neurolume, then getting cold feet. Realising what you'd been facilitating with the clinical trial data was being presented in a light not wholly beneficial to the end user. The affair with me. You eventually became an outlier. A renegade. Speaking up. And for that, you wound up dead.

And Lavinia. Her study. The tiny sunflower logo on that sheet of paper. What I now recognise as her investment portfolio, set up under a shell company under the name of her dead husband, Arthur Edwards. The pharmaceutical company linked to the Medical School's anonymous donor. That shadowy figure whose identity would always be protected. Who pulled all the strings. Lavinia, with her own financial skin in the game. Bellamy Ventures and their subsidiaries, Helianthus Holdings and Aurelia Wellness. God alone knows how much money she'd pumped into shares with them. I had spent hours poring over their external communications trying to find anything on them. Leads to other companies but there was nothing. Helianthus only had one page on the internet declaring that they were the leaders in the future of global health. There was no contact name. No contact number. The only link to Aurelia had been discovered by you. Clever you. A web designer who had used her email address as the creator of both sites. After weeks of research, the missing link. I think of you. I hear Jeff, the echo of my name. The people below me watching, waiting. And so I stride up onto the stage and take the microphone.

In the beginning I played the game, I admit. I keep thinking of the adoption papers, though. How if I stepped out of line, I'd lose it all. What had Jeff said at the beginning, shortly after you'd been murdered and he'd told me what would happen if I didn't pull myself together? *Look, this here will be over. Before you can say murder. The adoption. My career. Your place within this University. Finished.* I place a hand on my belly as I think of that pain, the way I'd hunched over in the Development office and I nearly let out a sob as I think about what I'd be giving up but as I keep on talking, I'm thinking more about the game. About how spectacularly I'd been played. I look around. Smile. I tell the crowd that I'm here for them. That I've learned so much about this innovative place and all the wonderful students within it, all thanks to our community. The donors who made all this possible. I look around me, eyes glistening. 'Imagine. A world where we come together to make the most incredible technological and pharmaceutical advancements that have the capability of transforming the health of millions.' I up the ante. I need to make everyone believe that like Lavinia, I'm also fully invested. I look down at Suzy, her hands clasped under her chin, smiling in delight. Jeff, who is nodding at me. Even Abraham. In their eyes, I've stepped into my feminine power as Jeff's counterpart and chosen them.

I tell everyone that they're now to watch the true stars of tonight, and the video we've had made of the previous Wickham Fellowship recipients is played amidst total silence other than the odd quiet sniff. The rustle of hankies and the ebb and flow of rousing music as the recipient of each award thanks this wonderful community from the screen for their generosity. All those donors, crying at how much they have changed lives. I wait a few beats after the video has ended. I wave, and out of nowhere comes a standing ovation. I wave again, doing exactly what

Jeff had done, then look down at the front two tables. Lavinia, Suzy, Harley and Abraham, all looking happy and healthy. Clapping hard, as though their lives depended on it. Lieutenant Newton, too, nodding, looking around the room. And my husband, Jeffrey Harker. The people a synecdoche of the University and Medical School itself, and how I see now that your death was exactly that. The sum of its parts. A necessity, delivered by the whole. The machinations of these bricks and mortar were your downfall. One person might have been the perpetrator. One person might have organised your death. I recall Abraham and Jeff at Cecconi's. *We have to carry on as normal. As though this never happened.* And you had all done exactly that. Carried on blithely. How neither my husband nor Abraham had slipped up with all those layers of lies and deceit, I do not know. Or maybe they had, and I hadn't noticed because until now I hadn't been looking out for it.

One person might have delivered the blow, or rather, the knife. But it was a collective effort that got you killed, and I will avenge your death.

The lights rise. My green dress shines under the lasers. I look at the gift bags lining the room, waiting to be collected into the eager hands of our guests, huge colourful bows wrapped around each handle. My face appearing on the front cover of every single magazine that has been popped so neatly into each bag. I look up, and there behind me is my photo on an enormous graphic. The front cover of the magazine. Me. The headline: I'm so excited about the Wickham Wing and out of nowhere I feel a cold, hard fury that my good name has been pulled into something so sordid. So evil. Even worse that it was under the guise of goodness. Grabbing the projector remote in one hand, I pick up your pen and hold it tightly in my other hand. Give a small nod to acknowledge that you are here with me now, in spirit.

'One more thing,' I tell the audience. 'A small surprise.' I don't look at Abraham. I had toyed with the idea of spilling it all on the screen. But I couldn't do that without him cutting the lot. Pulling the electrics. Setting off the fire alarm. I need to be one step ahead.

'I want to thank our incredible team, who have looked after us all behind the scenes after the tragic events of the past few weeks.' I press the remote control and, as I'd planned right before Harley had got up onstage, up flashes a picture with Jeff and Abraham's bios. 'You might not know this, but they've been working day in, day out to manage the fallout from this.' I look down, staring into the bright lights. Abraham is smiling, unaware what's about to happen. He genuinely thinks I'm about to hand him flowers. Then they are heads together, laughing about something, not listening. 'Am I boring you?' I want to shout down to them.

'And so I'm going to make a public thank you too, from all of us here at this wonderful institution, on one of our own social media accounts.' At this point Abraham's head snaps up, shadowing the path of light in his way. 'Here we go, everyone,' I start to shout. 'Just here. Look.' I press the remote control. 'This was started up by someone on our staff, so I know they won't mind at all that I'm using it here to post this big and special thank you.' I feel giddy. Abraham looks at Jeff and whispers something else to him. My husband frowns. Shakes his head. The murmurs from the crowd grow louder. Abraham looks up again at the screen as I press the right-hand arrow. There, on the next slide, I'd prepped a page with @StudentInvigilatorX's profile displayed on it. I'd been perfecting it this whole time sitting in Janet's office, and at home in the dead of night.

Next, I've set up a draft thread which will go live on X when I push the 'post' button. Ready for everyone to see. Thanks to the Development office's phone and with Janet's help in accessing the passwords spreadsheet, I'd managed to get into Abraham's linked accounts, where the passwords had been saved.

> @StudentInvigilatorX #NeurolumeTruth, I had typed. @— MedicalSchool and what they didn't tell you. The alleged injuries that have occurred from the drug.
> 🧐☠️🧐

'Ladies and gentlemen, I'd truly love for you to have a look at the @StudentInvigilatorX account for yourselves to see my special thank you. I'm sure you're deeply familiar with it all. The link, from the live @StudentInvigilatorX account, directs the user to neurolumetruth.com; a sole web page of photos and videos of every single person who had got in contact with me, all those hours and days in Janet's office and in the dead of night, after I'd posted on a health forum, asking for people who are of the 'belief' they had had adverse experiences from taking Neurolume either recreationally or not. The videos had been mostly shocking. Teenagers recording themselves having psychotic episodes during raves, or parties. Terrified voices in the background. Call 911. Hello? She's... I think she's dying. With eyes wide, bass pumping out around them. Photos of heart scans, the organ tripled in size. Videos of mainly young people having seizures, the whites of their eyes fluttering backwards like tiny dove wings. Addiction after just a few doses. Death. Parent testimonials, from a group called "Neurolume Survivors Unite".

I also post the before and after clinical trial data after it had been 'manipulated' favourably. The difference is stark. And then the fast-tracked external approval. Mainly, it's the stuff of nightmares. I hesitate. Squinting up at the bright lights, I press Enter, and it goes live, for all of @ StudentInvigilatorX's millions of followers.

For them to bear witness, just as I have done.

26.

Abraham appears on the stage next to me. 'Ladies and gentlemen, could someone help please? Any medics on duty? This lady. She's in desperate need of help. President's wife. Please. Anyone?'

It's started. The narrative. Again, I've got to hand it to him. There's a shuffling sound. The clink of glasses and the beep of phones. I'm not aware of anything else other than Abraham and one other person, I've no idea who, yanking out the HDMI cable from the screen projector and taking me firmly by the elbow.

'There there,' Abraham continues. 'It's okay. Let's get you safely out into the back.'

'Get off me!' I start to scream. 'Off me! Don't you touch me!'

The minute I set that post to live, it seemed to unleash all the emotion I'd held in since seeing the image of your body sprawled on the ground, blood blossoming around you. Jeff runs towards us, hands out as though I'm some untamed lion. My reflection in one of the huge silver balloons nearby shows me wild-eyed, looking around the room. I don't recognise that feral flare. We reach a small room at the side of the stage that looks like a janitor's cupboard. As soon as we're in, Abraham turns. He pushes me down onto a small blue plastic chair, the lights bright above me, and kicks a small metal mop and bucket out the way.

'Thank you.' Abraham motions to the other person in the room. 'That'll be all. Thank you though. Grateful. We've got it from here,' he manages. The person leaves. Visibly shaking, Abraham pulls out his phone. 'Lavinia. Room C42. Yes. Opposite you. There's a bolt. Get Harley on the stage again. Or Suzy. Get them to get the band to start up in about three minutes.'

We all wait in silence. We hear the echo of Harley's voice. *Ladies and gentlemen. A blip in tonight's proceedings. We wish her well. Maybe we'll give her some Neurolume,* he adds, dull the pain, which elicits a laugh until I realise the whole entire room is in on it. Of course. What had I been expecting? *No, seriously, seriously,* Harley carries on, *we are huge advocates of our pastoral care at this University so we will be doing anything and everything to ensure we look after the mental health of all our staff, and at times we need to be sure there aren't ulterior agendas at play, but look, let's all enjoy our night.*

It's doubtful, with all the money in the gala room, that anyone would stick their neck above the parapet. They had all invested in Neurolume, either unwittingly or not. By aligning themselves with the University, they had been implicit in it all. Their dreams had to stay alive. This building that had represented everything they wanted to be, either in their own lives or by association. Elite. The best, according to their own admissions process. Always just out of people's reach, dangling its philosophical self and its realised bricks and mortar into the hopes and dreams of people around the world. Or investing into others who were changing lives. The best by proxy. I listen to Harley's voice which has taken on a particularly sinister tone. 'Please, carry on the party.' Then Abraham lets out a sigh of relief as 'Twist and Shout' belts out of the speakers placed in all corners of the room. The guests start to cheer and whoop, stamp their feet on the floor. I feel the bass right through my body. Despite everything, I applaud myself as the smoke machines hiss and a saxophone plays over the top of the music. It has all worked. Everything I put into place. Even the @StudentInvigilatorX thread.

Finally, there's a bang at the door. Lavinia.

'Come in.' Abraham's voice is muffled behind his hand before turning to me. 'All this goddamn time.' I can see the tiny thread veins where his nose meets his cheek. 'All this fucking time,' he has the dignity to look at Lavinia after his expletive-ridden outburst. 'I knew. I knew you were trouble. The minute I saw you. Whining that you wanted this and that.' I don't have the energy to either reply or stand up. Jeff hasn't said a word, biting the inside of his cheek. 'And the amount of shit of yours I've had to sweep up. Are you even aware?'

'My dear,' Lavinia appears. She presses her hands against my arms and shoots Abraham a steely look.

'Please get off me,' I say as calmly as I can manage though my body is trembling.

'Dear, listen,' she carries on soothing. 'We're all on your side. Whatever you need, we'll give it to you. Anything at all. Any job role. Anything. We want you to be happy here. To relish in this wonderful space around us. We're doing such life-changing work. Don't you want to be a part of that too? Remember what I said? About your feminine power? This place needs that. It needs you.'

'Well…' I stop. I think of the videos I've just played of the fellowship recipients. The groundbreaking work they were doing. How they've also been unwittingly pulled into the game. 'It is rather wonderful. Watching them,' and for a split second, Lavinia thinks she's got me. 'It makes good business sense for you, doesn't it?' I spit. 'The Fellowships. Gets people flocking to you from all around the globe. You make quite the name for yourselves. And the Wickham Wing. Your shiny new baby.' I laugh, a wretched kind of sound. 'You thought you could put words into my mouth in that magazine.'

'I thought…' Lavinia tightens her mouth. 'I thought you were going to steer the ship as effectively as Suzy did.'

This time I've braced myself for that particular attack. 'I'm fine as I am,' I tell her. I stand up and they all move back a step, unsure what I'm going to do next. Abraham has pulled out his phone, no doubt masterminding his next move. 'And you,' I snarl. 'Abraham. Conspiring to take me down in public. Then lying about it. Gaslighting me.' But he's barely listening, instead staring at his screen with this weird, creepy smile on his face as though he knows a secret I don't or as if he's outwitted me. He's almost laughing. I launch myself at him.

'Look.' Jeff holds out his hands again, but that makes me even more furious. 'Lizzie Lou. Sit down.' He pushes my shoulders so I'm forced to take a seat. 'Let me take you home.'

'Wait.' Abraham steps forward, the smug smile still on his face. 'We need the password changed back. On the Student Invigilator X account. Neither of you can go until then.'

'No,' I snarl. 'No. Not until you get those damn drugs put back into the clinical trial and you do it properly.'

'So you can carry on your lover's good name and work?' Abraham sneers. 'Don't worry, Lavinia,' he carries on. 'I'll sort this. I've got some good ideas about how to work this out.' I try and work out what Abraham would do next. 'You've got scandal written right next to your name, after all,' Abraham smiles. 'Lots of it. People love a good old gossip. They really do. Give them some of that and they'll forget all about their moral nudge from you over here. Drugs having bad side effects? What do people care that much? It's never stopped them before, has it? You think people are going to stop getting high because they've seen a few scary pictures? Woooo.' He waves his fingers around in a faux-spectral fashion. 'And you, my friend, are the perfect fodder for that. You're now in the public domain don't forget.' I watch Abraham, his mouth moving, cheeks flushed. It's like he's forgotten entirely that any of us are here.

'The magazine? That was a stroke of genius. People know who you are. And your face is all over the internet now in relation to your boyfriend. That's the interesting story, dear. You. You're the story here. Not some people off their heads because they've maxed out on Neurolume dosage. Which is what half these people have done. You know that, don't you? There are clear instructions about usage here and keeping within the confines of recommended dosage. These people are shovelling pills down their throats like there's no tomorrow. Mixing it with all sorts. You think they're telling the truth about their drug intake? You think they're going to turn around and say, "Yes. Yes, I OD'd because I was also mainlining MDMA, ketamine and cocaine."' He doesn't stop. I'm as horrified as I am fascinated. 'Do you know what you've done? You've made yourself look even more of a goddamn idiot.'

I wonder how I can get in touch with Harbottle.

'A meddling one at that,' Abraham spits. 'You have no idea what you're dealing with or what you're doing. You think because your lover had some misplaced sense of moral duty that he was actually right?' He stops and shuts his eyes. 'You have no idea who he is. You have no idea at all.' I open my mouth to ask him to tell me, but he carries on. 'We cleaned up that sordid little affair of yours. You know that the hacks were sniffing around that story? Someone in Newton's office squealed, apparently. People were talking. I released it on X so they wouldn't get there first. We were protecting you. We made you the story to protect you. So you wouldn't be thrown to the wolves and this is how you repay us?' I look at Jeff, willing Abraham to stop. 'And don't worry your little head, Jeff knows everything. You think all your goings-on would remain a secret? In fact, I'd go so far as to say—'

'What?' My voice shakes. What do you mean?'

'Jeff. You knew?'

'Look, stop. Abraham, just stop.' Jeff takes my arm. 'I did what was—'

'You knew? All this time?' I say, horrified. So many betrayals already and still room for more. 'Let me get this straight. You knew I'd been—'

'Yes.' Abraham gives a mean laugh. 'Yes. He knew. All right?'

The cold, clinical way Jeff had been with me that night makes sense now. The first time we'd slept together after you died. The rigidity of his movements. He'd been almost angry. He'd used me as a vessel with the knowledge that I had been sleeping with another man, and yet he hadn't cared enough to call me out. Hadn't cared enough to ask me to stop. He cared more about the University. About keeping his own house in order. His own ambition.

'The babies? Our baby?' I whisper. His skin reddens and he has the decency to look down at the floor. 'My God, that was all a…'

I think I'm about to faint or be sick. It's too much information to process.

'Charade? That was all a charade. The adoption?' My voice is strangled as it comes out.

'I would have done. I was going to. I was going to do it. For you,' Jeff adds reluctantly. 'For this place,' he pleads.

What is it about this institution that has ensnared him too? That has held us all in its narcissistic embrace? I wrap my arms around myself and start to dry-heave. No one comes forward to comfort me.

'We're going to need the phone. It's not your property.' Abraham holds his hand out. He's still shaking with rage. 'Then we're going to need you to give us the password. That's also a private account. Oh wait, Newton. He's outside.' Abraham starts towards the door. 'So unless you'd like us to...'

I think about what else could unravel in front of Jeff. That I'd already seen Newton on my own terms? Except now I'm sure my husband also knew about that already.

'You nearly destroyed everything.' Abraham's voice is quiet now, and he sounds as if he's the one who's been betrayed. 'I'll never forgive you. Everything we've worked for. You decided you'd just try and wreck my entire life because you were sleeping with someone,' he hisses. 'And you thought you knew best. Every single thing I've worked for. Now hand over the damn phone before you do more damage. You think you're saving lives? You're causing more harm than you could possibly know. So hand it over.'

I ignore him, wondering if he's bluffing. Logging in to the phone, I go to Photos. There's the picture of the two of us the first time we met at that first fundraiser. The backs of our heads. At first, I hadn't been so sure it was us, but I'd looked at it a few times, replaying the scene again and again. The way you'd looked at me. The way we'd both known.

I glance up at Abraham and then back down at the photo. It's only then I realise that he is there. In the picture. He's facing the photographer. And his gaze is on us. How could I not have noticed that before? He's staring at us talking. I'd been so wrapped up in looking at you and me, I'd never noticed him in the photo before. He knew. About you and me. He knew. He knew from the beginning. Or even…

'Yes.' Abraham feigns a yawn. 'You were perfectly matched.'

I think back to when you and I first met. I had been the one to go up to you.

'I told him,' Abraham snaps. 'I told him you might need a helping hand. That you were a fish out of water and that he was to make himself clearly available to you. Of course I knew. Your type. Thought it would keep you busy whilst we let Jeff do his job. Keep you looking a certain way because you weren't doing much else, were you?'

'You didn't.'

And it's this that feels the cruellest. That Abraham had orchestrated our love for one another. Had I been that obvious? Career stalemate. Giving everything to ensure her husband was top dog. Older woman. I was easy pickings. I let out a gasp.

And had you seen me a mile off? Someone Abraham could use to keep me occupied? To keep me out of trouble so he could concentrate on Jeff and their ambitions for the University?

'And it's not the first time either, is it?' Abraham looks at me. I blush and look at Jeff. 'You've got form. You just used to be better at hiding it. I thought you two would keep each other occupied. Unfortunately, you screwed things up when you decided you were too high and mighty to carry on with your little affair.' He sneers at that last word. 'Password.' Abraham holds the phone near my hand. 'Now.'

William Harbottle. At this moment, he will probably be ferociously getting his editorial checked. Double-checked. I have to comply and play the game a little bit longer I can't risk jeopardising his part in this, but the anger snaking through me is making me feel faint. With shaking hands, I take the phone and unlock the X account and set it up for Abraham to change the password. By now, the entire globe will have seen it anyway, and I have nothing to gain by refusing. He snatches it back and taps something onto the screen.

'Jeff. You need to go back out.' Abraham nods towards the door. 'You're the face of tonight. Sort it out somehow. I'll take Elizabeth home. Escort her off the premises.' The colour has leached from his face. Jeff looks at me and shakes his head as Abraham pulls me by the elbow.

I hear Lavinia in the background. 'Lucky we sorted that little issue out. I always knew she was going to be a problem. I'm sorry, Jeff, to have to say that to you.'

The door swings open, and the noise and heat hit me. Abraham takes me around the side of the room through a fire exit, out into the cool night air around us. I think about the moment everything changed. That exclamation mark in Jeff's text message. That tiny omen that was a signifier of something none of us at — Medical School could understand. All playing into the machinations of something much bigger, the threads of the story pulling us tightly into their bonds as the walls of that great establishment created its own, juggernaut narrative.

27.

'In!'

Abraham slams the car door to the passenger side on me, as though I'm a child. I feel exposed in the green dress Suzy bought me, the leather seat sticking to my skin. He pulls off his black bow tie, throwing it into the back before getting into the driver's seat. The door lock clicks. I say nothing. I look out the car window, the building bathed in deep red lights. Abraham starts up the engine, and a male voice echoes out the car radio. I realise it's Jeff on a podcast, discussing AI in medicine and the Fellowships Scheme. Abraham jabs at the car screen and it powers down before he revs up the engine and pulls out the driveway. The bass is still pumping out the Medical School building, blasts of sound getting louder every few minutes as someone comes outside. We exit campus onto the main road, flashes of headlights passing us by as we make our way to The Lodge.

'You aren't getting away with this,' I state flatly. 'None of it. If you think you are, you're mistaken. I've got nothing to lose now.'

I look at Abraham's side profile; his jaw is clenched shut.

'Have I hit a nerve? I'm not someone you can keep down, you know. I'm not someone you can just shut up.' I can hear myself getting more and more frantic. 'You think I'm stupid? That you could make me think people were taking the wrong dosage and that I'd shut up?'

'No idea what you're talking about.' Abraham indicates and swings out of the campus. 'None. Now, if you don't mind, it's been a long day.' I watch as he turns the radio to Classic Moves. 'That's better. I'm going to drop you straight home.'

'I'm not leaving your car until you tell me who did it. Until you tell me what...' I try to keep my voice neutral, knowing that Abraham will have more control over me if he detects any panic in it. 'Until you tell me what happened to him.'

His mouth sets. 'Again, Elizabeth, no idea what you're talking about.'

'Tell me.' My core steels up into something totally unrecognisable. 'Now.'

'You like Brahms?' He turns up the volume. 'Your husband introduced me to this.' He starts to hum along, singing louder and louder as we drive through the dark roads. We're about fifteen minutes away from The Lodge. I grip the seat. I have no phone and I'm starting to feel the pitch of fear at the base of my spine as the velvety dark closes in on us.

'Tell me.' I grab his arm. 'Tell me. Now.'

Abraham tenses up, making the car swerve. 'Jesus damn Christ.' He gives a small laugh. 'What the hell are you doing? God, you really do need reining in, don't you?' But instead of slowing, he presses his foot down on the accelerator. 'Going to get you home soon. Calm the hell down. You're going to get us both killed if you carry on like this.'

Something is unleashed in me as he carries on speaking. 'You tell me!' I scream. 'You tell me who the hell did this. Who killed him!' I unbuckle my seat belt and move closer. I can see his pores now. 'Tell me, or I'll tell the world you did it. I know it was one of you. Who. Who carried out the hit?'

'And they'll believe you?!' Abraham laughs again. 'The picture we're going to paint of you as a madwoman, saying that the most respected university in the world had a hand in killing one of their staff members? Get real, Elizabeth.' He almost sounds hysterical now. 'People already think you've totally lost the plot.'

'They will believe me. You messed up, you see.' I start laughing myself. 'Truly. You messed up.' Abraham swerves again. 'And as I said to you, I have nothing to lose. It's already being looked into. Newton's counterpart.' The car jolts, almost undetectably. 'Tell me and I'll pull the evidence.'

'You don't have any evidence,' Abraham presses the accelerator again. 'Newton thinks you're crazy too.'

'You think?' I laugh, this time a manic sound that has no end, even though I know Abraham has one over me and he's probably right.

'Try me.' I will myself to sit back in my seat so as not to give him more ammunition. I hold firm in myself, embodying the Medical School as a whole. After all, I'm in the position of power here, being married to the president, something I seem to have forgotten in the past few weeks. I've let my own feelings of impotence mean they've got away with it for far too long now. 'Tell me,' I repeat. 'Tell me who did it. Or I will kill you with my own bare hands.' Abraham laughs again, a long, drawn-out sound as he bangs the steering wheel with his fists.

'Don't. I've told you, Elizabeth, you're playing a dangerous game here. Just leave it and get back to—' He waves a hand at me.

'Get back to what?' I hiss.

'Well, you won't be back on-site for a while after that silly little stunt you pulled at the gala.' Abraham grips the steering wheel harder. 'Really silly. You don't know what you're dealing with. I've told you. Just step back.'

The music crescendos, and for a second neither of us hear it. A ringing sound.

'Where's my damn cell?' Abraham looks around, and I see it before he does. His sleek, gunmetal-grey handset, nestled in the middle compartment between us, upright in the drink holder.

I look down. Jeff. My husband is calling Abraham. Grabbing the phone, I look at the screen before tapping on it to answer, except I don't manage to hit the green call icon.

'Give it here,' Abraham commands, and I can see I've trapped him. He swerves the car again. 'My cell. Give it to me now.' He holds out his hand, chest rising and falling. 'Elizabeth!'

'It's my husband,' I tell him. 'I think I should answer.' And as I'm about to tap on the screen again and look for the loudspeaker button, I feel the roughness of Abraham's right hand on my arm.

'Give that to me now.'

I swing my arm away from him, curling into the corner of my seat.

'Give it to me or—'

'Or what?' I answer the call. 'Jeff?' I say sweetly, but he's hung up. 'Damn, it looks like I missed the call, but that's all right.' I take the phone and start scrolling through his messages before the screen locks me out. 'Interesting.' I nudge Abraham away again as he tries to grab the phone off me.

He softens, trying a different tack. 'Look, Elizabeth, just give it back.'

'Oh wow,' I tell him. 'You've got some good stuff on here.' I click on his search history and glance through, gasping at what I've seen, but before I can take a proper look, I feel Abraham pinching at my arm.

'Don't you damn well dare,' he shouts. I carry on covering the phone with my arm, taunting him, realising it's way simpler to get at Abraham than I'd ever thought. I grab tight as he pulls at my arm again, squeezing my bare skin. I feel the pressure of his fingertips and I'm reminded of you, the day of Jeff's presidential appointment; the way you'd pressed your thumb into my wrist. I hold the phone between my hands as tightly as I can as Abraham seems to inexplicably speed up the car even more.

'Wow, who knew.' I laugh again, scrolling through his messages. 'That you held all these secrets. Who you really are.' And before I can say any more, I feel a force around my neck. I'm about to tell him it's a stupid thing to do. That his handprints would be visible to all. But I realise it must mean there's something on his phone that he'll stop at no lengths to hide. Just as I turn my head towards him, I feel the pull of the car as he yanks the steering wheel away from something in the road, and our eyes meet. My life becomes a series of freeze frames as everything kaleidoscopes in front of me, time contracting into something non-linear. And all I can think is that I've got Abraham's phone and I can't let it go. I squeeze tight, bracing myself. Segments of narrative flash through my mind. You. Us together. All at odds with what I see in front of me; a slow reckoning. The grey tarmac twisting upside down as the car caves in on itself. A strange sound next to me. Abraham. The crunch of something non-metallic. The blast of an airbag, the hiss as it inflates. The car is on its side, Abraham right cheek upwards. Still, I squeeze the phone in my hand. It would just take tiny movements, minuscule flexes of my muscles to press the three digits I'd need in order to get help. But something in my brain isn't connecting. I turn to face Abraham again. His neck is at a strange angle, face squashed against the inflated white material like some melted puppet. Everything is pitch-black around us. His eyelids twitch once, twice, and I can see the tiny movement in his throat, a sound escaping from deep within his belly. There's something truly repugnant about the flesh around his face, the hunted look in his eyes. A thin dribble of clear liquid releases itself from his nose. 'Eli...' he gasps. 'My...' He doesn't continue. I stare at him, the memories of the past few weeks playing through my mind. The moment I'd seen you lying in the dirt. My love. I look down at my own body. It seems like I'm unscathed, my body inured by the adrenaline and shock. I move my legs. My arms. There's blood all over my left thigh, my green dress has a huge rip in the side, and when I press my finger to my left nostril I feel warm, damp liquid, but I think I'm all right. Everything's working.

'Donny,' Abraham whispers. 'Donny.' He blinks slowly, his eyes vacant. He reminds me of those countless images and videos I've seen of people on Neurolume, souls dissipating from physical form. 'Donny,' he says again. 'Tell him...' The phone goes again. Our gazes meet.

'Jeff,' I say. I wait for it to ring out, wondering what the hell could be so urgent that he's called three times in a row. There's another strange sound from Abraham, and my finger hovers over the keypad. Three digits. That's all it would take. It's deathly quiet outside. The trees hang over us, and there are lights in the distance. Somewhere, about five minutes away, is my home.

'Please,' Abraham gasps. 'Please.' I stare at him, dangling the phone in front of his face. 'Give it.' A strange rattling sound is coming from his chest.

'No.' I shake my head. 'An eye for an eye,' I whisper. I sit, wondering if a car will pass us. Will they find me, unwilling to call for help? I stare at him again as his eyes start closing, opening, and then a surge of energy rises from within him.

'Elizabeth. Give me the damn cell.'

His voice fades. I move my hand over to him. His skin is cool, clammy to the touch. I wrap my hand around his right wrist. I feel the faint thread of a pulse. Abraham hangs on to life. I feel a kick of power. I squeeze his wrist tighter. Just a few more seconds. Then I'll call for help. A few more seconds. Everything sharpens around me. The phone is cool in my hands, its screen casting an eerie glow in the car, a digital halo around Abraham's pale face.

I lean my head back against the headrest, which is now at an angle, and think of you again. I'm sorry they murdered you for doing the right thing. I hear your voice. *I love you, Elizabeth.* The touch of you on my skin. The rhythmic meeting of our bodies. And your voicemail on my phone. Your last gasps for air. Your last words. And now, here I am, again listening to the desperate sounds of someone struggling to breathe.

I hold Abraham's phone before reaching over and placing his fingertip gently on the screen. It unlocks and I go to the Settings page, changing the fingerprint lock to my own personal PIN. It is mine now to keep. I hear the distant sound of a car. I type in 911. I watch Abraham's face, listen to the shudder of his breath.

I think of you again.

Just a few more seconds.

28.

'I want her checked over again.'

For the past half an hour, Jeff has been sitting on the end of my bed as I've been pretending to sleep and trying not to trigger even more pain by coughing. Now he's outside my hospital room and I strain to hear the conversation between him and the consultant, Mr Uko.

'Three broken ribs?' I listen to Jeff. 'Any concussion? Second opinion? Scans?'

The door opens and footsteps hurry towards my bed. Then Jeff again.

'Tell her I'll come and see her in a minute. Phone call. Keep her resting, please.'

'Hello, Elizabeth,' says a bright, female voice. 'Would you like some pain relief? Those ribs of yours are going to be sore. If I could get you sitting up a bit more? She taps me on the shoulder. I consider not responding to her, pretending to be asleep, but she's already plumping my pillows, moving my sheets up the bed.

'It's not Neurolume, is it?' I whisper, managing a tiny laugh. She doesn't respond, instead, placing a plastic thermometer in my ear. 'Good. Perfect temperature,' she says, wrapping a cuff around my arm and clipping an oxygen monitor on the tip of my index finger.

'Well, it looks like you're in excellent health,' she says. 'Quite the shock you had there. Your husband' – she places her own fingertips gently on the inner side of my wrist – 'he told me to tell you he's coming back to see you soon. Think someone's come to visit him. Nice strong pulse.' She counts and I think back to the way I gripped Abraham's wrist. I start to tremble.

'Who?' I whisper, even though I don't want to know the answer. 'Look, is it all right if I have a rest? No visitors. Not my husband, not anyone,' I beg, avoiding the question I simply can't bear to ask: is he alive?

I lie there, my legs twitching, moving around to try and quell the agitation that I now am a fully-fledged murderer. That my action – or inaction – has ended someone's life. My presence had already contributed to the chain of events that led to not only your death but had wider ramifications for the University and beyond. People's lives are at stake with Neurolume, and here I am with yet more blood on my hands.

Newton's voice comes from outside my room and I twist the sheets in between my fingers.

'No one, okay? I think it'll make me feel even worse.'

'Of course.' She places a hand on my forehead. 'I'll make sure no one comes in right now. Just rest. I'll ask that they give you some peace and quiet and I'll leave you to sleep.' She opens the door. Hushed conversation. The occasional beep of a monitor in my room. Newton's voice carrying.

Abraham's blood alcohol limit. Way over, he's saying. Just spoken to doctor. Terrible. Dangerous driving. Did you know?

I think back to Abraham's odd behaviour. The swerving of the car. The way he held his hands around my neck. I wonder how he would put his own spin on this.

'Look, I'm sorry, lieutenant,' the nurse is saying. 'Yes. I do understand the import. As I've said, you can go in in an hour or so. But she's not having any visitors right now. It's important that she gets a proper rest before you talk to her.'

Then the door closes and I only catch bits of the conversation. Something about Abraham. Something about not telling me yet. I strain my ears but the voices fade off into the distance along with the echo of footsteps down the corridor and I'm still left with the uncertainty as to whether he's dead or alive. When I'm sure there's no one around and using my left elbow, I drag myself across the bed slowly, carefully, wincing with pain, my limbs dragging but my mind going at full pelt. I manage to lift myself up, unlocking the bedside table drawer next to me before sliding out Abraham's phone.

Lying back in position, I prop myself up so I can see out of the windows around me. When I'm sure it's safe, I use the personal PIN I set up on Abraham's phone to access everything there is on there, and for the next half an hour I plough through all his data and communications. I use all the tricks you taught me on how to keep our affair top secret, along with the tips Laura had shown me when I'd been getting the USB unencrypted. Abraham has done well. Uploaded things onto the Dark Web. Hidden apps behind other apps. Locked his Telegram so it couldn't be accessed. But I find other clues, piecing together bits of evidence which make me wonder exactly how deep he is in all of this. I do a search on my name in his emails and WhatsApps, which he's surprisingly kept open, skimming through all the text and working out where everything fits in and all the bits of the puzzle that are accessible to me now. As I'm going through it all, I hear someone coming in, so I slide the phone under my pillow and feign sleep, rousing only slightly.

'Thank you,' I whisper, my voice hoarse as the nurse brings a cup of water to my mouth. 'Tired. Sleep more,' I tell her, grateful she hasn't asked to take my pulse again, which feels like it's thudding around my body at what I'd discovered on Abraham's phone.

'I can let you sleep all day and night, but for the moment...' She glances towards the door. 'Lieutenant Newton does need to see you. Just briefly.'

'All right,' I whimper. 'Please bring my husband in too.'

'Elizabeth.' Jeff swings the door open five minutes later and an antiseptic breeze hits me. 'I'm here with Lieutenant Newton. Are we all right to talk now?'

'Yes,' I mutter weakly. I can't let any part of me belie how I'm feeling and everything I now know. I thought the USB you'd given me would have been the end of it. And now, now this.

'Listen,' Newton stands by my bed, hands clasped behind his back. 'Ma'am. I'm sorry to have to ask you a few questions when you're like this,' he points to the bed. 'But I suppose you'd like an update on Abraham. Has Mr Uko told you?'

Jeff and Newton glance at each other. I shake my head.

'Look, there is no easy way to say this.' I clutch at the phone, thinking about everything I've found on Abraham's device so far. I'll have to contact Laura and get the rest of the info downloaded from it.

'And I know there might be such a thing as guilt that you got off this so,' Newton makes a gesture towards my ribs. 'Not lightly, but,' he bows his head. Have I killed him? 'He's had a bad bleed on the brain, and we're not sure,' Newton starts to choke up, and I remember they've known each other for years. 'I'm sorry.' He clears his throat. 'We're not sure he's going to make it.'

'Right.' I turn to face the left wall, terrified that if Abraham's alive, it'll all come out that I left him to die. That it will be my word against his and once again I'll be trapped in his lair. I touch the phone again and squeeze my eyes shut. 'What's the likelihood? I mean, is there a good chance he'll…' I can't bring myself to say either 'live' or 'die'. 'How likely?'

'I'm sorry,' Newton says again. 'We don't know, but it's not looking good. And I'm sorry about this too, but I do need to ask you some questions about the accident. I'm interested if Abraham mentioned alcohol at all before he got in the car with you.' It seems now that things have totally changed. Newton is interested in protecting Abraham's interests rather than questioning me and my involvement in the crash.

'He did say he'd been drinking a bit,' I push, praying Abraham would have forgotten everything if he ever did wake up fully. 'And come to think of it, he seemed a bit—'

'A bit…?' Jeff looks at me.

'He was talking a lot. Telling me things I was surprised about. Nothing you need to know about,' I say quickly, looking at Newton as Jeff's shoulders slightly relax. 'Stuff about the University. As he was dropping me off.'

'And just before the crash?' Newton continues. 'We've been down to the site. We can't see anything that might have led up to it. The tyre marks suggest he might have been avoiding something on the road. But we can't see any animal tracks or anything. Could you tell us what happened?'

'I'm so sorry. I don't remember a thing,' I lie, remembering the give of his flesh after pressing his finger to open up his phone's home screen. 'I think I blacked out. I can't seem to remember those last minutes.' I don't look at either of them. 'I only remember waking up and not knowing where I was.'

I think of Abraham's lessons about not saying too much. Being direct. Not being too wordy when being questioned. It puts you into a defensive positioning he'd always told us. I open my mouth but will myself to remain silent.

'That's not a surprise, is it?' Jeff reaches over and places a hand over my arm. I look down at the plastic bracelet around my wrist. Elizabeth Harker. DOB 22.10.1989. 'The doctor says you'll have residual trauma for a while. We're going to get you a talking therapist as well as an occupational one.' He looks at me. 'I feel terrible. I should have insisted on driving you. I had no idea he was over the limit. I feel like we're to blame.'

'Don't,' I manage not to sound too convincing. 'It's not your fault.' It was in my best interest for Jeff to feel in part culpable, so I retained some power over him. Not that I know if he's being disingenuous. I hold my left side and twist myself in the bed. Jeff finally gets the message.

'Look, I think we'd best leave her now,' Jeff says as he looks at Newton. 'And in any case, Donny and Abraham's mom,' he carries on. 'They want to come and see you. To say thank you. For doing all you could to save him. They know how frightened you must have been.' He points to my three broken ribs. 'How much it must have taken to call for help. They said you were holding his hand when they arrived. I'm not sure if you remember.' I shake my head.

'Right, Newton,' Jeff guides the lieutenant to the door. 'Thank you so much. I'll see Elizabeth gets some more rest now.' Newton nods and leaves the room, and Jeff comes back to my bedside. 'Here.' He passes me his phone. I scan through the words on the screen. 'To give you a break. And then it's time we put everything behind us. Don't you think? Everything that's gone on? No more...' He clears his throat. 'No more interest outside of our marriage. Let's focus on you and me, and this place. We can't afford any more—'

'Bad press?' I wince, trying to digest the words he wrote earlier that evening:

> Dear All (Staff, Governors, Students, and Alumni),
>
> Please find a letter attached from our University president, Jeffrey Harker, co-signed by Kevin Tang, Dean of the Medical School, and the Governors.
>
> Dear All,
>
> We write to inform you that Elizabeth Harker, wife of Jeffrey, our University president, will be taking a leave of absence. We do hope you'll join us in wishing Elizabeth all the best during her time away from the University, and we look forward to welcoming her back when she is ready.
>
> Sincerely,
>
> Jeffrey Harker, Kevin Tang, and the Governors
>
> Medical School Winner – Rosemont Development Award 2026
>
> *NYT* Number One University Endowment Fund in the USA! Donate here.

'Yes. Bad press. Listen.' Jeff pats my shoulder as though I'm a child. 'I'm sorry. I really am. That I didn't drive you. I'd seen him have a drink. Just didn't think after.' He doesn't explicitly reference what I did at the gala. Can't bring himself to, I realise.

'But you can relax now. Take your time to get better. Learn what is important to you. How we can make this world a better place than when we started here.' He takes my hand. 'We make a good team. Both of us. The things that happened, perhaps they were meant to happen for a reason. A clean slate.' Was he talking about my affair with you? Or everything I'd subsequently discovered about the University. I open my mouth to start talking but he carries on. 'Look. I've made up my mind. We need to do what's right. We can work out together what we believe that to be. But I need you, Elizabeth. I can't do this without you. You're the sole reason I'm here.' I remind him that this part is untrue. That he was filled with ambition the minute he set foot in this place and I've simply supported him with that.

'What about what I need?'

I look at Jeff's face, pleading at me. I think of you. You'd never have said such a thing, because it would have always been about me. What I'd desired. Us.

'That goes without saying.' He squeezes his fingers around mine, his gold wedding band cool on my skin. 'I was just saying how important you are to me. To this place. We can make a real difference. In whichever way you choose.' He stares at my face. 'I see now that maybe Abraham was too wrapped up in things here. We need someone like you. We can work on our marriage however you see fit. As long as...'

I feel the pull of my thought process towards familiarity; to keep going with the status quo that had been and gone before, me propping up Jeff's ego, but then I remember everything I'd been through. Your death would not be in vain.

'I want you to understand that I know everything,' I tell him. 'And I will not answer to you. Or anyone. So please, for once,' I wince as my ribs start to pound. 'Be honest about you and me. And about what you want from this place.'

'I want this to work,' he says. 'We have to make this work. We're a team and we always have been and if we keep things discreet, with some ground rules, we can do exactly that. Make it more than work. Create our legacy.'

'All right,' I tell him.

'I know I may not be young. Like him,' there's something resigned in his voice. 'But it takes a lot to run the University. And your home is within it now. With me,' he implores. 'In The Lodge. Whatever happens? All right? I'm your family. And I do want kids with you. Not just to make you happy.'

He guides his hand around the room, an imagined backdrop of our self-created perfection. I do not believe a word my husband is saying. The insinuation being that I do not have a choice about my own future and that it lies solely with him. That I am still a player within the University. It has reeled me in, and I sense that my time within its walls, not over yet.

The Day After the Gala

29.

The next day, I get a hospital visit from Lavinia. She's dressed as though she's on her way to a smart business meeting. A white, woollen skirt and jacket, her hair neatly coiffed into two tortoiseshell clips. I feel vulnerable and exposed lying on the bed in my hospital gown, but I remind myself of Abraham's phone and the power that lies within it.

'Dear.' She holds a newspaper under her arm. 'I just wanted to see how you are.'

'I'm fine,' I tell her. We make small talk. She tells me about her morning by the sea with her nephew. The cool breeze that has started across the land. A new restaurant she'd discovered.

'Abraham,' I tell her in the midst of a silence. 'I want you to know he told me everything. Absolutely everything.' I keep my head still. 'I think he saw that car ride as a confessional. He told me everything you all did. All the details.

I know. I know you were all in on it. I know it was him. Abraham. Who organised the stabbing. I know all of you knew. In parts. That it was happening.'

Lavinia looks to the door and shakes her head. I think of the information I'd seen on his cell. The routes he'd located, scoured and arranged for the coaches to come and collect us from the hall after you'd been stabbed. The policy that had been worded and reworded and sent round to Lavinia and Jeff for approval several times in the lead-up to your death, so everything was watertight in the event of 'anything untoward happening at the University'. The policy had been changed two or three times in those preceding days. It was why Jeff and Abraham knew what to do. It was why their actions were so smooth after that knife lodged itself deep into your flesh. My husband and his director of communications. Brilliant in the face of a crisis. A crisis that had been honed, planned and brilliantly executed to the second. I had found Abraham's internet searches on the Dark Web. Bitcoin payments to other countries. Nothing explicit about your death. Only a trail of scattered clues.

'He told me because he knew I had nothing to lose.'

I wonder if she'll call my bluff.

'And because he was drunk.'

'He did, did he?' I watch Lavinia's skin stain pink, the most I've ever seen her lose control. 'And there I was thinking he had dedicated his entire life to us. There's such a thing as too much loyalty, you know. And what do you want from all this?'

'I'm not going to say anything,' I tell her. 'I've tried that one already.' I think back to Abraham's words in the car. Him telling me they would paint me out to be a mad-woman. *Get real, Elizabeth. People already think you've totally lost the plot.* We both go silent and like I had been with you, safe with the thought that we both have something to lose should we ever speak out about the truth. The silence is punctuated by the beep of the monitor.

'Look. I'll leave you with this, shall I?' Somehow the power between us has evened out. Untucking the newspaper from under her arm, she slides it onto the tabletop next to me and taps on the paper. I watch her disappear, before I pick it up and read the words on the front page.

The Gazette

Painkiller or Party Drug that's 'killing thousands.' Inside Elite University 'Neurolume' Scandal.

By William Harbottle

Elite — University and Medical School faces questions over its role in the research and development of new drug Neurolume, a breakthrough in pain management, simultaneously touted as a nootropic for cognitive enhancement. Marketed for its benefits of providing non-addictive pain relief, as well combined with similarities to Adderall in memory and focus, the drug has been hailed as a game changer in medical science. However, documents seen by this newspaper show that the results of clinical trials conducted in the —

> *Medical School's Franklin Wing last year, may have been manipulated considerably to downplay serious side effects including dependency, a 'high risk' of psychotic episodes due to the pain relief element, and even death, outside of external regulations.*
>
> *A significant donor to the University's ongoing build of its new 'Wickham Wing' which is hailed as revolutionary in the field of teaching and medicine also has strong ties to the outcome of the trial data. Neurolume is also said to have had a large impact on recreational use, in clubs and raves because it induces feelings of euphoria similar to MDMA says one user. 'And my brain is still as sharp as a tack. Honestly, it's amazing.'*

I read through the rest of the article. I read about how the actual manipulation of trial data is a grey area, calling into question the ethics of the Medical School. There's no mention of you and your change of heart. William had told me it would be libel and that it was not possible but online, they've linked past stories about the University and Medical School under the 'Read more' section. Six highlighted articles about your death. The narrative was implicit. That your death and the Medical School's trial data were linked.

While I'm at it, I log on to the F&L Pharmaceuticals industry & Biotechnology index. Share prices in Helianthus have gone up since William's piece has been published and my little stunt at the gala. His feature seems to have had the opposite effect to what he'd intended, with Neurolume sales skyrocketing, as well as those of Aurelia Wellness, the shadow subsidiary company of Helianthus which used its ring to collect personal data, no doubt that they could then feed back into their own research. Something surfaces in the back of my mind and I click back onto @ StudentInvigilatorX's profile. 'Abraham', as I now know, had been telling his followers you had been stealing and selling drugs, and further down in his comments and replies he had started to mention the drug by name. #Neurolume, the new 'drug of choice' for all University students who wanted to 'kill a hangover headache and still be able to concentrate on a lecture'. I think about how appealing that would sound to the masses, to all the students who frequented the nightclubs in town or stayed up partying on campus, and about the crossover with those who fed into crime conspiracy theories.

The hashtag #Neurolume had been used thousands of times in @StudentInvigilatorX's profile. Your death and my actions last night worked absolute wonders for the drug, predominantly in the recreational sphere. So did Abraham in his strokes of utter genius on X. I google Jeff's book. Once a dead fish in the water, that is also stealthily creeping up the Amazon charts. I watch as the number of people talking about the drug rise. TikTok videos are going viral. People at raves, having the time of their lives. *This is amazing. Wild!* They're all saying. What have we done? We've started something. And we've wreaked havoc.

I'm devastated to say that your death was entirely in vain. And the ensuing whistle-blowing has served only those we've been trying to expose.

***

The day afterwards, a piece appears on the University website about the accident. I read the last paragraph twice over.

> Mr Cohen is currently under the rehabilitation arm of Maiden Valley Hospital and will not be returning to his position at our University. We wish him all the best and thank him for all his work and dedication to our educational establishment.
>
> Signed – the Governors.

I wonder who was behind the announcement. Jeff hadn't said a word about it. They'd thrown Abraham under a bus whilst using his own distraction techniques against further scrutiny. His own. Despite his loyalty to the University, he too has been dispensable, in order to protect the great Wickham legacy. How many lives in exchange for a reputation? No one, it seems, is immune.

Six Weeks After the Gala

30.

'Thank you, everybody.' I hold up the heavy glass globe and scan the audience in front of me, the crowd spotlit under soft yellow lights. I've had my hair done. Softly waved. I've even bought a beautiful new shimmering gold dress, courtesy of the clothing budget allocated a week earlier. I've been given a shiny new green credit card that has been put to good use. Megan came to do my make-up. I haven't let myself think of you once for the entire lead-up to the event. Jeff and I even arrived together to the huge, sparkling celebration held at the Rivermead Hotel, its front draped with an enormous purple and silver metallic crested banner. THE USA MEDICAL SCHOOL AWARDS, 2026. Then, in smaller writing, SPONSORED BY KOOKABURRA FOODS. The ceremony opens to the sound of Max Richter being blared through the speakers. I'm in prime position at the front, ready to make my speech, which I've actually written and rehearsed, and so when my name is called I hold my head up high and make my way up the huge central staircase and stand overlooking the crowd of people.

'Ladies and gentlemen.' I speak clearly, loudly, at the podium. 'I am so deeply honoured to accept this award tonight on behalf of Abraham Cohen, for best Marketing and Communications Strategy for Outstanding Fundraising and Development Programme. Abe dedicated his life to the University and as many of you know, was sadly involved in a terrible accident and could not be here tonight.'

I look down at Jeff and Lavinia on the table beneath the stage, Jeff in his black tie, Lavinia in a tailored lime-green Chanel suit. 'And I'd like to let you in on a little secret,' I continue. 'In light of Abraham's sad departure from the University, I'm highlighting a new initiative.' Lavinia lifts herself off the seat. I give her a small nod. It's okay. I'm no longer a loose cannon. I can't destroy this place and the dark, invisible forces behind it. I'm here now to play my own game.

'So tonight it is with great honour that I'm announcing a brand-new fellowship in his name that I've decided to implement. The Abraham Cohen Ethics in Medicine Fellowship.' There is a roar below me and the applause seeps into my bones. I stand up straighter, taller, and look around me, nodding at everyone, thinking of my earlier conversation with Harbottle. The front-page *Gazette* advertorial I've paid for from the Medical School's marketing budget, which tomorrow morning will announce the Medical

School Ethics Scheme and show photographs of me holding up the award along with the entirely new direction of the University Wickham Fellowships. *You've done a good thing,* Bill texted me an hour ago after working on the wording together for over a week. How to pitch it correctly. How to garner the most interest. *A human connection,* he pointed out. It's what Abraham always lacked. Placing a hand on my chest, I look around at the audience again, this time making eye contact with my husband. I think about our agreement about him turning a blind eye to any potential infidelity and my time with you, in exchange for my acquiescence over our marriage in the public eye. 'As long as you're careful,' he said. 'It'll be us cleaning up our own reputation now if you put a foot wrong.' We both at least managed to laugh at that. I catch Jeff's gaze again. He smiles at me. We've even discussed adoption lately, with the idea of me having full custody if we were to ever split, which, I told him, was still a possibility. Although for now things are good the way they are. For me, at least. I smile back at him.

'This' – I pause for effect – 'will go to a person who proves worthy of receiving this fellowship, to go alongside the new Ethics Wing at our University.' I hold the award up to the light and say a silent thank you to Abraham for this part of the story, and I think about what comes next in my own. My leave of absence. What I'll do with that time. The decisions I'll make about my own future and my place here. Whether I have the power to reform the dark forces around me into something new, something lasting and meaningful.

'And I know you'll join me in a big round of applause for the other people who deserve a mention both for this award, and the new Fellowship, even if they might not know it yet. Ladies and gentlemen, please join me in celebrating my wonderful husband, Jeffrey Harker and our inimitable chair of governors, Lavinia Edwards. And, of course, Abraham Cohen.'

I hold up the award again towards the light, the crystal refracting the light around the room into a burst of colour. Absorbing the reverberating sound of applause, I blow a kiss to the crowd. They're going wild. I think back to Abraham's first text to me, on behalf of my husband. *Good Morning, Mrs. President!* The tiny dot at the bottom of the exclamation mark is still present in my mind. It had been the marker of things to come. The marker of things that had been. I hold up the award again before walking off the stage. And here I am now. No longer the adjunct. I've made the story, and now it is mine and mine alone.

31.

I wake up early the next morning, my last day before a fortnight-long leave of absence. It had been discussed that I'd take at least three months away but there was so much to do in the University. I couldn't possibly take all that time off and in any case, me and Janet had meetings planned for an entire new initiative which involved moving our endowment fund into clean investing, something I'd been looking into for the past few weeks. I choose my clothes carefully. A new burgundy trouser suit. A pair of black suede heels. I slip on a pair of tortoiseshell glasses and shout out to Jeff, who is in his study, that I'm going to run some errands.

'Fundraiser tonight,' he shouts back. 'Meet me for a cocktail before. At Fellows?'

'Fine,' I tell him. 'Six.' For the most part, our marriage had settled into a steady rhythm of work and a mutual understanding of our individual ambitions, of which mine seemed to have ramped up in the past weeks since the gala and your death. I make my way to the car, turning on the radio and plugging in my Waze ready for the drive. The route takes me past your apartment. Pulling down my sun visor, I barely glance at the entrance to the Headway Woodland. It's not that I don't miss you. I do. I miss you so much. But at the same time, whenever I think of my desire for you and everything we had together, the way my body responded to you, I associate it with the terror and fear of the past weeks and that image of you, face to the ground.

I turn up the music, a pop song I recognise from around campus. I look at my bag on the passenger seat next to me, ready for my visit. Pulling into the large car park of Maiden Valley Hospital, I rub at my left side, the three cracked ribs still knotting themselves back together. When I arrive at the hospital, I get out the car and fill my lungs with the fresh air. My own stay here feels like a lifetime ago. Lifting my bag over my shoulder, its handle digging into my skin, I speed walk to the hospital entrance.

'Hi,' I say to the tiny, brown-haired woman at the reception, a long white desk with two vases of pink chrysanthemums on each end. 'I'm Elizabeth Harker. I dropped you an email yesterday?'

'Ah, Mrs Harker. I'm Eve. Pleasure. I was there last night. At the ceremony. A guest of the hospital. We had a table there. We won the award for best eco initiative.' She holds out a hand. 'What a beautiful thing you're doing with the Fellowship. If only he was awake to hear about it. Please. Go right ahead. Sorry I didn't get back to you sooner, but I have logged your visit. Sadly you've just missed his mother. She left twenty minutes ago.' I want to tell her that I know. That I've been liaising with Donny for the best part of a week trying to determine when I'll get a chance alone with his dear husband.

'That's so kind,' I say, pulling up my sunglasses and resting them on my head. 'I'll go right in, if you don't mind. I'm not going to be long. Just want to pay my respects.'

'Of course.' She clasps her hands to her front. 'So lovely to meet you again. Down the corridor. If you take the second left and take the elevator up to the Marigold Wing. There are only three patients in that part of the hospital. It's a specialist part of the building, so you can't get lost. He's in the Yellow Room. Very sad, the whole thing.'

'Isn't it.' I clasp my bag against my hip, wondering how disingenuous I could possibly sound. 'Thank you so much, Eve.' I wave goodbye as I walk down the long corridor, past the colourful modern art prints, the boards pinned with countless thank-you letters, inked baby footprints and huge paintings of daffodils, until I reach the elevator. I try not to breathe in the musty smell overlaid with sweet air freshener until I get to another receptionist.

'Abraham,' I tell her. 'I'm from the Medical School. Elizabeth Harker. I've booked in with Eve,' I say smoothly.

'Hey, honey.' The receptionist doesn't bother to look up, instead pointing a long, diamante-studded acrylic nail at a sign-in book. 'Just write your name there.' I do as I'm told, writing an indeterminate scribble, knowing she won't check, before sliding the pen back towards her.

'Thank you.'

***

Abraham's room is painted bright yellow, like a child's nursery space. His bedside table is covered in knick-knacks; an electric razor, books and poetry tomes, photographs of him, Donny. His mother. The University in all its glory. Him standing in front of it, in black tie. A huge smile on his face, holding Donny's hand. And then my gaze finally rests on Abraham in the bed. He looks tiny, shrunken, compared to the tall, bulk he once was. I'm reminded of a silicone sculpture I'd once seen, *Dead Dad by Ron Mueck* – a naked human-form replica of death, a prone body, lips sunken in on themselves, feet at resting position. Except Abraham is still here, alive. Still in a coma. 'We're not holding out much hope', Donny had told me. I'd spent extra time cultivating that relationship which no doubt would come in handy at some point. I sit down on the worn seat next to his bed, a permanent circular indent in the leather.

'Hello.' I clear my throat over the whirring of machinery. I wonder what it would be like to gently remove the plug. I stare at a large, rough patch of skin on Abraham's hand. 'It's me. Elizabeth.'

I watch him for a good few minutes before I speak again.

'I wanted to come here and tell you I accepted an award on your behalf last night. You won because of all the clever things you did around communications. Presenting the University in a very special light. I also have your phone. It was your greatest gift to me. But I'm not here for that. And I never will be.'

I reach down into my bag and pull out the globe, waving it in front of his face. For a second I think his eyelid twitches, and I nearly drop the award. I quickly move it to the bedside table, grasping the award by its brass base before pushing it into the middle, amongst all the photographs. It's engraved with — MEDICAL SCHOOL WINNER 2026. Your mother will be happy to see it,' I tell him. 'And Donny. If only they both knew. What kind of a person you really are. Were. Anyway, it's yours. I don't want it.' I wait a few minutes more, staring at the waxy skin on his face, his dry, cracked lips. 'And by the way, I'm not going anywhere,' I whisper. 'I've got a solid plan. Because you taught me incredibly well. And I won't ever let you change my narrative if you ever wake up and tell people what happened that night.'

I smile at him. I wonder what's going on in his internal world. 'You see, your own reputation at work preceded you, and now here we are. If you so much as open your eyes, I've got the perfect blueprint for your own murder. Your very own beautiful plans, where you had the love of my life killed. My darling John. I've got it all. Step by step. Your brains on a page. And thank you, by the way, for alerting me to the policy wording. That was helpful. I've already looked into that too, in the event of anything untoward happening at the University.'

I startle as I hear a clanking noise outside, but it's someone with a food trolley passing by the small window.

'I've also set up an anti-drink-driving campaign at the University for the students. I've set you up as the face of it, dear Abraham. An example of the awful things that can happen. You are now the barely living embodiment of your own worst fear. *Persona non grata.* It was drink that caused you to make your first mistake. Your loose tongue at Cecconi's when you talked about the Wickham Wing in front of me. And the main players. A helpful word to help me in my own investigations. And,' I lean forward, rubbing my hands over the smooth, cool glass of the award, 'I promise you, Abraham, you will never be coming back.' I stand up and look at him, a tiny sigh escaping his lips. 'Education. Isn't that what this great establishment is about? The University? The Medical School? Global change. The elite. The best of the best? It's about education. At least it's meant to be.'

I walk to the door and grab the handle. 'That's one thing, Abraham. One thing you've been. And one thing I'll always thank you for. I'm almost indebted to you for that.' I open up the door, ready to go back inside those walls which house the best minds in the world. 'A good teacher,' I whisper. 'You've educated me. And for that, I'm so grateful.'

Acknowledgements

Thank you to my phenomenal agent, Nelle Andrew. Some of my most life-changing moments have been from the words you've said to me.

My brilliant and wise editor at Oneworld Publications, Wayne Brookes; I've absolutely loved working with you. The fabulous Margot Weale, Rob Wilding, Kobe Grant, Paul Nash, Laura McFarlane, Sarah Terry, Tania Charles, Julian Ball, Francesca Dawes, Hayley Warnham; team extraordinaire – thank you all, so much, for your inspiration, brain power and expertise.

Huge thanks to everyone who spoke to me during the research for this book. Your insight was so helpful, many of you saved me from making huge blunders. Special thanks to Pippa, Izzy, Richard, Victor and Christine.

My forever thanks, as always, to Asia Mackay. My life is infinitely better because you are in it and every day I am thankful that you are. And to Caroline, Charlotte, Elizabeth, Izzy and Liz, I am so very, very lucky.

I once asked someone how I could repay their act of generosity. They asked that I consider giving to Tommy's and I'm also highlighting their work here. Each donation helps fund vital research into miscarriage, stillbirth and premature birth so that they can keep saving lives.

In memory of Leo – and with love to Chloe and her family.

Thank you to everyone at Papplewick School. Especially to Tom and Sallie Bunbury, for everything you have done for us; you will be sorely missed by everyone. I cannot thank you all enough for the time, dedication and energy you have brought to this very special school. It holds so many fantastic memories and it is absolutely everything that education should be. And of course the inimitable, inspiring and very dapper Jerry Ward for getting us there in the first place.

To the most incredible friends for pulling me through. You know who you are and I'm grateful for you every single day.

Thank you to the amazing Redfern Gallery.

Special thank yous, in abundance, to: Anna van Praagh, Anne Kriken Mann, Caroline & George Jones, Charlotte Wilkins, Clarissa Ward, Daniel Cavanagh, Edwina Gieve, Elizabeth Day, Emilie Bennetts, Gemma Morris, Helly Wilson, Izzy Cooper, Katie Woods, Karen and Ellis Spero, Liz Thornton, Lynn & Josh West, Maria Guven, Nerissa Martin and to everyone on the Girl Powder Retreat.

Alia, Alexander and Theo and of course my fantastic, hilarious and utterly brilliant siblings Emily and Jasper.

To Maggie and Adrian I count my lucky stars for you every day – the best parents I could ever have wished for. Thank you for everything.

And finally, to Walter, Dom and Sylvie, I love you so much, for all that you are.

R. L. Heber is the author of three previous novels and has been selected as a WHSmith Fresh Talent. She lives in London.